SHADOWBORN EXILE

BOOK ONE

SHADOWBORN EXILE

BOOK ONE

HARMON COOPER

Podium

Cover design by Mario Teodosio
Flashwraith designs by Sor

ISBN: 978-1-0394-7729-2

Published in 2026 by Podium Publishing
www.podiumentertainment.com

Podium

SHADOWBORN EXILE

BOOK ONE

PART ONE

THE TRIAL AND THE EYE

CHAPTER ONE

Death came after the light. It always did.

The Spiralrealm was vast—its depths uncharted, its tiers descending like a wound through the world. Flashwraiths roamed its reach: terrible things of searing energy, held at bay only by those willing to feast on shadow.

Like his father and grandfather before him, Attica had been born to hunt them. Now, at fourteen, he stood among the Vanguard, an ashling poised to take his place. His heartbeat was steady. His shade coiled restlessly at his back.

Tonight, he would take his first step toward adulthood.

"It's an emitter," Hadrian said, nodding toward the creature stalking the ridge below. "A small one. At your size, the best way to kill it is to cut the mana crystals at its heels." His voice was calm, shaped by years of survival. "Then—shadowblade to the base of the skull. Climb its back like you trained. And don't let it blind you. If it opens its mouth, you're dead. These next two minutes could define your future." A beat. A final weight behind the words. "Do as you've been trained."

"For the settlement," Attica whispered, jaw clenched. "And the Painter."

"For the settlement and the Painter," Hadrian echoed. He motioned to a Vanguard crouched behind a slab of broken stone. "It's time. Summon your shade, Attica. Prove yourself worthy to be Shadowborn."

Attica focused the darkness around him, his fingers curling with practiced control. His shade moved first, a shifting mass of ink that was both part of him and something else entirely. Every Vanguard had one—a living shadow, an extension of their will. Most shades reflected their hosts, merging cleanly.

But not his.

Attica's shade resisted. It disobeyed. It never moved quite as it should. "Stay with me," he scolded it. The shadow slid over him like a living cloak. "Good."

He glanced at Hadrian and exhaled. No nod. No approval. Just that same impassive gaze.

Everything Attica had learned since turning ten had led to this moment. And no lesson, not even Hadrian's, could prepare him for what came next.

His shoulders squared as he moved into position, circling the rock, his shade helping him vanish into the dark.

Stay behind it, he reminded himself. *They sense light shifts. That's why you strike from behind.*

Beyond, the emitter trembled with restless energy. Sinewy and angular, it raked the ground with slow, methodical claws. A faint halo pulsed around its skull, its mouth seething with raw radiance, enough to incinerate anything caught in its gaze.

It dug with eerie patience, carving a shallow pit.

Attica sank into the shadows, focused on his sworn enemy, and made the call.

"Now," he hissed.

His shade flared with him, dark essence coiling up his arms, prickling his skin as it shaped into a blade across his knuckles. Attica lunged, darkness surging with him as his shadowblade carved into the emitter's heels, splintering the crystalline growths with a sharp crack.

A garbled snarl escaped the creature's throat as it buckled.

By then, Attica was already climbing, fingers catching ridges in its body, shade shifting to steady him.

In a single, fluid motion, he drove the blade into the back of its skull.

Light erupted.

A final, searing pulse followed as the beast collapsed.

Panting, Attica stared down at the fading glow.

"I did it," he said, voice thin.

"Gather its resources, lad," was all Hadrian told him.

Attica crouched beside the corpse. Mana bled in luminous wisps from the wounds. He guided the energy into his family's gourd, corking it tight.

"To many more," Hadrian said, stepping closer. His shade flickered beside him—restrained, but eager. A faint smile touched his lips, gone as quickly as it came. "Remember this feeling. Victory. Survival. That's the way of the Shadowborn. Of the Vanguard." His gaze sharpened. "Not everyone makes it this far, Attica. Most ashlings don't."

Attica swallowed, the words sinking into his chest.

There would be more hunts. More kills. And soon, the trial.

But for now, this was enough.

Every potential Vanguard faced the trial on their eighteenth birthday. Only after a long trek through the upper tiers of the Spiralrealm—gathering essence, lighting lanterns with mana from the Seer's flask—could they earn their last name, their title.

It was a test of worth. A rite of passage, just as it had been for Attica's late father, Spiran, Knife of the Glintfang.

Attica had heard the tale a thousand times, how his father had slain a glintfang eight times his size. No, ten. Maybe twelve. The numbers blurred, but the legend endured.

Now it's my turn . . .

He met Hadrian beyond the settlement walls, where the greatest of the Vanguard stood, warriors whose names had shaped his childhood.

Standing before them was humbling. A reminder of what lay ahead.

Hadrian handed him the map. "You know what to do," he said. "And you know what's at stake. This is more than your life—it's the future of the settlement. You, and others like you, are why we endure."

"For the settlement and the Painter," Attica said. The words steadied him as the others echoed the phrase.

"You leave an ashling. You return a member of the Vanguard. Be brave, but be smart," Hadrian said. "Some flashwraiths should only be handled in parties. If you see signs of a flareback, leave the area. There are other ways to reach your goal." A pause. His voice dropped. "Don't let the weight of your father's legacy overshadow your task. Remember what I've taught you, lad. Remember it well."

Attica swallowed. "I will." His shade curled tighter against him. "We will."

Hadrian's dark eyes met his. For a moment, the world held still. Then, a hand on his shoulder. Brief. Firm. A gesture of quiet certainty. "The path is yours now," Hadrian said. "Walk it well. Don't rush. The trial takes as long as it needs."

Attica turned away from the Vanguard. The Spiralrealm stretched before him: vast, coiled, and mysterious, humming with forgotten history. Mist drifted like breath over abandoned settlements and crumbling stone. A light wind whispered in broken tongues.

And somewhere far below, something stirred in the dim.

One night, Attica thought, eyes fixed, heart steady. *I'll finish the trial in one night.*

CHAPTER TWO

Attica set off into the gloom.

The Spiralrealm's layers stretched endlessly below, each tier veiled in dense fog and fractured shadow, broken only by erratic flashes of light. A haunting verticality. Ancient stone bridges and jagged ledges jutted from the corkscrewed rock, some crumbling with age, others faintly aglow, none holding enough mana to be worth bottling.

There was history here, but much of it was forgotten.

His map guided him to the first checkpoint—a rocky outcrop made of the same stone as the settlement, its surface jagged and worn. *Here we are*, Attica thought. *Matches the map. We should reach the first lantern soon.*

Beyond the whirling fog, the other side of the Spiralrealm loomed, vast and unknowable, a chasm of shadow and mystery. It was a sight that never failed to unnerve him, no matter how often he saw it.

"Let's take a look," Attica told his shade. He produced a monocular from a satchel under his arm. He scanned the horizon until he found them. A band of flashwraiths carved through the murk, a beacon of searing light.

Too many, he thought. Attica lowered his monocular with a slight scowl. *No point. Not alone . . .*

Tucking it away, he continued along the path, only for a sudden gust of wind to snatch the map from his hands.

Hey—!

He bolted after the map, gravel sliding beneath his boots. The map twisted and fluttered like a bird learning to fly before the relentless wind snatched it higher, then farther—right over the edge of the first tier.

He reached the precipice and peered down, heart pounding.

Attica had been told that no one, not even the Seer, knew how deep the Spiralrealm went. Attica's people lived on its highest level, where it was supposedly safer. He'd heard of other settlements, but no one he knew had ever come across them, not even the most seasoned Vanguard. The farthest they would travel was the edge of the second tier. It was virtually unheard of to go to the third.

Shadows flickered off his fingers as he scanned the cliff face. The map had snagged on a hooked stone, just within reach.

It's not too far. I can jump to that ledge and climb down.

Without the map, Attica would have to return to the settlement in shame. Arriving empty-handed and without lighting the torches was unthinkable, and while they may let him go out again, he would never be able to live it down.

"Come on," he told his shade, which loomed beside him, silently judging him. "It wasn't my fault, and you know that."

His shade gave no reply.

"It's not that far down." He stepped forward, but the bond between them tightened—resisting. A subtle but deliberate pull. "I said, *let's go.*"

After a moment, his shade relented, its essence slithering over him like liquid shadow.

Attica dropped onto the ledge, his shade reinforcing his grip. The bond between them allowed him to summon a blackened blade made of dark essence, to anchor himself, to move as Shadowborn should. Yet, even now, his shade held something back, as if it doubted him.

"See? We're almost there," he said, gripping the rock as he continued his descent. Darkness slithered along his arms, sharpening his grip, yet his shade's presence remained tense, unsettled.

Attica reached the map and pulled it free, exhaling in relief. *Good.* He dropped down onto a lower ledge and paused to catch his bearings. "Told you," he said to his shade.

The fog was thicker here, curling around his legs like grasping hands. A faint light flickered in the distance, barely visible in the murk.

How far? Attica tied back his long dark hair and pressed on. "Let's go over flash-wraith traits," he told his shade, partly to focus himself. "When threatened, they can release a burst of toxic, suicidal light. We've seen it before—that one time."

Nearly a year ago, his group had crouched above a slot canyon, waiting for a pair of emitters to move into position.

Tarnal, then Attica's age, had jumped down to prove his bravery and impress a girl named Eve. He killed the first emitter but was caught by the second. The creature released a desperate burst of light from its terrible maw, killing Tarnal in an instant.

All that was left was a smoldering pile of dust, an image that remained burned in Attica's mind.

One moment there. The next, dust. Decide which existence you prefer. Hadrian's words at the time had been sharp, but not cruel. He always spoke plainly, without embellishment, as if facts alone carried the weight of wisdom. Where others might have offered comfort, Hadrian had offered truth. *Tarnal is dead. You are not. Learn from that.*

That was his way—his lesson in survival. Attica hadn't understood it then, and he didn't fully understand it now. But at least he knew enough to be aware.

"We have to be careful," he reminded his shade. "And if we see a flareback, be ready."

His shadow tugged at him again.

"I was joking. We're not looking for a flareback."

Still, the thought lingered. *If we do find one . . .*

The renown it would bring. The stories they would tell.

Spiran, Knife of the Glintfang.

Attica could surpass him. Not just match the name, but eclipse it.

Now on the second tier, Attica followed the map into a wider space scattered with ruins. "What's this?" He picked up a stone with carvings he didn't recognize. Dropping it, he noticed his shade shifting toward a crumbled wall.

Something was ahead.

Attica felt the shift as his shade stretched over him, cloaking him in darkness just as a single flaylight drifted near.

He froze, his shade doing the same.

The parasite hovered, its translucent wings humming softly, its body pulsing with a faint, shifting glow. Symbiotic, insect-like creatures, flaylights fed on the excess power of flashwraiths. But if their host was threatened, they became something else—merciless, swarming, and unrelenting.

Attica held his breath as the flaylight flitted past, vanishing into the ruins. Only then did he ease back against the crumbling wall, his pulse still hammering in his ears.

The sound returned, a low, resonant hum that rippled through the stone beneath him, shaking dust loose from the ruins. It wasn't just a sound. It was a presence.

His shade pulled at him, tense, urgent. It didn't want to be *there*.

"No," Attica whispered, excitement warred with fear. "We didn't come this far just to turn back."

But he knew.

That hum. That deep, bone-shaking tremor. He had felt it once before. Back then, Hadrian had been with him. They had heard it, seen the telltale light stirring in the distance. And they had turned back.

Better to hunt something big like that in numbers, Hadrian had said at the time. *Live to die another day.*

Attica eased forward, just beginning to peer around the wall when his shade protested again. Its tension bleeding into him, wrapping tight around his limbs. His skin hardened as its dark essence spilled over him, forming an armor.

"I'm in charge," he growled, anger flickering in his chest.

The sound came again—closer this time, deeper, vibrating not just the stone beneath him but *through* him, rattling his ribs as if something massive was stirring awake.

Attica relented, momentarily spooked. "Fine. Have it your way. Besides, I can see what it is from up top."

Without another word, he scaled back to the first tier, his shade surging with power to assist him. He crouched low, gripping the ledge as he surveyed the expanse below, his eyes bulging once he saw what had been trembling the earth.

The flareback was enormous.

Easily twelve feet tall, its hunched form bristled with pulsing, swollen nodules of light, like molten stars trapped beneath its skin. Some bulged outward like blisters, while others sat embedded in the dark, stonelike plates covering its body. Its core—an enormous, star-shaped nodule at its chest—blazed with raw energy.

Flaylights swarmed around it, their bodies flickering erratically, drawn to its excess mana.

Attica's breath caught. *If I kill it . . .*

The thought burned through him, tantalizing, undeniable.

A haul like this would secure his place among Vanguard legend. The Spectralists would have enough essence to fill their coffers, and Attica—Attica would have a title. A *legendary* one, like his father but better, one they would speak of for years to come. Spiran's son. The one who felled a flareback alone.

But the thought barely had time to settle before the flareback shifted.

It turned.

A searing eruption of light streaked toward him.

Everything blurred.

One moment Attica was crouched, the next, a force slammed into him, hurling him backward as if an unseen hand had shoved him. The impact sent him sprawling, his shade reacting faster than his own body, wrapping around him, the cocoon of darkness and whisking him to safety.

If his shade hadn't acted, there would have been nothing left of him—no second chance, no future at all.

Scrambling to his feet, Attica ran.

His shade bolstered his speed, shadows carrying him forward, but the flareback's light had burned itself into his vision, seared into his memory.

Attica ran until his thighs screamed, until his breath came in ragged gasps, until his heart pounded so hard it felt like it had been pried free from his chest.

The path blurred beneath him. He leapt over jagged stones, wove through the bouldered ruins without thought, without hesitation.

He reached a clearing and collapsed against the stone, hands braced on his knees, his breath still raw and uneven. His shade relaxed, the darkness flickering away. "Thank you," Attica said, ashamed.

I'm safe, he told himself.

But his hands betrayed him. Trembling. Unsteady. Refusing to listen.

Attica clenched them into fists. Forced control. Forced certainty. "Just you wait," he whispered. "I'll come back for you."

CHAPTER THREE

The Spiralrealm's sun bore red rings, though they were rarely seen through the fog that draped the world like a second sky. The haze clung to the air, shifting in slow currents, distorting distances, and muting colors into a palette of gray and deep shadow. Attica could count on one hand the number of times he had seen the sun unobscured, its crimson halo burning clearly against the abyss.

He rarely saw it from the settlement.

Most of the Shadowborn lived partially underground, and what remained above—crumbling ruins swallowed by time—was blanketed in dense foliage, a byproduct of the essence the Vanguard retrieved and the Spectralists refined.

Dayanne was one such Spectralist, responsible for refining the essence into something the Shadowborn could consume. Though they were the same age, Attica and Dayanne's paths had rarely crossed. His training had shaped him for the hunt, hers for her work alongside the Seer.

Dayanne had grown into a tall woman with slicked-back hair, always adorned in carefully chosen rings, ear cuffs, and fine threadwork that traced her ears and wrists. Each piece looked deliberate, never gaudy—just enough to make her unforgettable.

Attica had only ever spoken to her in passing when delivering essence, and each time, she had smiled at him. Each time, he had failed to say anything of substance.

But all that will change when I get back, he thought.

Ahead, a rare wellspring shimmered with concentrated energy.

These pools were scattered throughout the upper tiers of the Spiralrealm, a necessary reprieve for the Vanguard on long treks. The liquid mana gathered in slow, shimmering streams, pooling in the dips of the landscape before vanishing again into the deep.

Some of these springs also produced pearls—smooth, iridescent orbs ringed in red, reminiscent of the sun. Shadowborn artisans wove them into necklaces, earrings, talismans. They were rare. Highly prized.

It would be the perfect gift for Dayanne, he thought as he scanned the area.

"Keep guard," he told his shade, which had already slipped away from him.

Attica unslung his flask and lowered it into the flow of essence. The trickling mana shimmered faintly, moving like liquid silver under the dim light. It wasn't much, but it would fill his flask.

He took a sip and immediately felt the familiar tingling sensation that accompanied raw mana, energy crackling at the edges of his senses. It carried a faint metallic taste—sharper, earthier than what the Spectralists refined.

Stowing the flask, Attica stepped forward, his boots partially damming the shallow current. He knew he wasn't supposed to do this; most Shadowborn considered it disrespectful to disrupt a natural source of mana. But what the Vanguard did outside the settlement often differed from what was expected within its walls. The rules of survival and necessity didn't always align with those of tradition.

Hadrian had taught him that.

"Order keeps the settlement safe. Beyond its walls, they are mere words," Hadrian had said once, stepping into a similar stream, searching for something for his wife. They hadn't found a pearl that day, but they had uncovered something else—a bone, left so long in the flow of mana that it had crystallized into something unrecognizable.

"There has to be something." Attica stepped farther upstream, letting the mana swirl around his ankles.

He crouched, sweeping his hand through the dust, feeling for anything solid beneath the current. For a moment, nothing. Then, a flicker of red caught his eye. He pulled it free, a red-ringed pearl, just as he had hoped. But a piece of it was missing.

Broken, he thought, turning it in his palm. His jaw tightened.

His shade slithered back to him, shivering as it pressed against his form, sending a tremor through his body.

"I know, I know, we need to light the first lantern," he said. "I just wanted to get something for Dayanne."

He started to sweep his hand through the spring again, but this time, his shade physically stopped him. Its formless weight dragged against his wrist, tightening.

They struggled for a moment, a silent battle of wills.

In the end, Attica let his shade win. He could have overpowered it, but he knew when to pick his fights.

It will do for now, he thought, slipping the pearl into a pouch. *There will be more.*

Attica's people never strayed beyond the upper two tiers of the Spiralrealm. As far as he knew—and all his knowing came from the Vanguard—no one had ever gone deeper.

It was too risky.

The upper tiers stretched for miles, their ruins and landscapes vast, their secrets seemingly endless. There was no real need to go farther down, toward the bottom, yet they all wondered how far down it went.

Attica had spoken to numerous Vanguard as they stood on the edge of the second tier, gazing down into the abyss, speculating about what lay below, where the exiled had traveled. Some believed there were more settlements, more Shadowborn like them. Others whispered about creatures even more terrifying than the flarebacks.

Only one person had never speculated—Hadrian. *If there was anything worth finding below, the Spiralrealm would have dragged us down by now.*

Attica remembered those words as he crossed a narrow stone bridge. He'd checked the map recently. He was close.

He came to the other side and reached the first stone lantern. Chest-high, its bricks were stacked in a deliberate pattern, worn but intact. At its top sat a bowl, carved from petrified wood, its surface darkened by time.

"This is it."

His shade peeled away from him, its dark outline shifting as Attica leaned toward the bowl. It lifted its featureless head, its presence rippling like an unspoken thought, and then nodded.

Attica reached into his pack and produced the small flask given to him by the Seer.

Simply touching the stone ritual flask stirred a memory. It started with Dayanne, who had greeted Attica and the other Vanguard before leading them into the Seer's chamber, which glowed with essence.

Attica had only seen the Seer a handful of times. Each time, her brightness had been unbearable, forcing him to avert his gaze. This time had been no different— he wasn't even sure who had placed the ritual flask in his hands.

He liked to think it had been Dayanne.

"Just a small amount," he reminded his shade as he uncorked the flask and let a single drop of the strange essence fall into the bowl.

The reaction was instant.

A blue flame sparked to life, spreading in a sudden burst as Attica stepped back.

The land around the lantern shuddered—colors bleeding through the gray, saturating the world in hues so vivid Attica nearly lost his footing. The colorful light spread outward, climbing the ruins, painting the stone, igniting the very air with vibrancy until it reached its peak.

And then, just as quickly, the glory of it all collapsed.

The colors recoiled, rushing back to the lantern, vanishing into its core. The land returned to shades of muted gray.

Attica stood frozen, dumbfounded by what he had just witnessed.

His shade sealed the flask, silent and precise. Attica barely noticed. His mind continued spinning. He had never seen so much color variety before—so much *life*.

It left him weak, unsteady.

A trembling overtook him, the same unease he had felt earlier.

The body and the world are never fully in your control. In that way, they are similar. Hadrian's words settled him, grounding Attica once more.

He forced his focus back to the mission. "Three more lanterns to light." Attica pushed past his shock, masking the momentary dizziness with distraction, scanning his map again.

But even as he looked, a deep, aching yearning clawed at him.

Red. Black. White. Gray. These had been the colors of his world.

And now, they felt hollow.

Attica's fingers traced the flask's surface. What would happen if he drank from it? Would he see . . . more color? A firm squeeze on his shoulder jolted him back.

"I'm thinking," he said. His shade lingered, unimpressed. Clearly, it wanted to move on. "Have it your way."

Attica slipped the flask into his pouch and returned his focus to the map.

He located his next destination, a rock formation shaped like a crescent. Once there, he would follow the natural path to the second lantern.

The map wasn't to scale, but Hadrian had already briefed him.

From the first lantern, it will be several hours to the one near the crescent rock. The others are in that area. Travel via a lower tier to save time if you'd like. Or stay at the top where it is safer. There is no one right way to do it. This exercise is proof that you have what it takes. It is not a race, although ashlings often see it this way. Do not forget to fill your gourd before your return. Lanterns and the gourd—that is your mission.

"This way," Attica said with just enough confidence to make it feel real. His shade rejoined him, its presence settling over his form once more as they pressed on.

The journey carried them across uneven terrain, the path narrowing between jagged stone ridges before opening into a stretch of boulders twice Attica's height.

A glow flickering beyond caught his attention.

Attica pressed himself into the shadows of the rock, his shade tightening around him in response. "Can we?" he whispered.

The answer came as a subtle vibration, a sensation humming through his bones.

Attica let go.

His consciousness slipped forward, stretching out like a dark curtain lightly falling over a window. The vision was brief, mere seconds, but enough for him to see what lay ahead.

Two emitters were hunched before one another, their bodies pulsing faintly, light shifting beneath their skin. Their guttural sounds grated against the silence, a language he did not understand.

Attica's awareness snapped back. A dark blade coiled down his arm, forming from the depths of his shade.

Strike first or not at all.

The only thing that mattered now was the kill.

CHAPTER FOUR

Attica's pulse kicked hard as his shade wrapped around him—not like armor, like instinct. Ahead, two emitters hunched near the ruins of an old well. Their claws scraped broken stone, cracked mouths seething with restless light. Always digging. But for what?

Two at once. That had been Tarnal's mistake.

He exhaled slowly, forcing the memory aside. He wouldn't make the same mistake. He had to get back. Had to take a title, a last name. Had to be more than just another ashling, more than just Spiran's son.

Someone Dayanne might actually see . . .

The trick was speed. The trick was surprise. The trick was to overwhelm them—cut them down before they could react, and reap their essence.

His shade coiled as Attica moved in for the kill. The emitters startled, their reaction a fraction too slow.

He struck first, his shadowblade carving into the nearest emitter's heels. The creature reeled back with a hiss, but Attica was already climbing—fingers finding leverage where none existed, shade sharpening his grip like living gauntlets.

He wrenched its head back just as essence spewed from its maw—a raw surge of mana lashing out.

The second emitter was caught in the blast, its body flaring as it staggered backward.

Attica didn't hesitate.

His blade plunged deep into the first emitter's skull. Light flared from the wound—searing hot, then gone. The creature convulsed. Collapsed.

One down.

Attica dove. His shade snapped him back as a pulse of light streaked past— close enough to scorch the air, close enough to burn.

The second emitter shrieked, body curling, preparing for another burst.

Darkness swelled around Attica, snapping him forward. He surged past the creature's striking maw, past the boiling glow of its core, and drove his blade straight into its skull.

A final beat of light. Then silence.

The second emitter crumpled, twitching as what remained of its life flickered and died.

Attica landed in a crouch, chest rising and falling, gaze locked on the two emitter corpses. The satisfaction of victory came slow, curling up from somewhere deep inside him. He hated them. He hated all flashwraiths.

They had taken Tarnal. His father. Countless others.

Every one he killed was one less nightmare the Vanguard would face. One more reason to keep going.

A grin pulled at his lips as he uncorked his gourd. The shimmering essence bled from their husks, drawn into the vessel like mist curling toward an unseen force. The gourd felt heavy in his hands as the mana settled inside.

Attica spat on the first corpse. If he had been with the Vanguard, they would have stripped the bodies—harvesting bones, flesh, anything useful. But alone? Too much weight to carry this early on in the journey, even if he planned to light all four lanterns in a single night.

I was born for this, Attica reminded himself as his shade stirred, feeding off the rush of adrenaline, a reflection of his own hunger.

"Good work," he told his shadow. "The big flareback we saw? That's next." A flicker of amusement passed through him as his shade recoiled. "I'm kidding. You're too serious. Besides, we have lanterns to light first."

And then . . . Attica cast one last glance at the dead emitters, the whisper of a smirk still lingering. *We'll see about that flareback.*

The path to the crescent-shaped rock was long and arduous even after Attica shifted to the lower tier to ease his travel. The terrain remained unforgiving: uneven, winding, relentless. His shade hovered close, a quiet pulse against his dark skin.

The lantern awaits. The mission comes first, Attica reminded himself.

Occasional flashes of light flared in the distance, too far to be of concern. Some flickered alone, but others clustered together—a herd.

Attica remembered a particular herd he had encountered on a scouting mission with the Vanguard. Even with eight official members and four others like him, they had chosen to avoid it, especially after spotting a trio of glintfangs.

Glintfangs—wolves wreathed in electric-white fur—never ran *alone*. They moved with the herds, streaks of raw speed and light, impossible to isolate, impossible to outrun.

With that many glintfangs, a Vanguard named Cassian had said, *picking them off one by one won't work.*

Is that the only way to deal with a herd? Tarnal asked the older boy.

Depends on the size. But generally, yes. If you can't separate them, you don't fight. You run. Or you die.

Attica used his monocular to examine a bright cluster on the horizon. "Definitely a herd," he told his shade. "But it's on the other side. We won't be going that far."

He moved on, scaling back up to the first tier when the path allowed.

The crescent-shaped rock loomed ahead, jagged and ancient—a curved fang from some long-dead beast. Time and mana storms had scarred its surface, carving deep pits into the stone. At its peak, the rock split into a narrow gap, a wound torn open.

The lantern was nestled in the crook where the rock curved back toward the ground. The same petrified bowl rested at its peak, undisturbed.

"Found you." Attica unhooked the small ritual flask, uncorked it, and let a single drop of essence fall into the basin.

Blue fire ignited at once. Color rushed outward, racing across the land like spilled ink, swallowing the gray in waves too vivid to name. The stone beneath his feet brightened; the distant ruins, once muted, took on shades he couldn't name. His breath caught as the lantern's hues swelled, rich and blinding, flooding his vision with a world that was almost too much to bear.

Attica stood transfixed, drinking it in. *Is this what the Spiralrealm was meant to look like? Or what it used to be, before the dark took hold?*

His eyes burned. Not from the light. From something deeper. Something he couldn't name. Then, like before, the color collapsed.

Drained. Pulled back. Faded until only the dim, ghostly glow of the lantern remained.

Attica blinked hard, his vision slow to adjust. The weight of monotone grays settled in again, and for the first time, he felt something like loss.

His shade shifted beside him, a silent reminder.

"Two more lanterns to go," he exhaled, voice rough. "We're doing this tonight."

His shade curled around him, slow and deliberate. A silent plea. Stop. Rest. Recover. But Attica pressed forward. "I know," he told his shadow. "I know."

But I don't want to stop.

A bark rang out in the fog—sharp, distant, but unmistakable. Attica's shade surged, locking around him like living armor. He stilled, waiting and listening.

Nothing.

The sound had been far off. Not an immediate threat. His shade lingered for a moment longer, then loosened, drifting back into its natural form as Attica pressed on, descending into an ancient creek bed that had once flowed with essence.

Remnants of what had been lay all around him, the faint glow clinging to the rocks, the near-silver sheen of the dry riverbed. Once, something had thrived here.

There had been people in the Spiralrealm before the Vanguard. People who had lived freely, who hadn't been forced into old fortresses, hiding underground and behind thick walls, forced to adapt to dark essence.

We used to mean something, Attica thought as he ran a hand along the smoothed stone. *What happened to us?*

The Vanguard took what they could from the upper tiers of the Spiralrealm, remnants of a past no one understood. Over the years, Attica had seen all kinds of things—intricately carved bone tools, fragments of pottery with fading patterns, the twisted remains of metal contraptions no one could explain. Once, he had even seen a small figurine—a man and a woman locked in an embrace, their features smoothed by time. A moment of love, frozen in the ruin of a world long forgotten.

All of it was dust now. Just like he would be if he stepped into a flashwraith's light.

His eyes lifted after another long, winding trek through the gloom. The terrain had since blurred into shadow and silence, the weight of the Spiralrealm pressing in on all sides.

"There it is," he told his shade, just to say something.

Atop the next hill, half lost in the swirling fog, the third lantern waited.

Before he approached, Attica scanned the area for any track marks or flaylights. The mist was thick here, dense enough to shroud anything lying in wait. He'd heard rumors that some flashwraiths were capable of stalking, slipping through fog like drifting phantoms.

He wouldn't give them the chance.

Attica kept low, his shade sliding ahead, rippling in the wind. He climbed carefully, spreading his weight, staying close to the earth, always keeping his vision wide.

Only when he was certain the hill was empty did Attica rise. He uncorked the ritual flask and let a single drop of blue essence fall into the petrified wood bowl.

This time, he didn't just want to see the color, he wanted to experience it.

His eyes widened as the fire bloomed and light swelled outward, cutting color through the fog. It rolled down the hillside in rippling waves. The gray fog vanished—replaced by deep, brilliant tones that touched everything in sight.

Attica raised his hand to it, and for the first time, he noticed something.

Thin, delicate lines traced the skin of his fingers and palms, etched there as if carved into him long ago. They glowed faintly in the lantern's light, an intricate network of runes that flickered in the shifting glow. His ears filled with whispers, voices Attica couldn't understand.

"What's this?" His breath caught as he brought his hand closer to his face—

And then, just as before, the colors collapsed. The runes faded. *Gone.*

"Did you see that?" he asked, turning to his shade. The dark figure hovered over him, silent as ever. Attica lifted his hand. "There was something there. On my skin."

His shade remained still. *Watching.*

Attica flexed his fingers and frowned. The markings were gone. No trace of them remained, nothing but the usual roughness of his calloused hands.

"It doesn't matter now," he said, shaking off the unease, the exhaustion that was starting to creep up. Attica looked toward the horizon. He exhaled sharply, casting any lingering doubt aside.

One more lantern. One more climb.

CHAPTER FIVE

Attica pushed too hard.

He felt it deep in his bones, a dragging ache that no quick rest could erase. Every step had grown heavier, his movements slower, his thoughts dulled at the edges.

His shade had noticed long before he did. It clung to him now—thick, leaden, the weight pressing against his back, urging him to stop. But Attica ignored it.

One more hill. One more stretch. One more lantern.

His boots scraped over uneven ground, the fog swallowing the path ahead. He forced himself forward, but his footing wavered. The path wasn't even difficult—Attica had crossed far worse. But his body no longer responded the way it should.

"Come on," he said. "*Come on . . .*" When that didn't work, he checked his map, willing himself onward, until—

Hadrian's voice cut through: *The body bends before it breaks.*

Attica stilled. He had heard that phrase many times, during relentless training sessions where Hadrian had forced him to fight his own shade again and again, past the point of exhaustion.

"*For the settlement.* For the Painter," Attica murmured, conceding to his body and his mentor's words. "We will rest," he told his shade, finally giving in.

He soon found a narrow alcove where a fractured wall still held strong against time. It wasn't much, but it would do. Stretching just enough to ease the ache in his muscles, Attica let out a slow breath. His fingers brushed against the gourd at his waist.

Just a small amount.

Attica uncorked the vessel and inhaled. The raw essence inside carried a faint metallic tang—power without form, without shape, without control. It steadied his nerves, dulled the gnaw of hunger without actually imbibing the mana itself.

This was what the Vanguard were trained to do. Only in dire circumstances did they drink it outright. That would be depriving the settlement of what it needed to survive.

Better, Attica thought as he got comfortable. The moment his breathing slowed, he noticed it. A glow. Not from the sky above, but below.

Attica frowned and leaned forward. A shifting array of strobing light flickered through the ruins beneath him, pulsing across the second tier in shifting patterns. He had never seen anything like it before.

His shade curled around him, its presence thick with unease. Attica ignored it.

Without a second thought, he pushed off the ground, scanning for a new vantage point, one that would allow his shade to slip forward and see what lay below. But his shadow wouldn't budge. It lingered, knotted around him, its weight heavier than before.

Attica hesitated, fingers twitching at his side.

"If you won't help me, then I'll do it myself," he hissed. Attica took a step forward, but his shade resisted him, holding firm like an unseen tether.

A flicker of irritation burned through him. "Come on."

Still, it wouldn't let go. His shade resisted—not just cautious, not just wary, but something deeper. A warning. A refusal.

With a sharp inhale, Attica forced his tethered shadow to move, pushing their connection forward. Their bond loosened, reluctant but yielding. Attica pressed on and slipped behind a rock, where he finally got a clear view of the ruins below.

A chill ran down Attica's spine as he saw a type of flashwraith he had never encountered before. *What . . . is that?*

From its broad, sinewy shoulders, the creature's upper body unfurled in two directions at once, splitting the fracturing bone of its upper back. Two distinct stems extended upward, each narrowing into a skull-like dome ringed with ridges of sinew. At their crowns, an ever-flickering aura of searing light pulsed, radiating a spectral glow.

It was unlike any flashwraith Attica had ever encountered before.

I have to kill it, he thought, his hands trembling.

He slipped into the shadows, moving with silent precision. His shade remained tense, still resisting. Attica ignored its unease. His hand drifted toward the stone flask given to him by the Seer. *How much is in there?*

He knew the flask held something stronger than any essence he had ever known. Power beyond measure. Power sealed away. And yet, it was forbidden. He had already seen what a mere drop could do—how it ignited the lanterns, spilling sacred color into the world before pulling it back into nothing. Whatever was inside the ritual flask, it was far stronger than anything the community normally used.

Dayanne had reminded him of this before he left the Seer's sanctum.

"You mustn't drink it," she had warned.

"Why?" had been his reply, a smirk tugging at his lips. He knew he had failed to flirt the moment Dayanne's expression shifted—her eyes narrowing, the faint trace of incredulity hardening into disappointment.

"I was just joking," he had added quickly, but the damage was done.

A beat passed before she exhaled, the tension easing just enough for a small, knowing smile to form. "Good luck," was all Dayanne said before turning back to the Sanctum.

Now far beyond the settlement, Attica imagined the renown that would follow him if he not only completed the trial but returned having slain a new kind of flashwraith. But with his waning energy levels, and without knowing how strong it was, this could prove challenging.

We're not supposed to consume the essence we bring back to the settlement either, Attica thought, his hand still on the ritual flask. *But I've seen the Vanguard do it before. Sometimes, it's necessary.*

Hadrian's words echoed in his mind. *Out there, the rules are different.*

Attica moved his hand away. For once, it wasn't his shade guiding him. It was his own will. All of his training, his respect for the laws of his people, his reverence for the Seer—all of it told him to leave the flask untouched.

He did just that as he reached for the gourd instead, only for his shade to stop him.

Attica froze. His shade moved on its own, curling around his wrist. Not guiding. *Forcing.* His fingers twitched. His shade pressed harder, guiding his hand back toward the ritual flask.

"What?" he whispered. "You know I can't drink the Seer's flask. Why do you want me to—?"

He wrenched his arm free, the tension snapping between them.

"I'm in charge," he reminded his shadow. With deliberate intent, Attica reached for his gourd instead. He uncorked it and inhaled the raw essence. His shade eased in response, as if momentarily appeased.

If I do this, I have to kill whatever that is down there and replace the essence. Attica lifted the gourd and took a small sip.

The effect was immediate.

Power coursed through him, hot and sharp, racing along his veins. His vision sharpened, the edges of the world hardening into perfect clarity. His muscles coiled with newfound strength, the dull ache in his limbs vanishing. His shade flared outward, blooming with dark energy, its form pulsing as if feeding off the excess mana.

He capped the gourd and slipped it back into place at his belt right next to the ritual flask.

He locked eyes onto the two-headed flashwraith. *This is it,* he thought, emboldened by his newfound strength. *For the settlement. For the Painter.*

CHAPTER SIX

The pure essence from his gourd made Attica feel unstoppable.

The essence burned through his veins, sharpening everything—the jagged terrain, the shifting light, the very air. Every motion felt fluid, his body weightless yet powerful, as if the world had slowed just enough for him to move through it like a shadow.

He leapt soundlessly from his vantage point, his shade stretching and gripping the stone, an extension of himself.

Attica descended, slipping down the jagged rock formations with an effortless, predatory grace, his shade anchoring him in silence. The terrain here was rougher with craggy overhangs, deep fissures where essence had once flowed, and towering spires jutting skyward in unnatural formations.

Attica reached the bottom and melted into the darkness, his shade pressing close.

The two-headed flashwraith stood motionless, its eerie, masklike faces lowered, as if in silent contemplation. The stillness felt *wrong*.

What is it looking at?

The monster remained unnervingly still. Then, as if reacting to some unseen thought, the creature lifted a clawed hand and traced the ridges of its left face—a slow, deliberate motion, almost . . . melancholic.

Attica barely had time to process before the flashwraith shifted, revealing the object it had been examining.

A stone?

Something about the way it studied the stone unsettled him. But there was no time to wonder about its motives.

Attica moved, dark energy rippling over him as he shot forward, his shade coiling tight, lending him speed. Shadowblades flickered to life along his forearms as Attica zeroed in on the creature's exposed flank.

The strike was perfect. Precise. Lethal. Just as he had trained.

But the flashwraith had two heads. At the last moment, one of its twisting skulls snapped toward him, its empty sockets erupting in a flare of searing light.

Attica barely had time to react. He twisted away, throwing himself sideways as a blast of energy tore through the space he had occupied moments before. The rock shattered, fissures burning deep into its surface as he hit the ground hard, rolling.

His shade tightened around him, absorbing the impact.

Attica came to a stop. He sucked in a breath, blinking against the afterimage of the creature's light.

This one wasn't like the others. It didn't react. It anticipated. It tracked him. It was smarter. Both heads, moving independently, hunting in tandem.

The flashwraith turned fully toward him, claws burning brighter, the light intensifying.

A pulse of energy flared and the creature released another blinding blast of light. He sprinted left just as the attack sliced through the mist, carving a jagged scar into the rock. Stone erupted around him, shards crashing in a violent cascade.

Attica took advantage of the chaos that followed, augmented by his newfound power and speed. He sprang forward as his shade latched onto the spiral-shaped formations overhead. Using the formation as leverage, Attica swung himself forward, propelling his body over the beast and twisting midair to land on the opposite side.

His shadowblade tore into its torso, carving through sinew and light-flesh alike. The wound flared violently, sparks of essence bursting outward as the two-headed flashwraith reeled back.

For a moment, Attica thought he had done it.

Then, the creature slammed into him, its weight driving both of them back into the rock wall. His shade reacted instantly, hardening over Attica's ribs, yet the sheer force still sent him crashing into a jagged formation.

Pain flared through his back as he kicked the beast away.

The flashwraith lunged for him again, claws igniting with light, slashing in a frenzied blur of burning arcs. The creature grew rabid, twin heads shifting independently, tracking him, predicting him.

Attica barely had time to react.

He twisted; his shade pulling him into the shadows between the fractured stones.

Attica feinted left, then pivoted sharply, sliding beneath the creature's lunge. His shadowblade struck true, driving upward into its abdomen. The flashwraith convulsed as Attica held it there for a moment, certain he had won, certain he had killed the monster.

But the two-headed creature wasn't done.

A flash of movement was followed by a sharp, searing white-hot burst as claws drove into his left eye.

Attica's vision fractured.

The world twisted in on itself as something inside him ripped.

My eye!

Attica clutched his face, breathing ragged, panic rising in his chest, his remaining vision fraying at the edges. The flashwraith advanced, twin faces glowing like spectral masks of judgment.

His shade surged. But this time, it didn't just follow his will—it acted.

Dark tendrils whipped forward, faster than he'd ever commanded, lashing out with a force beyond Attica's command. The flashwraith reeled, caught off guard as Attica's shade ripped into it, striking like a spear of pure darkness.

The tendrils pierced its torso, unspooling its essence in jagged, unraveling threads. Light flared, desperate and wild, as the creature let out a soundless scream, its twin heads snapping upward in a final, broken spasm.

The flashwraith's body buckled inward, crumbling in on itself, essence scattering like dying embers across the stone as his shade killed it.

My . . . eye . . . was all Attica could think as his shade ripped the wraith's core apart, leaving the beast's heads intact, still fused at the base where sinew and searing light had once held them in place.

Its last remnants flickered, then faded.

Silence fell.

Attica dropped to his knees, fingers trembling as they touched the cauterized wound on his face.

A rising wave of something cold swelled inside him, but he shoved it down.

He forced himself upright, breath sharp, body unsteady, swaying as darkness pooled at the edges of his sight.

Attica's knees hit the ground again.

The world tilted, warped. Half of his vision was blackness. Gone.

His shade tightened around him, but there was no fight left.

Attica collapsed. And this time, he didn't get back up.

CHAPTER SEVEN

For the settlement. For the Painter. For the settlement. For the Painter . . .

The words drifted through Attica's mind, circling, slipping, warping.

He gasped, his body jolting as awareness slammed back into him. His shade huddled over him, trembling in fear. It swelled toward him in relief, wrapping around him, steadying him.

Attica sucked in a breath. "I'm fine," he said as his shade helped him up. "I'm fine."

But then it all hit him. The sting in his face. The raw, unfamiliar ache beneath his brow. The way the world tilted wrong, less whole than before. He blinked, once, twice, but the distortion remained.

Not just distortion. Absence.

The world wasn't whole anymore. His left side was nothing—a void where light should have been.

Attica's stomach twisted. *No . . .*

He lifted a shaky hand to his face, fingers ghosting over the wound where his eye had been. His touch met ridges of cauterized flesh, the seared path of the flashwraith's claws—a ruined socket, cauterized and raw. A scar that would never fade.

Slowly, his gaze flicked to the motionless body before him, its fading essence casting a pale glow against the stone. And then, just beyond his narrowed vision, he saw it.

The flashwraith's two heads were gone.

"Where?" Attica rasped, forcing himself to move.

His body felt heavier than before, as if the weight of what had just happened was pressing down on him. He finally spotted them a few feet away, both heads, their twin necks conjoined, still held together by a sliver of exposed spine. His shade lingered near the severed heads—silent, still.

Attica exhaled sharply. "You did this?" he asked.

His shade didn't respond, only loomed, waiting.

"You did this," he said again, quieter this time. The words felt like stone on his tongue, heavy and immovable. A beat passed before he forced himself to nod. "Good . . . thank you."

Hadrian would have said, *The eye was never yours to keep.* Or worse, *You're lucky it didn't take them both.*

Cold, unflinching words, but not untrue.

And yet, this was *not* the legacy Attica had wanted.

Bitter as ever, Attica uncapped his gourd. The remaining essence trembled toward him, drawn in as he absorbed it, reclaiming what little the battle had left behind.

Attica took another breath, slow and uneven, before staggering toward the severed heads. His shade flickered uncertainly beside him as he reached down, gripping them. The flesh was stiff, fused at the point where the creature's unnatural light had burned away. His hands trembled, but he didn't let himself stop.

This was proof he had fought something new, something no one else had seen. And he had won. He had done what the Vanguard were trained to do, even if he had lost his eye in the process.

Pride swelled in his chest: sharp, stubborn, unbroken.

Attica turned the heads in his grasp, angling them just right, then secured them onto the hook at his belt, the one meant for trophies. They swayed slightly, grim, but they were secure.

Once he got out his map, his good eye traced the rough, hand-drawn markings, searching for his final target. The trial had been meant to take two days. Hadrian had already told him to pace himself, conserve energy and return in one piece.

But Hadrian wasn't here.

One night. That's all I need.

His shade pressed against him, tense, disapproving.

"One lantern left," came his reply. "We've made it this far."

The Spiralrealm stretched before Attica, its winding tiers spiraling into infinity. Attica paused only once—not to rest, but to glance with his one good eye across its vast expanse.

Lights. Clusters of them, burning bright on the far side of the realm. *A herd. If they were closer, I'd have to do something . . .*

Attica swallowed down his nerves, watching the distant glow. They were too far away to see him. That didn't stop him from running his fingers over his ruined left eye, tracing the uneven contours of the wound. His shade curled against his ribs, pressing close, as if to remind him that this injury was real. Permanent.

The thought made him feel sick, but he pushed on.

Soon, the climb to the top tier turned brutal. The Spiralrealm's stone was uneven, brittle in places, yet he moved with the practiced ease of a hunter. His shade coiled and uncoiled, anchoring him when the terrain threatened to shift beneath his weight.

Attica's body ached, exhaustion gnawing at the edges of his mind, but he refused to slow.

Hours blurred together. His only points were the landmarks on the map, unchanging, indifferent to his suffering.

Then, he saw it, the final lantern.

It waited at the heart of a crater—a hollowed wound in the earth, its edges cracked and dry. A place where water may have once gathered, but no longer did.

And yet . . .

Something felt wrong.

Attica slowed as he stepped into the crater, boots crunching against the brittle earth. The air was heavier here, unsettlingly so. A silence lingered, thick and motionless, as if the land itself were holding its breath.

Altars. Scattered along the crater's rim, half buried in time. Their stone faces were smooth, worn by wind and something older, something unseen.

A strange feeling settled in his chest.

He had seen ruins before—remnants of those who had lived freely, long before the Vanguard. Maybe even before the settlement. But this place . . . this place felt like it remembered him.

His shade clung closer, uncertain. Attica tore his gaze away. He couldn't let himself get distracted. With a shake of his head, he unhooked the ritual flask from his belt, his grip tightening around the carved surface.

Dayanne's warning echoed faintly in his mind. *You mustn't drink it.*

He uncorked the flask, and a single drop of concentrated essence fell into the petrified bowl of the lantern. Blue fire blazed to life and the world awoke. Color surged outward, racing across the crater, spilling into the dry lakebed, climbing the altars in impossible hues.

For one fleeting moment, the world felt whole.

And then, like the other times, the color collapsed.

Drained. Swallowed. Gone.

Attica stood in the dim, gray light, staring at the final lantern. His breath came slow and uneven. Something gnawed at the edge of his mind.

But the trial was done.

All four lanterns were lit, his gourd was filled, and the trial was complete. He closed his eye, inhaled deeply, and steadied himself.

Attica had done it in one night.

Now, I just need to make it back to the settlement in one piece . . .

CHAPTER EIGHT

The journey back to the settlement stretched late into the night. Above, the red-ringed sun had dimmed. The Spiralrealm lay draped in deep, shifting shades of gray.

He pushed himself harder than he should have, his body protesting with every step. The rush of victory—of survival—had long since faded.

My eye is gone. The thought returned again and again, a cycle he couldn't break. His fingers fretted over his face, tracing the ruined skin. His other eye strained, darting too fast, overcompensating.

Depth faltered, edges blurred.

The terrain beneath his boots, once second nature, became treacherous. Every uneven ridge in the stone, every sudden shift, was a misstep waiting to happen.

Still, he pressed on, determined to do it all in one day no matter what it cost him. Slowing meant weakness.

He moved carefully, his shade stabilizing him when his footing wavered. "Thank you," he said from time to time, ashamed of his own clumsiness, humiliated by how he would return and whatever name he would be given.

Every Vanguard had one—his father, Knife of the Glintfang; Hadrian the Unshaken. Even if he hoped it wouldn't be the case, Attica knew his would center around his missing eye.

At least I have this.

Attica's hand found his trophy, the conjoined heads of the new flashwraith swaying heavily at his belt. Proof of his triumph, despite everything else.

Ahead, faint glows flickered through the mist, shifting like ghostly beacons, indicating that a flashwraith was in the vicinity.

He soon spotted an emitter within striking distance, crouched on the tier below, hunched over something half buried in the dirt. Attica paused, his shade moving fluidly to keep him concealed.

He could have killed it.

He had done something similar before, aided by his vantage point. Yet, standing at the ledge, something in him hesitated. Not fear—never fear—but the cold realization that the world no longer aligned as it should. The drop below seemed farther than it likely was, the angles all wrong. His body tensed, instinct warping against uncertainty.

His shade hovered close. Not a push forward, not a restraint. Just there. Watching. Waiting. Ready. The emitter let out a squawk and scuttled away before Attica could decide. He remained frozen, anger at himself welling in his chest.

He exhaled as the shame within burned hotter than any pain. *I just need to keep moving. Keep moving, and I'll make it home.*

Attica reached a familiar ridge, where the land dipped sharply toward the tier below. He could see the swarming flaylights beyond, their eerie glow pulsing in tight pockets of movement. They hovered over the same place where he had encountered the enormous flareback before, their presence a clear sign that the beast still lurked below.

"It's still down there . . ." The prideful urge to go after the flareback swelled inside him, sharp and reckless. A surge of energy coursed through him, his shade trembling in response. *I've already survived the worst*, he thought as he glared into the abyss. *I've already suffered—why not make it mean something?*

His shade bristled against him, coiling tighter, a silent plea.

"Relax," Attica said, though his own voice carried little conviction. The rational part of him knew better. His body was already at its limit, his mind running on the last fumes of sheer willpower.

If he went down there, he wouldn't make it back.

Even at his peak, taking on a flareback alone was suicide. No one fought the massive creatures without a plan, without backup. Even the most seasoned Vanguard didn't try.

His fingers brushed his face again, and he hesitated. Only then did he realize his shade had guided his hand there. He pressed his fingers to the ruined flesh, tracing the edges of an injury that would be with him for the rest of his life. The skin was tight, raw. The nerve endings still burned beneath the surface, phantom pains flickering in the hollow where his eye had once been.

I've already lost enough.

Attica turned, forcing himself forward, away from the sight of the flickering flaylights and the flareback below.

The final stretch toward the settlement was the hardest. The familiar landmarks should have been a comfort, a sign that home was close. Instead, they filled him with dread and unease. Attica had survived. He had lit all the lanterns in one night. He had killed something unseen before. But he had come back tarnished.

Some of the Vanguard would see him for what he was—a fool who had over-reached. A child who thought himself untouchable and paid the price.

The very thought made his stomach twist.

Would they consider him unfit? Strip him of his chance to be Vanguard? Would they mock him for coming back broken?

His shade shifted against him, sensing his spiraling thoughts. It pressed against his shoulder in a familiar, grounding way. Attica exhaled, straightening his back.

"Almost there," he said, his words hollow.

By the time the first signs of the settlement flickered into view, Attica was staggering. He forced himself upright, squaring his shoulders despite the exhaustion clawing at him.

He heard the sound of drums in the distance, noting his return. Two figures emerged near the outer perimeter—Vanguard scouts, Menzel and Paderborn.

Their shades reached him first, rushing ahead in sleek, fluid tendrils before retracting just as quickly. The scouts said nothing on arrival. They only exchanged a brief glance before stepping forward and grabbing him by the arms, dragging Attica the last few paces.

The black banners fluttered weakly in the wind as he passed through the gates, the great stone archway stretching over him—unmoving, unchanging. This was home. It had always been home. And yet, it felt different now as he was brought to the front of the Vanguard's lodge.

His heart caved in once he saw Dayanne standing among a small gathering. His mother. Hadrian. Eve. Others he had learned from and trained with. No one spoke. No one moved to greet him. They only watched.

Attica's fingers curled around his trophy, the twin heads of the mysterious new flashwraith.

Has Dayanne been waiting for me? he wondered as a new wave of shame washed over him.

He could already hear Hadrian's voice in his head. He knew his mother's ways—this was a woman who hadn't cried a single tear when his father had died beyond these walls.

There would be opinions. There would be judgment. But in that brief moment, after everything, only one opinion mattered to him. And the moment their eyes met, he knew one thing for certain.

Whatever had once been there, whatever had lingered between them before he left was gone.

Dayanne wasn't looking at him the way she had before.

CHAPTER NINE

Attica had barely gathered his thoughts when Hadrian stepped forward. A firm hand came down onto his shoulder. "You made it back," Hadrian said, his voice even, unreadable.

Attica swallowed, suddenly unsure of how to respond. He wanted to say something profound, something that matched the weight of the moment, something to explain his wound, his change. Instead, the words tumbled out gracelessly. "I—I brought this."

With the help of his shade, he unclipped the heavy weight from his belt and lifted his trophy. The conjoined heads dangled by their fused spine, their eerie masklike faces twisted in eternally empty expressions. A murmur rippled through the gathered Vanguard and scouts.

Hadrian's fingers tightened slightly on Attica's shoulder as he studied the prize. His usual impassiveness flickered—just for a second, a subtle narrowing of the eyes, a shift of his brow.

"A brighthowler," one of the older warriors said. "I've only seen it once before down on the second."

Brighthowler? Attica felt his stomach twist. He had expected awe, admiration—something other than this quiet unease. His fingers hovered over his ruined eye again, an anxious, restless motion. The wound ached, a phantom pain thrumming beneath his skin.

Hadrian's face remained unchanged, but Attica could tell that name meant something. He glanced at the others, waiting for someone to say what the older man was thinking.

"I did it in one night," Attica said in earnest. "I lit all the lanterns."

No acknowledgment. No reaction. The words simply dissolved into the late night air.

Instead, Hadrian's focus remained on the severed heads. "There shouldn't have been one above the second tier."

Before he could say anything, another figure broke from the crowd. His mother moved with quiet authority, her sharp features betraying neither relief nor worry. Without a word, she reached out, her calloused fingers brushing the edge of Attica's face, tracing the contours of his cauterized wound.

"A worthy scar," she said, satisfaction clear in her voice. And then, with a faint smile, she spoke the words that would change him forever: "Attica, the Lone-Eyed Wolf."

The hush deepened. Then, slowly, whispers rippled through the gathered crowd.

"Lone-Eyed Wolf," Hadrian repeated it, as if weighing the name against the boy who now carried it. "It is a good one, lad. Attica the Lone-Eyed Wolf, son of Spiran, Knife of the Glintfang." He took Attica's trophy and raised it into the air. "To the Lone-Eyed Wolf!"

For the first time in his life, Attica heard true pride in Hadrian's voice.

The others joined in. The Vanguard. The scouts. The gathered Shadowborn. His name solidified in their voices, taking root in the history of the settlement. Attica wanted to revel in it, to let the pride wash over his exhaustion, but his gaze flickered past the warriors, past the gathered elders.

He searched for only one face.

Dayanne.

She stood near Eve, slightly apart from the rest, watching with intent. When their eyes met, something unspoken passed between the two—acknowledgment, curiosity, something else he couldn't quite place.

And then Dayanne stepped forward. Without a word, she reached for the gourd at his waist, her hands careful but certain as she unhooked it. "Come, Lone-Eyed Wolf," she said as the crowd started to part. "The Seer is waiting."

"We're going to the Sanctum now?" he asked.

"Come," was all she said as she started off.

The Sanctum lay beneath the main halls of the settlement, carved deep into the bedrock. The deeper they descended, the colder the air became, the scent of damp stone thickening around them.

Dayanne continued on, her movements sure. For once, she did not simply rush him through the corridors, the Spectralist taking her time.

They reached a chamber jutting off a long, spiraling stairwell.

The walls bore intricate carvings, ancient and deliberate. Twisting skeletal forms intertwined with dark symbols, a record of the dead, those whose bones hadn't been destroyed by the light of the flashwraiths. Some were full remains, others just pieces, skulls set into alcoves, femurs woven into the architecture like supports, and ribs hung from silvered rope. The entire room had a faint glow, the essence of the past lingering.

Dayanne traced a hand along the carvings, glancing at Attica. "Recognize any names, Lone-Eyed Wolf?"

Attica touched his face at the sound of his new name. His shade curled back—not just hesitant, but resistant.

Dayanne brushed her fingers against his arm, gentler now. "I'm only teasing. It's a fitting name." A pause. "What happened?"

"The brighthowler. It had two heads. I didn't calculate that part."

"So it's the one that took your eye?"

"It is."

"And for it, you took its two heads?"

"I did."

"Fitting." Her eyes softened slightly, her pupils dilating as she reached up and, without hesitation, placed a hand against his cheek. "But you didn't need to push yourself so hard."

A lump formed in his throat. His body shuddered, not from pain, but from something else, something he wouldn't understand for years. A strange ache that had nothing to do with his wounds.

She must have felt the tremor in him because she pulled back. "Did I say something?"

"No," he exhaled quickly. "It's been a long night."

"You didn't have to do it in one day."

"I did it for you." The words slipped out before Attica could stop them. His shade tensed. So did she.

Dayanne stilled. "Me?"

"And me," he corrected, stumbling over his words. "No, I mean I did it for the settlement. That's what I meant. Sorry. Long night, like I said." He reached for a pocket and produced the pearl-like manastone he had found for her. The stone was chipped, but its swirling red bands still shimmered like fire trapped in pearl. "This is for you."

Delight spread across her face. "For me?"

"Yes," Attica said, ignoring the way his hand suddenly trembled. "You like jewelry."

Dayanne took the stone from him and examined it. She glanced down at the bracelets on her arms and the rings on her fingers, all of which gleamed in the darkened space. "You know me so well," she finally said as she put the stone away.

"Not really, but . . ." Attica cleared his throat. He gestured at the bones. "Not exactly the place for this conversation."

"Certainly not. In that case, come." She motioned for him to follow. "I can tell you some of their stories later. But for now, the Seer is waiting. And Attica?"

"Yes."

"Thank you for the stone. I think I'll have it turned into a necklace."

The corridor led to a chamber bathed in light. Not the flickering glow of lanterns, but something harsher, more absolute. Attica stepped forward, and his remaining vision blurred. His shade recoiled, shrinking back into him as the brightness overwhelmed his senses.

He squeezed his eye shut as a voice echoed through the chamber.

"You have done well, Attica." The Seer's voice was thin and aged, yet it seemed to sink into him, ensnaring his thoughts, a whisper that could not be ignored.

Attica kept his gaze averted, head slightly bowed. The light threaded around him—not warm, not cold, but something else entirely. Something unnatural.

"He is now the Lone-Eyed Wolf," Dayanne said as she stepped forward to present a different flask, one made of carved bone that belonged to the Seer. The slightest brush of her hand against him sent a spark racing through his body, igniting every nerve at once. He exhaled, steadying himself.

The Seer examined the ritual flask with a quiet, knowing hum. "Had you drunk all of this," she mused, "you would have been banished, Lone-Eyed Wolf."

"They never told me that," he managed to say.

"No," the Seer admitted. "They did not. It is a test of character, a test you have passed. You have completed your task. You are now a full-fledged member of the Vanguard."

The words struck deeper than he expected. A shiver coursed through him, exhaustion momentarily forgotten. "I . . ."

"Despite your wound, you have done it—what few men and women have been able to do." Her voice turned ceremonial, her words falling into place as if they had been spoken a thousand times before. "For the settlement."

"For the Painter," Attica echoed automatically.

The light pulsed once more, and then dimmed.

When he opened his one good eye, Attica found the Seer seated before him, sagging into her chair, her frail body nearly swallowed by its mass. Her skin resembled wax that had melted and then hardened again. Deep-set eyes peered out from beneath heavy lids, ancient and knowing.

The chamber, once an unbearable void of light, now felt different. Smaller, more intimate.

"Do you know what these words mean, Attica?" The Seer watched him closely, her fingers tapping against the arm of her chair. "Hmmm?"

Attica hesitated. "I know what the settlement is. I know the Painter is . . ." He faltered. The words had been drilled into him since childhood, spoken without thought. But now, when asked directly, he found himself at a loss.

"The Spiralrealm was once ruled by the Baffled King, a creation of the Painter," she said. "The Baffled King is responsible for the loss of the color in our world. Now, flashwraiths bring violent light. Shadowborn maintain the dark. Vanguard like yourself protect us. And thus, the balance. Without it, the spiral would collapse into itself."

Attica listened, the weight of her words settling uneasily in his chest.

The Baffled King. He had never heard of such a thing. He glanced at Dayanne, searching for some confirmation, but she only lowered her gaze.

"It is time," the Seer murmured. She produced a different flask, one made of intricately carved bone, and uncorked it. "Come forward," she told him as she placed her finger over the opening. The Seer let a single drop of shimmering essence cling to her fingertip—thick, slow, reverent.

Attica stepped closer, lowering to one knee before her. A scent wafted toward him—not unpleasant, but old, like the dust of forgotten halls. His shade quivered at his back, seeping away from the Seer, reluctant.

"This part of the ritual may bring visions," she warned, her finger still in the air. "Are you ready?"

"I am," he told her as he swept his hair aside.

She pressed her finger into his forehead.

For a heartbeat, the world exploded with color.

The walls swelled, their carvings shifting in impossible ways, the very stone stirring like it remembered something lost. And then it all went gray again.

The vision struck him. The settlement, burning. Shrieks tore through the air. The Vanguard, vanquished. Flames raged where stone had once stood, the walls crumbling into ruin. The banners, the halls, the people—all were gone. Bodies scattered in the chaos, lost beneath the destruction.

And in the center of it all, a child of light.

Attica gasped, staggering back, his chest heaving. His knees hit the ground, his hand shooting to his forehead, as if trying to wipe away whatever she had placed there.

Dayanne was already at his side, steadying him. "Attica—"

But the Seer's voice halted her. "Wait."

Attica turned, breath unsteady. "Yes?"

The Seer lifted a frail hand. "Dayanne, you may leave."

A pause. "Are you certain?" Dayanne glanced at Attica, uncertainty flickering in her eyes. But when the Seer did not respond, she turned and left.

Once she was gone, the chamber pulsed again, light rising from all corners. The Seer's gaze did not waver. "What did you see, Lone-Eyed Wolf?"

Attica hesitated.

"Please, tell me."

"I saw the destruction of the settlement," he said, his voice catching in his throat.

"And?"

"A child made of light. I do not understand."

"Whose child?"

"I do not know."

She studied him, the dim glow shifting across the deep lines of her face. "Yours?"

Attica's breath caught. "I . . ." He swallowed. "I do not know."

The Seer exhaled, her body sinking deeper into her chair. The light around her swelled until Attica had to avert his gaze. The chamber felt different now. The ritual was over, but something had changed. Something that would not leave him.

Finally, her voice came, low and knowing. "That is all, for now."

Attica stood slowly, unsteady. The moment lingered—unspoken, unfinished. A pressure he couldn't name. A question without a shape.

It would be many years before he fully understood what he had seen.

PART TWO

THE LAST CRAZED GRIN
OF HADRIAN THE UNSHAKEN

CHAPTER TEN

S even years since the trial. Seven years since Attica carved his place into the Vanguard—since his mother gave him a name that would not be forgotten. Attica the Lone-Eyed Wolf.

A fitting name for a warrior who never wavered, never faltered. A fitting name for a man who refused to break.

But the ominous mist never truly settled in the Spiralrealm. It hung in the air, a gnawing afterthought shifting with the unseen breath of the colorless world.

And things were changing.

Certain flashwraiths, once rare, had grown common, like the two-headed brighthowler. The Vanguard had adapted, just as they always had, but each year brought new challenges, new threats.

Attica had changed as well.

His hair had grown even longer, enough to partially obscure the scarred remains of his missing eye. His shoulders had broadened, his frame thickened through years of hard-earned survival. The brashness of youth had sharpened into something colder, more deliberate. The Spiralrealm didn't forgive softness, and neither did his shade. While they still didn't always get along, Attica had learned to live with it . . .

Attica crouched at the edge of a narrow ridge, his one good eye locked onto the hulking form that lumbered through the ravine below.

A flareback, easily ten feet tall at the shoulder, its cracked, stonelike plating shifting as it moved. The monster's swollen mana nodules pulsed erratically, glowing like molten veins beneath its hide.

"Not yet," he whispered to Tiago, an ashling, the youngest of the hunting party. Sixteen—restless and reckless. Still trying to prove himself.

Attica had complained about the boy to Hadrian once. "He moves like a fool. Takes too many risks."

Hadrian had barely lifted his gaze. "Reminds me of someone."

Attica scowled at the memory.

"Give him time," Hadrian said on the tail end of a cough. "If death decides to take him early, it will be his own doing."

Below, the flareback's core, a massive star-shaped nodule, flared in uneven bursts. Attica knew what that meant. These large flashwraiths didn't just die—they detonated. If that happened, the mana they carried would disperse too fast for the Vanguard to harvest. Wasted essence. Wasted effort.

He signaled to the hunting party with a sharp, silent motion, tightening his fingers into a fist.

They responded immediately.

Three ashlings and Eve, a seasoned huntress, shifted into formation. They moved like shadows, their shades suppressing their presence. All except one, Tiago. His shade flickered unevenly, edges fraying, restraining him.

Attica's jaw tightened as he watched the boy struggle with his shade.

The plan had been simple.

The flareback was powerful, but not invulnerable. Its chest plating protected its core, but its underbelly was exposed in the right moment—just before it released its stored light. They would use their shades to push through the flaylights hovering in the air, confuse the hulking monster, strike before it could combust, and slay the beast.

This had been the technique they had found worked best on flarebacks that were especially vibrant, signaling they would soon explode.

Attica glanced at Tiago, hoping to communicate what he was thinking through the harshness of his gaze. *Don't move too quickly. Let Eve and I do the work. Watch and learn.*

Tiago huffed, bristling as if he could feel the weight of Attica's unspoken command. Then, before anyone could stop him, a stone dislodged beneath his boot. It clattered down the ravine, a sharp, grating scrape against the rock.

Attica's breath caught. He motioned to the young man and his shade surged forward, snapping around Tiago like a living vise, yanking him back into the shadows before the sound could betray their position any further.

The flaylights reacted first.

The symbiotic parasites, once clustered in the air like drifting embers, exploded into motion. Their glow flared, an erratic spark of gold and white, casting eerie illumination through the mist.

The flareback lurched in their direction, the earth trembling before Attica even registered the movement.

The beast reared up, light surging through its body like molten veins.

Too fast. Too soon. The eruption was imminent.

Attica reacted on instinct: "Scatter!"

The Vanguard broke apart just as the flareback unleashed a searing wave of essence.

The blast ripped through the mist, turning the air into a storm of raw essence. It struck the ground where they had been moments before, reducing stone to splintered slag. The shock wave sent Tiago tumbling, his shade thrashing against the storm of flaylights attacking him.

The flareback locked onto Tiago and charged, the ground cracking beneath its weight, claws shearing into the stone as it barreled forward, an avalanche of living fire.

Attica moved to protect the youth.

His shade unfurled, wrapping around his legs, amplifying his speed as he surged forward to intercept the charge. His enormous shadowblade formed just in time to carve a deep gash along the flareback's plated shoulder.

The beast reeled, snarling, yet its armor held.

Eve flanked left, vanishing into the terrain, striking when the flareback's attention wavered.

Attica wove through the chaos, his movements fluid, tactical, instinct honed by years of survival. But the flareback's sheer power unraveled the battle, each stomp a quake, each flare of light a disorienting blast of brilliance warping the terrain, casting phantom afterimages that made it impossible to tell where the real threat stood.

The heat warped his vision, bending the mist like molten glass.

Attica barely dodged a swipe from its burning claws. He countered, shadowblade slicing along its flank.

But its armor held.

Then, a misstep. One of the ashlings, a quiet young man named Vilken, stumbled into the open, overwhelmed by the flaylights. The flareback pivoted, light building at its core. A direct hit would kill the young man. The boy's shade reacted instantly by slamming Vilken into an outcropping of jagged rock, the impact knocking him out cold.

"Get them clear!" Attica barked to Eve.

"On it!"

The flareback shifted. Its stance lowered. Attica's shade pulsed, recognizing the moment before he did.

He exhaled, then lunged low, his shade gliding him beneath the beast's guard, shadowblade angled for the exposed underbelly. At the same time—Tiago moved. Still reeling from his mistake, the young buck threw himself into the fray and drove his shadowblade deep into the flareback's exposed core and used his shade to fling himself away.

The flareback shrieked, an ear-splitting, agony-filled wail as it staggered, mana pouring from its wounds in chaotic, luminous streaks of light. Its star-core nodule twitched violently, flaring as it prepared to release a final, violent surge.

Attica didn't hesitate.

His shadowblade plunged deep, striking alongside Tiago's opening attack, finishing the job the younger warrior couldn't.

The flareback convulsed.

Its body shuddered, light unraveling, folding in on itself. There was no time to react as the air thickened, the very essence of the beast threatening to rupture.

It was too late. The flareback would tear itself apart, and it would take them all with it.

CHAPTER ELEVEN

The flareback's light writhed—boiling, resisting, fighting its own death.

For a breath, Attica was certain this was it. The light swelled, a heartbeat from detonation—a final, blinding rupture that would consume them all.

He had pushed too hard, risked too much.

He wouldn't make it back to the settlement. Wouldn't see Dayanne again, not now, not on the eve of something so important, so life-changing.

But then the light cracked.

A final, shuddering death rattle escaped the beast's chest as its massive form gave out. It crashed down in a heaving, thunderous collapse, the impact shaking the ground beneath their feet. Its star core pulsed once, flickered weakly, then went dark.

Silence settled in the swirling dust.

Attica exhaled slowly, his chest rising and falling in measured breaths. He felt Eve watching. He didn't need to look to know what expression she wore.

Attica turned sharply, locking eyes with Tiago. "You."

The youth had barely risen to his feet. His head dipped slightly, his expression caught between shame and stubborn defiance. "I didn't know if you would—"

Attica loomed over Tiago, dark hair falling into his face. His shade snapped forward before he even realized it had moved, curling around Attica's shoulders. Tiago cowered for a second but held his ground. Attica could feel the weight of his own fury, could sense the others watching—especially Eve.

Hadrian's voice surfaced in his mind. *Strike the ones who will carry your name forward, and they will strike in turn.*

At the time, it had felt like a riddle, something the old man had said just to sound profound. But now, in the heat of his frustration, it landed differently. The Vanguard had their ways. But violence out of sheer frustration? That wasn't their way. That wasn't the mark of a leader.

He glanced at the other ashlings, who were all watching him intently.

Attica finally exhaled sharply and turned away, his shade deflating around him. "Do that again, and I won't step in next time," he told Tiago, his voice cold. "You make that kind of mistake on your own, you die on your own."

Tiago nodded stiffly. "Understood. And . . ."

"And?" Attica asked, turning back to him.

"Sorry."

Attica let it go, but his hands were still shaking. He gestured toward the flareback and unclipped his gourd. "Gather its essence; that's always the first step. Then we can deal with its body. We'll need its skin, at least the parts that are usable. Use the skin to make bone sacks. It'll take time."

"So we'll camp here tonight?" Eve asked.

Attica answered with a grunt.

Normally, Attica and Eve would have pushed through the night and made it back to the settlement by morning. But with a trio of ashlings? Things went much slower, and it was best for them to spend as much time in the field in preparation of their trial. Out here, the Spiralrealm was alive, shifting with unseen forces beneath a red-ringed sun and a mist that concealed, a fate that could turn without warning. One misstep and it wouldn't be a lesson—it would be a grave.

After gathering the flareback's essence, the group got to work butchering the massive thing. Flesh was peeled from muscle, packed into sacks made of its own hide. Bones were freed with careful cuts, their edges honed for later use. Its armored plating, still warm, was pried loose—valuable, if reforged.

By the time they finished, the battlefield had grown still. The only trace of the hunt was the residual hum of energy that still clung to the air, like the ghost of the battle refusing to dissipate.

They made camp beneath an overhanging slab of ancient stone. The land settled, the air thick with the scent of earth. Attica sat cross-legged on a flat stone surrounded by the others, his gourd turning over in his hands, the essence inside shifting faintly, pulsing. Across from him, Eve leaned back against a rock, her eyes closed for a moment.

"Eat," Attica told the ashlings. He raised his gourd, watching as the others uncorked their own. "One or two inhales."

Attica demonstrated what he meant as he inhaled deeply, letting the raw power fill his lungs.

The metallic tang was sharp, intoxicating. It lingered in his lungs, stirring something distant. It was the smell of the Sanctum, the same scent that clung to Dayanne's skin when she returned from long hours beneath the halls. He corked the gourd and glanced toward Eve, who did the same.

She caught his gaze, a faint smile flickering at the corner of her lips.

"I heard the Seer has an even stronger essence," Tiago said, soon breaking the silence.

Vilken elbowed him hard in the ribs. "Quiet."

"You're the one that told me—"

Attica allowed himself a quiet chuckle at their bickering. He rolled his gourd once more in his palm, then set it aside. "She does."

Vilken frowned. "But the Seer's is forbidden."

"It is."

The final ashling, a girl named Ione, hesitated before speaking. "And the ritual with the Seer . . . we'll be required to handle it then, right?"

Attica nodded. "You will. But not her flask, her flask is made of bone. The ritual flask is made of stone and only has a little essence in it. That said, it's much stronger than this."

He could feel their eyes on him—not just as their leader tonight, but as someone who had already passed the trial, as someone who had stood before the Seer herself.

A beat of silence. Then, the question he had been waiting for.

"What is she like?" Ione asked.

Attica rested his hands on his knees. He pictured the Seer as she had been that night of his trial—the heavy stillness of her chamber, her ancient form draped across the chair, her sagging skin bathed in unbearable brightness. Her voice had hung in the air, neither here nor gone, just echoing inside the light.

"She's . . ." Attica started, then stopped. He thought of the first time he had stood before her, the light, the weight of her words.

"No one has really seen her, have they?" Tiago asked.

Attica ran a hand over the rough stubble on his jaw. He remembered the vision the Seer had given him when she pressed her finger into the center of his head, the settlement burning, the child of light. It was too much. "You will one day," he finally told the boy.

Tiago shifted closer, lowering his voice like he was sharing a secret. "What about Dayanne? She's a Spectralist. She works in the Sanctum. She could become one, you know . . ."

Attica's fingers stilled. He didn't react outright, but something in him stirred. Yet again, he could feel Eve's dark eyes on him, her gaze sharp, but he didn't turn to meet it.

"You're asking if she'll become a Seer," Attica said, his voice carefully neutral.

Tiago hesitated. "I mean . . . she's already with her. Already in the Sanctum. If anyone would—"

Attica cut him off with a shake of his head. "I would hope that isn't her fate."

No one spoke. Even Tiago knew better than to push further. Attica couldn't shake the thought that followed, especially with what was going on back home. *I shouldn't be out here. I should be back at the settlement . . .*

Later that night, once most had settled into a restless half sleep, Attica sat at the camp's edge, listening.

The Spiralrealm never truly slept.

It shifted in the dark, silent movements just beyond sight, unseen flashes of light stirring in the mist. A random beam of light flaring in the distance caught his attention, shifting just beyond reach—too far to touch, too close to ignore.

Eve approached, moving as she always did, smooth and deliberate. Her shade curled faintly around at wrists, shifting in a way Attica never quite understood. Feminine, but sharp, like the edge of a blade drawn slow.

Eve didn't speak at first, just settled beside him, her presence slipping into the quiet.

Attica didn't look at her. He didn't have to.

The spark between them was there, flickering at the edges of his awareness, something unspoken, something he refused to name.

The quiet moments after battle. The nights spent too long away from the settlement. The way Eve always sat just a fraction closer than necessary. This had happened before. Attica felt it. But he never acknowledged it. Dayanne existed in his mind, in his chest, in the spaces between these long nights.

Yet he couldn't deny there was something between them. A bond forged in battle, in blood, in nights spent at the edge of the world. Something that didn't ask for permission. Something that had always been there.

She never pushed. Never tried to break past the lines he had drawn. But tonight, when she exhaled, resting her arms on her knees, her gaze settling on him, the silence between them felt heavier.

Attica ruined it before it could settle. "We'll be back in the morning."

"I know. We didn't have to camp here."

"I want them to have more experience doing that, especially with a fresh kill."

"I know," she said. "But—"

"It will be fine," Attica said, cutting her off before she could say it. Before she could say her name. "Can you imagine at their age, taking on a flareback with a group that small?"

"Huh."

He shook his head. "We wouldn't have dared."

Eve smirked. "We're not that much older. You make us sound like Hadrian."

He gestured toward the resting ashlings. "They're sixteen, seventeen. The world is changing too fast for them."

"It always does. Are you sure it's not changing too fast for you? It will soon."

Attica glanced at her, catching a flicker of something in her expression before she looked away. His shade stirred, an uneasy ripple against his skin. "What do you mean?"

"You know what I mean. We think the world is different now—and it is. But it was different when the others were our age too, and it will be different for future ashlings."

Attica frowned. "Flarebacks, glintfangs, brighthowlers, emitters. Flaylights. There are more now than ever. And there will be more in the future." His jaw tensed. "Remember the strange bones Cassian found?"

A knowing look crossed her face. "I do. Maybe that's why the ashlings had to try for a flareback. Is it wrong for them to want to prove themselves?"

"You're defending Tiago?"

"If I recall, you told me once you were going to take one down alone."

"I would have."

Eve arched an eyebrow at him. "Then why shouldn't they?"

Attica didn't answer.

"The next generation will be bolder," she continued. "They might need to be." She nudged his shoulder, her shade brushing against his—light, fleeting, the same way she had always tested boundaries.

Attica tensed.

"I'm just saying." Her tone was playful, but her eyes were unreadable. "It's natural to feel the way we do about them. About the future of the settlement. I never thought I'd see the day you, the Lone-Eyed Wolf, became the cautious one."

"I'm not cautious."

Eve's smile faltered slightly. "That's a ridiculous thing to say. Especially now, with Dayanne waiting . . ."

Attica grunted a reply.

For the first time that night, Eve looked away first. "I should try to get some sleep," she said, standing. She hesitated, something unsaid lingering between them. But instead of voicing it, she simply added, "You should too."

Eve left before he could stop her. The mist swallowed her whole, shifting like something alive.

Attica sat in silence, the weight of her words pressing against something deeper—something he didn't want to name.

CHAPTER TWELVE

Attica woke to movement. A cool tendril of darkness curled over his shoulder. Not a warning, but something familiar. Watchful.

Eve.

His shade rippled against the stone, fluid and restless, like wind skimming over a black pool. He exhaled slowly, grounding himself before opening his eye to the dim glow of the Spiralrealm.

"You're awake," she murmured, her voice sliding into his mind without sound. "I know you went to bed later than all of us—"

"What is this about?" Attica pushed himself up, muscles protesting after the strain of the hunt.

"Want to take a wild guess?"

"No."

Eve paused for a fraction of a second, before stepping closer. "Tiago is missing."

"He . . . what?" Attica glanced toward the two ashlings, Vilken and Ione, standing near the spoils they had stripped from the flareback. Their gazes kept shifting, shoulders tense. A subtle fear—not of the Spiralrealm, but of Attica's forthcoming reaction.

A slow breath left him, measured, controlled.

Eve continued: "I've already checked the perimeter," she said. "He left before dawn. I can track him, but someone needs to stay with the others."

"Agreed."

"I don't know how far he's gone."

Attica dragged a hand down his face, wiping away the last dregs of sleep. "I'll handle it. Take Vilken and Ione back to the settlement. We've pushed them far enough."

Eve inclined her head and stepped past him. She paused, just within reach. For a moment, her shade stretched ever so slightly toward his, a brush of something unsaid, something felt but not spoken. The tension coiled tight before it broke. "I'll see you back there." Then, without another word, she turned and left, leading the others away, their packs heavy with the spoils of the hunt.

Attica watched her go, exhaled, and turned toward the horizon. His shade shifted restlessly, mirroring his irritation.

Tiago. If that idiot has gotten himself killed . . .

Attica crouched, pressing his palm to the cold stone. "Find him." His shade stretched forward like a second breath, rippling forward.

A second sight. A second awareness.

Attica's consciousness wavered, untethering ever so slightly, a disorienting sensation creeping in. And then—whispers. Faint. Fleeting. Not voices, not fully. Just scraps of sound, too soft to form words, too persistent to be ignored. They had always been there, lingering at the edges of his senses. He had never understood them, had never even been certain they were real.

He didn't let himself linger on them now as he moved on, following Tiago's tracks.

The climb down was easy. Years ago, scaling the walls of the Spiralrealm had been a feat in itself, but now, his shade anchored him effortlessly, extending and retracting like muscle and sinew.

Attica moved fast, silent, his anger simmering beneath the surface.

He has no right to do this. To just vanish and leave the others without a word, acting like he isn't responsible for anyone but himself! Attica clenched his jaw. "Reckless. Stupid," he muttered.

His fingers curled tighter as he landed on a lower ridge, scanning the mist. He knew this feeling—the part of himself that had once been young, reckless, and unafraid.

He wanted to tear into Tiago, to make sure the youth never made the same mistake again. But then he spotted the boy crouched on a narrow ledge, silhouetted against the shifting mist. Not panicked. Not lost. *Watching.*

Attica frowned. He scaled down in an instant, his shade flickering over the stone.

Tiago didn't flinch. Didn't move.

"Tiago—" Attica spit the name out through clenched teeth.

The boy didn't even glance at him. He simply passed his monocular to Attica. "Look. Between here and the third tier."

Attica hesitated, then took the instrument. He raised the monocular to his eye and saw it.

A floating shield—no, not a shield, but something shaped like one—hovered just above a lower ledge. The thing was massive, easily twelve feet tall, with dark chitinous plates wrapped around a glowing, pulsating core of light. It drifted weightlessly, suspended by forces Attica couldn't begin to understand. The light at its center burned steadily, controlled, precise—nothing like the wild, erratic bursts of a flareback.

"Have you ever seen something like it?" Tiago whispered.

Attica lowered the monocular. "I have not."

Tiago's grin widened. "A new one!"

"This is not the cause for celebration you think it is."

"Should we try for it?"

"Wh-what?" Attica's instincts warred with caution.

If Eve were here, they would do it. She would flank left, Attica would go right. The two would maneuver in sync, like they always did. But Tiago wasn't Eve. And Tiago wasn't ready.

"No."

Tiago blinked. "Why not?"

Attica handed the monocular back to him. "Did I ever tell you what happened to my eye?"

"The others did."

"Do you not see the lesson there?"

"There are two of us," Tiago countered.

"We will report it to the other Vanguard and send a party out. We don't go to the third tier."

"Why not?"

Attica had often wondered that himself. "It is more dangerous," he finally said, the words automatic, an answer that closed rather than invited.

"But it was on the second tier when I spotted it. I was up before everyone. My shade . . ." Tiago hesitated. "It wakes early. Sometimes it forces me to work out. It heals me faster too; I can't explain it."

Attica gave him a long look, finally taking in the boy properly. Now that he was paying attention, Tiago seemed stronger than he had been at that age. Leaner, but with more definition.

Attica ran a hand over his jaw. "Be that as it may, you left the group without waking any of us—"

"I just wanted a better look," Tiago admitted, shoulders rolling back. "And then . . . I kept following it."

Attica let out a slow breath, tension draining. He had been angry, but looking at the boy now, he felt something else. Understanding. If it had been him, years ago . . . would he have done any different? Probably not. He sighed, rubbing his temple. "We're going back and will report what we've both seen to the others. Understood?"

"So we'll send a party out?"

"We will."

"And I can be the one that tells them about it?"

"You can, but only if we leave now, Tiago. Some tasks aren't meant to be tackled blindly."

The journey back to the settlement stretched longer than Attica liked—mostly because Tiago wouldn't shut up. It wasn't that the boy was slow. If anything, his energy was expected. But after hours of travel, the endless stream of questions wore at Attica's patience.

"What do you think the Seer is actually like?" Tiago asked for what felt like the tenth time.

Attica didn't bother looking at him. "Why do you care?"

"I mean—what's she like when no one's watching?"

Attica exhaled through his nose. "Same as she is when you're watching."

"So . . . weird and brightly terrifying?"

"Probably."

Attica shifted around a rock, catching a faint glow through the mist ahead. Too distant to be a concern. He didn't slow.

Tiago continued, undeterred. "But Dayanne works with her as a Spectralist."

"We've already been over this."

"What has she seen? I'm sure she tells you things. My sister says she's heard other Spectralists talking about the Seer. Livia says they're always talking about the Seer."

"Your sister is not a Spectralist. She's like you but . . ." Attica thought of Livia. From what he'd heard about her silence and dedication, she was nothing like Tiago.

He finally turned his head, just enough to give him a look. Tiago grew quiet—for fifteen whole minutes, until he could no longer contain the silence. "What about shades?"

Attica sighed. "What about them?"

"What are they, really?"

Attica knew the answer, but he didn't say it.

Oddly enough, it hadn't been the Vanguard who had explained the origins of a shade, it had been Dayanne.

Years ago, before they had officially formed their union, Attica had stopped by the Sanctum to find her adjusting vials of essence on a stone shelf, each bottle faintly glowing in the dim chamber. The older members of their community took them in careful doses, rationed and precise, yet she handled them with effortless ease, as if she could read the mana within by touch alone.

When he asked what Dayanne was working on, the conversation had turned to shades.

"Think of them as remnants," she said, casual as ever, her fingers trailing over the glass. "Not ghosts, not exactly. Just . . . echoes. Pieces of something left behind." She gestured to the space beside him, where his shade hovered in its usual, flickering form. "Your shade was once something else," she had said, turning the vial in her hands. "Not someone. Not exactly. Just a . . . piece. There are more out there, you know."

Attica had stared at his shade then, something crawling beneath his skin. "Why aren't we told this?"

Dayanne offered up a playful shrug. "You're asking the wrong person."

The next day, as they were preparing for an excursion, Attica brought the question to Hadrian. "Why is this not common knowledge?" he asked. "Why don't they tell us shades were once alive?"

Hadrian hadn't even glanced at him as he responded. "Because not everything should be known."

Attica snorted at Hadrian's remark. "That's not an answer."

The older man paused, cracked his knuckles, and then turned to face him properly. "Vanguard who have known this in the past acted differently toward their shades. Some treated them as lost loved ones. Others began to hear things that weren't there. Think of shades as instruments of mana, of essence. No longer alive, even if they have . . . tendencies. It's best to see them this way, and not humanize them."

Attica let it go. There was finality in Hadrian's voice—the kind that closed doors before you even reached them. Now, walking beside Tiago, he finally responded. "Trust your shade," he told the boy. "It usually has your best interests at heart."

"Usually?"

Attica smirked. "Yes, even when it forces you to exercise in the morning."

Tiago groaned. "But what is it, exactly? You never said."

They crested a rocky incline, a jagged ledge that gave way to a mesa. Below, the crumbled outer ramparts of the settlement came into view, partially obscured by the shifting mist.

"Think of your shade as an instrument of essence," Attica said.

Before the boy could ask any more questions, movement caught his eye. A figure broke through the mist, moving fast. Too fast.

Attica went still, his shade flaring instinctively, poised for an ambush.

Something was off. The way the scout ran, frantic, but not in fear. Urgent, but not desperate. And then—

Dayanne.

He launched forward, his shade propelling him ahead in a blur of motion. The scout stumbled as Attica landed in front of him.

"Attica—" The man caught his breath, his face flushed from exertion. "Dayanne's in labor."

The world snapped into focus.

His shade surged, and Attica vanished into motion.

CHAPTER THIRTEEN

Attica cut through the winding stone corridors, his shade pulsing in time with his breath, coiling and unraveling in anticipation.

He reached the Sanctum and stepped inside.

The chamber was bathed in the soft glow of essence, the air thick with the scent of stone, crushed resin, and the faint metallic tang of mana-infused herbs. The Spectralists maintained a quiet ceremony, their shades pulsing faintly as they passed a small bundle between them. Their murmured blessings wove through the air, low and rhythmic, a chant of protection as they cradled the child in arms both physical and shadowed, brushing him with strands of flickering dark.

Attica's breath caught in his throat when he saw her.

Dayanne lay on a bed of woven cloth, her face pale but her eyes sharp, the necklace she'd made out of the stone he had given her gleaming against the sweat on her chest. "A boy," she told Attica as a single tear had started to slip down her cheek. She caught herself, exhaling sharply and straightening. She was Shadowborn, as were they all—she had endured worse pain than this before.

"My love," Attica breathed, barely aware he'd spoken aloud.

He moved closer, his heartbeat thundering in his ears. He took her hand, his grip firm but careful, his fingers tracing over her skin as if confirming she was real. His shade trembled toward her—unsteady, stretched thin by a feeling it shouldn't have known.

Attica nearly told his shade to get itself together, yet he refrained, choosing instead to focus on the warmth of Dayanne's palm against his own.

His mother stood at Dayanne's side, unmoving, an unshakable presence in the dim light. The last Spectralist whispered a final blessing, then stepped aside. Attica's mother reached forward, lifting the bundle in her arms. "Lone-Eyed Wolf," she said softly. And for the first time, Attica saw his son properly.

The infant was impossibly small, his skin warm and dark, his features delicate but unmistakable. A soft tuft of dark hair covered his head, and his body, untouched by a shade, seemed almost fragile without its presence. That would come later, when he was old enough to withstand the bond.

Attica's mother turned to Dayanne, her voice steady. "Strange."

"What do you mean?"

She brought the child to her ear as if to confirm. "He hasn't cried."

Murmurs spread around the space from the other Spectralists as they all confirmed what Attica's mother had said.

"He is Shadowborn," Attica said, pride swelling in his chest. "He has no need for tears."

"No, no, he does not," his mother told him as she turned the child toward Dayanne. "What will you name him?"

Dayanne looked up at Attica, searching his face. They had spoken of this before, on quiet nights, when the weight of the future had felt distant, when things like this had still been far-off dreams.

"Eli," she finally said.

"Eli," Attica repeated.

He hadn't realized how tight his chest had been until he let out a slow breath. He reached forward, fingers grazing the child's tiny hand. Eli stirred, his movements sluggish, impossibly soft compared to the harshness of the world waiting outside these walls.

"Eli," his mother echoed softly.

Dayanne smiled. Just barely. Just enough to stay whole. The moment should have lasted forever, but as it often did, the world had other plans.

A shift in the air made Attica's shoulders stiffen.

He didn't turn immediately, unwilling to tear himself from this moment, but he knew the weight of a summons when he felt it. A younger Vanguard stood at the doorway, arms at her side, gaze expectant. "They need you at the lodge."

Attica clenched his eyes shut and bowed his head. He had known this was coming. Tiago had likely gone ahead and explained the shield-shaped flashwraith they had encountered. The Vanguard wouldn't let something like that go unanswered.

Dayanne reached out to him, fingers curling lightly around his wrist. Attica turned back to her, meeting her gaze.

She was exhausted, but her eyes held a quiet understanding. "Go," she said.

"I—"

"I'll be here when you return, my love."

"My love." He pressed a kiss to her hand—light, lingering. He rose and his shade coiled around him, mirroring his reluctance.

Then, he was gone.

*   *   *

The lodge was carved deep into the rock, its walls reinforced with slabs of prismatic stone hauled from the second tier of the Spiralrealm. At its center lay a circular recess, a pit of fine white sand enclosed by a raised ring of stone. It was here that the Vanguard mapped their hunts, their battles, their futures.

And now, their next move.

Attica stepped inside. The first to acknowledge him was Eve, who pressed her tongue briefly against the inside of her lip, her expression unreadable. She offered him a curt nod, a quiet acknowledgment, nothing more. Even now, in a room full of their peers, she remained measured—curious, perhaps, but disciplined above all else.

The gathered warriors stood in a loose formation, their conversation low but charged with the weight of the unknown. At the center, Tiago stood over the sand pit, his movements exaggerated as he gestured toward the sand.

His shade seeped into the dust, bringing it to life. Shadows carved rough lines into the surface of the sand, shaping a crude but unmistakable rendering of the flashwraith's shield-like body compared to the size of an average man.

Attica bit his lip, unease curling at the edges of his mind. A brighthowler, the two-headed creature that had taken his left eye, was dangerous. But this? This was something else.

"With plating like that, it will be hard to kill," Hadrian said, the other elder Vanguard grunting alongside him. "Did you get a look at its backside?"

Attica's gaze shifted toward the far end of the chamber to his mentor, who sat in his throne of carved basalt, the dark stone absorbing the flickering light of the lanterns. Aside from a long, gnarly beard, he had not changed much over the years— his presence was as solid as ever, unshaken, but time had thickened the lines in his face.

Hadrian leaned slightly against the armrest, and though he made no outward show of it, Attica caught the flicker of movement—a cough into his fist, too controlled to seem casual. He had been unwell for some time now, but he had survived longer than most, and that alone commanded respect.

"What's the plan?" Attica asked.

Hadrian's gaze lifted, meeting his evenly. "We handle it," he told him simply. "But only if it comes back up to the second tier."

"I can lead the hunt," Attica said.

Laughter rumbled from a few of the older Vanguard. It was a knowing sound, a brief and unexpected break in the tension. Hadrian's lips twitched in something that might have been amusement. "You've just had a child, Lone-Eyed Wolf," Hadrian said on the tail end of a cough. "Enjoy the day off."

The laughter grew, rippling through the chamber as Attica bristled. "Something like that doesn't belong in the Spiralrealm."

"And it won't be there much longer, at least not this close to the settlement," Hadrian replied, tone even. "Others will handle it. You trust us?"

Attica clenched his jaw but knew better than to argue. He had earned his place here, but Hadrian's word was final.

He looked back to the sand pit, where the shape of the shield remained etched in faint, ghostly lines. It would be retrieved and studied. That much, he was certain. But even now, standing over its image, he felt an unease he couldn't quite name.

Hadrian leaned back slightly, expression unreadable. "Go home, Attica. Be with Dayanne."

His shade coiled tighter, resisting. Something about this felt unfinished. *But Hadrian has spoken, and Dayanne is waiting*, he reminded himself.

Attica turned, jaw tight. "Come on." And with that, he was gone.

The rest of the day blurred into ritual.

Soft chanting filled the Sanctum's innermost chamber. The Seer's words threaded through the dim light, ancient and intangible. Her thin voice rising and falling in a rhythm older than the settlement itself, words shaped by generations past. Attica couldn't understand them, but they carried weight—lacing the heavy air with something unspoken, something absolute.

Eli stirred against his chest, his tiny body shifting, a hiccupping breath escaping him.

"It's fine," Attica's mother whispered beside him, her hands firm around his arm. "The child must know."

"Know what?" he asked with another glance toward the Seer as the chamber pulsed with a deeper glow, the light swallowing her form entirely.

"Know his place," his mother said.

Attica ran a steadying hand down Eli's back, grounding himself in the warmth of his son's body. The child barely weighed anything, but somehow, he was the heaviest thing he had ever held. The weight settled him. Grounded him. Yet as the ceremony dragged on, Attica wished he could go back to Dayanne, who was recovering.

Soon, the hum of gathered Spectralists filled the chamber, low and resonant, a single note threading through the Seer's chant. It built upon itself, a vibration in Attica's chest, sinking into his bones. He barely noticed when Eli's quivering lip stilled, when the soft sound of his breath evened out against him.

For the first time in as long as he could remember, Attica let himself breathe.

He had loved his life—or, at the very least, he had accepted it without question. The Vanguard's purpose was clear. The hunts, the disturbances beyond the wall, the investigations—each day shaped by duty. He had thought he had understood the meaning in it all, but now, standing before the Seer with his newborn son, something in him stirred.

How much had he missed?

For the settlement. For the Painter. The words had been drilled into Attica since childhood, a mantra woven into the very fabric of his being. But now, for the first time, they rang hollow.

He forced his doubts away, let them fade into the flickering gray. Not to the Spiralrealm. Not to the flareback, or Tiago, or the strange shield-shaped flash-wraith that floated in the lower tier. Not to the Vanguard, or the Seer, or even to the whispers of rising change among their enemies—like something unseen was shifting, evolving.

Attica tried to be present, to truly be here. But it felt the same as when he was on the hunt, the moment before the strike. His shade tensed, a familiar pressure curling at the edges of his being, sensing what he could not.

And then Eli's fingers curled against his chest, impossibly small, impossibly warm, anchoring him before the thought could fully form, bringing him back to the present. Attica pressed a kiss to his son's forehead, breathing in the scent of him—new, untouched by the violence beyond these walls.

The warmth of home awaited both of them.

He left, Attica drifting back to Dayanne as if floating through a dream. The settlement faded, the world narrowing as he reached the quiet space of their two-room home with Eli. She awaited him, wrapped in a blanket, half sitting in bed, exhaustion softening the sharpness in her features.

"Attica," she murmured, her voice syrupy and warm, her eyes half lidded.

He reached the bedside, hesitating. He didn't want to let go of Eli—not yet. "Do you . . . mind?"

She let out a quiet laugh at his serious expression. "Why would I?"

Attica glanced over his shoulder, only now realizing his mother had gone. "I didn't see her leave."

Dayanne laughed again, softer this time. She brought a small gourd to her lips, one he hadn't seen before.

"What's that?" he asked.

"A mixture of the community's essence and the Painter's—" She stopped herself. "The *Seer's.*"

His brows furrowed. "Are you sure it's safe?"

"All mothers are allowed a full ritual flask on the day they give birth. I told you. It's important later for the bonding of the shade."

"You did?"

She took another sip. "I told you."

Attica didn't press the point. The last time he'd come into contact with the stuff, it had brought on a terrible vision. He wanted nothing to do with it. He sat on the edge of the bed, shifting carefully to avoid waking Eli. "He's so small." The words slipped out. "So small . . ."

Attica wasn't sure what else to say. The room felt too quiet, too fragile—like sound itself might shatter the moment. They had tried for so long and failed. Month after month, year after year. For a time, Attica and Dayanne had both wondered if it would ever happen at all.

Yet now, the impossible has been made real, he thought as he glanced down at Eli, the infant asleep against his chest. So light. So impossibly real. "He's perfect," Attica said. "So quiet."

"He's ours," Dayanne told him softly. "And he'll make noise when he wants to. You'll be a great father."

"And you, a great mother. And our son . . ."

"A great member of the Vanguard," Dayanne said firmly, the teasing lilt in her voice shifting into something fierce.

Attica met her gaze. Her lips were still curved, but her grip on the Seer's flask was tight. A rare seriousness glinted in her dark eyes.

"Eli," she continued. "Son of the Lone-Eyed Wolf. Grandson of Spiran, Knife of the Glintfang."

Attica exhaled, shaking his head. "Hopefully, he won't let youthful hubris take his eye."

"Youthful hubris?" She laughed. "You are still young, Attica, two years younger than me, if I recall." She smiled, tired but certain. "He'll hear of your misadventures enough to know better."

He shifted beside her carefully, cradling Eli between them. The house was quiet, the only sound the steady rhythm of their son's breath.

For once, Attica let himself rest.

He didn't wake when Dayanne stirred in the night, when she took Eli from his arms to feed him, when she whispered to Attica softly, her voice thick with a prophecy born of the Seer's flask, fragile and half lost to the dark.

For years, the memory would remain frayed along the edges, blurred by the strain and triumph of exhaustion. A moment half lived, slipping between wakefulness and dream. But one day, he would recall that night in full, remembering the quiet certainty in her tone, the meaning woven into her words.

And when he did, the memory would return whole, and the Spiralrealm would never be the same.

CHAPTER FOURTEEN

The morning felt wrong, almost too still, as if the Spiralrealm itself was holding its breath.

Attica woke to the sensation before his mind had fully caught up. A weight, not physical, but something deeper—a pressure that sat heavy on his chest, winding through his bones. His shade curled at the edge of his senses, restless, seemingly happy to find that he was finally up.

Nearby, Dayanne sat at the edge of their bed with dark robes draped over her shoulders, her form bathed in the gray light that filtered through the stone slats of their home. She rocked Eli gently against her chest, speaking softly to him in a voice that barely rose above a whisper.

"You should go," she said without looking at him.

Attica sat up, rubbing his face. "You feel it too?"

"We all do." Dayanne kept her focus on Eli, tracing the curve of his tiny fingers. "Or at least, those of us who are in tune with the essence. With the Painter. A disturbance."

"Yes, a disturbance. That would be a good way to describe it."

She finally glanced over at him, her gaze steady as a strand of her long dark hair fell into her face. "And if you can't feel it, you can hear it. The Vanguard have returned."

Attica closed his eye and listened, realizing she was right. The low murmur of voices carried from beyond the walls, a hum of tension that wasn't there the night before.

"I usually hear them," he said.

"No, you don't," she teased. "You usually snore so loudly they hear you."

A small smile tugged at his lips. "I've never snored a day in my life," he told her, shifting closer to look down at their son. "I still can't believe it."

"That we're parents?"

"That," he said. The word held everything they'd endured up until that point, from their intimate moments to losses in the community, the harsh times they had shouldered together, like the days during the storm that shrouded the uppermost tier in dust, making it impossible to gather essence for nearly a month.

Attica didn't want to leave.

Everything he had was within arm's reach. The way Eli's breath warmed the space between them, the way Dayanne's presence had changed, softer now, but no less powerful—Attica's world was now complete. They had survived so much, endured loss and hardship, yet somehow, this moment felt even more monumental than all the battles before.

And now, it was being disturbed by what he knew was the return of a hunting party.

"The first night wasn't so bad," Dayanne murmured. "Aside from . . ." She trailed off, finally looking him in the eye. "Do you remember anything I said?"

"Did you say something?"

"Good," she said simply. Dayanne gestured toward the door. "Go. Check on them. Then come back so I can sleep."

"As you wish." He pressed a hand briefly to her shoulder before slipping out into the settlement.

The return of the hunting party came with none of the usual fanfare. No cheers of victory, no triumphant boasting. Instead, there was only quiet unease, a gathering of warriors standing just beyond the settlement's walls, surrounding the hulking form of a new flashwraith.

Attica didn't have to push to the front. The Vanguard parted for him, some clapping him on the back in greeting, others simply stepping aside. Eve squeezed his arm as he passed, but her expression was unreadable.

He barely registered them, his focus now on what lay in the center of the gathering, the strange shield monster that young Tiago had discovered.

Attica stopped short, his gut twisting as he took in its impossible form.

The flashwraith was massive, its outer shell dark and jagged, its core now hollow, stripped of the blinding eye of light that had once gleamed at its center. Its barbed edges curled inward. Parts were rough, charred like brittle stone; others gleamed with an unnatural sheen, as if reforged in fire and cooled in a world that had forgotten color.

It was supposed to be dead and yet, the giant shield creature floated. Not high, just an inch or so off the ground, as if refusing to surrender.

Attica's breath slowed, his shade tensing around him.

He finally looked over to Hadrian, who stood beside the carcass, his arms folded behind his back, his shade shifting faintly at his feet to support his stance. Even from a distance, Attica could tell something was different about him.

"Ever seen anything like it?" Attica asked, stepping forward.

Hadrian's lips pressed into a thin line. He brought a hand to his mouth, coughed once, and shook his head. "No. But that doesn't mean anything. The Spiralrealm is full of things we've yet to see."

Attica's eye flicked toward the ashlings, who all stood at attention. Tiago could barely contain his excitement. He kept glancing his way, seeking acknowledgment. Attica ignored him for now.

He turned back to Hadrian, who seemed to interpret what Attica was about to ask next: "We don't know why it is still floating." A long silence, then: "That's the question, isn't it? Why does it still float?"

Attica crouched before the massive thing. He ran a hand just beneath the creature's edge without touching it. The space between his fingers and its shell hummed faintly, an energy he couldn't quite place.

Hadrian continued, "The others believe it could be used for armor, but none of our shades can pierce it. Not yet."

Attica straightened, meeting Hadrian's gaze. "What do you propose we do with it?"

"I do not know. But I do know this: It cannot stay here."

The Vanguard stirred at Hadrian's words, their reactions split between generations.

The older warriors—those who had survived more years than most—nodded in grim agreement, their expressions unreadable but their silence heavy with understanding. They had seen too much to believe anything good could come from something so unnatural.

The younger Vanguard shifted restlessly, casting uneasy glances at one another. Some had expected a decisive order, a challenge, a call to arms. A few of them—Tiago among them—looked disappointed, their excitement over the rare find souring into frustration. To them, the creature was an opportunity, a discovery worthy of immediate action, not something to be cast aside.

"This is the first of its kind," Tiago said. "Shouldn't we be studying it? Finding a way to use it?"

"Use it for what?" Ione shot back, who was next to Tiago's younger sister, Livia. "You want to strap it to your back and see if it makes you invincible?"

A few snorts of laughter followed, but the tension remained, thick and uneasy.

"We've fought flashwraiths for generations," another Vanguard named Garax chimed in, younger but not reckless. "We know what to expect from them. But this? It didn't die the way *they* do. It doesn't fall, doesn't settle. And now it's just . . . waiting?" He gestured at the floating husk, his wariness clear.

Hadrian let the voices rise for a moment, absorbing their doubts, their eagerness, their fear. Then, with a single look, he quieted them. "It does not belong here," he repeated, firmer this time. "And if you think that means it should be ours, then you have not been paying attention."

"I can take it down to the third tier," a Vanguard named Cassian volunteered.

Hadrian shook his head. "The Vanguard do not go down there."

"Then I tip it over the edge."

"It's not a bad idea," Attica said, echoing Cassian's suggestion. "Better there than here."

Hadrian's voice remained firm. "No, you don't tip it over the edge, Cassian. I do, and I head down with it to make sure it doesn't come back."

"What are you saying?" Attica asked.

"It is my time." Hadrian coughed into his hand again, softer this time, as if trying not to let them hear. "It is imminent."

A lump formed in Attica's throat. He already knew what Hadrian meant, but he asked anyway. "You're choosing . . . exile?"

Hadrian's eyes flickered, his shade flaring then settling. "It's been coming for some time. I'm no longer fit for the field. I will take the shieldwraith with me. This is my decision."

Attica clenched his jaw, expecting the Vanguard around him to protest, but none did. It was not an announcement to be taken lightly. "That's not necessary."

"All Shadowborn must exile themselves if they live long enough," Hadrian said firmly. "It is our way."

"It doesn't have to be."

Hadrian's expression didn't change. "It has always been."

The moment settled between them, heavy with the finality of it. Then—the giant shield twitched. A sharp buzz, more vibration than sound, thrummed through the air.

Attica's shade snapped to attention and so did the others, a synchronized ripple of instinct.

The creature lurched upward, flying ten feet above them. It tilted midair, rotating toward the depths of the Spiralrealm.

"Get back—!" Attica shouted.

The monster fired a blast of light. The moment the light struck downward, the focused beam vanished into the abyss below, swallowed whole by the darkness of the Spiralrealm's lower tiers.

For a breath, no one moved.

Then, with a heavy, almost reluctant *thunk*, the shield collapsed. The impossible force that had held it aloft was gone. It struck the ground like deadweight, its jagged shell scraping against the stone.

A few of the Vanguard flinched, stepping back instinctively, as if expecting it to spring back to life. But it didn't move. Whatever power had sustained the shield had been spent.

"A signal." Hadrian's voice cut through the hush, grim and steady. "It was a signal."

Attica turned to him. "To what?"

"I do not know."

The younger Vanguard stirred uneasily. Some shifted their gazes to the distant horizon, others toward the mist-wreathed depths below.

Attica turned to the others, his voice sharp. "Get it to the edge and push it to the second."

"Yes," Hadrian said, taking over from there. "And prepare a harness. I will take it with me on my exile, but first I must bid farewell to the Seer." He gestured at the shield. "Make sure my shade can drag it."

"No," Attica said, standing firm. "You're not doing it alone."

Hadrian paused, watching him. The Vanguard quieted again, all eyes drawn not to the shield, but to the old man and the Lone-Eyed Wolf.

Hadrian finally relented. "Yes, fine. That's fine, Attica. You can help me some of the way."

CHAPTER FIFTEEN

The corridors of the settlement twisted around him, narrow and dim. Attica barely registered them—Hadrian's words looped through his skull, colliding with the image of the shield creature collapsing after sending its signal below.

Whatever it was, something had changed.

Attica suppressed the urge to return to the Vanguard. He kept walking, intent on seeing Dayanne before he set off.

Attica tried to steady his breath, to slow the pounding in his chest, but it was proving difficult. The weight of it all pressed down on him, the anxiety of fatherhood and the recent developments heavier than it should have been.

He reached the threshold of their home and pushed inside, going straight down the steps, where he found Dayanne exactly where he had left her. She sat at the edge of the bed, Eli curled in her arms, a soft look on her face. She barely lifted her gaze as he entered. "You won't be staying this afternoon," she said, not as a question, but as a statement of fact.

She always knows, Attica thought as he took her in, the love of his life, the person whose spirit had guided him through his trial. He stood there dumbfounded for a moment by her beauty, the way her eyes always drew him in.

"No," he admitted. "Something happened. As you know, Tiago and I spotted a new type of flashwraith yesterday. They retrieved it and brought it back to the settlement, but it . . ." He ran a hand through his hair, exhaling sharply. "It did something, Dayanne. It released some kind of signal down into the Spiralrealm."

"A signal?"

"I think. I don't know. But it was something, and the light was not like others I have seen. It felt focused, more deliberate. And then the thing just fell, lifeless again. I don't know what it means, but it's wrong. It's all wrong."

"Surely you aren't keeping it near the settlement."

"Of course not," he said quickly, his voice tight. "We can't risk keeping it here, even if it doesn't appear to be alive anymore. The elder Vanguard agree. They—" He clenched his jaw, pacing. "That's not all of it. He . . . Hadrian—" Attica faltered, struggling to say the words aloud, as if speaking them would make them irreversible.

"He's leaving," Dayanne finished for him, her tone even as she continued to rock Eli.

Attica stopped pacing and turned to her. He couldn't hide the accusatory edge in his voice. "You knew?"

Dayanne held his gaze, hers unreadable, holy in its own way. "Hadrian is dying, Attica. And he has made his choice. He will drink from the flask and exile," she said softly. "The Seer has spoken of this."

Attica's stomach twisted. "What? Why didn't you tell me?"

"There is much that happens behind closed doors that's not meant for others to know." She studied him for a moment, as if weighing how much she should say. "And Hadrian requested it. His choice."

Attica took a step closer, his mind racing. "What is it really, Dayanne? What's in the flask?"

She sighed, shifting Eli slightly in her arms. "The flask contains the essence of the Painter, all that our settlement has. Think of it like that."

"But what does it do?" His voice was sharper than he intended, but he needed answers, needed something solid to grasp onto.

"It does . . ." She hesitated, fingers tightening around the fabric of Eli's wrap. "It changes your eyes. I know that from experience. If you take enough, it changes your eyes."

Attica exhaled through his nose. "Your *eyes*?"

"Yes, but not in a way you can imagine. Will you go with Hadrian?" she asked, changing topics.

"How did you . . . ?" He decided not to finish the question. Dayanne always knew. "Yes, I will go with him and help him the best that I can."

"Surely not past the third tier."

Attica swallowed. He had fought beside Hadrian for years, had learned everything he knew from the older man. The man had become a father figure he never had. *And now, just like that, he is leaving? It makes no sense . . .*

"I won't go to the third tier," Attica promised, "but I will help him get it there."

Eli stirred against Dayanne's chest, tiny fingers twitching in his sleep. Attica's gaze softened as he looked down at their son. He was so small, so unaware of the world beyond these walls, all the joys and pains that were in store for him.

A new thought came to him as he stared at the child. "Has he made a sound yet?"

"He has not," Dayanne said. "But that means nothing. Eli and I will be safe here. But you, you, you must be careful," Dayanne murmured, cradling Eli closer. "You have two people relying on you now."

Attica's breath caught. "I understand."

"Don't go to the third tier."

"I won't."

"Hadrian will not be himself. Be ready for that."

"I will try my best."

He stepped back, his weight shifting onto the balls of his feet, itching to leave, to move, to *do* something. But as he turned toward the door, Attica felt it—the pull of something unfinished, something unspoken lingering between them.

Dayanne's voice was barely above a whisper. "Be careful, my love."

The tiers twisted beneath them were covered in fog as they descended toward the unseen depths of their world like the remnants of a long-dead leviathan, the ancient ripples in its petrified skin creating the crumbling layers of the Spiralrealm.

It was not a perfect spiral—not truly.

The layers wound downward in uneven steps, each tier smaller than the last, yet filled with vast stretches of stone and shadow, their edges hidden by the ever-present mist that feathered through the chasms.

The uppermost tier, home to the Shadowborn and their settlement, spanned several miles in width. It was their refuge, their last line against the encroaching light, and for generations, it had been enough.

The idea of pushing the settlement farther inland had been raised before. But no one truly knew how long the ruin they called home had sheltered them. The walls—weathered and scarred—stood as silent sentinels, strong, protecting the Shadowborn and whoever had come before, whoever had built them, was now dust.

The deepest points of the Spiralrealm were unknown, unreachable, obscured by mist and rumored to be perilous. The farther one descended, the more treacherous the world became, which was why going past the second tier was strictly forbidden. It was said that light pooled in the lower depths, not as salvation, but as something else entirely, something that should never be reached.

Attica pushed these thoughts aside as he approached the gathered Vanguard outside of the settlement's walls.

Their formation was tense, quiet. They stood along the ridge, their focus locked on the thing they had dragged back from the wilds.

The shield-like flashwraith had been secured with thick ropes wound around its jagged frame, its once-floating body now unnervingly still. A harness had been rigged, made of heavy flashwraith-leather straps and braided cord designed to loop over a body and distribute weight for the long descent.

Hadrian was already prepared.

The older man stood near the edge of the first tier, his frame draped in a heavy cloak, his movements sluggish but deliberate. Two Vanguard assisted him, adjusting the straps over his shoulders, securing the bindings at his waist. His breaths came in uneven bursts, his gaze flickering between lucidity and something else entirely.

Attica's stomach tightened the moment he finally saw his face.

Hadrian's eyes were too wide, and his tongue flicked out occasionally, wetting his lips like a man tasting something only he could perceive.

Hadrian whispered to himself. He pointed to a rock near the edge, one with symbols on it, and mumbled incoherently. He reached his hands out as if trying to grasp something unseen. His shade flickered at his back, warping at the edges, its form struggling against whatever force was unraveling him from within.

His gaze snapped to Attica, and for the first time in years, there was something bright behind Hadrian's eyes, something too bright.

"Ah! There you are, lad!" He clasped Attica's hand with surprising strength. His grip lingered, as if testing to make sure Attica was real. "You are so much larger than you used to be. Why, you're a man . . . you're a man!" Hadrian's eyes watered. "A good man, good lad." He peered off into the distance. "You see it, don't you? The way the light bends? The way it moves?" He motioned to the rock with symbols carved in. "The words? You see them, yes?"

Attica didn't answer.

Hadrian let out a breathy laugh. It was not the dry chuckle of the stoic man Attica had known his entire life, but something else, something unmoored. "It's all there, just waiting! We have all been so blind! I thought we had forgotten, but I hadn't! Not really!" He started to sob and stopped, his eyes once again flashing with intensity. "The flask—it opens the door, lad. Do you see? Do you see now?"

Attica exchanged a glance with Eve, who had moved up beside him. Concern darkened her expression. "You're really going with him?"

"I am."

"What does Dayanne think?" Eve asked, a question that took Attica by surprise. Eve rarely mentioned Dayanne, if ever.

He hesitated. "I won't go past the end of the second. That's her only concern."

"Attica . . ." Her voice was barely above a whisper, meant only for him. "Hadrian has drunk from the flask. His mind isn't his mind any longer. You must understand this about him."

Attica hesitated, watching Hadrian pull against his harness with the restless energy of a man half his age. The flask had given him a new strength—but at what cost?

"I will be back," Attica promised Eve. "I will make sure he completes his . . . mission."

A hint of sadness flickered across her eyes. "When?"

"By tomorrow. Or sooner."

Her lips parted, a thought caught between silence and speech.

"We do not know the extent of what may happen," he told her, the words forming before he could fully process them. "And the Vanguard must always be ready. Have the ashlings assist the scouts. The settlement must be prepared."

"The ashlings are not ready."

"No one ever is," he said, though his tone was distant, his thoughts already moving ahead of him.

"Attica—" Eve began.

Hadrian turned abruptly, clapping his hands together. "Enough of this waiting! Let's go, let's bring the shieldwraith to the depths together, lad!" The older man slipped the last part of the harness into place, gripping the lead rope in his hands, dragging it taut. "Argh!" He took a staggering step forward. The shieldwraith scraped against the ground as it shifted, its weight unnatural even in its stillness.

Attica's shade unfurled, wrapping around his legs, steadying him. He didn't look back to Eve and the rest of the Vanguard.

He didn't need to.

Attica was certain he would return.

CHAPTER SIXTEEN

The descent was silent at first, Hadrian erratic at the front as he led with the harness while Attica and his shade pushed the shieldwraith from behind. The massive, jagged thing scraped against the stone, its unnatural weight a constant reminder of the task at hand. The mist clung thick to the air, curling around their feet, filling the spaces between the broken terrain.

Hadrian whispered half-formed phrases under his breath that made little sense. He spoke of the Baffled King, the Council of Torn, the shattering of the Crown of Shadows. Twice, he spoke to someone he called the Mother of Whispers, Hadrian assuring her that he was on his way.

It pained Attica to watch the old man unraveling. This wasn't exhaustion. This was erosion—of mind, of memory, of meaning. The man who had once led the Vanguard with absolute clarity now spoke in riddles to ghosts that weren't there.

"Let's keep going," Attica told him again.

As they pressed on, Hadrian's breath grew ragged, his steps uneven, not with strain, but with the slow decay of something vital unraveling inside him.

Attica knew it wasn't the weight of the wraith that burdened him. *It is the Seer's flask.* Whatever Hadrian had consumed had unraveled his mind, threading through his thoughts, a needle through cloth. The stoic, inspiring man Attica had looked up to for years was slipping away.

"You'll see it one day, lad," Hadrian said, wide-eyed, gazing out into nothing. "If you make it that far . . ."

The pair came to the bones of a long-dead flareback, its ribs removed, skull smashed to bits. Attica hadn't been part of this hunt, but he had heard the story from Eve, how the Vanguard had left it behind when their gourds were filled, marking the place as if to ward off the unknown.

"You'll see . . . you'll see . . ." Hadrian kept saying. "One day, lad."

"See what?" Attica asked, not entirely certain he wanted to know the answer.

"It all makes so much sense now. And at the same time . . ." The older man trailed off, his expression shifting. He dropped a hand from his harness and smoothed it over his twisted beard. "At the same time, it makes absolutely no sense. Why did we *not* go after the shards ourselves? Why did we allow the dukes and duchesses to hoard them away in the lower tiers? Why are the exiled only granted these powers now? We . . . we could have done something!" His shade flickered wildly, distorting at the edges. "I know, Arminius, I know."

Attica frowned. "Who is Arminius?"

"That was my shade's name. It still is."

"We are not supposed to name our shades."

Hadrian scoffed at this suggestion. "Arminius doesn't need a name. He already had one, long before we were joined. There were other names, but that was his last. Yours is—"

"I'm not interested in knowing," Attica said, which caused his shadow to tremble. He remembered what Dayanne had told him about the shades, how they were once members of the Shadowborn community. "Why didn't you become a shade? Why exile?"

Hadrian snorted at the thought. "Me? I have served my role. There comes a time . . . not all can continue, young man. And I'm curious, boy. I want to know what it is I've been hiding from all my life."

"I'm no longer a boy."

Hadrian continued: "Not all are forced to remain in the community, to further it along, to delay . . . delay the inevitable. We earn the choice through sacrifice. I chose to drink from the flask, yes, I chose to have my eyes opened. I did this for my shade. For the shades before him. Because I wanted to know . . . selfish. I am selfish."

"No, you aren't," Attica said, his voice firm. "You are the most selfless man I've ever known."

Hadrian laughed, short and brittle. "I wanted to know, and now . . ." He slapped the side of his head. "Now, I do." He slapped the side of his head again. "I know! Ha! And now? Now, I don't want to know, now I can't forget, now I must endure. It was all folly, all . . ." He trailed off, babbling phrases Attica didn't recognize until he finally grew quiet.

Later, they came within about a mile to the edge of the second tier, the sky dimming into the half light of the Spiralrealm's eternal dusk. The terrain here flattened as it pushed toward the edge, its surface fractured by jagged fault lines— the remnants of some long-forgotten shift in the world's bones. The mist was thinner too, less oppressive, yet it still was impossible to see straight through to the other side of the Spiralrealm.

"We camp here," Attica said, though every part of him wanted to push forward, to return to the settlement, to Dayanne and baby Eli. "You're in no condition to keep going."

"It's only over the edge."

"We rest," Attica said. "It's better. You taught me to take rest whenever it is offered."

Hadrian made a sound in the back of his throat—something like a laugh but tinged with sorrow. "Aye, lad, I suppose you're right. And Arminius agrees. A night beneath the open sky, then. Like old times. The Painter's blood is our protection."

Painter's blood? Attica thought, trying to recall where he'd heard that before. Rather than respond, he busied himself with unfastening the harness, finally freeing his mentor. Hadrian staggered slightly but held himself upright, his hands trembling as he pulled his cloak tighter around his body. His eyes darted about, catching on things Attica couldn't see.

"They're here," Hadrian murmured. "Do you see them, boy?"

Attica stiffened, the hair on the back of his neck rising. "See what?"

Hadrian's lips parted, but before he could answer, a flicker of movement cut through the mist. Attica reacted instantly, his shade coiling around him in a predatory manner. His hand went to his weapon, eyes locking on to the figure emerging from the gloom ahead.

A flashwraith. An emitter.

Attica and his shade had been too distracted to notice it earlier. It was smaller than the others he had seen—almost humanoid. The emitter's body was hunched over, its luminous core pulsing softly beneath dark chitinous plating. It seemed like it was lost.

Hadrian's hand shot out, gripping Attica's wrist with surprising strength. "No," the older man whispered.

Attica's muscles tensed, his shade mirroring his unease. "It has seen us."

"It can't see." Hadrian's grip tightened. His lips moved, but no sound came.

The emitter stilled, its core flaring once, twice, as it shifted toward the two of them. Attica felt a pressure in his skull, an odd, whispering static just out of reach. It was neither light nor dark, neither a threat nor a retreat.

And then, impossibly, the flashwraith hesitated.

It should have attacked. It should have released its core's energy and killed them both. But it didn't. It froze, as if it had seen a ghost.

"There," Hadrian said, overcome with remorse. He loosened his grip on Attica's wrist, and his shoulders lowered as though in quiet relief.

Attica didn't hesitate. He moved in a blur toward the emitter, who had yet to act. He drove his shadowblade forward, slicing into the creature's core. The emitter shuddered. Its light faltered, flickered, then vanished into the mist.

"What have you done?" Hadrian let out a strangled noise, his body sagging forward as though Attica had driven the blade through him instead.

Attica ignored it. He knelt, retrieved his gourd, and filled it with what little essence remained of the creature, sealing it tight.

When he looked up, Hadrian was weeping, his face twisting with grief.

Attica frowned, uncertain how to respond. "It was a flashwraith, Hadrian. Get hold of yourself, man!"

"You don't understand. You don't see!"

Attica said nothing. He grabbed the creature's remains and dragged them away from their campsite.

When he returned, Attica found Hadrian sitting with his hood drawn, staring into the sky, whispering prayers of forgiveness. "Please," the older man whispered. "For the Painter, for the settlement . . ."

Attica uncorked his gourd, inhaling the faint traces of essence inside. "Would you like some?"

Hadrian didn't answer. Once it was clear he wouldn't respond, Attica stowed the gourd and settled across from him, spine pressed to jagged stone.

They sat in silence for a long while before Hadrian spoke again, his voice softer than before: "You were always a stubborn one. A headstrong boy. But loyal. The makings of a true Vanguard. A good lad. The very best."

Attica turned, frowning. Hadrian wasn't looking at a fellow Vanguard. He was looking at a boy. A son.

"I'm no longer a boy. I've told you this."

Hadrian rubbed his hands together like a man trying to remember warmth. "You mustn't be too proud. Too sure of yourself. That is how ashlings die, you know."

"I am no longer an ashling. I have a child myself," he admitted, the words much quieter than he intended.

Hadrian's expression flickered, caught between realization and disbelief. He squinted at Attica, as if trying to reconcile the image in his mind. Then, after a long pause, his lips curled into a weary smile. "A child," he echoed. "You, a father? Ha! That's a good one."

Attica's chest ached, though he wasn't sure why.

Hadrian chuckled again, but it faded quickly, his gaze drifting toward the mist beyond their camp. "Strange lights out there," he mumbled. "Not for us, though. Not yet."

Attica followed his gaze, watching as faint glimmers pulsed far beyond the reaches of the settlement. They were too distant to be a threat.

As Hadrian drifted off to sleep, Attica watched the lights beyond, waiting for something. Though he wasn't sure what. The world grew quiet, and soon, the mist swallowed the distant glow.

Whatever lay beyond would have to wait.

CHAPTER SEVENTEEN

Attica couldn't sleep.

He sat upright against a jagged stone, arms crossed, shade pooled around him like the living shadow it was. His gourd glowed faintly at his hip, its light barely illuminating his surroundings. It felt too bright in the oppressive gloom.

Hadrian was mumbling again.

The old man lay wrapped in his cloak a few paces away, muttering in the rasp of a fevered dream. Occasionally, his shade twitched beside him, shifting in ways Attica had never seen before.

The words that slipped past Hadrian's lips were nonsense—disjointed fragments of history, myths, and battle hymns. He continued speaking to the Mother of Whispers about something called the Realm of Recumbency. He assured her that he would reach there, that it was his duty to serve.

Sometimes, in the quiet moments between his ramblings, Hadrian spoke as if addressing someone unseen, as if responding to a conversation only he could hear. *"Arminius,"* he whispered. *"Tell me more. Tell me all."*

It wasn't just Hadrian keeping Attica awake.

There was also the shieldwraith, which lay motionless at the far end of their camp, dark and inert, its mere presence gnawing at the edge of his thoughts. Attica kept thinking of the signal it had sent before it fell. A light, not like the flarebacks, not wild or erratic, but focused. A potential beacon.

The urge to return to the settlement itched at his thoughts—a low hum beneath everything else.

The mist had thickened since nightfall, pressing in around them, shifting in slow, deliberate currents as though something unseen was stirring just beyond his vision. Attica told himself it was nothing; he told himself that the paranoia creeping up his spine was just exhaustion. But at the same time, he knew to trust his instincts.

As much as it troubled him, Attica let his head rest back against the rock. He closed his eye just for a moment and eventually, rest came in shallow bursts.

The sharp scrape of stone against stone jolted him upright. This was followed by the howl of a glintfang, a sound Attica was all too familiar with.

Attica's shade flared out instinctively, searching the blue morning twilight, his breath caught between sleep and waking. It took Attica a second to register the source of *both* sounds.

Hadrian.

The old man had harnessed himself up again.

He was already several paces away, dragging the shieldwraith toward the edge of the second tier. He stopped occasionally, cupped his hands around his mouth, and made the howling sound.

"Ha!" he said once he heard a reply in the distance. "It actually worked."

Hadrian's posture was hunched but determined, his boots digging into the gray dirt with each step. His breath came in steady huffs, and though his movements were labored, there was something methodical about them. Focused. Strong. Determined.

Attica surged to his feet, irritation flaring as he reached his mentor. "Stop howling," he told him.

"Lad! Did you hear? One howled back." A curious look came across his face. "I can't remember a time one ever howled back. I saw Sevus pull it off once . . . or was that Garax?"

"Glintfangs are the last thing we want. And you couldn't wake me?"

"You were dreaming," Hadrian told him without looking back. "Dreams are important glimpses into your mind. And it's not every day I get to drag a bloody monster to the edge of the second tier. What a fascinating thing, our world, and to know . . ." His eyes twitched. *"To know it was once bathed in color."*

Attica fell into step beside him, grabbing the ropes to help. As they pressed on, the shieldwraith scraped against the ground, its jagged edges catching on loose rock, the sound grating in the silence.

Visibility grew worse by the minute. The descent to the second tier's edge was still nearly a mile away, and the mist thickened even more, curling low around their ankles.

A fog this dense . . . Attica thought. *If something's out there, we won't see it.*

He scanned what little of the terrain he could make out, his shade extending in thin tendrils, searching. Nothing.

Not yet.

They pressed forward.

It wasn't long before they encountered their first real obstacle, a jagged outcrop of rock that jutted from the earth like the broken ribs of some long-dead giant. It stretched across their path, the hoodoos too numerous and too high to drag the shieldwraith over.

"We'll have to go around," Attica muttered. "It's the only way."

Hadrian nodded, though his gaze had drifted again. "Yes. Around."

They turned, maneuvering along the outer edge of the formation, but the new path was uneven, riddled with fractures in the stone that made hauling the shieldwraith even more difficult. Their progress slowed, the sound of metal scraping against rock ringing louder than Attica would have liked.

He heard a howl in the distance. "We're drawing attention to ourselves," he said, eye flicking to the mist.

Hadrian only laughed. "We had their attention long before now."

Attica tightened his grip on the rope, shifting his weight as they navigated another stretch of broken ground. The shieldwraith scraped across the uneven terrain, sending small showers of dust cascading into the abyss.

Hadrian's breathing had changed. At first, Attica thought it was exhaustion, but when he glanced over, he saw the strange gleam in Hadrian's eye, the way his lips moved without sound, as if reciting something in his head. He continued rambling about the Crown of Shadows, and the Council of Torn—of forgotten history, spoken like prophecy by a man unraveling.

"What are you saying?" Attica asked.

Hadrian blinked, then grinned. "All of it, lad. I understand all of it now. The Seer showed me after she gave me her drink. On her walls."

Attica remembered the Seer's room, how it was normally bathed in light. The only time it hadn't been was after his trial. Thinking back, he now recalled that there were etchings on the walls, glyphs of an ancient language he couldn't read."

And what a task!" Hadrian laughed. "How could the Shadowborn ever accomplish such a feat? The Crown of Shadows exists! We could restore color. It's no wonder the truth has been obscured. The success of our community depends on it."

Attica frowned. "What truth?"

Hadrian chuckled, the sound dry and distant. "The way things move. The way things break. The way things change." His gaze drifted beyond the mist, as though looking at something Attica couldn't see. The way the world is shaped."

"Hadrian—"

"We're almost there," Hadrian cut him off, nodding ahead. "Come on, now! No time for second thoughts or questions with obvious answers, my boy!"

Attica exhaled sharply and kept moving. They reached the drop-off at last. The ground leveled, stretching out in a final, flat expanse before the sheer descent to the third tier. The mist thinned; Attica could see flashes of something bright beyond.

Hadrian unhooked the harness. "Here, finally!" He stretched out his arms and rolled his shoulders. "And see? No glintfangs."

Attica stared down into the abyss. It was darker than he expected. There was light, but it was faint, diffused, as if struggling to reach them.

Hadrian looked to Attica, eyes suddenly solemn. "Come with me."

Attica's head snapped up. "What?"

Hadrian smiled, but there was something different in it—something knowing. "Come with me," he repeated. "See the third tier for yourself. *I know, I know, Arminius, there are risks, but he's a growing lad! He must know the truth! Yes, I keep telling him, I agree, but—*"

Attica hesitated. For as long as he could remember, Hadrian had been the one to warn him to never go past the second tier, never stray too deep. There were places even the Vanguard dared not tread. "You told me to never go there."

Hadrian burst out laughing. "You, of all people, should know when to heed the words of a man of fear and faith, and the words of a man determined."

Attica stared down at the edge again, his shade shifting at his feet, uncertain.

Hadrian didn't wait for an answer. He fastened the harness once more, securing the ropes, preparing himself for the final descent.

Rather than test the rock himself, Attica extended his shade forward, feeling for footholds, ensuring he could climb back up if needed. His shade stretched out, seeking, anchoring, their consciousness united. It returned, cautious as ever, but Attica had long since learned how to read its wary nature.

It's possible, he thought. *I can climb back up if I go down.*

"You're thinking about it, aren't you?" Hadrian asked, still with that hallucinatory grin on his face.

"The settlement. Dayanne. My son—"

Hadrian smacked the harness with his fist. "Aye. That's a good lad! Help me get the shieldwraith down there. I suppose at that point . . ." He let out a short grunt. "You can decide if you will continue or return."

"I will return."

Hadrian waved his statement away. "Decide for yourself once we reach the bottom. Let's go, lad!"

CHAPTER EIGHTEEN

Attica used the strength of his shade to help Hadrian shift the shieldwraith toward the edge of the second tier, positioning it carefully for its inevitable drop. Hadrian had already slipped out of his harness. The ropes hung like tattered garlands across his shoulders, his posture vibrating with some mix of purpose and unraveling.

His wild-eyed gaze flickered between Attica and the abyss below, excitement and something deeper, something unsteady, woven into every short breath. "I've never been, you know," Hadrian said suddenly, his voice cracking. "But she's there. We get this down, and we meet her."

"Who?" Attica asked, though he wasn't sure he wanted the answer.

"Vespasia, the Mother of Whispers," Hadrian murmured, his lips twitching into something between a grin and a grimace. "She resides on the third tier, lad, her ghost. You'll see."

Attica stared at him, a stark sadness threading through his ribs. Hadrian had always been a man of certainty, of quiet resolve. Now, his words tumbled from his lips like loose stones, disjointed and slippery. He wasn't afraid—if anything, the older man seemed overjoyed—but it was the wrong kind of joy, the kind that came from a mind no longer fully tethered to itself, to reality.

Hadrian coughed and gestured toward the shieldwraith with a quick jerk of his chin. "Well?"

"I already said I would help you." Attica positioned himself at the opposite side of the shieldwraith. He felt his shade boil around him, liquid shadow surging through his limbs, strengthening his grip.

"On my count, then." Hadrian lifted his end higher, surprising Attica with his strength. "One . . ."

Attica's breath steadied.

"Two . . ."

His shade coiled, tendrils bracing against the stone.

"Three!"

Together, they heaved the shieldwraith over the edge.

The shieldwraith tipped over the edge, scraping as it vanished into the mist. A second later, the impact rang through the air, sending a ripple of unease up Attica's spine. His shade flared instinctively, forming jagged tendrils and bristling like it expected an ambush.

"Off we go!" Hadrian bellowed.

Before Attica could react, the older man hurled himself over the side, the loose ends of his harness trailing after him. Attica's hand shot forward but stopped short, fingers curling against his palm.

He waited until a voice rose from below, distant but strong. "You coming, lad?"

Attica swallowed, his throat dry. He pushed through the tension he was feeling and took a step forward. His shade resisted, curling against his ankles.

"You must believe me," Attica told his shade, yet it held firm, preventing him from going over the edge of the second tier. "I will not stay. I gave Dayanne my word. I have Eli. I will not stay."

A slow moment passed. Then, reluctantly, the shadows holding him back uncoiled.

Attica placed his foot on the edge and began his descent. His shade stretched out, tendrils spidering into the grooves of the rock face. The air thickened as he dropped lower, the mist swallowing him whole. The cold hit next—a sharp, biting thing that felt unnatural, as if the very air resisted his presence.

He pushed through. The moment his boots touched smooth stone, Attica knew something was wrong. Hadrian stood motionless near the shieldwraith, his mouth agape, spittle dripping from his lips, his gaze lifted toward the sky. His entire body trembled.

Attica scanned the thick fog of the third tier, expecting to see something, some Mother of Whispers, but there was nothing. No ghost. No apparition, or whatever Hadrian had spoken to earlier. Just the unsettling quiet and a fog thick enough to obscure a mountain.

Hadrian wiped his face with a shaky hand, sniffled once, then turned—his eyes hollow and shining. Whatever fire had burned in him was burning out. "You made it."

Attica stepped forward. "Let's get your harness—"

"Do you hear her, lad?" Hadrian's arms hung loose at his sides, his stance unsteady. He swayed slightly. "Vespasia speaks. No? He can't hear you . . . I see . . . But I want him to hear you. I've come all this way? Can't you grant my single request?"

Attica hesitated. "I don't hear anything."

Hadrian's lips formed a smile, but his eyes glistened with unshed tears. "It's real," he whispered. "You are real. I am real. And she is real." He turned his face toward the abyss. "Introduce yourself, Vespasia. Show the lad you are here."

The hair on the back of Attica's neck prickled. He had heard whispers before. But now—now there was only silence, thick and suffocating, as if something was muffling the sound just beyond reach.

"Hadrian, your harness," Attica said, his voice edged with urgency and sadness.

A shift passed over the older man's expression, something fragile breaking beneath the weight of realization. His body sagged, his shoulders lowering. Attica could see it clearly now. The loneliness setting in. The slow, sinking understanding that this was the end.

"I am to carry the shieldwraith further," Hadrian said with finality.

Attica nodded. "Only if you want to."

"I promised the Vanguard I would, as far as I can."

"As far as you're able."

Hadrian's fingers twitched. He exhaled, rubbing his temple before looking at Attica again. "She is still here, the Mother of Whispers, Vespasia, yes, guide me to the Gate of Whispers. That will be fine."

Attica's stomach clenched. "If she's really there, ask her how many tiers there are."

Hadrian's head tilted, as if listening. His expression shifted, his ears perking at some unseen voice. "Nine," he whispered. "She says there are nine, not including the . . . Realm of Recumbency." He coughed, wiping the smear of spit from his lips. His body shook. "I'm going to be alone soon."

Attica swallowed. "You are."

His eyes welled with sadness. "You cannot come with me, lad?"

"I cannot. I have a family."

"But . . . but you're just a boy."

"I have a child, Hadrian. The Seer's flask has warped your mind. Do you see a child standing before you?" Attica asked forcefully. "Look, man, look for yourself!" His voice sharpened, Attica unable to bury the pain. "Look at me, dammit! Vespasia be damned, look at me. I am real."

Hadrian lifted his gaze, his watery eyes locking onto Attica's. Slowly, he reached a trembling hand toward Attica's face. Then, through the tears, he smiled. "You are a tall lad." Hadrian exhaled, as if the last remnants of some illusion had finally faded. "And if you must go, I understand. The Mother of Whispers says it is not your time. Not yet."

"She . . . did?"

The older man turned away abruptly, shaking his head. "Help me with the harness, and I will continue."

Attica hesitated only a second before securing the straps once more. His hands moved automatically, each motion practiced and precise. But his throat felt tight, his chest heavy. He felt bad for scolding him; Attica didn't know how to say goodbye.

It made it worse that Hadrian didn't speak as Attica worked. His mentor merely stood there, bewitched by whatever he was seeing in the fog. When it was done, Hadrian rolled his shoulders, testing the fit. "For the Painter," Hadrian whispered.

"For the settlement," Attica replied.

"For all of us."

"Go with the Painter at your back, Hadrian."

"I will, lad, I will."

Attica took one last look at the man who had trained him, fought beside him, raised him in ways no one else had. Then, slowly and deliberately, he turned away.

Staying any longer would break him.

His shade shot toward the wall of stone, and he began his climb. Attica reached the second tier and hauled himself over the edge, breathless, doing all he could not to give in to the emotion running through him.

"I need to get home," he told his shade.

He shifted toward the direction of the settlement, but the mist was thick. Too thick.

He heard the howl of a glintfang on the other side of the tier.

Attica stepped forward, his shade bristling at his feet. Far in the distance, beyond the mist, something flickered. Attica narrowed his eye. He took another step, heart still, until he heard Hadrian's final cry from below. "Good luck, lad!"

Then, silence.

PART THREE

ALL THE DARKNESS

CHAPTER NINETEEN

The hunt had been long, but it had been good.

Attica led the returning party, his gourd's weight a steady, familiar presence at his hip. The others carried theirs as well—Cassian, Sevus, Eve, and Varro, their expressions weary but triumphant. Tiago lagged behind, the young man tossing a shadowdagger, ever casual.

"Not a bad haul," Cassian remarked, shifting the weight of his pack. "Would've been better with another glintfang or three." He placed his hands around his mouth and mimicked a glintfang howl.

Eve scoffed. "You're insatiable, Cassian."

Attica let their voices fade into the background as the settlement's walls came into view. He quickened his pace, the group crossing through the gates.

It had been nearly a week. A long trip across the first tier. Longer than he would have liked.

Dayanne. Eli.

The weight in his chest eased the moment the settlement's rhythms wrapped around him as they entered through the main gate. Shadowborn moved through the ancient streets, tending to their tasks, the quiet hum of survival unbroken.

Yet Attica saw only one person. Dayanne stood at the threshold of their home, watching him approach, already aware of his return. Eli was balanced on her hip, his small fingers gripping at her tunic as he squirmed.

Attica barely had time to set down his bag before Eli reached out, his hands grasping the air with clumsy urgency. The boy let out a rasping sound, a noise that tugged at something deep in Attica's chest.

Eli didn't make sounds like the other children did. At two years old, he still hadn't spoken a word. No names, no cries, only quiet, breathy noises shaped in his throat.

Some in the community whispered their concerns. Others gave Dayanne pitying looks when they thought she wouldn't notice.

But it didn't bother Attica and it never had. He loved Eli all the same.

He scooped the boy into his arms. Eli kicked with delight, a broad, toothy grin spreading across his face.

"Look at you," Attica said, pressing his forehead to Eli's. "Did you behave for your mother?"

He set him down, but Eli clung to his leg, unsteady but determined.

Dayanne laughed, shaking her head. "He always behaves, even better when you aren't around."

"You keep saying that."

She arched a brow, stepping closer. "What kind of father disappears for so long?"

"A week? I've been gone longer. It was a good haul."

Dayanne exhaled sharply, and when she spoke again, her voice softened: "It felt longer." Then her nose twitched. "You smell like beyond the walls."

"That checks out," he told her with a smirk.

Before she could scold him further, Eli reached for Attica's shade, his small hands batting at the dark tendrils curling around his father's wrist. His shade reacted instantly. It swirled around the boy's fingers, shifting playfully, lifting him gently off the ground. Eli giggled, hoarse but bright, delighting in the way it moved.

Attica watched, his chest tightening, something warm, something heavy and real. "He'll have his own in a few years."

Dayanne scoffed at the suggestion. "And I will make sure he enjoys his childhood before then." She nudged Attica's ribs, her teasing gentle. "You'd have him hunting flashwraiths by the age of three if I let you."

"Better for him to start early."

She rolled her eyes, but her fingers found his hand, squeezing once. "Get in here. You've been missed thoroughly."

"The Vanguard—"

"The Vanguard can wait," Dayanne said with finality.

The training grounds stretched along the northern edge of the settlement, a wide clearing of compacted earth bordered by towering slabs of stone. Even now, in the dim red morning twilight of the Spiralrealm, it was alive with movement—Vanguard clashing in practice bouts, shades twisting in sharp, fluid bursts as their wielders tested skill and instinct alike.

Attica stood at the edge of the sparring circle, arms crossed, watching as Tiago and Vilken faced off in the dust. The two moved fast, their weapons a blur of shifting darkness, Tiago wielding his shadowdaggers, quick and aggressive; Vilken responding with a whip of shadow, striking in looping, controlled arcs. Their combat was relentless, both young men pressing each other hard, neither willing to concede ground.

Both had changed since their trials a year ago. Tiago had returned with a streak of white in his hair, something no one could quite explain, while Vilken bore burn scars trailing up his forearms from a near-fatal encounter with an emitter. Now, both stood as full-fledged Vanguard, no longer boys, but warriors.

Their sparring match had drawn a crowd. Seasoned Vanguard stood among ashlings, all watching with quiet intensity, their gazes sharp. Some discussed the fight, gauging strengths and weaknesses. Others stood in silence, their expressions unreadable.

Attica's eye flickered between them, taking in every detail.

Tiago took a blow that would have felled another Vanguard—his shoulder snapping back, then realigning in a blink. Not a reflex. Not brute strength. His shade was doing it. Quietly, instinctively, mending what broke. In a real fight, that kind of recovery wasn't just rare, it was lethal.

Vilken feinted left, his whip snapping out toward Tiago's ankle. Tiago dodged at the last moment, pivoting sharply, his spear twisting in a deceptive flourish. The movement forced Vilken to commit. And in that single instant, Tiago cheated.

Or at least, that's what the others would call it.

Instead of pressing his advantage with his dagger, Tiago let his shade surge ahead—a quick, darting tendril that flickered past Vilken's defenses and wrapped around his wrist, yanking him off balance. Before Vilken could react, Tiago lunged, the bladed tip of his weapon stopping just before the other's throat.

The match was over.

For a moment, there was silence. Then—

"That was cheap," Vilken spat, yanking his arm free. A few of the gathered Vanguard murmured in agreement.

"You should've seen it coming," Tiago shot back, grinning.

Attica sighed. He had seen this before. The younger Vanguard had their own set of unspoken rules—guidelines on what was "honorable" in a fight, what separated a practice duel from a kill beyond the walls.

Tiago was right. If this had been a real battle, Vilken would be dead. Still, Attica knew the weight of perception. Attica stepped forward and placed a firm hand on Tiago's shoulder just as Vilken got to his feet, his shade flaring in agitation.

"Come with me," Attica said. Tiago hesitated but followed, his stance still taut with the energy of the fight. The intensity in his eyes hadn't faded, but Attica could see it, the anticipation, the way his shoulders stiffened slightly—Tiago was already bracing for a lecture.

"What?" he asked once they were away from the others.

Attica exhaled slowly. "You know what they're saying."

Tiago's jaw tightened. "That I, Tiago the Ghost-Touched, am too fast for Vilken."

"What does that have to do with your last name?"

Tiago flashed a grin. "Because I move like a ghost?"

"Our last names aren't always about who we are," Attica said. "I'm the Lone-Eyed Wolf. They gave me that name because I lost my eye during my trial—and because I did something I should've done with others watching. It's a name that's both strong and mocking. Smart wolves hunt in packs." He glanced at Eve. "Eve was named the Blood Measured because she managed to light each lantern twice—and because she's cautious. Overly so." Then back to Tiago. "And you're Ghost-Touched. Not just for that streak in your hair, but because you always seem to get under someone's skin. Like a ghost that never left."

Tiago's shadow flickered. "Understood."

"Listen carefully: You are no longer an ashling. You are the only one besides me to light all four lanterns in a single night." He held the young man's gaze, letting the gravity and hidden praise of his words settle. "The younger watch you now," Attica continued. "The older watch for cracks—not because they want you to fail, but because they need a cautionary tale."

Something flickered in Tiago's eyes. Pride. Uncertainty. He clenched his fists at his sides. "I know that."

"Then start acting like you know it."

"I—"

"You don't have to prove anything anymore." Attica's voice was firm, cutting through whatever excuse Tiago had been trying to make. "Not to them, not to me. You could lose. Vilken could win. Do so with honor."

"Would you let Eve beat you?"

"She has beaten me," Attica said dryly, aware that Tiago was baiting him. It was no secret that Eve had feelings for Attica, yet no one ever spoke of it. No one dared. "She has beaten me more times than I can count. Her shade is stronger than mine."

Tiago's smirk twitched at the edges, but Attica didn't indulge it. He met the younger man's gaze, unshaken.

"And if you think she'd let me win, you don't know her at all." Attica let out a slow breath. "But enough of this talk. There's something else. Your sister is heading out for her trial soon. She will become a member of the Vanguard."

Tiago nodded, something unreadable flickering across his face. "Livia." A beat of silence. Then, a sharp nod.

"How does she feel about it?"

"Livia is ready." Tiago paused, then let out a slow breath. Hesitation traced across his face. "But that doesn't mean I am."

Attica studied him for a moment. He understood. Watching someone you cared about leave the safety of the walls, knowing they might never return—it never got easier.

"You'll have to trust her," Attica said finally. "And like all of us, she must face the trial alone."

Tiago exhaled sharply. "I know."

Attica glanced toward the dark horizon beyond the walls. The world outside had always been treacherous, but something about it had felt . . . different lately. Two years ago, the shieldwraith's signal had gone unanswered. No attacks had come. No sign that the message had reached anyone or anything.

And yet, he couldn't shake the feeling that something was watching. Beyond the walls, something waited.

Attica turned back to Tiago, his voice quiet, steady. "You're Vanguard now. That means you follow the rules—even when they feel wrong. The world beyond is unknown, and it will kill us if we let it. Don't forget that."

Tiago nodded. He didn't argue. Neither of them said what they both knew— one simple mistake could cost them everything.

CHAPTER TWENTY

The lodge could wait. The Vanguard could wait. Life could wait. For the first time in what felt like forever, Attica had let himself remain in the settlement, ignoring the usual pull of duty, of expectation.

A week passed this way—Attica at home with his family while the Vanguard managed the hunts beyond the walls. Instead of going on the hunt, instead of sitting in the lodge listening to reports or playing politics with the senior membership, or heading out for an expedition, Attica spent his days sprawled across the floor, locked in a fierce battle with Eli.

The two-year-old shrieked, a breathy rasp of delight, as he flung himself at Attica's shade, tiny hands grasping at the shifting tendrils. His shade responded playfully, weaving just out of reach before curling around Eli in a loose embrace. Attica caught him mid-pounce, scooping him up and flipping him onto the bed, eliciting another hoarse giggle.

"You're getting too fast," Attica murmured, nudging Eli's cheek with his nose. "A few more months, and I won't stand a chance." He grinned, echoing something Hadrian had once told him. "Speed is the difference between the living and the dead."

Eli wobbled upright, hands planted against his father's chest. He made another soft, breathy sound, his mouth forming a shape, but the word never came.

Attica stilled. The air in the room shifted.

"What is it?" he asked, his voice quieter now, his skin prickling with unease.

Eli tried again, frustration flickering across his small face. His brow furrowed, and Attica reached forward, his hand falling on the child's shoulder. He met his son's gaze, holding it for a moment longer than he normally would.

"It's okay," he said. "You'll get it. Speak whenever you want. Or don't. The world's already full of noise. No need to add to it until you're ready."

The door creaked open.

Dayanne entered, the faint scent of incense clinging to her clothes. Attica glanced up, immediately recognizing the weight in her posture. The Sanctum.

She's been with the Seer, he thought as he looked her over. Attica pulled Eli into his lap. "How was it?"

Dayanne exhaled as she untied the dark scarf from her shoulders. She draped it over a nearby chair. "Strange," she said at last. "But that would be my work for the last few months."

Attica frowned. "Strange, how?"

Dayanne crossed the room and lowered herself beside him. Her fingers drifted absently through Eli's curls as she spoke. "The others have started to notice it too. The Seer . . . she's different. More erratic than before. Let's call it that."

"Can she be more erratic?" Attica asked, his tone dry.

"She can. Even I don't know the full details of what's going on. And now, she speaks in riddles, in half sentences, then forgets them entirely. And she keeps talking about time, as if it's running out."

Something in the way she said it twisted in Attica's gut. It reminded him of Hadrian. "Could she exile herself?"

Dayanne shook her head. "She would never. She can barely move."

Attica hesitated. "And if she passes? What then?"

Dayanne's gaze lowered. "She's already given specific instructions. Someone would be chosen through a conclave, they would take a drink from her flask and get instructions. The last time it happened was a long time before we were born, but I remember learning about it as a girl."

A silence stretched between them as she came into his arms. Attica's eyes drifted to the necklace—the pearl-shaped stone with red rings he'd given her, once upon a time that now felt distant.

"You're remembering the day you found it?" Dayanne asked, watching him closely.

"I think about it every day," he muttered, brushing the pad of his thumb over the stone's smooth surface. Dayanne caught his wrist and pressed a kiss to his knuckles. "I've never taken it off. It was a gift from the Lone-Eyed Wolf. The other Spectralists are jealous."

"I'm certain that's not true."

She shrugged playfully. "You wouldn't know. How was Eli today?"

"He almost spoke earlier," he admitted quietly.

Dayanne's gaze flickered to Eli, now waddling across the room toward a wooden toy. "Did he?"

"I swear it." Attica leaned forward, closer to her. For a moment, the world was quiet, the warmth of her presence grounding him in a way nothing else ever could.

"Did he now?" she asked.

She smiled. "Then it's only a matter of time."

For a moment, the world narrowed. Dayanne, the warmth of her presence, the safety of their home. Attica let himself exist in it. Let himself believe, if only for a breath, that things would remain this way.

A sharp knock at the door shattered the moment. Attica's shade flared before settling.

Dayanne sighed, smoothing her tunic as she stood. "I'll get it."

Attica was already moving. "No. It's probably for me."

He braced himself as he opened the door. Tiago stood on the threshold, his usual easy posture gone, his expression drawn tight.

"She's still not back," he said, voice low. "I'm sorry to disturb you, but she's still not—"

Attica's stomach tightened. "Livia?"

"It's been a week, Attica. After a week . . ." Tiago's throat quivered. "After a week, she should be here."

Attica didn't need him to finish the sentence.

Longer than any ritual in recent memory, Attica thought as he looked Tiago over, allowing the young man a moment to get hold of himself. Three days was already pushing the limit. Attica knew what the Vanguard would say, what the settlement would assume if nearly a week had passed. *And to think I've missed all of that by just staying at home . . .*

"At the very least," Tiago continued, his voice edged with desperation, "we should recover her body. So she can be buried in the Sanctum. I want my sister to be buried there, not left out in the Spiralrealm to be picked apart by . . . Please, Attica, Dayanne—"

Attica turned—Dayanne was already standing behind him.

"Yes," she said, her voice quieter now, like the weight of the words was settling into something permanent. "There's room for her there, Ghost-Touched. But you must find Livia first."

"I'll go out with you," Attica told the young man.

"You will?"

"Yes, this is important." Attica started to leave, but his steps faltered at the threshold.

He glanced back, expecting Dayanne to say something—to caution him, to tell him she'd wait. But she only stood there, Eli clinging to her tunic, watching.

For a moment, he thought of crossing the room, of pressing his forehead to hers, of holding Eli once more before he left.

But he didn't.

Instead, he put on his boots and fastened them with the efficiency of a man who had done this too many times before. When he stepped through the door, Attica felt Dayanne's gaze on his back.

"Take care, my love," she called after him.

Attica reached the lodge just as Eve stepped from the side path, Ione and Vilken trailing behind her. Tiago blinked at the sight of them, the young man surprised, maybe even uneasy, especially after his bout with Vilken, where a shade-assisted move had handed him the win.

"You're coming too?" he asked, voice caught between gratitude and disbelief.

"Of course, we are," Vilken said. "She's your sister."

"And she's my friend," Ione added. Fear flickered in her eyes, but it was quickly smothered by the kind of quiet resolve Attica had come to expect from her. Like Livia, Ione kept to herself. And like all Vanguard, she knew how to kill.

Eve crossed her arms as she looked Attica over. "Took you long enough. You've been gone so long I thought maybe you'd retired."

He almost smiled. "Vanguard don't retire—"

"We expire," she finished for him. No trace of humor. No trace of fear.

That was the truth of it. The only exits were death or exile. One of them would come for him too, in time. *Better to walk with death than wait for it*, Hadrian had once told him.

Tiago's shade twisted, agitated. "We have to find her body. We have to—"

"Don't assume she's dead," Ione snapped.

"No one has ever taken this long to light the lanterns. Right, Attica?" Tiago asked Attica and Eve.

"Maybe," Attica said, "but it's best not to assume the worst." He turned to Eve. "Do you have a map?"

"I do."

"And the others?"

"They've been informed."

"Then we move."

The five Vanguard slipped past the outer gates, boots scuffing against packed stone, breath misting in the heavy air. Fog pooled low, thickening as they descended. Eve followed close behind Attica, who led the group in silence, flanked by Ione and Vilken. Tiago kept to the rear, his shade twitching with every step—tension made visible as he rolled his shadowdagger across his knuckles.

They reached the first lantern by sunset. Its flame had long since died, its pedestal cold. Attica traced his hand over the still bowl. *Where are you, Livia?* he thought as his shade pulsed outward, rippling across the stone in waves.

Ione crouched beside a faint impression in the dirt. "She was here. One set of prints, eastbound. Upright. Not limping."

"She lit it, then kept going," Vilken confirmed. He glanced at Tiago. "This is a good thing, Ghost-Touched."

"And toward the second lantern too," Eve confirmed, eyes on the map. "She made it that far, at least."

Tiago said nothing as he approached the lantern and stared down at the darkened bowl. Attica gave him space, and once Tiago seemed ready, he motioned them onward. The air grew heavier with each mile. As they neared the second lantern, the wind shifted—wrong, angled sideways across the stone like something crawling against the grain.

Eve frowned. "This isn't wind season."

"No," Attica said, "but the world has changed." He glanced to Ione, whose shade moved in careful loops ahead of them. "Anything?"

"Just a faint trace," she said as her eyes went black, the young woman entirely possessed by her shade. The white of her eyes returned. "Residual essence. She refueled here."

"Still eastbound?"

"I think so."

"Then she lives," Eve said. "And we continue."

Attica's gaze drifted outward. In the distance, past the lantern ridge, pale lights drifted through the fog—wavering, distant. He saw and heard the lighthowl of a glintfang.

"Too far to matter," Attica replied, though the movement burrowed beneath his skin, his shade hesitant as always.

They pressed forward, weaving along the rim of the Spiralrealm until the trail curved toward a crescent-shaped ridge of stone, one that Attica had visited nine years ago.

Ione halted. "There."

They fanned out, the group trailing down to the center of the basin, where they found a dozen flashwraith corpses, cores dimmed to gray. Some were burned through, others cleaved. They lay scattered like shed husks, all facing inward, curled toward a figure at the clearing's heart.

"Livia!" Tiago broke rank and ran to her side. Her gourd was still clutched in one hand, nearly full. Dried blue blood streaked her temple.

"She did this?" Vilken whispered as he gestured to the dead flashwraith. "She killed them all?"

"She did," Eve said, awe in her voice. "Livia held them off by herself."

"Livia. Why didn't they finish her?" Tiago seethed. "Why leave her like this? I don't understand . . ." No one answered as Tiago pulled her to his chest and hugged his sister.

Ione pointed past the bodies. "There are drag marks." She started moving toward the markings. "Let's see if we can't find something."

"They don't normally drag away bodies," Vilken said, stepping closer to her.

"Her shade?" Attica asked.

"It's not here any longer," Eva said as Tiago clung to his sister, his breathing ragged. He didn't want to let go. Attica recognized that posture—grief resisting the shape of reality.

He was about to say something when Eve's gaze locked on him. "This is going to sound crazy, but I think . . ." She glanced around again, alert as ever as her whipsword took shape. "They left her as bait."

Tiago looked up sharply. "What? Bait? What flashwraith uses bait?"

Attica's shade shuddered along his spine as the realization came to him. His eyes snapped to the edge of the basin, where Ione and Vilken moved among the prints. The fog had thickened, too thick, too still.

"They wanted us to find her," Eve said, the pieces coming together. "This was an invitation."

The mist erupted. Light flared as two figures shimmered into existence.

Vilken was the first to fall, his body split open in a single stroke. He instantly turned to dust as a bolt of light tore through him.

Ione stepped back, hand rising to call her weapon as a blade of pure light burst from her abdomen, disintegrating her before her shade could even react.

They'd walked straight into it. This wasn't a rescue. It was an ambush.

CHAPTER TWENTY-ONE

The two figures tore free from the fog, bending the air as they moved. Their limbs shimmered with sinew and light, torsos braided in prismatic glow. At their cores, false hearts pulsed with radiant essence. Light warped around them like a second skin.

The first flashwraith struck again, lunging toward Tiago, who met it with his own ferocity. His shade surged up, wilder than it had ever been, roaring in defense. He ducked low, rolled beneath a lash of condensed light, and struck the alien flashwraith with a blade of concentrated shadow.

It barely flinched.

Eve flanked the other, her shade exploding outward in spirals of darkness. It was chaos, fast, bright, and wrong.

Attica tried to focus, tried to keep track of positions, shadows, the patterns of light, but the only thing that mattered was survival. Vilken and Ione were gone—burned to dust in seconds. No bodies. No future graves. Nothing left to mourn but memories.

This wasn't just an ambush. It was worse—something planned. Coordinated. The kind of ambush the flashwraiths weren't supposed to be capable of.

And that means . . .

Attica couldn't finish this thought as the nearest monster shimmered into existence. Its arm split, bent unnaturally, then reformed into a blade of gleaming essence.

It struck low as Attica moved to shield Tiago.

His shade met it; armor thickened in an instant and shattered as the blade punched through Attica's side.

There was no time to scream. Only breath—then heat—then nothing but pain.

The pain wasn't like the cauterizing burn that took his eye. It was colder, deeper. Hungry. By the time his knees gave out, Eve was already moving, dragging Attica back, her shade protecting them from incoming strikes, lashing out with bursts of jagged darkness. "Stay with me . . . Attica, stay with me!"

He coughed, blood thick in his throat.

It was the worst wound he'd ever taken, deeper than any shade-bound strike, deeper than the claw that stole his eye. His shade wrapped around it, trying to seal it shut. Eve's shade joined, binding the edges, pressing essence into his body as she continued to fend off their attackers.

Tiago lunged with both fists forward, shadow-forged blades exploding from his knuckles like curved shards of night. He drove them into the chest of the flashwraith, Tiago screaming into its blank face as Eve circled the second, her shadowy whipsword slicing with precision.

Together, they brought the second one down—its body cracking as the core dimmed, light guttering out. They stood over the corpses, blood-streaked, breaths ragged. Then they rushed to Attica's side.

Tiago dropped to his knees, panting as he examined the wound.

Eve grabbed Attica's chin with one hand. "Don't you fucking do it. Don't you fucking leave—"

His eye drifted. She tapped his face—once, twice—just enough to jolt him.

"So . . . much," Attica whispered, staring at the blue blood on his fingers, his own essence leaking like water from a cracked shell.

"We can heal you," Eve said, voice breaking.

Attica noticed she also had blue blood on her face. "Are you . . . ?"

"It's yours," she told him. "Just stay with me, Attica! Just . . . stay . . ."

Just stay . . .

The words echoed—louder than they should have. Time bent. Seconds stretched like hours. He couldn't tell how long he'd been lying there, only that his shade felt thinner now, weaker. Like it was pulling too hard just to keep him whole.

All he felt was a flash of energy, and the draining hush that followed it.

"What's . . . happening?" he whispered as Tiago uncorked his gourd and fed the essence to him.

"Why's it not working?" Tiago asked. "It should be healing him!"

"I don't know," Eve said. She took it from there, lifting the gourd to Attica's lips. "Essence should work. It should heal a wound like this. We have to get him back to the settlement—"

"The settlement!" Attica rasped, lurching upright.

Both of them froze.

"This was . . . it's not random," he said, finally giving words to the thought that had come to him earlier. "It was coordinated."

"Attica, please—" Eve reached for him.

"I will survive," he told Eve, his voice raw but steady now. "Tiago. Get your sister. Take her back. She deserves a proper burial. Ione and Vilken . . . they're gone. Nothing left. The settlement. If I'm wrong . . ."

He faltered. Tiago leaned in. "What? What is it? What's happening at the settlement?"

"Years ago . . . I had a vision of the settlement. I saw it burning. After my ritual, I saw it."

"The Seer's flask showed you?" Eve asked.

"Yes, the—" He inhaled, forcing his thoughts into order. "Go, Tiago. Carry your sister. If I'm wrong . . . she'll be buried properly. If I'm right . . ."

He didn't finish. Tiago rose slowly. "I should stay with you two. What if there are more of these flashwraiths that can disappear? I can help—"

"No," Attica said, his voice harder now, final. "Get to the settlement—now."

Tiago looked from Eve to Attica. And then, after a short nod of determination, he ran.

They moved slowly.

Eve shouldered most of Attica's weight, one arm wrapped around his back, the other gripping his wrist to keep him upright. Every few minutes, his legs gave out—and every time, she caught him. Both their shades helped keep Attica up, but the weight of what had happened continued to take its toll.

"Drink more," she said, bringing the gourd of essence to his lips.

"It's not . . . not working." He looked down at the wound. Blue blood pooled steadily. "I'm dying. I just want . . ."

The Spiralrealm shifted around them. The mist thinned. The stones deepened in hue, shadows spreading like bruises beneath their feet.

"You *will not* die on me, Attica. You'll make it," Eve said, picking up her pace. "You have to."

"How far?" he whispered, sight swimming, the world dripping away at the edges.

"Don't worry about that."

"I just . . . want to see them. Dayanne . . . Eli . . ."

Eve didn't answer. A long silence followed—broken only by their footfalls, by the hush of wind through gullies, over ridges, across familiar ground worn thin by memory.

"I'm sorry," he murmured.

Her eyes flicked toward him. "For what?"

"What?"

"What are you sorry for?"

"I . . . I . . ." He couldn't say. The words got caught in his throat.

She shook her head. "The world's not ending. Not yet. Save your breath, Attica. The settlement will be fine."

He glanced at her again and saw his blood smeared across her cheek. "I should have held back," he said. "Should've—"

"You did the right thing. You men always worry you acted too late, too early, never just *enough*. But you saved Tiago. You survived." She exhaled sharply. "We were ambushed by . . . something. I don't know what. No one could have predicted that. They were hunters, hunters who can vanish on a whim. We've never fought something like that before."

"We are hunters."

"Not like them," she said. "Light bent around them, Attica. You saw it for yourself. How do you fight that? Even our shades didn't see them."

Attica didn't reply. He only drank when she pressed the gourd to his lips again.

They kept going. His sight blurred. Hours dragged through the fog-choked dregs of the uppermost tier, where the Spiralrealm felt older, heavier. Attica lost track of how many times he fell, how many times Eve hauled him back to his feet—sometimes swearing, sometimes pleading with him to hold on.

"They weren't like the others," he said, voice thinned by pain, his shade vibrating around him. "Flashwraiths . . . hunters . . ."

"Save your strength," Eve told him. "Please. I can't . . . *we* can't lose you."

Spittle tinged with blood slid down his chin. Attica looked at his side. The bleeding had slowed, but the cold had crept inward. The wound felt deeper than flesh—like something vital had been carved out of him and left behind in the basin.

"They knew what they were doing," he said.

She didn't reply as the pair crested the final ridge and the fog began to peel back.

Below them, sprawled across the jagged rise and ruin, was the settlement—burning, the gates ripped open.

Flames and flashes of light tore the night apart, casting twisted silhouettes of broken homes, collapsing towers, and fleeing shades. Dozens of flashwraiths swarmed the perimeter. Vanguard held the line where they could, but they were losing.

It was exactly as Attica had seen in his vision. But something new loomed beyond the vision—something worse than anything he had imagined.

Above the chaos, a monstrous being moved through the heart of the settlement unlike any flashwraith Attica had ever seen before. It moved like a walking solar storm: towering, molten, unreal. Its limbs flickered like shattered suns. Its form was a tangle of brilliance that refused to settle, ever shifting, ever burning.

And inside its blazing skull, a child. Suspended at the center of the glow, curled in a fetal cradle of flame.

Attica collapsed to his knees, and this time, Eve didn't stop him.

"You were right," she whispered, sinking beside him.

He summoned what little strength remained, rose, and took one trembling step toward the firelit horizon.

Dayanne. Eli . . . I'm coming.

CHAPTER TWENTY-TWO

The flames pulled him forward.

Attica staggered down the ridge, legs weak beneath him, breath caught in a broken rhythm. Every step jarred the wound in his side, sending fresh flashes of pain racing through his body. He should have collapsed. Should have crawled. He shouldn't have been able to run.

Yet the screams carried him. The smoke. The light. The towering monster with the child inside its skull . . .

The settlement had become unrecognizable, his home razed, its order shattered, its safety a thing of the shattered past. All crumbled to madness as the Vanguard tried to save what was left.

Flashwraiths spilled through the broken gates, emitters by the dozen, their bodies pulsing with pale brilliance, limbs twitching with hungry light. Two emitters with wings, the likes of which Attica had never seen before, perched atop the inner wall, releasing concentrated bolts of light that tore through stone and armor alike. Vanguard met them in furious clusters, weapons drawn, shades flaring in all directions.

In the distance, a two-headed brighthowler loomed, surrounded by swarming flaylights, the symbiotic parasites flitting through the haze like fireflies fueled by dormant mana.

A cluster of civilians ran past him, bloodied and gasping, led by a single Vanguard missing her arm.

Attica didn't stop. He couldn't. Not until a shriek tore through the smoke to his left—raw, human, real. It was followed by a burst of light as an emitter lunged toward a fleeing child, core glowing.

He summoned his shadowblade; dark essence rippled down his arm as his shade surged forward, intercepting mid-strike.

Attica drove the blade into the emitter's chest. Once. Twice. The creature convulsed and fell.

"Keep . . . running," he told the wide-eyed child, one he didn't recognize.

The girl took off as Attica turned to find Tiago fighting with unadulterated rage. His twin shadowdaggers sliced in wide arcs, cutting down emitters in a blur as his shade bled outward with rage. He locked eyes with Attica as he drove his blades through another flashwraith.

"I looked for her!" he shouted. "Dayanne—Eli—I couldn't find them!"

Attica's heart seized. *The Sanctum.*

Eve appeared beside Attica, her shadowy whipsword cutting clean through an emitter's neck. Blood spritzed the air as the monster fell away. Not far, a flareback barreled through a shrine to the Painter—its body pulsing with heat, its trail one of ruin and molten stone. And beyond that, the towering flashwraith with the glowing child in its head continued its carnage.

Eve's shade flared across her form, jagged and sharp. "Attica—"

"The Sanctum," he said through gritted teeth, already staggering forward.

"Have you lost your mind?" She caught his arm. "You can barely stand. Attica—!"

He shook her off and shouldered forward. "I'm fine . . ."

The lie stuck in his throat as his vision swam, edges dimming to gray. Every heartbeat felt slower than the last—thick, syrupy beats that echoed in his skull.

His legs threatened to fold.

The wound on his side, given to him by that vanishing flashwraith, throbbed with a cold, creeping pressure, as if something inside him had come loose and was leaking out into the world.

But Attica kept walking, dragging his left foot now, determined to reach the Sanctum.

Eve caught up with him. "What are you—?"

"Focus on the emitters. Push the civilians out first and fast. Watch . . . watch the brighthowlers. They're clever. And that thing—" He pointed to the colossus stomping through the back wall, light pouring from its body. "I don't know. Not yet. But we will bring it down."

"There are more of the vanishing flashwraiths, like the ones who killed Livia," Tiago said, his shade pulsing with rage. "I've seen them appearing and vanishing. They're fast. Too fast. Killing everyone. We have to—"

A Vanguard screamed to their left as something leapt from the rooftops.

A glintfang, fluid and sleek, clamped its jaws around the man's skull and flashed. A burst of searing lighthowl erupted from its mouth, frying him from the inside out.

His body dropped in a twitching heap, a husk of dust. The man's shade flickered once, then vanished.

Eve turned to intercept, but another emitter barreled into her, knocking her off balance.

Tiago caught it mid-leap and sliced it clean down the middle. He didn't stop. His eyes locked on the glintfang, Tiago's shade launched him forward in a blur of motion, lost in the smoke and light.

"I have to go," Attica told Eve as his side flared again, vision blurring. "I'll be back."

"Attica!" she shouted, but by this point, he was already gone.

The wound throbbed as he hobbled along. His skin burned. But he could see it now, the path through broken stone and flame. The path to the Sanctum. The only path left. To Dayanne. To Eli.

He increased his pace, pushing past the pain, the delirium.

The outer Sanctum had been breached. Pillars cracked. Doors shattered. Blood smeared across the stones, bright blue, still fresh. Essence hung in the air like smoke without anchors, all of it reaching Attica at once, the calamity, the ruin, the catastrophe.

With a quick breath out, Attica started down the winding stairs and through the broken gate into silence. He found her near the Seer's chamber. His peripheral vision dimmed. Everything narrowed onto the first and only person to truly touch his heart.

Dayanne.

Bleeding. Kneeling. Seething. Her hands cupped around a small, still form. Eli.

Lifeless. Gone.

Attica froze as reality fizzled all around him. All the fire above—the ruin, the screaming, the rage—all of it fell away. Background noise.

Dayanne looked up, face smeared with blue blood, eyes soft. "I told you. Attica . . ."

He opened his mouth, but no sound came.

"I told you this would happen," she said again, voice hoarse. "The night after he was born. I drank from the flask. I saw it. Remember? Remember what I told you?"

"No," Attica whispered, heart heavy with remorse. His voice cracked. "I don't . . . but I remember . . ." He struggled to find the words for his own vision. He collapsed beside her. "The settlement. The child of light . . ."

"Yes, that! It's all related. There is hope. Attica . . . there is hope. I didn't know what it meant at the time, my words then," she confessed, tears slipping free. "But I knew it would come." She clenched her eyes shut and glanced up to the ceiling as the floor above them quaked.

"I'm sorry."

Dayanne returned her focus to him, her eyes dropping to his side. "Drink from your gourd?"

"It's not working," he said. "But I can give you what I have left."

"Attica." She touched his face. "This . . . Eli is—"

A tremor cracked through the ceiling, splitting stone.

Eve burst through the doorway, her whipsword catching a brighthowler just as the two-headed beast surged into the room.

Its first blast hit Dayanne as it went down.

The beam of pure light flared into the chamber, blinding and final.

Dayanne folded without a sound. The second beam grazed past Eve's shoulder and slammed her against the wall.

The brighthowler stepped through, and Attica's shade moved. It erupted from his spine, a rush of pure shadow. It caught the monster and drove a single spike through its core, killing it.

Attica crawled to her, pulled Dayanne into his arms, the weight of her limp body confirming what he already knew. Then, trembling, he reached for Eli.

No breath. No light. Both dead.

Attica's lips parted, but nothing came out.

Ahead, the Seer's door stood open, pale light pulsing from within.

Attica was ready to die. To stay in this moment. To let the wound take him, quietly, beside the only two souls that ever truly knew him. And then, just as he was about to give in to death, a voice cleaved the silence.

"Lone-Eyed Wolf . . ." The Seer spoke—not loud, not strong, but clear. "It's time."

Attica turned to Eve, who was on one knee, clutching her wounded arm. She sipped from her gourd and looked up at him. "Go," she said, tears in her eyes. "For Dayanne. For Eli. For . . . me."

CHAPTER TWENTY-THREE

Attica's shade pried him away from Dayanne's body. It dragged him forward, his limbs too heavy, his will too splintered to resist.

"Please," he whispered, the word frayed as tremors rolled through the stone overhead. The Sanctum shook, dust spilling from the ceiling. A crack opened in the stone, followed by the sound of something larger giving way on the floor above. "Please . . ."

His shade hauled him to the door, the Seer waiting beyond. The light around her had faded. No more radiance—just the dim hush of someone already half departed. Just a frail, trembling figure seated on a throne and hunched forward, stringy hair in her face, eyes locked on him.

"Attica," she murmured. "You must . . ."

"Why?"

All at once, the trauma surged through him—Dayanne, Eli, the slaughter, the giant flashwraith storming through the settlement. It feverishly tore through his thoughts. Too much to contain. He turned toward the antechamber—toward Dayanne and Eli, unmoving on the stone.

"There is a way," the Seer whispered. "The Crown of Shadows . . . its shards . . . Find the shards, repair the crown . . ."

He looked back at her, and the woman came into focus slowly, her body flickering as shadows crept closer to her. She looked older now. Brittle. The whites of her eyes had dulled to yellow, each breath a struggle.

"How?" he asked the Seer.

"You must drink." She pulled the flask from within her robes, bone-pale, etched with ancient art. "All of it. It's yours. The Painter's blood."

"The . . . what?" he stared at her, dumbfounded. "Drinking will exile me."

"Look around you, Attica. Exile is the only way." She tilted her chin toward the ceiling. "I will die with the settlement. All are almost gone now. I'm dying . . ."

"Dayanne, Eli—"

"You can still save them." Her voice broke as she dropped the bone flask. It struck the base of her throne, rolled once, then settled at his feet with a hollow clink. "There is a way, but you must drink now, before it's too late."

"Eve could—"

"No. You're the one who had the vision. You and Dayanne. You saw it before it came."

"I don't know what she saw," he said, voice raw.

"You will one day," she said. "Drink."

His shade moved again. It pulled him forward, placed his hand on the flask.

"I will make the decision," Attica told his shade through clenched teeth. But even as he said it, he knew it wasn't true. His shade wasn't forcing him. It was helping him. It turned his body slightly, giving Attica a glimpse of the wound in his side, still seeping blood.

It's trying to save me, he realized.

He closed his fingers around the flask. The Seer leaned back in her chair, eyes lifted to the ceiling. "It's coming," she whispered, yet there was no fear in her voice, only certainty. "Goodbye, Attica, and good—"

The ceiling gave way. A slab of stone collapsed from above, killing her with a sickening crunch.

Above, screams echoed through the settlement. The ground groaned as the Sanctum trembled, more stones falling.

"Attica!" Eve's shout pierced the dust.

Attica raised the carved bone flask to his lips.

For Dayanne. For Eli.

The taste hit like fire and rust: bitter, ancient, laced with iron and memory. It was like swallowing lightning and ash, a violent heat that scalded his throat and seared through his chest.

It burned and bloomed.

Light unfurled behind his eye. Heat hammered through his heart, each beat louder, deeper, layered with something other. A second heartbeat joined his own. Then a third as color filled the room.

Voices rose, not from the room, but from within, creating a kaleidoscope of color and sound, a thousand whispers speaking the same word in a language he didn't know until clarity struck, radiant and new.

Everything snapped back to how it had been just moments ago, Attica's world once again a swath of gray tones. But something had changed. Knowledge hovered before him as if it had been awakened, as if it had always lived inside him, waiting to be remembered.

Name: Attica, the Lone-Eyed Wolf
Designation: Shadowborn – Tier I
Rank: Vanguard (Exile)
Shard Fragments: 0 / 11
Current Traits:
Shadowblade – Your weapon is born of will and shadow. Its shape reflects you.
Resonant Shade – You can extend your awareness through your shade.
Shade Swarm – Summon nearby shades to overwhelm a target. May fail.
Shadow Phasing – Press through surfaces.
Shade Devour – Absorb the essence of slain foes to empower your shade.

"What is this?" he breathed, eyes locked on the strange script unfolding before him.

Attica rose to his feet effortlessly and attached the bone flask to his belt. The pain was gone, the wound on his side completely healed. His skin shimmered with veins of living shadow, and for a moment, he could see miniature glyphs tracing across his skin. It felt like waking from a years-long sleep—his strength bottomless, his mind razor sharp.

Attica stepped into the antechamber. Eve was still on the floor, propped against the wall, her eyes wide. "You're . . . glowing."

He looked down at his hands and watched the light fade into something darker.

The foundation above groaned. More stone cracked overhead.

Eve pushed herself upright, bracing against the wall.

"Are you—?"

"I'm fine," she said. "But the building's going to collapse."

Attica moved to Dayanne. He lifted her easily and pressed his lips to her forehead, the world falling away for just one heartbeat. "Please," he told Eve, "get Eli."

She came forward and took the boy into her arms.

"We'll bury them after," Attica said as he started up the stairs.

"After?" she asked. "After what?"

"After I erase every last flashwraith in our settlement."

"Attica—"

His shade flared. "And then, I'm going to bring down that giant."

CHAPTER TWENTY-FOUR

Attica stepped into the burning night. The Sanctum groaned behind him, its ancient supports cracking in protest as fires raged all around him. Eve followed at his side, Eli in her arms.

"No . . ." she said, her voice filling with pain as smoke billowed around them, the stench of ash tinged with the strange electric tang of dying light.

Attica barely heard her. His eyes were on Dayanne, her lifeless body cradled in his arms. "I'm sorry, my love," he whispered. "I'm so sorry." He kissed her forehead and pressed forward, past corpses and flames, through a place that had once been sacred, a home for generations of Shadowborn.

Behind them, the Sanctum collapsed in full. Stone screamed overhead as the upper levels collapsed, vomiting ash and grit into the sky.

Attica clenched his eye shut, his way of saying goodbye to a place he would never visit again. He found a flat piece of ground between the shattered gates and the wall that had once marked one of the inner rings of the settlement. After clearing a space with his foot, he laid Dayanne down and carefully took her stone necklace. He placed it around his neck. Eve approached in silence and laid Eli gently at Dayanne's side.

Flakes of ruin fell around them once the two bodies were settled.

"I'm sorry," Eve began to say.

"We will be back," Attica told her as the shadows all bent toward him. His blade formed across his forearm—longer now, darker, alive, pulsing with dark essence, a sleek extension of his will and power. His shade threaded down his arm, coiling toward his fingers as it fed the weapon's edge. It hummed with pressure. With purpose. With hunger.

An emitter burst from the smoke, mouth filled with light.

One stroke and the emitter vanished, cleaved from core to throat.

Another charged. His shade lashed out at the emitter mid-strike, pinning the creature with ten black tendrils. Its core cracked. Essence bloomed and vanished.

"Attica—" Eve said, summoning her shadowy whipsword as the air around them shimmered. A hunter emerged, one of the light-warpers they'd faced earlier. Tall, fluid, alien, and incredibly lethal.

Attica turned and impaled it through the chest, lifting the creature with an angry grunt before slamming it into the ground. He felt the surge this time, raw and clean. Power flooded into him with sharp clarity. When he looked back, Eve was staring.

A slow grin curved across her dark face, her breath catching just slightly before she spoke. "Incredible," she said, voice low, almost reverent. Her eyes lingered on him for a breath too long . . . then flicked past his shoulder. "Tiago," she said, the moment broken. "He's going to get himself killed!"

Attica turned and spotted the young man just beyond another inner wall, trying to hold off a flareback, *alone*.

"Dammit!" Attica took a running step forward and vaulted toward Tiago and the flareback. His body soared over the beast in a blur, the shadow surrounding him trailing like a torn banner. Attica landed behind it, spun mid-strike, and brought the flareback down. He drove his blade through its spine, straight into the glowing core.

Tiago stood wide-eyed, his face covered in streaks of blue blood as he tried to process what Attica had just done. "What the—" He swallowed hard. "H-how?"

"We need to finish here," Attica told him as he stepped around the beast.

"What did you do?" Tiago asked. "Your power . . ."

"The Seer's flask."

"You drank it?" Tiago asked as he noticed the flask now looped to Attica's belt.

"She gave it to me." His gaze locked on the giant flashwraith, now well beyond the northern wall. It moved with a terrible grace, each massive stride carrying it farther from the burning ruins. The child of light floated absentmindedly inside its skull, a soft glow in a body built for ruin.

"I have to kill it," was all Attica told Tiago as he started forward, steps steady, vision narrowing to that distant glow.

But the world wouldn't let him go.

Movement surged at the edges of his focus. Emitters. Glintfangs. Swarms of lesser flaylights poured from the wreckage like insects, their forms twitching with fractured light.

He staggered back as one emitter caught him square in the chest with a blast of essence, a strike that would have normally killed him even with his shade. The force broke against him, scattered across the surface of his shadow-wrought armor.

Before Tiago could shout a warning, Attica moved—a blur of motion, a flash of black steel. The emitter split apart mid-lunge, its core cleaved in two.

Tiago didn't hesitate.

With a shout, the young man surged toward the next one, his twin daggers igniting with shadow as his shade coiled tight around his arms. He ducked a searing beam, rolled low, and came up inside the flashwraith's guard. Both weapons struck in unison—one slicing through its limbs, the other stabbing deep into its chest.

The emitter buckled, cracked, and burst apart. Tiago stood panting over the corpse as he looked up to his next opponent. His eyes went wide. "Attica, watch out—!" he shouted as a glintfang leapt from the rubble, jaws open.

Attica *caught* the wolflike flashwraith in midair, one hand on its upper jaw, one on the lower, the beast mere seconds away from releasing a blast of light at the back of his throat. Attica tore the glintfang open like he was splitting kindling and tossed it aside.

He glanced ahead to Eve, who was handling her own against a brighthowler, Tiago moving to assist.

Good, he thought as he bound toward an incoming flareback, which locked onto his movement and released all of the power from his core. The blast should have completely disintegrated him, yet Attica *phased* right through the attack, warmth trailing over his shoulders as the beast fell.

He landed on top of a crumbled structure. Attica patted his chest with his hands. "How?" he whispered. His mind flashed to the information he had come to understand after drinking the flask. *It has to be one of my new powers . . . Shadow Phasing . . .*

He remembered following Hadrian down to the third tier. Hadrian hadn't exhibited any new powers, but he had been stronger.

Maybe he drank less than I did. He must have drunk less. Attica turned, hoping—praying—to see more Vanguard behind him. His heart sank as he found no army left. Just Tiago, Eve, and one other. Cassian limped across a courtyard, the tall man dragging his leg.

He was too far behind. Too slow. Cassian went down as another glintfang took him from behind, ripping into his spine with a burst of light.

Attica surged toward it, rage pushing him forward. He landed near the glintfang and caught it mid-turn, his hand clamping down on its tail. Before the creature could react, Attica yanked it backward and drove his shadowblade up through its spine, slicing through flesh and bone alike. The blade erupted from its throat coupled with a burst of light.

The glintfang twitched once, then went still, dissolving into streaks of essence.

"Cassian," Attica breathed as he looked down at the body. For a moment, the chaos receded. He remembered laughter around the fire. A quiet night outside the wall. The way Cassian had always used his shade to cheat at Vaultstone—a game of strength and balance the Vanguard played to prove who could throw the farthest.

That moment was gone now. Now, only Eve, Tiago, and Attica remained.

He grimaced. His lungs burned from the ash, but his body thrummed with unnatural energy.

Then, he felt it.

The essence wasn't just around him anymore. It was inside him—burning, binding, becoming. Every flashwraith he had killed fueled him, fed his shade and augmented his dark powers. The Seer's flask had opened something deeper. *And it has given me new powers*, he thought as he recalled the power he had received known as Shade Swarm.

The rest came to him instinctually. Attica dropped to one knee. His shade curled around him, its edges flickering with anticipation.

"I'm ready," he whispered.

The world went still for half a second, then broke. Shadows erupted from every shattered wall, every scorched doorway, streaking across the settlement like lightning laced in smoke.

They tore through flaylights in a frenzy, converging on Attica. Dozens. Hundreds. Shades—both his and not—rising from the ruin like smoke made flesh.

They swarmed the remaining flashwraiths, and the night's sky dimmed.

Flarebacks screamed as their cores burst, spewing light in wide arcs, tearing through stone and flame alike. Watchtowers collapsed. Gates imploded. What little structure remained was scoured in those last, desperate bursts of brilliance.

But it wasn't enough.

By the time it ended, the only thing left was silence, the dead, and the occasional fire.

Attica turned back to where he'd last seen the enormous flashwraith. His shade lifted him toward higher ground, clinging to fractured stone and smoke-slicked walls. He climbed until the firelight faded below, until there was nothing but wind, ruin, and the ghost of what once was home.

"There you are," he growled as his eye settled on the towering flashwraith, the child of light glowing in its head. The giant was far off now, a silhouette of burning gold at the edge of the first tier.

The colossus paused—head tilting, light flickering—as if it felt his gaze.

Then it stepped over the rim, and vanished into the dark below.

CHAPTER TWENTY-FIVE

Attica turned from the ledge, his focus still fixed on where the giant flash-wraith had vanished. He was about to leap after it when a voice reached him from below.

"Attica!" Eve's tone was sharp, grounded, what he'd expect from her. "Hey!" Tiago called to him as well, his voice heavy with urgency.

Attica exhaled. "Let's head down," he told his shade.

The climb down was slow. With each foothold, exhaustion crept deeper into his bones. His limbs trembled with the weight of what he'd done, and more pressing, what he had lost. By the time his boots hit the stone, his breath was ragged. Still, he inhaled deeply and stood tall, Attica keenly aware of all that had just taken place.

Eve approached, watching him closely. Her face was streaked with soot and blood, her lip split, but her eyes held him steady.

"I have to keep going," he said as he leveled his broken gaze on her. "We can't lose that thing."

"That *thing* is too large to lose. Besides, you won't catch it in your current state," Eve told him, firm as ever. "Even with your newfound strength. Fill your gourd. We handle the dead, and—"

"We hunt it," Tiago said, stepping forward, voice low and burning. "We do it together."

Attica hesitated. Then gave them both a slow nod. "Together, then."

They passed through what was left of the settlement, their boots crunching over crumbled brick and kicking through ash. Buildings that had once held warmth—barracks, homes, the quiet alcove where Vanguard carved murals into the stone, the place where they held essence feasts—all of it nothing more than burned-out husks, the makings of a ruin.

The walls still breathed heat, ash twisting in the wind as shadows flickered all around, remnants of shades. Some moved like echoes. Others lingered in corners, nearly faded. Attica could hear their whispers at the edge of thought, yet he still hadn't received any other communication from them—not like Hadrian, who had been able to seemingly communicate with his shade.

Attica hadn't believed him then. Back when they were hauling the shieldwraith over the edge, he was certain Hadrian had gone mad from the contents of the Seer's flask. He was starting to see that their experiences in drinking from the Seer's flask were radically different.

Maybe because I drank more? Maybe because it was the Painter's blood?

His eye caught the edge of a familiar half-crumbled wall. Once, he and Dayanne had argued near it, the topic of their quarrel one he no longer remembered. *I fought with her so little that the fights we had seem even less so,* he thought as he placed his hand on her necklace.

He whispered her name and pushed on, continuing through the remains in silence with a heavy heart.

They came across a trio of dead Vanguard. "We should get more gourds if this is . . ." Tiago cleared his throat and tried again. "If this is the last time we will visit the settlement."

"Yes, smart. More gourds. Two each," Eve told him, newfound strength in her voice. "And you should fill the Seer's flask, Attica."

Attica placed his hand on the bone flask, which felt heavier now. Hollow and strange. "I agree with the gourds, but maybe it's best to save this vessel."

Eve slowly nodded. "Yes, that makes sense. Drink from your gourd, then. Even with what you just did, you could use it."

Attica did as instructed, and his energy levels returned, the mana like fire and breath threading through his veins all at once.

"There is so much here," Tiago said, a wild look in his eyes. "Maybe we will come back."

"What do you mean?" Eve asked as she drank from her gourd as well.

"For essence and to pay our respects for the dead. I don't want to speak out of place but . . . where?"

"Where?" Attica echoed, realizing Tiago was looking at him.

"The graves. Where should I dig them? I figured I could do that part. While you, you . . ."

Attica opened his mouth to speak, but the words failed him.

Eve spoke for him after a long pause. "Put the graves in the training grounds. Bury them there so that their souls may return as warriors. And thank you, Tiago."

Tiago left, Eve now alone with Attica.

The silence that followed was thick with ash and absence, broken only by the distant crackle of dying embers. He turned toward the husk of a flareback and absorbed essence into his gourd, Eve still focused on his flask.

"The Seer's wasn't like our normal essence," Eve said. "We both went through the trial."

"Before she died, she called it the Painter's blood."

"Did she?"

"She did, but it might have been metaphorical."

"Look what it did to you. I don't think it was metaphorical at all, Attica."

He put the gourd away and picked up another gourd that belonged to a fallen Vanguard named Paderborn who was burned almost beyond recognition. "Maybe it's best to save this vessel."

"Agreed," she said as she found a gourd as well.

They came to the heart of the carnage, the place where fire had pooled longest and bodies still steamed.

Shadowborn lay crumpled around in unnatural poses, some only fragments. Others were little more than piles of soot and armor. The ground still smoked and the smell was terrible. Most were beyond recognition, but they found the ones they needed—Dayanne, Eli, Livia, Cassian.

"Take a moment," Eve told him.

Attica whispered an incoherent reply.

While Eve brought Livia and Cassian to Tiago using the assistance of her shade, Attica sat with Dayanne and Eli.

He didn't say anything. He didn't know what to tell them aside from this constant urge to apologize. But in looking at Dayanne's face, he knew she wouldn't have accepted an apology. She would have said that he was doing what he was born to do as a member of the Vanguard, and that . . .

"The best way to show my remorse is to get revenge," Attica said, knowing full well Dayanne would have hated that answer.

But it was the only one that felt honest. It was the only one that he could come up with as he gathered her gently into his arms, the weight of her body unfamiliar and final.

Attica carried her dead body through the ruins toward the training field— where Tiago, face still smeared with ash, had carved shallow graves into the scorched earth with the help of his shade.

Attica laid Dayanne down with care, and for a moment, he didn't move at all. Then he turned, his eye stinging as he walked back through the smoke to retrieve Eli.

"You would have been the strongest of them all," he told the toddler as he brought him into his arms and returned to the graves, where he laid Eli with Dayanne.

There were no prayers. No rites to follow.

Just the three of them, heads bowed, the ash curling around their ankles, the dead still warm in the earth.

When it was done, Attica, Eve, and Tiago gathered at the gate of the settlement and made for the path to the second tier. Neither looked back.

The world grew dimmer as they started off.

Attica's head pulsed as he relived all that had just happened—from the ambush to the moment his mind had opened to a string of text he could have never imagined. Just thinking about it caused the information to flicker before his eyes again:

Name: Attica, the Lone-Eyed Wolf
Designation: Shadowborn – Tier I
Rank: Vanguard (Exile)
Shard Fragments: 0 / 11
Current Traits:
Shadowblade – Your weapon is born of will and shadow. Its shape reflects you.
Resonant Shade – You can extend your awareness through your shade.
Shade Swarm – Summon nearby shades to overwhelm a target. May fail.
Shadow Phasing – Press through surfaces.
Shade Devour – Absorb the essence of slain foes to empower your shade.

The new traits were certainly something.

As he glanced toward the shadows stretching along the jagged terrain, Attica wondered if Shade Swarm had limits. *Will the ability fail in places where there were no nearby shades? No dark essence? Is the power tied to proximity or simply potential?*

He remembered phasing through a flareback's blast. It had happened so fast that it barely registered in the moment.

And Shade Swarm . . . *That may be the only way I can bring down the giant.*

Then there was the last trait, Shade Devour, which still felt mysterious.

Did I use it? Was that the reason my shade felt stronger during the fight? Or did it trigger automatically, feeding on the dead without my command?

His thoughts shifted again to the Seer's final words.

Shard Fragments . . . Fragments of what?

His eye widened slightly as a memory surfaced—Hadrian's voice, ragged from the effects of the Seer's flask: *The Crown of Shadows exists . . . in pieces. Shards. It's no wonder the truth has been obscured. The success of our community depends on it.*

Tiago turned back to him. "We're almost at the second tier. Why are you stopping?"

"Yes, let's keep going," Eve said. "We find the giant—which we should be able to see soon—and rest before we kill it. We *will* kill it," she added, her voice like stone. It wasn't a hope. It was a vow.

They came to the edge of the first tier, where a broken cliff curved over a long descent into mist. As they prepared to trek down with the aid of their shades, Attica noticed a stone set into the ledge that he'd seen countless times before. It jutted from the cliffside—a warning etched in script so old no one could've known how to read it.

He paused, stepping closer. The symbols burned faintly in the gloom. He blinked once, confused.

Then the symbols shifted—not into letters, but understanding.

Attica could read it.

CHAPTER TWENTY-SIX

For a moment, Attica stood there, dumbfounded by what he was looking at. The symbols were carved deep into the stone, older than the walls around them, untouched by the destruction above. He remained at the edge of the first tier long enough for Eve to climb up beside him, brushing ash from her gloves.

"What is it?" she asked.

He pointed to the symbols. "I understand it."

Her brow creased as she looked at the ancient glyphs. "You can actually read it?"

"They're instructions."

"For what, Attica?"

He kept staring at the stone, unable to look away. "Part of it is missing. But . . . I can't believe I'm saying this. It's a description of the third tier and what to expect there."

"What does it say?" Tiago asked.

"For those that seek it, the Realm of Recumbency can be accessed on the third tier, through the Gate of Whispers. Vespasia, Mother of Whispers, will guide you. Beware—"

"Beware what?" Tiago asked, interrupting him.

"That's where the text cuts off. But Hadrian mentioned Vespasia, Mother of Whispers, when we were taking the shield down."

"Realm of Recumbency?" Eve frowned. "What could that mean?"

"I don't know," Attica said. "But I will find it."

"After the giant flashwraith is dead?"

"Yes. And the child in its head is destroyed." He turned to her. "There is nothing left for me now, Eve. My family is gone."

She opened her mouth like she was going to speak, but stopped. Her jaw tensed. Eve turned away instead and began her descent without another word, though her presence lingered long after.

Attica's shade squeezed his shoulders in a familiar way, the sensation one he was all too familiar with. "I don't need your input right now," he told it as he took a step forward and his shade stopped. "Release me," Attica said, his voice just above a whisper.

"Are you coming?" Tiago called to him.

"Yes." Attica had dealt with the stubborn shade long enough to know better than to be too harsh with it. Yet his shade persisted. "What are you doing?" Attica's head shifted back to the symbols. "You want me to . . . reach the Realm of Recumbency?"

His shade released him so quickly that Attica actually took a lumbering step forward.

"So that *is* what this is about. We have other plans first."

His shade's presence surged again, bracing his shoulders.

"*After*. We have to kill the beast first for what it did. Can't you see that? I do not want to argue this with you."

Attica's shade relented, its influence pulling back and all but disappearing until he scaled down the side of the cliff, where it assisted him with his climb.

At the bottom, Tiago crouched in the dirt, examining the trail the creature had left behind. "Look," he said. "It burned the ground as it moved. Cratered it too. Each step . . . six feet wide, maybe more."

Eve stepped into one of the tracks without hesitation. Her boots vanished nearly to the shin. "See?" she said, looking back. "Just as I suspected: it will be easy to follow, and incredibly hard to kill. We need a place to rest."

"We will rest once we are able to get eyes on it," Attica said. "We can take turns tracking it."

"And if it goes over the third tier?" Tiago asked.

"We go with it," Attica said. "I'm exiled."

"So we can go too."

"Of course," he told the younger man. "There are no longer any rules."

Tiago ran his hand through his white-streaked hair. "Good. I was afraid you'd leave us up here."

"You're afraid to be left with me?" Eve asked.

"That's not exactly what I said . . ." Tiago offered a crooked grin, but it faded almost as quickly as it came. "Actually, I don't know why I asked what I asked. But I'm in this until we reach the bottom, or . . . or whatever it is we plan to do. That's what I mean."

He cleared his throat, his shoulders twitching with tension. "I'm saying too much."

"It's been a long night," Eve said, glancing at him without judgment.

"It is no longer night," Attica replied. His voice was low, steady. "We find the flashwraith first."

They pressed on, following the monster's trail through a narrowing pass. The path coiled around the cliffside, forcing them to navigate loose rock and wind-scoured ledges before it widened again. Ahead, the trail burned across the massive steps punched into the Spiralrealm's hardtop like ritual scars.

It soon became clear that the giant flashwraith wasn't heading toward the third tier as Attica had anticipated. It was circling the second.

Moving with purpose. With calculation.

But toward what? Attica wondered.

The trio crested a final rise and halted. There, across the broken stone, stood the monstrous flashwraith, immense and unmoving, its twisted frame silhouetted against the dim glow of the Spiralrealm. It faced the abyss beyond, as if watching something none of them could see.

Waiting.

"You're sure we should do it now?" Tiago asked, his voice even, but the strain in it betrayed him. The young man rarely showed fatigue, Tiago known for pushing himself past reason. But Attica had seen that glint in his eyes before, the kind that came right before a collapse.

Attica glanced at Eve. Her gaze was steady, flint hard, that familiar fire still burning behind her exhaustion. But she was visibly tired. Her stance said it all. Too still, too tight. She'd been holding the line for too long.

His gaze returned to the massive flashwraith. He could end it now. Attica felt it in his limbs, in the unnatural stillness of his own breath. Power pulsed in him. But—

"No," Attica said at last, every word dragged from the well of his restraint. "We study it first, we rest, and then we kill it."

Attica knew he wasn't going to be able to sleep, not with the giant flashwraith standing nearly a mile away, its massive frame haloed in mist and light, practically daring him to act.

But he also knew better than to go at it alone.

Hadrian had drilled that into him. There was strength in unity, in formation. Vanguard were not meant to die one at a time. *A shade may follow only one Vanguard,* Hadrian had once told him, *but it fights for many.*

Yet every time Attica shut his eye, the anger tightened inside him—coiling, hardening, becoming something sharp.

Sleep didn't come. It couldn't.

Not with the image of the burning settlement scorched into his mind. Not with the memory of Eli's stillness, Dayanne's death. Their absence carved through him.

He paced. His shade moved with him, coiling and uncoiling in sync, mirroring the storm beneath his skin. It didn't try to stop him. It didn't soothe. It simply watched, a silent witness to his unraveling.

There were moments he nearly surged off into the dark alone, shadowblade drawn, vision tunneling on the monstrous figure that still loomed somewhere beyond the ridge. He could feel it even now—that distant wrongness, that impossibly patient malice.

He always stopped short. Always.

But each time, it took longer to pull himself back.

His restless fury eventually cooled into something sharper. More dangerous. *How do I kill it?* he thought. *How do I kill the child of light inside its skull?* He knew it had to be done. There was no question.

But every time he braced himself for the act, every time the resolve solidified into certainty, Dayanne's voice returned. Not clearly. Just fragments. He strained to remember the words she spoke the night Eli was born, spoken through the haze of the Seer's flask. Delirious. Prophetic. Lost.

He couldn't remember what she had said. Not fully. Just the weight of it, the tremble in her voice. "Why can't I remember?" he whispered into the dark. "What did you try to tell me, my love?"

Attica sat down on a fallen pillar, worn smooth by time. His eye drifted into the mist, vision pulling and blurring. The distance shimmered, then it shifted, a veil being drawn back.

For a breath, he thought he saw Dayanne. Her long hair, the way the world seemed to sway with her, the softness of her gait.

"Dayanne?" he whispered as the mist stirred, then dissipated.

His heart sank. *You're seeing things*, he thought.

He glanced back toward Eve and Tiago, both asleep. Eve was propped against a ruined wall, one hand still wrapped around the hilt of her blade.

Attica turned again toward the mist.

Something moved. It didn't just swell toward it, it arrived.

Banshee-like at first, a figure was suddenly there hovering above him, robes swirling in the mist. Power drained from the air. His shade recoiled as though struck. Even Attica's thoughts seemed slower, muted under a pressure he didn't understand as he looked up at the ghost of a woman.

Two sharp, porcelain-pale hands extended from her sleeves. Fingernails black and curved. She lifted one hand, pulled back her hood.

Her face was bisected by a vertical stripe of darkness, and her skin pale like frozen clay. Her eyes were red—so red they shimmered like the rings around the Spiralrealm's sun. And yet, she was calm, nothing about her monstrous or resembling a flashwraith.

His shade surged in front of him, armor flaring—then *shrank* back, its jagged ridges rising only to fall again, deferential. "Good. Your shade now understands. Do not be frightened, Lone-Eyed Wolf," she said. Her voice was *layered*. It didn't echo, but it *felt* like it should. Warm, yet impossibly still. "I am Vespasia, the

Mother of Whispers. You are exiled." She gestured toward Eve and Tiago. "They are not."

"No, but they are with me," he said, finding his voice. "Your name was mentioned in the message near the edge of the first tier."

"Then you know who I am, and like all exiles, I implore you to visit the Gate of Whispers on the third tier. Go there, and I will lead you to the gate, which will grant you access to the Realm of Recumbency, where you can meet Duchess Corvenna. I cannot open the way, but I can point to the path."

"That can wait," Attica said, the edge in his voice unmistakable.

"You will not succeed in your endeavor without understanding what it is you've become," Vespasia said. "You have consumed the Painter's blood. You now see the world as it truly is."

Attica touched the flask. "So it is truly her blood?"

"Yes, the blood given to your community long ago, nurtured and sustained over time. But that doesn't matter now. You will soon find your pack, Lone-Eyed Wolf. Or you will not. That is not for me to decide. But if you hope to continue, you will go to the third tier and enter the Gate of Whispers."

Vespasia hovered back. Mist coiled around her lower half and rose to obscure her face. A flurry of whispers followed, soft, layered, and impossible to trace. They swirled like wind through dead leaves. Only her blazing red eyes remained, suspended in the fog like twin embers.

"I hope you survive long enough to visit the Realm of Recumbency," she said, her voice now echoed by a dozen unseen mouths.

And then she was gone, the night silent again.

CHAPTER TWENTY-SEVEN

The giant flashwraith hadn't moved.

It stood at the far end of the scorched plateau, tall as a tower, backlit by drifting clouds, its silhouette pulsing with essence. Its head hung slightly, arms loose at its sides.

Attica had stared long enough to memorize its shape—the horns curling from its shoulders, the faint shifts in its stance, the way the essence flared along its form, and the child suspended in a pool of light within its head.

That was his target. Nothing shielded the child—no armor, no barrier. Attica was certain he could punch through the giant's semitransparent skull, certain it would kill the creature that had destroyed the settlement.

He had watched the child intently, the way it flickered, the way the creature housing it responded. Like the core of lights Vanguard often targeted on flashwraiths, *this* was the fastest path to a kill.

Has to be.

And right now, that was all Attica really wanted, a fast kill. Revenge.

"It's just standing there," Tiago whispered as he approached, light on his feet as always.

"It's been like that all night."

"You never slept?"

"No. I don't need to right now." Attica turned just as Eve joined them. "Are you ready?"

He ignored the warning in her eyes—eyes that didn't match the words she chose next: "We do it now," Eve said, her voice flint sharp with resolve.

"And after?" Tiago asked. "What then?"

"Don't worry about the future until you've seen to the present," Attica told him, which felt like something Hadrian would have said, only hollow.

The three Vanguards moved carefully in the direction of the giant flashwraith, spreading out along the edge of the broken path.

The plateau was cracked and uneven, its surface fractured like old bone. Fissures veined the stone, some narrow, others wide enough to swallow a man. Weathered outcrops jutted near the edges, remnants of a time when the land had been whole. At the far end, a collapsed bridge clung stubbornly to a shattered ledge, its span now a ruin dangling over a vast gorge—an open wound at the edge of the second tier. Beyond it, the third descended in a sheer vertical drop, lost beneath folds of fog. Wind funneled up through the broken escarpment, laced with the scent of moss and raw, metallic ore.

Eve was the first to sense danger. "Attica—!"

The elite flashwraiths blinked into existence from nothing, bending light around their tall and sinewy forms. Two, four, then *six* of them in total.

Attica's shade snapped tight against his back as he summoned an arm-length blade made of dark mana.

Faster than thought, Attica surged forward—his blade cleaving through the nearest elite flashwraith in a single fluid stroke. The creature collapsed inward, folding into itself as light poured from the wound. He was already turning, shadows trailing him, eyes locked on the next, when another blurred out of existence and appeared behind Tiago.

It lashed out with a bladelike arm; Tiago blocked it just in time, but the force sent him sprawling backward.

Eve intercepted the next one, her whipsword cutting arcs of shadow into the air as she held it back. "I've got this one! Keep moving!"

Attica met his opponent head-on, shadowblade clashing against the wraith's strike, dark essence flaring from his shoulders as the elite flashwraith's eyes burned with searing light.

The ground trembled beneath them. Beyond, the giant flashwraith lifted its head as it noticed their presence. Its absent gaze locked on Attica, daring him to come forward.

Fueled by a sudden sense of fury, Attica killed his opponent by driving his blade through its stomach just as it was starting to vanish, the monster going limp. He was just about to move toward the giant flashwraith when Tiago screamed.

Attica turned as Tiago went down, a deep gash carving through his shoulder, blue blood soaking his tunic. His shade collapsed across his chest, trying to hold him together.

"Fall back!" Eve shouted, dragging Tiago behind a crumbled wall. "We're outnumbered!"

But Attica refused to hear her.

He surged forward, propelled by dark essence. Another elite flashwraith fell beneath his strike. As its body disintegrated, he was already turning back to the giant.

"Attica—" Eve started to say, but by this point, he was gone.

He blinked across the battlefield. One elite gave chase. It appeared in front of him, and met only empty air as Attica stepped behind it and drove his blade into its spine, the creature spitting a flash of light out of its mouth before it expired.

Beyond, the giant moved. The towering flashwraith stepped forward with impossible weight, the ground quaking beneath each step as it approached the gorge.

Attica vaulted toward it, his shade propelling him forward. He landed near the horn sticking out of its shoulder, closer than ever to the child of light. *If I can just get to it—*

A sweep of the giant's massive hand sent him flying forward. The backhand strike caught him clean, flinging Attica like a stone across the sky. He slammed into the gorge wall and tumbled, skidding down the incline, rocks trailing in his wake, the drop pulling him into the dark.

Attica hit the bottom of the third tier with a thud that should have killed him had it not been for his shade, which took the worst of it.

His vision swam as whispers rose around him. They came from every crevice of the gorge, spectral, writhing, clawing at his limbs. His shade moved again, forming a ring of hardened spikes that flared outward, keeping the whispers at bay.

"We have to get back up there." Attica told his shade as he crouched, head down, gathering power.

He launched upward and shot back to the second tier, his body trailing shadow, his blade glowing dimly at the edges.

The giant turned to meet him, misjudged, and slipped. Its massive form tilted, then crashed sideways into the gorge.

The ground convulsed.

Stone shattered beneath the weight, and a shock wave of dust and essence tore outward in a low, thunderous howl.

Attica landed hard on cracked stone beside the creature's ruined head. The air around him thick, essence bristling toward him, raw and endless, drawn by something deeper than instinct.

This was his chance, his one shot to pierce the veil and kill the child of light. It would not undo what had happened, but it was the closest thing to justice he had left.

There was no final roar. No fury.

Only the child, rising slowly, still tethered to the fallen flashwraith's remains by an umbilical cord of light.

It was too bright for Attica to fully make out its details, but judging by the child's size, Attica could see it was an infant, younger than Eli, the child wrapped in a nearly blinding white flame.

It didn't cry.

Didn't make a sound.

Just like Eli . . .

Attica took a step back, breath tight in his throat as the child turned to him.

Then a pulse of power radiated outward. No light, no sound, just *pressure*. The remaining elite flashwraiths and the giant's body vanished, drawn into its wake, the child disappearing with them.

Gone.

Attica stood frozen, chest heaving, mind racing. *What was that?* He cursed himself for not delivering the finishing blow. "What's wrong with you?" he hissed, slapping the side of his head. "Are you no longer Vanguard?"

Eve's voice rang out behind him. "Attica!"

His blade fizzled away as he turned to find Eve crouched beside Tiago, cradling him with one arm, blue blood pooling beneath them. Her face was twisted in anger and grief. "You just left us," she said as he finally approached. "You ran off like . . . like we didn't matter!"

Attica opened his mouth to speak, but nothing came.

Her glare cracked. "Are you okay?"

"Don't worry about me," he said quietly, gaze drifting to Tiago, the young man pale and unconscious, his shade flickering faintly. "We will go to the Realm of Recumbency. He will be looked after there."

Eve didn't answer. She just looked away, her jaw tight, her eyes wet with fury.

And somewhere deep below, the Spiralrealm waited.

PART FOUR

OPEN THE FLOODGATES

CHAPTER TWENTY-EIGHT

S tay strong, Tiago," Attica said, carrying the young man on his back. "You will survive this. You must."

He could feel Tiago's shade trembling against him, doing its best to slow the bleeding, to keep him conscious. Some shades could do that—lend their essence to their wielder in moments of crisis. It was rare, but Attica had seen it before. Tiago's shade was one of the few with healing traits, and it had saved him more than once. That was part of why Tiago fought so recklessly. He knew he could take wounds others couldn't.

But not these.

The elite flashwraiths had cut too deep. And now, even with his shade's help, Tiago was struggling just to breathe.

"Why won't you tell me what happened back there?" Eve asked Attica as they stopped at the edge of the second tier. "Why didn't you—"

"Because . . ." He recalled the moment the child of light opened its eyes. Even with how bright it was, he could see the glow of its pupils, he could still feel the child's eyes on him, not judging, but curious.

Just like Eli, he thought, remembering the way his son would look at him.

"Why?" Eve asked again, her voice quieter this time.

"Because." He lowered his chin. "Because it reminded me of Eli."

"The child?"

"Yes. The giant flashwraith tripped. I could have ended it right there, but then the child looked at me. I can't explain my actions, but I can say I was wrong," he told her through gritted teeth, "and I will not let it happen again. I won't, Eve. I swear it. Next time, I won't hesitate. I will kill the child of light."

Eve stared at him, her expression caught between judgment and something softer. She didn't look away. "You cannot forget what that Lightborn monster did to our home, Attica. It is *not* Eli," she said quietly. "It is nothing like Eli. It is a demon. And it was in control of the giant."

"We shouldn't have brought that shieldwraith to the settlement," he said bitterly. "That's when it started."

"What do you mean?"

"It released a signal, two years ago." Attica bit his lip. "You remember. And they finally came from the depths. Now, Dayanne, Eli . . . all the others . . . that was our fatal error."

"It is common for us to bring new flashwraiths to the settlement. You did the same with the brighthowler after your trial. But enough. You can feel bad, and we can debate things later. We need to do something before Tiago dies."

Tiago exhaled painfully. "I'm not . . . going to die . . ."

"Just focus on breathing," Attica told him. "We're heading down to the third tier, and from that point . . ." He didn't finish the sentence. He didn't know what would happen next.

The descent was slower than Attica would have liked. The wall of the second tier was slick not with living moss, but with the dark stains it had left behind, remnants etched into the stone like old burns, the memory of life long gone. Eons of erosion had cracked the surface further, turning the climb into a slow, cautious slide.

He moved with Tiago slung across his back, his shade helping to keep the young man in place. Mist curled around their ankles, then climbed to their knees. The light dimmed with every step. The whispers grew louder. Something in the air pressed down on them—dense, unseen, undeniable.

But soon, Attica's lungs adjusted. His breaths came slower. Deeper. As if the third tier had chosen to accept him.

He glanced at Eve and saw the opposite. She was still struggling, her breaths short and staccato. Her shade pulsed heavily at her back, wrapping her in layers of stabilizing shadow, trying to hold her together.

Eve was frightened. It was written in her eyes, in the way she moved. Like him, she had been taught never to descend past the second tier. And now, their home was ash.

The whispers thickened around him, threading through his thoughts like smoke laced with memory.

They prickled the back of Attica's neck, voices without breath. Menacing at first. Then less so. He began to grow used to their presence, as if they'd been waiting for him. He raised his voice into the dark: "I am here, Vespasia. Mother of Whispers. Lead us to the Realm of Recumbency."

The whispers spiraled through the mist, clear yet visible as Tiago looked up at them. "Where . . . are we?" he asked, growing increasingly delirious.

"We are nearly there," Attica told him. "You must keep your composure and focus on healing."

"For . . . for the settlement. For the Painter."

"Yes," Attica said as the whispers pressed through the mist, creating a narrow path ahead. They took it, Attica and Eve on edge, prepared for an ambush. *With the elite flashwraiths, there is no telling*, he thought, shadowblade at the ready.

The path narrowed, and the rock began to change beneath their boots, older, more marbled, veined with silver, Attica could almost hear words inside the whispers.

No language. No structure. But *intention*.

It didn't take long for Attica to realize the third tier wasn't just another descent. It felt alive in a way the upper tiers hadn't, as if the mist itself was listening. The whispers cut through the fog like breath through lungs, giving the entire place a sense of watchfulness. And with that came unease. It was impossible to tell how close danger might be.

His shade reacted in the same way, as it tensed and relaxed several times.

Ahead, something huge moved through the mist, cycling in and out of it resembling a fish moving against the current. The whispers seemed excited by it, their sound growing louder until it disappeared.

Attica was certain it was a flashwraith.

"How would we kill something like that?" Eve asked.

"We . . . we couldn't . . ." Tiago said, who had also been watching the movement.

"Please, Tiago," she said softly, "you're supposed to be resting."

"I'll fight if . . . if I have to." He wheezed "Hard to . . . breathe here."

"Focus on your breath and healing," Attica told him as the whispers continued to part the mist. They traveled down a sloping stone, one slick enough that Attica's shade had to help him with balance. He reached the flowing stream of mana before Eve did.

"Drink from your gourd," he told Tiago as he carefully set him down. "You can refill here."

Eve approached and ran her fingers through the iridescent current. "This is strong," she said as she ran her hand through the iridescent energy. "Stronger than what we have. I don't know if we should consume this or not." She waved her hand through it and brought it up to her nose. "Odd."

Attica ran his hand through as well. "Strange. I've never seen something so abundant. Our streams are always . . . well, you know," he told her as Tiago drank from his gourd. "I'll fill it for you," Attica told him once he had finished.

He took the gourd from Tiago and slowly ran it through the stream of mana. He handed it back to him.

"Should I drink this as well?" Tiago asked.

"Take it easy. It will help you and your shade," Attica told him. "But it might be too powerful. Let's keep moving." Once again, he lifted Tiago onto his back.

"You don't have to carry me."

"We don't know how long this journey will take. It is best that you save your strength."

"It's because . . . because I'm short. You can carry me because I'm short."

"Tiago, enough," Attica told him.

They continued through the whisper-parted mist, and came to a break in the path, where a crooked arch of stone led to a natural tunnel slick with condensation and silence. There were no lanterns here. No signs of flashwraiths. Just the smell of earth and something far more ancient.

Attica paused, the fog peeling back at his presence, revealing a figure barely visible in the dark—a shape wrapped in robes, not fully real, not fully present.

Her voice reached him first. "You come carrying the wounded," said Vespasia, the Mother of Whispers.

Attica stepped forward. "He needs help. His shade is failing."

"Who are you speaking to?" Eve asked.

"It's her, Vespasia, Mother of Whispers. Can you not hear or see her?"

"All I see is fog . . ."

Vespasia motioned to Eve. "And you bring another who has not tasted the Painter's blood. Neither are awakened, exiled. You are at the Gate of Whispers, the entrance to the Realm of Recumbency. All must pass through this gate before they may access the realm, and to do that, they must be awoken. There are rules."

"We are all that's left," Attica told Vespasia, his temper flaring. "We seek help. I did not ask to drink from the flask. I did not ask for you to come to me. But I have come to you seeking your help, seeking whatever this Realm of Recumbency is."

"You did not ask for it, yet you drank it all," Vespasia told Attica.

"Then I will give him my blood, if that's what it takes. This is all that is left of my people. My partner, my child, all are gone. You can help me."

Vespasia drifted closer. Her red eyes pierced the gloom, locking onto him with a weight that slowed the air around him. She hovered above the ground, robes trailing mist. "You don't know what I can do. But others may be more able to help. First, you must pass through the Gate of Whispers. Only you. Only those who are exiled, awakened."

Attica looked at Tiago, then Eve. He returned his focus to Vespasia. "If I do this—?"

"I can protect them while you are within. I cannot promise more. But in the realm . . . you may find allies. And perhaps more than that." She extended her arm, the sleeve falling back to reveal an impossibly old hand. Behind her, the stone breathed. A door rose from its surface—veined with faint script, etched in bone-white carvings, as if it had always been waiting beneath the skin of the cliff. "All who wish to pass must prove they are ready."

"What kind of trial?" Attica asked.

"Nothing you aren't capable of."

"Go," Eve said as she came forward. "If she's telling you that you must pass a trial to save Tiago, that is what you must do."

"But—"

"I will stay here with Tiago."

"We will . . . survive," Tiago said. "Lone-Eyed Wolf, we will survive."

"See?" Eve asked. "Now go. Do what must be done."

CHAPTER TWENTY-NINE

Attica stepped through the Gate of Whispers, the mist pressing in behind him, swallowing the tunnel leaving Eve, Vespasia, and Tiago in its wake.

Some sort of trial, he reminded himself as the stone behind him closed with a slow, seamless fold, as if it had never existed at all. His shade tightened, and for once, Attica didn't push it away.

He felt the same way, a deep apprehension as he looked ahead, as he prepared himself for whatever came next. The corridor ahead was dimly lit by faint veins of essence running along the walls and floor, just enough to see his hands.

He stood still for a moment, listening as his shade tightened around him.

It was the first time he had felt *truly* alone since the settlement burned. Attica closed his eye for a moment and remained motionless. He saw Dayanne's hand reaching out to him. Still warm. Beyond her, Baby Eli extended his hands as well.

If I'd been faster . . . if I hadn't been injured . . .

The grief coiled inside him, quiet and constricting, like something best left unspoken.

"Only one way forward," he said, repeating something that Hadrian had once said to him.

He moved forward into the dry air. It wasn't heavy here, and the whispers were no longer swarming around him. A welcome reprieve.

Still, his shade clung close.

"I know," he whispered. "Something's ahead. You're not the only one who feels it."

The corridor widened into a circular chamber—an ancient arena, or perhaps a trial ground long abandoned. The walls rose high into shadow, disappearing into a dome of black above. The only light came from embedded essence-stones in the floor, their glow pulsing slow and rhythmic, like the echo of a heart no longer there.

Two statues stood at the chamber's center. Three times his height, they were carved from the same marbled stone as the walls. Brutalist armor encased them—massive pauldrons, thick breastplates, gauntlets like stone anvils. Each rested both hands on a greatsword, the blades buried point down in the floor. Both seemed like they were breathing, their shoulders rising and falling.

"No exit," Attica said, eyeing the edge of the chamber. "This must be the trial. Ready?"

His shade coiled into a defensive tendril and surged ahead as the statues came to life.

They pulled their swords free and slammed them down in unison, stone ringing like a subterranean bell.

Attica's shade hurled him backward just in time.

He hit the ground, rolled, rose, and charged in again, shadowblade drawn. He lashed out at the left statue. The strike hissed against its armor—and recoiled. The backlash flung him across the floor.

He landed hard, scrambled to his feet.

"Again!" Attica said through gritted teeth.

His shade launched him up the wall. He flipped through the air, striking clean at the grief statue's arm and met the same result. The shadow snapped back, like he'd struck molten steel.

My attacks aren't working. Then what is this trial for?

The statues moved slow enough for him to keep his distance. One raised its sword again. The other didn't, opting to throw a stone-crushing fist in his direction instead.

Attica darted between them as the two statues struck, just slightly offbeat. The second's fist hit the first's raised shoulder. A deep, shuddering *crack* echoed through the room. Lines of silver veined out from the floor where the blow landed.

He backed away, breathing hard. "Get them to fight each other," he said aloud. "Get them to fight each other . . ."

The statues reset.

Attica darted right, drawing one's attention. Then slipped left, provoking the other. They moved and almost collided.

Not every attempt worked. But each clash landed hard—triggering another shock wave, lighting more veins across the stone, cracking their armor.

Clumsy, he thought, but that was not quite the right word. *No, frenzied.*

"You try," Attica told his shade as he held back.

It rushed toward the statue on the left, which tried to strike it with his sword.

They can detect my shade, Attica thought, a plan forming as the shadows returned to him. "Distract the one on the left; I'll distract the one on the right!"

His shade bristled with anticipation and moved.

They moved in tandem, circling like wolves, drawing attacks, slipping between them again and again as Attica's plan fell into place. The damage mounted. Each collision exposed something deeper, layers of glowing runes beneath their stone exteriors, fractures along the joints, hollow sockets behind the armor.

Then came the opening.

Attica and his shade surged toward each other, and at the last second, they split, both diving aside.

The statues collided. Stone cracked. Blades crossed. Their heads shattered and both figures fell to one knee, lowering their weapons. The air went still.

Attica turned as a soft glow rose behind him.

The far wall had begun to change. A doorway grew from the stone, arched, seamless, as though it had always been there. At its center, a single rune burned to life and fizzled away, revealing an open pathway.

Attica stepped toward it. His shade hesitated. "Yes?" he asked. Then repeated, quieter, "Yes."

Attica pressed forward as an iridescent fog slipped past him, leading the way.

The stone sealed behind Attica without a sound. No path back. No light from where he'd come.

Before him, spiraling stairwells arced in every direction, upward, downward, many vanishing into open air like broken threads of thought. Bridges looped in impossible curves, some suspended in midair, others folding into themselves like snapped ribbons of stone.

None of it should have stood. Yet somehow, it *did*.

Like the kind of spinning top Attica had played with as a child, there was an ethereal balance here. At the center of it all, resting in a basin of carved stone, flowed a large fountain. It didn't babble. The glowing pool of essence churned like liquid moonlight.

Attica looked up to a woman who sat on a bone-pale throne above the fountain, still as death, her body tilted slightly as though caught mid-turn. Her robes pooled like black silk. Her face was beautiful, but utterly frozen, her eyes wide, her bloodred lips slightly parted. Not asleep. Not dead. Somewhere in between.

"Hello," he called up to her, unsure of the protocol. ". . . Duchess?"

Movement on one of the stairs caused Attica to tense.

He turned as a boy approached, walking with a pronounced limp. His gait was awkward, twisted. A hump pressed high from his back beneath a woven cloak, and his face was hidden behind an ornate fox mask, white with a single red slash down one cheek. "Ah," said the boy, voice light and strange. "You've met my mother, then. She hasn't spoken since I was a child."

"Who are you?" Attica asked.

"You might know me as Sebastian the Limp."

"I've never heard such a name in my life," he told the masked boy.

"And you are from which tier, hmmm?"

"The first. I journeyed from there to here through the third tier, if that is indeed where we are."

"We are and we are not," Sebastian said with a half laugh. "You are exiled. There was one like you not so long ago. Or was it long? My sense of time in the Spiralrealm isn't what it used to be." He brought his hands together. "In any event, welcome to the Realm of Recumbency. What is your name?"

"Attica, the Lone-Eyed Wolf."

"Ah, you too have a disadvantage, I *see*," he said, examining Attica further. "I have found that what others see as our weaknesses are often our strengths."

Attica didn't have a response for this.

"May I ask what challenge you faced? The Gate of Whispers always presents a challenge. These can vary."

"The challenge back there?" Attica gestured behind him, even though there was no longer a wall or a pathway. "Two statues. My powers didn't work against them. I had them fight each other."

He grew excited. "Ah, yes, that's one of the easier ones. You are lucky!"

Attica bit his lip. "Luck is just a name we give to things that don't kill us. You manage this place?"

Sebastian stopped beside the fountain. "You have seen my mother, but let me officially introduce you to her." He gestured toward the woman on the throne above. "That, Lone-Eyed Wolf, is Duchess Corvenna. She once sat on the Council of the Torn, and for a short time, even wore the Crown of Shadows. Now, she sits here. Silently."

"So . . . you manage this place?" Attica asked him.

"Yes, I manage them all. She oversees . . . in a manner of speaking."

"I don't understand."

"I didn't expect you to."

Attica looked up at the woman again. "Are you the only ones here?"

"We're the only ones you can see," Sebastian corrected. He raised a hand, gesturing to the stairwells and the empty platforms. "The Realm of Recumbency is a sanctuary between tiers. It exists for all exiles, but we don't always share the same space. The paths shift. Sometimes they cross. Most often, they don't."

Attica's eye narrowed. "So I'm alone."

"Only in this moment, yes, but these spaces can grow quite lively depending on how well you do."

"How well I do?"

"You are newly awakened."

"I am. You still haven't told me what this place is for."

"It's for you," Sebastian replied. "Was I not clear? The Realm of Recumbency is for you and those who may one day serve you. A refuge. A place to begin again. If you can collect the eleven shards of the Crown of Shadows," he said calmly, "you can restore the Spiralrealm to its former strength."

"Do what?" Attica asked. "Collect the shards? Why would I do that?"

"To restore the Spiralrealm to its former shape. Its former strength and color. To bring it back to glory. That's another way to think of it."

Attica stared at him. "I care nothing for its former glory."

"No?"

"I care about Tiago, one of my men. He's dying. That's why I came here. The Mother of Whispers said—"

"Tiago." Sebastian rolled the name in his mouth. "I'm sorry, I do not know a—"

Before he could finish, Vespasia stepped into the chamber without sound, her silhouette gliding from the mist. A flurry of whispers followed the cloaked woman in, the whispers vanishing.

"He speaks of another Shadowborn, my sovereign," she said. "A companion left beyond the gate. Along with a woman named Eve."

Sebastian brought his hand to the bottom of his mask. "Odd. Have they not drunk the Painter's blood?"

"They have not."

Attica turned to Vespasia. "If you are here, who's watching them?" he asked the cloaked woman.

"I am," she said simply. "I can be in many places at once."

Sebastian tilted his head. "Three Shadowborn, one exiled, two not yet awakened. Vespasia, what has happened above? This is rare."

Vespasia regarded him for a moment, then briefly explained how the first-tier settlement had fallen.

Sebastian listened without interruption, his masked face unreadable. "I did not know," he said when she finished. "That changes things."

Attica stepped between them. "Then help me. I need to help Tiago."

"Simple enough," Sebastian said with a shrug. "There is a settlement of Shadowborn on the third tier. If there is aid to be found, it will be there. They would have some access to the Painter's blood."

"I thought as much," Vespasia said.

"Then why didn't you tell me out there?" Attica motioned to wherever there could be.

"It is not my role to point you in any other direction aside from the Realm of Recumbency."

Attica turned sharply. "How do I leave this place?"

"You're not interested in learning more about the Crown of Shadows and its shards?" Sebastian asked.

Attica's jaw tightened. "No."

"The fate of the Spiralrealm—"

"My fate has already been decided," he cut in. "My partner and my child are now dead. I will see that Tiago survives. I will kill the child of light. And then . . . then I will be done with this constant madness."

A long pause. Attica clenched his fists. His shade swirled around him like smoke made of fire, blistering at the edges as it fed on his fury.

"What if there's a way?" Sebastian finally asked him.

"A way to what?" Attica turned slowly. His voice came quiet, hoarse. "Do not play with me, boy—"

Sebastian stepped forward. "To bring back the ones you lost."

CHAPTER THIRTY

Attica looked from Sebastian the Limp to Vespasia, the Mother of Whispers, who remained near the man, still half-shrouded in mist. Above them both, Duchess Corvenna held court, the woman frozen and delicate.

"Is he telling the truth?" Attica asked, not to Sebastian, but to the duchess herself.

The duchess didn't speak. Her gaze remained fixed on something far beyond the room until she blinked, once. The gesture alone chilled Attica—not from fear, but from what it implied. It was the first movement he'd seen from her.

The only one.

"Mother will not speak to you," Sebastian said gently. "But she's acknowledged your question. Yes, what I'm telling you is the truth."

Attica's shadowblade formed on his arm, crackling with power. "Do not lie to me."

"You threaten me? In the Realm of Recumbency?" Sebastian almost smiled. "That would be a true test of your strength. And a short one. You'd die before you gathered what you need for . . . who was it again? Your partner and your child?"

"Dayanne and Eli," Attica said bitterly as his blade started to retract.

"I see. Then let's begin with this: While I may appear powerless here, this is Mother's realm—one of many. As I said already, she wore the crown, briefly, and used its power to create the place before the crown was destroyed. But by the looks of it, you aren't here for a history lesson."

"I am not," Attica said flatly.

"Another time, then. But you should know this part: The Crown of Shadows was what the Baffled King once wore, a gift from the Painter. Whoever wears the crown can have anything they'd like, really, yet that is impossible at the moment because the crown has been shattered. Getting the pieces would be nearly impossible for someone like you, at least at this very moment."

"You're saying if I can find the shards—"

"Eleven of them, yes."

"And reform the crown, I could bring Dayanne and Eli back?"

"You would have the Painter's grace," Vespasia said for Sebastian. "She is the crown, Lone-Eyed Wolf. If you are able to obtain even one of the shards, you will better understand what he means."

"How do I know you don't want the crown for yourself?" he asked her. "What about you or your silent mother?" he asked Sebastian as he motioned to the woman on her throne above them.

"You don't know that," Sebastian said, "but I've already told you my mother used it to make this space, and I quite enjoy it here." He brought his hands behind his back and looked around, Attica getting just a glimpse of his heavily scarred chin beneath his fox mask. Sebastian seemed to study something far above, distracted by the ceiling's spiraled glow. "Vespasia will open you to whispers. They will help. Once you get better at understanding them, you might even be able to speak with your shade."

Attica's mind reeled. Too much, too fast. Too many truths layered atop one another. "How do I leave this place?"

Sebastian looked at him curiously. "After all you've just learned, that is your concern?"

"How do I get out of here and how do I come back?" Attica asked, clarifying.

"Vespasia," Sebastian said, voice now distant, almost reverent.

The mist curled closer as Vespasia floated forward. "There are access points known as portalstones to the realm on every tier. When you find the stones, you can return—and once found, they remain linked to you. For now, you only have access to the gate here, on the third tier."

"Got it. Access points across the Spiralrealm."

"Indeed," Vespasia said, her eyes glowing red. "As much as you can't see it now, you will need this place. It will serve as a sanctuary. A place to replenish your strength, gather whispers . . . and eventually, others."

Sebastian spoke: "As I always do for new guests, I will show you the power of one of our echoes. There are many out there."

"Who do you mean when you say *our*?" Attica asked.

"Well, I mean my mother and myself, but others like me. The echo I give you will be temporary. While you remain on the third tier, you may call upon the power of my mask. Once you leave it, the effect will fade. But others, they will give you powers that are permanent."

Attica didn't move.

"You will soon find others," Sebastian continued. "Remnants of what once was. Spirits. If you find them, through Vespasia's gift, they may grant you an echo of their own. Now, hold still."

Attica felt a tingling sensation pull at the corners of his face, one that came with a slight pinch. He brought a hand to his face and gasped. "What have you done to me?"

"Show him, Vespasia."

The robed woman formed a reflective surface out of the mist, so Attica was able to see his face. He now wore the mask of a white fox, one that seemed to be fused to his skin.

Attica tried to pry it off.

"You won't be able to," Sebastian said, "but it will dissolve when you leave this tier. Until then, it will serve you. It will also give you permanent access to the Codex, something that may help you as you discover what the Spiralrealm has to offer. But we will get to that next. First, the mask's ability. Rather than explain it myself, look at your status."

"My status?"

"The information that you were presented after drinking the Painter's blood. Invoke it."

Just thinking of the words he had read back at the settlement caused them to appear:

Name: Attica, the Lone-Eyed Wolf
Designation: Shadowborn – Tier I
Rank: Vanguard (Exile)
Shard Fragments: 0 / 11
Current Traits:
Shadowblade – Your weapon is born of will and shadow. Its shape reflects you.
Resonant Shade – You can extend your awareness through your shade.
Shade Swarm – Summon nearby shades to overwhelm a target. May fail.
Shadow Phasing – Press through surfaces.
Shade Devour – Absorb the essence of slain foes to empower your shade.
Echoes Granted:
Glimpse of the Unmade – This mask will grant you ghostlike impressions of past figures to uncover lore, paths, or patterns. Unlocks permanent access to the Codex.

Attica touched his face as he looked around the Realm of Recumbency.

Vespasia seemed pleased. "It is a good gift, and the Codex alone is worth it."

"What is this Codex?" Attica asked.

"You will thank me later for it," Sebastian assured him. "Vespasia, your gift."

"Yes, my gift is one that the exiled have found quite helpful. Come to me," she said as she opened her arms. "It is not an echo, but rather an awakening."

Attica hesitated.

"If I wanted to hurt you, I would have done so by now."

It went against everything he knew, yet Attica stepped closer to the woman, who remained partially covered by mist. She pulled him into a slow, cool embrace. Whispers coiled around him, soft at first, then singular until a clear voice reached him: *"Listen for me in the Spiralrealm. I am always there."*

She stepped back. The scent of brimstone lingered.

The whispers around him died down. "What have you done, exactly?"

"You can now understand whispers. Follow them and find their hosts. In doing so, you will be given tasks, and upon completing them, granted other echoes. You may also bring them here."

It dawned on Attica what she was saying. "So each exile has their own Realm of Recumbency," Attica said slowly, the pieces falling into place. "These are accessed throughout the Spiralrealm, where the spirits we meet along the way can gather?"

"Yes, and now you understand why your companions cannot come here—because they do not have access. To gain access, one must drink the blood of the Painter," she said. "If you try to bring one through a portalstone, it will kill them."

"I'm glad you told me that, otherwise I might have tried it."

"You aren't the first exile who thought they were clever," she said.

Sebastian clasped his hands together. "Vespasia, please show him how the portal-stones work. I am going to tend to Mother now." He turned from the two of them and headed up the spiraled steps to his mother.

"Your gourds are filled?" Vespasia asked Attica.

"They are."

"This way." She led him to a pile of stones. Beyond was nothing like Attica had ever seen before. A shimmering void stretched beyond—a tapestry of stars, lights drifting in an endless dark.

"Is there anything else I should know?" he asked as Vespasia came to a stop.

She waved her hand over the stones, and they formed into a doorway. Attica was not able to make out what was on the other side. "Step through, and you will join your companions. To return, look for a glowing pile of rocks etched in runes. The same gateway will appear and bring you here."

"Can you point me in the direction of this settlement?"

"I don't need to. The whispers can help you. Just follow them and see the world for what it once was." She leaned in just a bit closer to him, eyes shining beneath the hood of her robes. "Maybe you are the one to restore order. Or maybe you'll be driven by matters of the heart. But you already know what must be done—if you ever hope to see your family again."

"Can the Crown of Shadows really bring them back?" he whispered.

"It can do much more than that, Lone-Eyed Wolf. Much more. Now go."

Attica stepped through the gate, the mask tight to his skin, the whispers already rising again.

Behind him, the Realm of Recumbency vanished. And ahead, the Spiralrealm waited—brighter, darker, and now stranger than before.

CHAPTER THIRTY-ONE

The stones that had once formed the portal collapsed behind Attica in a soft crumble of dust. The shimmer of the gateway faded as he staggered forward into the mist, where he soon found his companions. Eve stood first, weapons half drawn. Tiago lay beside her, breathing shallow, his shade cradling him like a tattered blanket.

Both stared at Attica.

Not at his body but at his face. The white fox mask was fused to his skin, its edges melted into him like old bone.

"Attica?" Eve said cautiously. "What the hell is this mask?"

"Yes, it's me. Sorry if that took longer than I would have—"

"What happened to you?" she demanded. Eve approached and reached for him. Normally, he would have pulled away, but he didn't this time. Attica let her touch the mask and see it was fused to his face. "Attica, are you sure about this?"

"I'll explain everything. But first, we move. I found a way."

"A way to what?"

"To save Tiago," he told her quickly.

The young man stirred weakly at the sound of his name. "I'll . . . I'll be fine. I—"

"No, you won't," Eve said. "The only thing that can save you is in the Seer's flask."

Attica stepped forward and knelt beside him. "Stay strong. If anyone can survive this, it's you. We're going to find a settlement. One with access to the Painter's blood. We will use that to heal your wound."

"People like us?" Tiago asked.

"I would assume so, but . . ." Attica imagined other Shadowborn approaching their settlement, how the scouts might have reacted. There would be questions, certainly, but his people were cautious, not cruel. There was a good chance they would have been overjoyed.

Just to know that someone else is out there, that someone else cares . . .

If there were Shadowborn living on the third tier, they likely shared a common enemy in the flashwraiths. He had no doubt those creatures prowled the lower tiers just as relentlessly as they did the upper ones.

"And you know where this settlement is?" Eve asked, skeptical.

"No. But they do."

"They?"

"Just trust me." Attica turned to the mist, to the endless curling of silver and ash. It began to part, but only to allow whispers to rush forward. He closed his eye and lowered his head, giving in to the influence until the voices blended together. "I'm looking for a settlement," he said aloud.

"I know the way," came a woman's whisper, soft as breath. "I can show you," the voice said, louder this time, speaking in Attica's other ear.

The mist parted slightly, revealing a crooked path that led through a rocky outcrop.

"Just like that, huh?" Eve asked as she watched the path form.

"Apparently so." Attica turned to Tiago. "I will carry you."

"I don't—"

Rather than listen to his protest, Attica approached the young man, and with the help of his shade, transitioned Tiago to his back. "Relax. I know you can hold your own."

"I can," Tiago said, voice weak.

"You have always held your own."

"I try. I learned it from you."

"And I learned it from Hadrian," Attica said. "Eve, let's go."

"Do you want me to take the lead?" she asked him.

"Sure, just follow the path that has appeared in the mist," Attica said as the trail wound down through broken ground, splintered rocks, dead brush, and slick black moss. The third tier felt emptier than the ones above. Thinner. As if something had drawn most life away.

"You still never explained where you went," Eve told him as they continued on, past the remnants of an ancient well.

"I went through the Gate of Whispers, where I faced a trial."

"What kind of trial?"

"Against two statues. Once I figured out they'd beat each other to death, I used my shade to force them into each other and went to the Realm of Recumbency from there."

"Realm of . . . what?" Tiago asked.

"The Realm of Recumbency was created by a woman named the Duchess Corvenna, who once sat on the Council of Torn. From what I have put together, this is the council overseen by the Baffled King, who wore the Crown of Shadows and controlled the Spiralrealm."

"And the Painter?" Eve asked.

"Yes, the Painter created the Spiralrealm. She forged the Crown of Shadows for the Baffled King. Before it was shattered, Duchess Corvenna used it to create the Realm of Recumbency, a refuge for those who have drunk the Painter's blood, those who are exiled. And that's why you two must drink from it as well."

Eve stopped. "Then we'd better find this settlement."

"I doubt they will give us enough to awaken the two of you, but I can ask. If anything, we can get a small amount, a few drops, to heal Tiago. But I will try. The Painter's blood is incredibly strong. You were there, Eve. I was on the shores of death and I am back, stronger than ever. I've been given powers, and there are more out there. The whispers I hear. They will lead me to some. And if we can get enough Painter's blood to awaken the two of you, you will also have access to the Realm of Recumbency."

"Yours?" Tiago asked him.

"No, your own. I think. I'm not fully aware of how it works, but they said others who are exiled have access."

"The Unshaken lives?" Eve asked.

"I don't know what has become of Hadrian."

"I would've thought that'd be your first question."

"My first concern was Tiago. Then . . . the child of light." Attica paused, his voice growing quieter. "But I've learned something else."

Eve glanced at him as they took a path that curved beneath an overhang of stone, mist trailing in the crevices. Their footsteps echoed faintly. "What is it?" she asked.

Attica didn't answer right away. The truth felt too large in his mouth. Too heavy. It took him a moment to finally get it out. "If I capture all eleven shards of the Crown of Shadows, the one the Baffled King once wore," he said finally, "I can bring Dayanne and Eli back."

Eve stopped. "You really think it would be that easy?"

Attica turned back to her. "Which part?"

"Both."

"Getting the shards; bringing them back. I don't know," he told Eve. "I don't know. But first, Tiago. And—"

A shimmer flickered to their left.

Attica spun as Tiago slipped to the ground. "Stay low," he told the young man, shadowblade forming.

The air bent and a lightreaver blinked into existence. It was alone, taller than the others Attica remembered fighting before.

And this time, something new happened. As it blinked out of his existence, a pulse flashed across Attica's vision, words burning into his mind.

Codex Entry Unlocked!
Name: Lightreaver
Origin: Lower Spiral Variant, Possibly Engineered
Known Strengths:
– Invisibility through refracted light
– Coordinated tactics, can hunt in packs
– Adaptive melee weapon formation from limb-core essence
Known Weaknesses:
– Overloads when forced to clash with matching light frequencies
– Susceptible to prolonged darkness saturation
– The knees are its weakest point
Classification: T-IV | Rank B | Cog 2 | Predator
Notes: Entry incomplete. Further observation required.

He could *see it now*, the lightreaver's knees flickered faintly when it shifted, the armor there weaker, thinner, unfinished.

"The knees!" he shouted to Eve, who had already moved on the defensive as she summoned her shadowy whipsword. "That's its weak spot! Cut low!"

Eve didn't question him. She moved in a hard arc to the left. Attica went right. Together they flanked the creature as it shimmered and blurred. It tried to vanish, but Eve lashed her whipsword low, snagging one leg.

The lightreaver stumbled.

Attica's shade propelled him forward with incredible force as the lightreaver went down. Attica thrust his sword through its stomach and held the creature there for a moment longer than he should have as the lightreaver convulsed, light flaring violently.

"Attica!" Eve shouted, yet he bore down on the lightreaver, the light glowing around its body fading. It collapsed, core dimming into dust.

Attica let it fall off his blade. He stepped on its head and turned back to Eve. "It works!"

"Are you crazy? You don't know what it can do—"

"Why do you think I told you to go for its knees?" Attica tapped his temple. "I've been given access to information. That one was called a lightreaver. Their knees are their weakest points, but they can also be overwhelmed by shadow, or as the Codex calls it, *darkness saturation*." Attica paused and focused on the one part of the information he didn't understand.

Classification: T-IV | Rank B | Cog 2 | Predator

I will have to ask about that, he thought. *Next time I visit the Realm.*

"You should still be careful," Eve finally said. "Knowing too much can make you reckless. Do you know who told me that?"

"Do I even need to guess?" Attica asked.

They moved again, faster now, following the woman's whisper as it weaved between the broken rocks ahead.

Every so often, Attica caught glimpses of long-dead figures pacing just out of reach, vanishing when he tried to focus on them. *It must be my mask,* he thought, occasionally touching his face. The mist thickened as the three reached a break in the path that narrowed to a tunnel of gray.

And there, barely visible, stood another figure. Larger. Steadier. Half formed from shadow and memory.

"Ah, you can hear me," said an older man's voice, filtering in and out of the mist. His outline shimmered, tattered by time. "You are exiled."

"I am," Attica replied.

"Who are you talking to?" Eve asked behind him.

"A whisper."

Attica set Tiago down carefully, cradling his head against the slope of a broken stone. Then he stepped forward. The figure extended a hand, long-fingered, dripping mist, and for a heartbeat, Attica thought he saw real eyes behind the haze.

"Help me," the old man said. His voice was hoarse, low, barely holding itself together. "I could use . . . your help."

Eve came up beside him, breath uneven. "What's going on? Why's the fog thickening like that?"

"He wants my help," Attica said quietly. "He's asking."

The figure didn't move closer. Didn't threaten. It just lingered, waiting, and then, with a slow turn, it drifted back into the mist. Whispers followed him like trailing smoke.

A strange, weighted silence followed, one that pressed against the ribs, leaving only the heavy thud of Attica's own heartbeat in his ears. He stood there for a moment, uncertain.

"Are you coming?" the female whisper he had heard earlier asked from somewhere farther ahead.

Attica blinked, shaking himself loose from whatever had tried to root him there. "Yes," he said aloud. "Sorry." He turned to Eve. "Come on. I will chase whispers later."

They gathered Tiago again and pressed on, weaving through the mist. The path wound downward sharply, the ground shifting underfoot. Then the mist thinned. Attica and the others crested a ridge, where they came to a stop.

Below them, carved into the jagged slope of the third tier, was a settlement. Not ruins. Not dust and memory. A *living* place. Lights burned in the windows. Shadows moved along the massive stone walls.

While their settlement had more angles, this one seemed more rounded, with domed roofs and arched doorways. At the gate, scouts had already spotted them.

Dark-cloaked figures rushed forward, shades rippling at their backs, shadow weapons drawn.

Attica placed Tiago down and shifted into a ready stance. "Eve—"

"We will engage if necessary."

Attica glanced at Tiago, who managed to produce one of his shadowdaggers. "Let them try," Tiago said, his voice thin but unwavering. "I'm not afraid."

CHAPTER THIRTY-TWO

The third tier Shadowborn scouts converged fast, seven dark shapes cutting through the thinning mist, weapons drawn, shades rippling at their heels like lean hunting dogs.

"Get behind that slab of stone," Attica told Tiago as he produced his shadowblade, power rippling through him as it unfurled down his arm with a quiet hiss.

"But I—"

"No, Tiago, Eve and I can handle this."

Beside Attica, Eve kept her whipsword low and coiled, a viper at her side.

"Let them try," Tiago said again, grinning.

"Please. You are in no shape," Eve started to say.

"I'm not afraid of anything," Tiago shot back.

"You should be," she told him as the new group of Shadowborn surrounded them. They were taller than most of the Vanguard Attica had fought alongside, thinner and harder.

Their armor was crafted from flashwraith bone, its polished surfaces catching the light with a faint, unnatural glimmer. Dark thread bound the pieces together— breastplates shaped from curved ribs, pauldrons from splintered femurs. The helmets were slim, bone-curved and wicked, each bearing the twisted contours of human jaws. Their skin matched Attica's in hue, blackened and shadow-marked, but it was etched with sharp white tattoos that coiled down their arms and over their throats like thorned vines.

The leader stepped forward, a massive figure, his shade slithering in the air behind him like a living noose. His voice came harsh, broken at the edges. "Claim yourselves," he said.

"I am Attica, the Lone-Eyed Wolf. We are Shadowborn, Vanguard of the first-tier settlement. I speak for my companions."

A flicker of tension rippled through their ranks.

The leader's gaze sharpened. "What is the mask you wear? And what is the Vanguard?"

"We protect the settlement," Attica said, voice steady. "Or we did. Until it was overrun by flashwraiths."

"Flashwraiths?" one of the Brethren asked.

Their leader answered: "An old word for *Lightborn* that I haven't heard since I was a child."

Eve stepped forward. "Lightborn? I've only heard the Seer use that term."

The leader's attention snapped to her, sharp and sudden. "And there is a woman among you." Disbelief crept into his tone. "Surely she is not part of your Vanguard?"

"She is," Attica said.

Murmurs rippled through the scouts, low and distrustful. "We are the Brethren," the leader said coldly, "and I would say we perform a similar role to your Vanguard, but there are no women among us, and more importantly, we take no refugees."

Attica straightened. "We're not asking for refuge. One of ours is wounded. He needs the Painter's blood. We know you have access. We are only asking for enough to heal our wounded, and then we will move on."

"The Painter's blood?" the leader asked, skeptical.

"Have you a Seer?" Attica pressed.

"We do." The leader's shade slithered wider, a warning. "Our blood is for the Brethren only."

"You said yourself," Eve told the man, her voice cutting, "we serve a similar purpose. We only ask for enough to heal him. A drop, maybe less."

The Brethren's gazes snapped to her as one. Hostility flickered, sudden and raw. Their shades grew leaner, looming in size over them.

"There are no women among the Brethren," another scout growled.

"She fights as well as any of us," Attica said. "Better, even. You might be surprised—" He stopped himself from saying what he wanted to say. While their leader looked fierce, and all of them had armor, Attica had sparred with Eve. *She is a devil to fight against.*

A tense silence stretched between the two parties.

The leader's mask shifted slightly. "That remains to be seen."

Attica let his blade fade away. "We didn't come here to challenge you. We came for aid. Just enough to heal the wound given to him by an ambush of lightreavers."

"Where are you from again?" their leader asked.

"The first tier."

"We do not venture to the first tier," the leader said, dismissive, "and there is nothing on the second tier worth hunting. You said that the Lightborn destroyed your settlement."

"Yes," Attica told him. "They seemed to be led by a giant flashwraith with a child in its head."

Murmurs again. The leader silenced them with a raised hand. "I've never seen such a thing," he said at last. "But any member of the Brethren would have died protecting their settlement, and to see the three of you, one wounded, one with a demonic mask, and the other a woman, tells me that you have all failed. If you had any honor, you would have died alongside your people."

"I have a better idea—" Tiago started.

"No," Attica told him, cutting Tiago off before the young man's sharp tongue could jeopardize their discussion.

The Brethren leader stared at him. And then, slowly, he shook his head. "No entrance for the Vanguard. No blood for those not brave enough to defend their settlement. Return to the mist or face the consequences."

The others tightened their shadow weapons.

Attica's shade flared, curling over his shoulder. Eve's grip tightened beside him. *They don't know that I'm exiled,* he thought. *I could end it all now with Shade Swarm. If it comes to a fight, it would be brutal, but it would be no contest.*

He glanced at Eve.

Or I could let her handle a few of them at first, just so they can die knowing what the Vanguard are capable of . . .

Attica had enough rage built up inside of him to actually go through with it. The leader of the Brethren had insulted them, but . . . *These could just be the scouts,* he thought, recalling the brashness of the settlement's scouts at times. *I do not know their hierarchy.*

"I will say it once more," the leader said, stepping forward with deliberate weight, his chest lifted, voice steady beneath his bone helmet. One hand hovered near the hilt at his side, a signal his warriors didn't need spoken. "Return. Or face the consequences."

Something higher pulled at Attica's senses. A different way. A better solution. His fingers brushed the fox mask still fused to his face, and he felt a pulse answered him from the mist. "Have it your way, then. We're leaving," he said at last, his voice carrying weight, finality.

The weight in his words settled like a dropped blade. Near him, Eve ground her teeth but gave a single nod.

The Brethren didn't move at first. Then, one by one, they stepped back, silent, weapons raised but still. Not striking. Not yet.

The standoff held a breath longer, then passed.

Attica moved to help, but Tiago pushed himself upright, swaying slightly. "I can do it myself," he said, fierce and breathless, blood still wet at his side.

"Are you certain?"

"By the Painter," Tiago told him.

Attica watched the young man a moment, then gave a single nod. "Good," he said, a flicker of pride in his voice. "Eve."

She shot him one of her glares but fell in silently beside him as they backed away.

Only when they reached the broken ridge did Attica release a slow, steady breath. Below, the Brethren moved as one. They withdrew in formation, weapons never lowered, steps echoing faintly across the stone. The lead warrior turned last, giving one final glance before vanishing into the fog.

"We could have done something," Eve said once they were gone.

"I know," he told her, his voice was low, measured. "But there's another way." Attica looked out across the wall. In the mist, faint as memory, faint as dream, he saw it. A path. Footsteps burned into the air by something older than any of them.

A forgotten pathway.

Attica's lips curled into a grim smile. "The mask is how we'll get the blood," he said.

Eve frowned. "I still can't take you seriously in that mask."

Attica's eye followed the ghostly shimmer winding toward the far edge of the Brethren's settlement. "You will if this works."

CHAPTER THIRTY-THREE

The spectral footsteps grew clearer as Attica led his two companions into the fog. He took a wide berth around the Brethren's settlement, always wary of additional scouts lurking in the mist.

"You still aren't being clear with me," Eve said, falling in step behind him as he paused near a rough wall of stone.

"I told you already. The mask lets me see imprints. Things hidden to others." Attica gestured with his chin to the ground, where the footsteps led directly into a solid wall of stone.

"And you're tracking what, exactly?"

"Footprints," he said. "Ancient ones, I think. Tiago. How are you holding up?"

"I'll be fine," the younger man said.

"Be honest."

Tiago grimaced. "I feel like I might pass out soon."

"Let me help you," Eve said, already moving to steady him.

Attica turned his attention to a wall of weathered stone, thick with old carvings, worn down to almost nothing. It wasn't natural. He placed his hand on it and finally found the outlines of a sealed doorway.

He stepped back and examined them again, confirming the spectral footprints led straight into it. He rapped his fist against the stone. It sounded hollow beneath the surface.

"This is it." Without hesitation, Attica summoned his shadowblade and drove it into the seam. The door crumbled, a plume of dust clouding the fog around them.

"The mask helped you find . . . a cave?" Tiago asked.

Attica peered into the opening, the darkness thick and damp. "No, a passageway." Attica turned back to Eve and Tiago. "Can you hear me?" he called into the mist.

"I can," came the woman's voice, the childlike whisper that had guided them before.

"May I ask you something?"

"You may."

"Where does this passageway lead?"

"Would you like me to check?" she asked, almost coy.

"I would be grateful."

The mist swelled and coiled into the broken doorway. It returned moments later, before Eve could even speak. "It leads to a cellar," the voice told Attica. "Inside the Brethren's settlement. Old and forgotten. Perhaps an escape route once designed by the settlement's founders."

Attica smiled grimly. "Thank you yet again. Your name? You have been so helpful."

"Joan."

"I will remember that name." He turned to Eve, who was helping Tiago to his feet. "It leads inside."

"What are you proposing?" she asked.

Tiago gave a shaky grin. "Heh. We break in."

"Quiet," Eve told him. "There are two and a half of us against an entire settlement of heavily armored, aggressively territorial Shadowborn."

"She's right." Attica continued to peer into the opening. "I will go."

"With that mask?" Eve said, eyeing him like he was the foolish one. "You won't blend in any better than I would. Even without the mask, you do not have the tattoos that their Shadowborn exhibit."

"True. But I can do things that they can't. You've seen me do them, Eve, you know what I'm now capable of after drinking from the Seer's flask."

"You were never this reckless," Eve told him.

He cracked a grin at this. "You forget the boy you grew up with." Attica tapped his finger on the temple closest to his missing eye. "We do not have another way to heal him, not to my current knowledge. Could we explore the Spiralrealm for the next few days in search of an alternative? Certainly. But would he make it? I do not know."

"I . . . I'm fine," Tiago said.

Attica looked the young man over, pale, struggling to stay upright even with Eve's help. "You will be once I get some of the Painter's blood." He touched the empty bone flask attached to his belt. "I wish I knew more about this substance."

"What more is there to know than what is in the name?" Eve asked.

"If Dayanne were here, she would explain better how the Seer's flask and her access to the Painter's blood worked. That's what I mean. But that is an unknown, and even if they were hostile, it is not my desire to doom an entire settlement by doing something like . . ."

"Stealing the flask?"

"Yes," Attica said. "That is not the way of the Vanguard."

"No, it is not."

"There are only three Vanguard now," Tiago said.

"We still have our code. No, you will stay here." Attica turned toward the mist. "Vespasia, are you there?"

The mist thickened—and the Mother of Whispers stepped free, her hooded form half seen, half felt. Her red eyes glowed, eyes that only Attica could see. "I am here, Lone-Eyed Wolf."

"May I ask you to watch over them yet again?"

She tilted her head slightly, considering Attica's request. "You may ask," Vespasia said, voice soft and dangerous. "But in exchange . . . I will claim a favor later. And you are running low on future requests."

Attica didn't flinch. "Name your favor."

"You will know when I call for it." The mist around Vespasia's pale hands knotted together.

He bowed his head once. "So be it."

The mist surged outward, cocooning Eve and Tiago in its quiet shelter.

"She will protect you for now," he told the two of them.

Eve looked like she wanted to say something, but refrained.

"Good luck," Tiago called to him as Attica turned back toward the crumbled doorway, pulse steady, blade forming again in the dark.

Attica pressed into the tunnel, his eye naturally adjusting to the dimness. "Lead the way," he told the whisper who continued to aid them. "And . . . thank you, Joan."

"It is my pleasure," she said, voice brushing the stones around him.

"You do not seek an exchange for your help?"

"Not at the moment, no. I was once part of the Brethren's settlement. When it belonged to Duke Tiberion Astor."

"When this path was made?" he asked the spirit as they pushed farther into the darkness.

"No," she said, "long after. This passage is ancient."

"I see what you mean," he told her as the passage narrowed into a corridor, the walls slick with condensation and carved symbols almost worn away to nothing. Attica saw spiral patterns, hunters with spears, and twisted beasts that looked nothing like the flashwraiths he had encountered.

The question of the Spiralrealm's true age came to him as the path descended sharply. The mystery, the wonder of it all. *How old is this world? Older than the Painter?*

The path steepened sharply. Shadows pulsed at the edges of his vision, his shade coiling tighter around his back in silent warning. Yet nothing moved, no enemy waited in ambush as he continued into the depths of the world, the bones of the spiral itself.

Attica felt the steps beneath him shift and buckle, the path moving from smooth stone to gravel. They came to a large space with old clay pots. *Some sort of storage area*, he thought as he reached his hand out to one of the pots. His fingers returned covered in dust.

They moved on, traveling another twenty minutes before he spoke. "How much farther?" he whispered into the mist.

"Not far," Joan's voice answered, closer now, almost at his ear.

The tunnel tightened into a crawlspace. Attica ducked low and moved carefully, every sound swallowed by the heavy air. Soon, a faint light illuminated the space. He gravitated toward the dim glow ahead, where he found a ladder cut directly into the stone, a narrow shaft rising into the glow. Slots of light patterned the ceiling, like stars scattered against the dark.

Attica climbed carefully, pushed aside the old slab at the top, the stone grinding quietly. He pulled himself up into a cellar hollowed beneath the Brethren's settlement.

Dust hung thick in the air. Barrels lay shattered in corners. Racks of armor, forged of bone and thick with dust, lined the walls.

He let his shadowblade reform as the mist feathered around him, Attica's shade tense as ever. "I need to find the Sanctum," he said softly to the whisper that had guided him there. "The settlement's Seer."

It was faint, yet he could see the outline of Joan's face take shape mere inches away from his. "He has already found you," she said, voice curling upward like smoke.

Attica looked up a set of stone steps to the cellar's exit. He was about to send his shade forward when the door opened. Two cloaked figures came inside, women, their features obscured by thick gray mantles and their movements almost too smooth.

While his shade remained rigid, Attica didn't sense a threat from the two. As the two paused at the bottom of the steps, he recognized what they were. *Spectralists, like Dayanne*, he thought.

"You are a Shadowborn of the first tier," the taller one called into the dark.

He stepped out, his weapon fading. "I am. I'm merely seeking—"

"A gift." The woman produced a dark cloak woven from something rough and patchworked, clearly stitched from many different fabrics. "You must cover yourself before we take you to the Seer."

"How did you know?"

"The Seer knows," she said. "He speaks with whispers."

Attica turned toward the mist behind him. "You gave away my presence?"

"No," Joan said. "You gave yourself away. I merely told them your need."

Attica didn't know if the Spectralists could hear her or not, but he knew it was best to cover his tracks. "I came alone seeking something. I do not wish to do either of you harm," he told the two women standing before him.

"We are aware," the taller Spectralist said. "Cover yourself, warrior of the first tier. Your mask will bring attention."

Attica's shade pressed away as if it trusted them. He took the cloak and pulled it around his shoulders. He brought the hood over the fox mask.

Without another word, the two Spectralists turned and motioned for him to follow.

After his disguise was set, the three moved quickly, weaving through narrow alleys and crumbling stairwells that spiderwebbed through the heart of the Brethren's settlement.

Attica caught glimpses of what he would have been up against had he tried to breach the walls alone. The parapets were lined with scouts and there were guards posted at every major turn, yet none paid any attention to the three of them.

Everywhere he looked, the Brethren moved like a colony of ants—efficient, brutal, paranoid.

The Spectralists never paused as they led him up broken steps, through alleyways where even the stones seemed to whisper with old warnings. Then past a church dedicated to the Painter, the Brethren's rendition angular, almost violent in its carvings.

They worship differently here, Attica thought grimly.

The tall Spectralist paused as they reached a narrow side passage carved into the sandstone wall, its entrance framed by a crumbling arch etched with faded script. She knelt beside a mosaic of broken tiles and pried loose a stone slab, revealing a low, tunnel-like corridor beyond. The air that poured out was dry and warm, scented faintly with dust and old incense.

Vaulted supports ribbed the walls, their curvature suggesting a path once sacred—now forgotten. The tunnel was just wide enough to crawl through, its floor worn smooth by centuries of passage.

"This way," she said quietly. "We are almost there."

Attica hesitated, listening.

From somewhere nearby he heard the low rumble of guards speaking, the occasional scrape of a weapon against bone-forged armor.

No alarm yet.

"Hurry, Shadowborn," the woman told him. He ducked into the passage, the cloak muffling his outline, the Spectralists flowing silently behind him.

They entered into a hallway that ran beside the Sanctum's courtyard, one with arched openings revealing two guards stationed near one of the entrances.

The Spectralists moved like shadows, keeping their heads down. Attica remained beside them in his disguise, pulse hammering.

Tiago needs him. Eve is counting on me.

One of the guards shifted suddenly, his gaze sweeping in their direction. He frowned and took a step toward the archway.

The Spectralists froze, silent as the stones.

Then the guard's voice cut the silence, low and sharp, "Mara?" he called, uncertain.

Attica stiffened under his cloak.

The guard's voice rose slightly, more questioning than hostile: "Mara, is that you?"

CHAPTER THIRTY-FOUR

M ara?" the guard called out again, squinting into the hallway. His hand lowered and a jagged shadowblade formed, his eyes narrowing as he tried to make out their shapes through the dim light.

The taller Spectralist didn't hesitate. "We went for a walk," she said as she stepped out, her tone calm but edged with quiet command. Her voice carried just enough weight to make the guard flinch upright, adjusting his stance without realizing it. "Rosaren, Emelia, and I are returning to the Seer."

The guard hesitated.

Attica didn't move. He willed his shade to stay still, every muscle now tight beneath the weight of the cloak. Only when the footsteps began to fade into the mist did his heartbeat begin to slow.

"Safe night," the guard called, his voice already distant.

"Same, brother," Mara replied.

They moved quickly after that, slipping through another hallway and ascending a final flight of worn stone steps. Candles flickered on each landing, their flames casting long shadows against the walls. At the top, an arched doorway waited.

"Come on," Mara said as she ushered Attica inside the room.

Bones lined the walls in intricate, deliberate stacks, the spirals, lattices, and broken patterns too intentional to be random. Hundreds of flashwraith skulls stared out from the gloom, their surfaces dulled to a pale sheen. All were too old or mangled for the Codex to recognize, yet their curved remains still caught the dim candlelight like half-buried relics.

At the center of the chamber, seated on a throne, was a man around Attica's age, cloaked in the same radiance as the Seer from Attica's settlement. His hair was cropped short, his robes unadorned and threadbare. And yet there was a sharpness to him, quiet and exact, like something waiting for permission to strike.

"Welcome," the Seer said, his voice even and oddly kind. He seemed at ease among the dead, accustomed to the grotesque spectacle that defined the Brethren's inner sanctum. "It is good to meet one sent by Esmeralda."

Attica stiffened. *Esmeralda?*

"Your Seer never told you her name?" the Brethren Seer asked, tilting his head.

"No," Attica said, "and I never asked. I don't think anyone knew." *Not even Dayanne*, he thought.

The man waved his surprise away with the flicker of his hand. "She was much older than most Seers. I do believe she had plans to pass the mantle, but seeing you here tells me that this never happened."

"How would you know? Right, the whispers."

"Indeed. Mara, Rosaren, please." The Seer gestured to a place in front of him. The two Spectralists stepped forward in perfect sync. They bowed and placed a small dark pillow at Attica's feet, one stitched with demonic images.

"Sit," Mara said softly. "Please."

Attica hesitated, just for a breath, then sank to his knees. The women flanked him without a word, settling beside him like guardians carved from stone as their robes draped around them.

The Seer watched him for a long moment before the smile touched his face. The chamber dimmed around him, the light withdrawing back into the bones. "Beyond the whispers, we Seers have ways of speaking to one another," he said. "And believe it or not . . . you are part of that."

Attica touched his chest. "Me?"

"The lanterns you lit during your ritual. That is how we speak to each other."

Attica blinked, a memory stirring as he saw the world in all its color, just briefly, when lighting the lanterns. He recalled the ritual flask he had been given during the ritual, different from the one now at his waist. The ritual flask had been smooth. This one was carved, intricate, and ancient.

"We were given flasks, but they are different from this one," Attica said slowly.

"Yes, yes, they are. It would be unwise for a Seer to give anyone their true flask of the Painter's blood. The flasks you were given? Temporary. Symbols. But the lanterns—those matter." He leaned forward slightly. "They show that we endure. They remind others we are still alive. What is your name?"

"Attica, the Lone-Eyed Wolf."

"The Lone-Eyed Wolf." The Seer let the name sit on his tongue, as if tasting its shape. "Interesting. And your reason for disturbing the order here?"

"Your whispers didn't tell you?"

"Some are more cooperative than others."

Attica took a breath, organizing the weight of what he needed to say. "As you may already know, I've come here because one of ours is wounded. I do not seek to take the Painter's blood that your community protects, only to heal my companion. Enough to stabilize him. He has proven to have a natural healing capability with his shade, but the lightreavers that injured him are new to us."

"Ah, yes." The Seer's eyes sharpened. "Being from the first tier, you wouldn't likely encounter something like that."

"It was an ambush," Attica said, his voice lower now. A tension coiled in his chest, tightening with the memory. "They raided our community. Killed . . . everyone."

"I am sorry to hear that. It is troubling to know that this has happened again."

"It has happened before?"

"Yes, on the second tier. That is why there isn't a settlement there. It's the only tier to my knowledge without a settlement. It happened here as well, when the duke ruled this place and led to its downfall. But we rebuilt. I find it interesting you are from the first, you know. Yours was the most distant settlement, the farthest from the bottom. I always found that intriguing."

"Yet your people never visited."

"No, we rarely go to the second tier. There isn't much worth our time there. Our hunting grounds are here and the fourth tier. The fifth is too dangerous. Anything below that would be absolute madness."

"And do you have a relationship with the Shadowborn on the fourth tier?"

"We do, a trading one . . . for now. In the past, we have gone to war with the Centurions, quite a bit, actually. Their way of life is quite different from ours, but we've learned to respect that. The Brethren that protect our community are a strong group, perhaps one of the strongest in the Spiralrealm, but with that strength comes . . ." He grinned at Attica. "You are a man. You know what can happen when too many get together."

"Our *Vanguard* had both men and women," Attica said, not able to hide the pride in his voice.

"The fourth-tier Centurions are similar in that regard," the Seer said, "but when they meet with our Brethren, they leave the women behind." He waved a hand, brushing the thought aside. "A deeper understanding of Spiralrealm politics won't help your companion." He shifted in his seat. "May I see Esmeralda's flask?"

Attica unhooked it from his belt. Before he could rise, Mara stepped forward and took it from him without a word. She carried it to the Seer, who moved to a pedestal at the rear of the chamber—where another dark flask rested, nearly identical.

"Two drops," he said, inspecting the vessel. He brought the bone flask to his forehead, touched it, and placed it down. "Two drops, no more. Apply it directly to the wound. If there are several, treat the worst of them." He carefully uncorked his darker flask. "After, let your companion rest through the night. Give him your cloak. Keep him warm."

"Understood," Attica said.

The Seer tipped the flask with practiced care, transferring two shimmering drops into Attica's bone vessel. The liquid caught the light like quicksilver, glowing faintly as it swirled into place. Even from across the chamber, Attica could feel the essence humming—low and steady, like the beat of some ancient heart.

The Seer sealed both flasks and returned to his seat. Mara took it from his hand and brought it back to Attica, placing it gently into his palm. The warmth from the drops lingered even through the bone.

Attica held the flask for a moment, then nodded. "Thank you."

He paused, his voice lowering. "Are you familiar with the Realm of Recumbency or the child of light?"

The Seer's expression shifted almost imperceptibly. He turned to the two Spectralists. "Mara, Rosaren. Leave us."

The two women bowed and glided from the chamber without a word, leaving Attica and the Seer alone in the heavy air. He leaned in again, examining Attica. "Tell me about the child of light."

"Of all the flashwraiths—Lightborn—that attacked our settlement, the child of light was the most destructive." He stopped and took a breath, his jaw hardening. "Imagine a baby bathed in light, suspended in the head of a giant. I can't . . . I'm by no means a poet or a bard, not one for fancy words. But I can tell you this: It was as tall as a mountain, the giant, and the child in its head was like the wick of a burning candle."

The Seer pressed back, studying him. "I have heard rumors of a child moving across the fourth tier. A disturbance that matches what you describe."

"So others have seen it."

"They have." The Seer's voice was grim now. "And if it destroyed your settlement, then perhaps it is time someone dealt with it."

Attica's throat tightened. "And the Realm of Recumbency—"

"Yes, that. You are exiled, then, yes?"

"I am."

"I thought as much. Unless Esmeralda gave you access to information, there is no way that you would know of the Realm of Recumbency."

"I have visited recently."

"The Mother of Whispers showed you the way?"

"She did," Attica said, "and I met Sebastian the Limp and Duchess Corvenna there as well. They—well, Sebastian, he speaks for his mother—said if I gather the shards of the Crown of Shadows that I could do something remarkable."

The Seer didn't respond at first. He shifted slightly in his seat, a brief tightening around the eyes betrayed something unspoken as his fingers tapped once, slowly, against the armrest. "Define remarkable," he said at last.

Attica's hands curled into fists against his knees. "My partner and my child were killed in the disaster. With the Crown of Shadows, I was told I could bring them back. Is this true?"

"With the crown reforged, you would have the Painter's favor," the Seer said carefully, "enough to heal. Enough to raise the dead. Enough to do anything you'd like, really."

Attica's breath caught. "Dayanne," he whispered, solidifying his plans in his mind. "Eli."

The Seer's gaze softened. Not with pity, but with understanding. "But the shards are scattered—hidden, guarded. Some by beings you are not yet ready to face. One of them is Duke Tiberion Astor, the former ruler of this very settlement. He now lives in a manor on the fourth tier, where he demands tithe from the Centurions and makes the lives of anyone who encounters him a living hell."

"I will keep that in mind." Attica straightened. "Then a question for my companions, then."

"Go on."

"I know it is possible for them to gain access to enough of the Painter's blood to be granted powers and visit the Realm of Recumbency, but where would I go about getting such a thing?"

"Where to get the Painter's blood? Why, from the Painter!" He laughed. "But good luck finding the Painter anywhere above the fifth tier. In that case, the second tier might be your answer."

"How so?"

"The abandoned settlement that was once there, the one I mentioned earlier. They would have had a Seer too, who died with the community. It would take some searching, but perhaps there is enough there in a flask hidden beneath some ruin for them to both awaken."

"Could whispers help me?"

"They could help you, but they wouldn't be able to help your companions if they are not exiled. They simply wouldn't have access to their influence unless . . ." The Seer scanned some of the bones that line his walls. "I suppose our dear Vespasia, the Mother of Whispers, could part the mist and lead them to it. You have established a relation with her?"

"Barely."

"It's worth an ask, Lone-Eyed Wolf."

A long pause. Then Attica went for another question that he was increasingly starting to wonder about. "Are Seers like you exiled?"

"No, we are not. I suppose you're wondering how we would know of the space that Duchess Corvenna set up," he asked, eyes gleaming.

"I am. It seems like hidden information."

"The Seers serve a different purpose. We were set in place by Margrave Hallow of the fifth tier—one who holds a shard, or at least, she once held one. Consider us archivists. Record keepers. Witnesses. Not rulers. We have power, but not the kind of power it would take to gather the shards. That must fall to someone like you." He studied Attica. "I will say this, however: If color were to return to the world, it would benefit us all."

The Seer fell silent for a moment, weighing Attica with his gaze.

"I appreciate the Painter's blood," he finally told the man. "And I appreciate what you have told me. I will not forget this night and what you have done."

"Maybe you will, maybe you won't. The Spiralrealm's fate is as murky as its mist. Regardless, next time you visit, come through the front gates. You will be welcomed as a guest, I assure you."

"Thank you."

The Seer turned slightly toward the doorway. "Mara."

The tall Spectralist reappeared almost instantly, stepping from the shadows as if she had never left. "Yes?"

He motioned to Attica. "Escort him back. Quietly. Tell the guards nothing. We will hold counsel with them later."

Without another word, Attica pulled the rough cloak tighter around his shoulders and stepped into the darkened corridors of the Brethren's settlement, Mara at his side.

Behind him, the chamber of bones stood silent. The Seer remained at its center, on his throne surrounded by frightening bones, lost in thought. Waiting.

CHAPTER THIRTY-FIVE

The walk back through the Brethren's settlement was quiet. Attica and the two Spectralists moved swiftly through the tight streets, cloaks drawn against the deepening dark. Shadows stretched long beneath the stone arches, their footfalls muffled beneath layers of dust and old memory.

As they neared the outer quarter, the Painter's church loomed into view—its structure angular, its stonework harsher than any shrine Attica had known. He slowed as they passed beneath it, his gaze drawn upward. On the second floor, half veiled by mist and angled light, a stained-glass relief shimmered faintly in the gloom.

Set into the wall, the fractured panes depicted a spiral of color bursting outward from a single red sun. The glass was old, flawed, its edges dulled by time—but something about it held him.

It didn't stir memory. It stirred meaning. He lingered there, unmoving, looking up at it until Mara placed a hand on his arm.

Attica flinched, breath catching. She said nothing and they moved on.

The three reached the cellar not long after. Mara turned to him. "Good luck in your exile," she said, soft but steady—as if she knew just how far he had to go.

"So, you figured it out," he said.

"How could I not? We are on the third tier, where the Gate of Whispers is located. We get visitors from time to time. And just so you know, my brothers often greet the exiled and bring them to the Seer themselves. I don't know why they didn't with you—"

"I didn't tell them I was exiled, and I was with a woman."

"Right, that might explain it. The lower tiers are accustomed to the exiled roaming around. What is rarer would be the other two in your party. I do not know how the other settlements would react to that. But now, you may simply approach. They will know Attica, the Lone-Eyed Wolf."

"I might not have my fox mask next time."

"They will know that as well."

"Why are they so afraid to take in their own kind?" Attica asked, motioning between them. "We are all Shadowborn."

"We are," Mara said. "And I do not speak for everyone . . . but I understand their suspicion. During my childhood there were many issues that arose from lower settlements, not to mention the occasional crazed exile." Her smile faded into something more knowing. She pressed back, joining Rosaren, who offered Attica a short and slightly stilted bow. "Good luck."

"Thank you." Attica descended the stone ladder into the darkened corridor. Joan, the whisper who had guided him there, stirred in the gloom. Her voice seemed softer now, frail. "You got what you needed?"

"I did," Attica said, moving deeper into the darkness. His shade flared once, then settled, more at ease than it had been for the past twelve hours.

Rest. The thought took root as his foot slipped on loose gravel. *Rest would be good; rest before we try to find the child of light. Or . . .*

"The shards," Attica said, breathing life into the thought. "For Dayanne and Eli. I could . . ." He started up toward the exit of the tunnel, his hand faintly touching some of the glyphs on the wall. "I could try. What would it hurt to try? Once the child of light is dealt with . . ." He laughed bitterly at himself. "You're starting to sound like Hadrian, an old man mumbling to himself."

"I've met Hadrian," the whisper told him, taking him by surprise.

"You . . . you have?" Attica asked Joan.

"Hadrian the Unshaken, yes? A while ago. He was dragging a monster—it came alive once he reached the fourth tier."

"He made it?" Attica asked. Then, the next question. "The shieldwraith came back to life?"

"It did, but he handled it. And yes, Hadrian the Unshaken made it to the fourth tier. I do not know of his fate from there."

"You can't move freely between tiers?"

"Some spirits can. Some cannot. I was once part of this settlement . . . then, I became a shade. So I stay closer."

"Do you think he's still alive?" Attica asked.

"I do not know. But there are others whom you could ask."

They reached the exit, where a thin gray light filled the entryway. Attica stepped out to find Eve tending to Tiago, who could barely keep his eyes open. "Attica," she said. "Did you . . . ?"

"Show me the wound," Attica said, letting his cloak fall from his shoulders. He crouched beside Eve as she gently rolled Tiago onto his side. Blood had soaked through the wrappings. The injury was worse than he'd feared.

"See?" Eve said.

"Listen carefully," he told them both. "I have exactly two drops of the Painter's Blood. It will be enough to close the wound—but tonight won't be pleasant."

Tiago stirred, eyes unfocused, breath shallow. "Attica?" he mumbled, voice thick with pain. "I . . . I'm sorry if I slowed you down . . ."

"You did nothing wrong," Attica said, already reaching for the Seer's flask. His voice softened. "But I'm going to need you to hold still—and let the blood do its work." As his fingers brushed the stopper, a flicker of memory struck him: the night of Eli's birth, the way Dayanne had cried out as the Painter's blood took hold—visions, light, unbearable beauty. Her grip on his hand had turned to steel. Attica exhaled slowly. "Don't be afraid," he said, more to himself than to Tiago.

"I've . . . I've never been afraid," Tiago said, head lowered.

"You are a good Vanguard, strong and brave," Attica told him.

"You will survive this," Eve said as Attica dripped the Painter's blood onto the wound.

The change was sudden. Tiago arched backward, eyes wide with visions only he could see. "Color . . ." he gasped, barely a whisper.

And then, he fainted.

Attica made sure Tiago was bundled carefully beneath his cloak. The wound had closed cleanly, and Tiago's breaths came easier now. Still shallow, but steady.

Rising slowly, he walked a few paces away and found a low rock near the edge of the clearing, sinking down against it with a quiet grunt. "Vespasia," he called into the mist.

The fog shifted and the woman emerged, her indistinct figure shaped from vapor and voice. "You have healed your companion," she said as her eyes settled into a deep red glow.

Attica glanced back. Eve crouched beside Tiago, her body angled protectively over him, eyes fixed and alert. She glanced toward Attica and looked away in an attempt to give him some privacy.

"He will recover," Attica said at last, his gaze drifting toward the mist form that hovered near him. "He's one of our strongest—and if not that, certainly one of our most stubborn." He managed a thin smile. "I'm glad to see you."

"Are you?" Vespasia's tone held a trace of knowing amusement. "You're about to ask for something else, aren't you, Lone-Eyed Wolf?"

"What makes you think that?"

"You're in a unique position," she said. "Exiles rarely arrive with companions. Not living ones. They seek them out, sure; they also go mad for them once they've drunk the Painter's blood. But the situation you have presented is quite rare." Her head tilted, eyes narrowing as if peering into something beyond him. "It was you . . . wasn't it?"

"Me? What do you mean?"

"With the Unshaken, the man dragging the shield."

"Hadrian?" Attica asked.

"Yes, I see it now. You were with him."

The memory came to him, Hadrian's crazed grin, how he had gone from fee-ble to incredibly powerful after drinking some of the Painter's blood. "He was my mentor. I helped him bring it down."

"And then you quickly departed, yes, I remember."

"I had to. We were forbidden to go to the third tier." Attica decided to ask her the same question he had recently asked the whisper. "Is he alive?"

"Is that why you called me? I assumed you wanted another favor."

"I—"

"I am forbidden to speak of other exiles. This is part of my soul contract that I made with Duchess Corvenna."

"A favor it is, then," Attica said.

"Yes, a favor. Even with the fox mask, your face and demeanor are easy to read. What is it you would request of me?"

Attica glanced back to Eve and Tiago. "The Brethren Seer told me there was a settlement on the second tier. I would like you to lead my companions there. They cannot speak with you, but they can follow your trail through the mist. The Seer seems to think there could be some of the Painter's blood there. If they were awakened, our task would be easier."

"Our task?" she asked. "And what task would that be?"

"Getting the shards for the Crown of Shadows."

"Ah," she said softly. "That would be your first mistake. Exiles work alone. Your companions may have different desires than you."

He lowered his voice. "Is the Painter's true power so limited it can only save one life? Surely if the crown is restored, it can help more than just me."

"Things change as you descend," Vespasia said instead of giving him a firm answer. "I remain within the top three tiers. But a crown is worn by one head." The words lingered between them, heavy in the stillness. "As for your companions, yes, I can guide them to the location. I would assume that means you have other plans."

"I'm going to kill the child of light," Attica said, an ember reigniting in his chest. "The Seer mentioned that the child was seen on the fourth tier. I will go there."

"Revenge," Vespasia mused. "It drives you still?"

"It must be done," Attica told her with finality.

"You are not ready, Lone-Eyed Wolf. The fourth tier will challenge you. I sug-gest you stay here and prepare. Build alliances with the Brethren and other whis-pers. Seek out new entrances to the Realm of Recumbency before you descend. Remember Sebastian's fox mask will not survive beyond this tier. But that is merely my suggestion. I do have a task for you."

"Name it," Attica said.

Vespasia motioned a misty hand across the Spiralrealm. It was too foggy here for Attica to see the other side, but he understood her gesture. "I lost a necklace on the other side of the third tier. Retrieve the necklace and I will lead your companions to the settlement on the second tier, although I can't say for certain if the Seer's blood is indeed there."

"I will find your necklace," Attica said. "Is there anything I should know about it?"

"It is buried in a hive."

"A hive?" Attica asked.

"Built by what you call flashwraiths, particularly what's known as a broodmother that has moved on to the fourth tier," she said. "Dangerous. But you seem capable." She began to withdraw into the mist but paused. "Do not forget to look for entrances to the Realm of Recumbency," she added. "They may prove critical in the days to come. And trust your shade more."

Attica bowed his head once, then back toward Eve and Tiago. "I will find your necklace," he said. He brought his hand to his neck, to the stone that he had once given Dayanne. "You have my word."

CHAPTER THIRTY-SIX

Sleep took Attica—deep and dreamless, the kind that swallowed time. No whispers. No light. Just quiet.

When he finally stirred, the mist had thinned, the pale morning light curling through the ruin, cast from the Spiralrealm's red-ringed sun. He blinked, disoriented. For a moment, it felt like Dayanne was there beside him. That familiar shape. That quiet presence. The warmth.

But it wasn't her, it was Eve. She sat with her back to the same stone, shoulders nearly touching his, arms resting loosely on bent knees. Her eyes were already open—distant and unreadable. She'd been awake a long while. "Good," she said softly, still not looking at him. "You're up."

"How is Tiago?"

"Alive. Shivering and talking to himself most of the night, but alive."

"I saw Dayanne do that once," Attica said. "After she gave birth. The Seer gave her some of the Painter's blood to ease her pain. She was fine the next day."

Eve exhaled through her nose. "I'm not worried about Tiago," she said. "He's stubborn and young—good traits in our line of work." She turned slightly, gaze narrowing. "I'm more worried about whatever it is you're planning."

"You know what I'm planning?"

"You spoke to the Mother of Whispers again last night, yes?"

"I did."

"But I wasn't able to hear what you were saying. And as you very well know by now, I can't hear her."

Attica stretched his legs, working stiffness from his joints. "I may have located a flask of the Painter's blood on the second tier. I want you and Tiago to go for it. Vespasia will guide you as best she can."

"The second tier?" Eve repeated, doubt unthreading her voice.

"Yes."

She folded her arms, eyeing him. "And the Mother of Whispers just agreed to that? What did you promise her this time?"

"A necklace buried in a hive on the other side of this tier. I will handle it."

Eve stiffened. "A hive? We've encountered a herd before, but nothing like that. Do you know how many there might be?"

"I do not."

"How will you find it if the Mother of Whispers is aiding us?"

"Using the mask."

"And how do you know you can handle it on your own?"

"I can do it. I'll kill them all; you don't need to worry about that. You've never needed to worry about that. And I'll find her necklace." His voice was steady, sharpened by resolve. "Your job is to find the Painter's blood alongside Tiago."

Eve didn't answer at first. She looked away, arms tightening around herself, fingers digging into the fabric at her sides. "So we can become like you?" she asked finally, the words barely above a whisper. Not defiance, uncertainty.

"It's the only way to survive," Attica said, though a quiet resistance stirred in his chest. He didn't believe Vespasia. Not fully. *The Crown of Shadows can be shared.*

Eve stared at him. "And then what? You get her necklace—and then what?"

"And then I will find you on the second tier."

"You're so sure."

"What do we have to lose at this point besides . . ."

"Each other," Eve said, looking away from him. "We've lost everyone. And now you want to split up and put us in a position where we could lose each other."

"You've spent a lot of time on the second tier. You'll be safer there than you will here."

Eve turned her head slightly. "What aren't you telling me, Attica?"

"What?"

"What else did the Brethren Seer tell you? There's more."

"He has heard of the child of light. He said there were reports it was on the fourth tier."

She leaned back and stared up at the hazy gray sky. "I knew it. I knew that there would be more to your little side mission."

"It is not little. I'm doing it to help Tiago and you."

"Then let me ask you this: You won't be going down there, will you?"

He hunched forward, annoyed by her line of questioning. "That wasn't my plan."

"Attica."

"Eve?"

"Promise me," she said. The way she spoke, the softness and the weight behind it, reminded him of Dayanne.

Attica didn't answer right away. He looked past Eve, toward the mist, as if something might be waiting there to give him a reason not to lie. *If I have a chance to kill the child of light, I will take that chance*, he thought, solidifying this vow deep inside him.

His hands tightened at his sides. "I won't go there," he finally told her. The words tasted false the moment they left his mouth, but he said them gently, like they might still do some good. Attica cleared his throat, forcing his voice steady. "The Seer also explained that all Seers are connected. The lanterns we lit? That was part of that connection. Our Seer's name was Esmeralda."

"Esmeralda? I've never heard a name like that before." Eve paused, the edge in her voice softening. "There's so much we don't know."

"I keep telling myself that."

"And yet you keep digging deeper, like you're trying to reach the bottom of something that doesn't have one."

"The Spiralrealm has a bottom. The ninth tier."

She turned to him. "Attica, you can't be serious."

"I am dead serious. If that's where I have to go to bring back Dayanne and Eli," he said, voice tightening, "then so be it."

Eve shifted away, jaw clenched. "Then there's nothing left to say." Silence hung between them—cold, brittle, final. Attica felt the urge to say something else to her, to undo the words, to offer something gentler. But nothing came. Not now. Maybe not ever.

She broke the silence first. "We'll leave when Tiago wakes. I'll follow your ghost guide to the second tier. And if you don't meet us there . . ."

She didn't finish the sentence. She didn't need to. Attica watched her retreat into the fog, her silhouette swallowed too quickly by the gray.

Tiago was up when Attica returned.

He sat on a flat rock, his hair with its white streak combed back, eyes still a little too wide. Yet by the looks of it, the worst had passed. "Well," he said, grinning despite himself, "that was something."

"You're lucky you didn't scream," Attica told him as he offered the young man a hand.

Tiago took it and got to his feet. "I think I did. I don't really remember."

"Trust me, you didn't. I would have heard you. Were the visions strong?"

"Just my sister, Livia. But . . ." Tiago flexed his fingers. "I'm good. Thank you for getting the Painter's blood for me. I feel strange. Stronger. Like I'm still waking up from something I will never fully understand."

"That feeling too will pass. Well, at least until you drink the blood. Then, it becomes . . . I don't want to say worse, but more complicated."

Eve approached and motioned to Tiago's gourd. "Have a little," she said. "We will be able to get more on the second tier."

"About that . . ." Tiago said, glancing between them. "What happens now? I think I heard you two arguing."

"We weren't arguing," Attica said firmly.

"You'd know if we were," Eve added, her tone cool but not unkind.

Attica stepped in again, keeping his voice calm. "Next, you and Eve will head to the second tier. Vespasia will guide you. She can't speak to you, but she can part the mist and create a path. Follow it. The Seer believes there may be another flask of the Painter's blood there."

Tiago shifted, propping himself up slightly. He looked at Attica, not just with curiosity, but with something heavier. Trust. Expectation. The kind that made walking away harder. "What about you?" he asked.

Attica held his gaze for a moment. "I have something else to do," he said quietly. "A debt to repay."

"What kind of debt?"

"How do you think I convinced Vespasia to agree to help the two of you, Tiago?"

He scratched the back of his head. "I get it now. She's helping us because you promised her something."

Eve gave him a sideways glance. "You catch on quick, don't you?"

"I'm still a little bit fuzzy from last night, but I'll be fine." He flexed his arms and grinned at her as his shade intensified around him. "I feel good as new."

"I'm sure you do," Eve told him. "I think it's best we start off. Where do we meet you?" she asked Attica.

"The settlement, *our* settlement. It will be hard to see, I'm aware, but it would be the most logical place for us to meet again. You two can easily get there from the second tier. I'll work my way up once I'm finished."

"Works for me," Tiago said. "Do you want your cloak?" he asked, already starting to remove it.

"Actually, yes." Attica took the cloak from him and fastened it over his shoulders. "It will help me blend in, especially while I have this mask."

"There's one more thing—if you run into lightreavers up there, aim for the knees," Attica reminded them. "It's their weakest point."

Tiago gave a low whistle. "So that's what you and Eve were doing when we encountered that one."

"Exactly."

"I can barely remember any of it. All I know is that the two of you killed it rapidly." He cleared his throat. "Honestly, that might be the closest I ever come to dying."

"The closest?" Eve asked Tiago.

"If I get any closer, I might as well push through to the other side." He produced one of his shadowdaggers, flipped it, and caught the blade. "But like I said, I'm good as new. For now."

Attica turned to Eve, who still hadn't looked at him since their earlier conversation. "Keep him alive," he said.

"Keep yourself alive," she shot back, sharper than he'd hoped.

"I'll do my best. But I mean it—"

"I'm not an ashling anymore," Tiago said, his voice steadier than before. "We'll take care of each other. And we'll see you at the settlement. Hopefully by then, we'll have some of those powers you keep going on about. If you're late, which I'm guessing you will be, we will tidy up the place."

"Tidy up the place?" Eve asked. "You say that as if you plan to move back in."

"No, no," he told her with a shrug. "But I'd at least like to make sure any bodies that can be buried are. I'll never live in a settlement again. Even though he's the only one that is technically exiled, we are all exiles."

"Yes, that is a smart way to think of it." Attica gave a faint smile. "Good luck."

He stepped into the mist. For a moment, he nearly kept walking, like he had with Dayanne that last time, a memory that would never loosen its grip.

This time, he turned and waved. Only Tiago saw him at first. He nudged Eve. She raised her hand in reply, just a small, reluctant motion, but still didn't meet his eye.

Suit yourself, Attica thought. Then he disappeared into the eternal gray.

The Spiralrealm held a silence that was heavy and close. The kind that settled on the skin like damp ash.

Attica moved cautiously ahead, the fox mask veiling his face, the cloak blending him into the drifting mist. He followed faint, shimmering footprints, residual impressions from the past. They veered off the common paths, winding between jagged stones and broken causeways long since claimed by moss and shadow.

I hope this is the right way, he thought, as an old quote surfaced from memory: *The best way to cross the Spiralrealm is to fly. Since no one can fly, the second-best way is to walk.*

"Who used to say that?" he murmured, scanning the fog as the names of his favorite Vanguard rose in his mind—Cassian, Sevus, and Varro. All funny, dark in their own ways that only someone who lived their lives on the frontlines could appreciate.

All gone now . . .

He continued forward, pausing now and then to send his shade ahead. A silent scout. There were flashwraiths nearby—he could feel the tremble of their presence—but distant enough that he chose to avoid them. Better to conserve his strength for the hive.

"Vespasia," he said at one point, voice calm but edged with impatience. "Perhaps you could show me the way yourself, instead of leaving glowing footprints in the dark."

The mist offered no reply. No shifting veil. No flicker of her form or glow of her red eyes. The Mother of Whispers remained silent, either unwilling or simply uninterested.

He gave a quiet, dry laugh and kept walking.

So much for guidance, he thought. She was already doing more than he had any right to ask, leading Eve and Tiago to safety. Whatever came next, Attica would face it alone.

The day wore on, and Attica kept low, kept quiet. The cloak helped. It made him feel less like a man, more like a shifting shadow. Something half born of stone and silence.

His shade moved with him, a silent sentinel, its form melted into the terrain.

They encountered no travelers. Only bones, dust, and the remnants of forgotten ruins, so eroded by time they no longer looked like structures at all. Halfway through the journey, a whisper rose from the edge of an old cistern. The voice was young, male, and uncertain: "Wait . . . please . . . someone—"

A shimmer took shape near the edge of the cistern, coalescing slowly into the faint outline of a boy no older than twelve years of age. His features were soft and incomplete, shifting slightly as if the mist hadn't finished remembering him.

"I'm lost," the boy said, his voice light and hollow. "I don't know where I went. I was Brethren once. I think. Will you help me?"

Attica paused, his hand at the edge of his cloak. "How were you lost?"

"I left for my Trial."

At your age? Attica thought as he looked him over. "You didn't make it back, did you?" he asked.

"I did not. I failed. But I can still make it there . . ."

Attica studied the flickering outline. A breeze moved through the broken stones, and the shimmer wavered. He hesitated, then chose honesty: "I'm sorry to be the one to tell you this . . . but you are no longer among the living."

The boy's face twisted with something close to grief. "I'm dead?"

"You are. This is your spirit I'm speaking with. You don't have to believe me. And if you're still trying to reach the Brethren's settlement, it's behind me, through that mist." He pointed without turning. "But I'm afraid the path would lead nowhere."

The whisper blinked. His form flickered once. "Then what do I do?"

Attica remembered Vespasia's words—how whispers might choose to follow him, how bonds could form. He nodded slowly. "You may journey with me. I'm searching for a hive. If we find portalstones, a way into the Realm of Recumbency, I should be able to take you there."

The boy's outline steadied, drawn by the offer. "You would allow me to travel alongside you?"

"I would. I'm Attica. The Lone-Eyed Wolf."

"Luther," the voice replied. Then, after a pause, "Wolf? But you wear the face of a fox."

Attica touched the mask, his fingers brushing the smooth edge. "For now. What will it be, Luther?"

"I'll go with you," the whisper said. "If you don't mind."

"I don't. But we need to stay quiet."

"I can be quiet," Luther said quickly. "I can also help you. You mentioned a hive."

"I did."

"There is one not far from here. I . . . I don't remember the path the way a living person would. But I can feel it. Like pressure in the fog. Follow me."

Before Attica could respond, the boy's form vanished into the mist. A moment later, the fog began to shift, parting in slow spirals, the same way it had when Vespasia took the lead.

Attica followed without a word.

The trail wound through broken stone and slick black moss, the terrain growing more unstable with every step. Luther didn't reappear, but his presence lingered in the subtle shifts of the mist, guiding Attica forward, always just ahead.

Eventually, they reached a low ridge. Attica stopped.

The air here felt wrong—thick and humid, laced with a sharp, chemical bite that clung to the back of the throat.

Below, the mist had thinned enough to reveal movement.

The hive churned in the basin, alive with soundless activity. Emitters crawled across its surface in tight clusters, their bodies glinting like shattered glass beneath the red glow of the sun.

Attica crouched low, his cloak tightened around him.

Beside him, Luther pointed. Attica followed the gesture and felt a slow, sick weight settle in his chest.

They were standing directly above the hive, and the flashwraiths hadn't sensed them.

Not yet.

CHAPTER THIRTY-SEVEN

Attica crouched at the ridge, the mist clinging to his cloak, the Spiralrealm stretching away in every direction.

Below, the hive pulsed, half living, half built, a festering wound in the land filled with light and monstrous beings. Emitters crawled over it, their bodies sparking faint bursts of light as they shifted and jostled against one another. *Mindless monsters*, Attica thought as the Codex produced information for one of them:

Codex Entry Unlocked!
Name: Emitter
Origin: Common Upper Spiral Variant
Known Strengths:
– Emits concentrated light-bursts via oral cavity
– Agile and erratic in close quarters
Known Weaknesses:
– Crystalline mana nodes located in heels—primary kill point
– Light burst has a cooldown; vulnerable afterward
– Panics when isolated or cornered
Classification: T-I | Rank D | Cog 0 | Swarm
Notes: Frequently encountered in packs. Low individual threat—lethal only to the careless or overconfident.

Everything it described was true. Attica's first kill had been against an emitter. He could still remember the light it gave off in its final moment, the way its body convulsed in a stuttering burst of energy before collapsing into itself. It was that hesitation, those final spasms, that marked the difference between surviving and dying.

One of his fellow Vanguard, a boy named Tarnal, hadn't recognized the emitter's pause for what it was. He'd moved in too early, confident and careless. The emitter had unleashed a searing blast of essence, and they found what was left of him fused to the stone mere moments after.

For a long time, Attica assumed Tiago might suffer the same fate. The boy had that same reckless gleam in his eye, always pushing forward, trying to prove something. And yet, he hadn't broken. He hadn't hesitated either. Tiago had adapted—quickly, and not through precision or discipline, but through grit. Through raw, bull-headed determination and an almost irritating refusal to quit.

"I can do it," Tiago would always say. Not as a boast, but as something he was willing into truth. He spoke with the kind of conviction that bent reality. And more often than not, he pulled it off.

Thinking of him gave Attica a flicker of resolve as he crouched low, eye scanning the hive below. It sprawled in uneven rings, dense at the center and thinning toward the edges like ripples caught mid-collapse.

Movement stirred near the base. Just a flicker, but enough.

The best way to do this is to hit it all at once, Attica thought as he once again took in the structure.

He tensed once he saw a brighthowler, the two-headed flashwraith that had taken his eye.

Codex Entry Unlocked!
Name: Brighthowler
Origin: Mid-Spiral Mutation, Possibly Naturally Occurring
Known Strengths:
– Dual cranial nodes allow simultaneous tracking and threat projection
– Emits a resonance howl that destabilizes nearby shadows
– Highly aggressive; difficult to flank due to bifurcated awareness
Known Weaknesses:
– Head-strike vulnerability; severing one disables coordination
– Reduced physical force compared to ancestral forms
– Often overcommits in melee, exposing flank
Classification: T-III | Rank B | Cog 2 | Predator
Notes: Rare but increasing in number. Intelligence borderline strategic; prefers direct engagements over ambush tactics.

Scanning this information made Attica wonder more about the Classification section and what it actually meant, something he planned to ask Sebastian. *Cog 2? Rank B?* He also noted something he hadn't seen or really thought of before: *Possibly naturally occurring? Does that mean there could be flashwraiths that are . . . engineered?*

Attica continued scanning the hive, looking for any other types of flashwraiths. He noticed a sudden sparkle of light heading toward the hive above. It grew in size, joined by several others.

This one was new.

Codex Entry Unlocked!
Name: Avian Emitter
Origin: T-IV Variant; initially mistaken for ground-based class
Known Strengths:
– Capable of true flight despite skeletal frame
– Emits shriek-light while airborne; can target from above with precision
– Exceptional burst speed and vertical mobility
Known Weaknesses:
– Bone structure is hollow and brittle under sustained pressure
– Light gland is throat-centered, not heel-bound
– Becomes disoriented in high winds or enclosed spaces
Classification: T-IV | Rank C | Cog 1 | Predator
Notes: Often underestimated due to resemblance to standard emitters. Do not engage near cliff edges or open air unless prepared for aerial pursuit.

Beside him, his shade tensed slightly. "Don't like the winged one, do you?"
His shade bristled.

"Heh. Come on. One Vanguard against a legion of Lightborn monstrosities? You don't think we can do it, do you?" Attica asked, the words touched with challenge more than confidence. He wasn't trying to be cocky; he had experienced firsthand what he was capable of back at the settlement, when his true powers had been unleashed.

The emitters could be torn apart with Shadow Swarm. The brighthowlers would be more difficult. *The avians . . . that is the wild card. But if they're like the normal emitters, only with wings, then I will handle them.*

His shade settled again, just barely.

"That's what I thought," Attica said.

Small exhaust ports along the hive hissed open and shut, venting pale mist and radiant bursts of pressure. The structure pulsed with life, a bulbous tangle of silicate and light-veined chitin, its surface crawling with thin, luminous filaments that slithered in and out of view.

Beyond it, something else caught Attica's eye.

A soft, steady glow—too faint to be threatening, too focused to be natural.

He narrowed his gaze toward a low pile of stones. Haphazard at first glance, but no . . . too cleanly stacked. Too deliberate.

Portalstones, he thought. *Maybe . . .*

He sent his shade ahead, the shadow coiling wide around the hive before sweeping toward the stones. Though he remained at a distance, Attica could sense the stones now. Could nearly see them in front of him, even through the fog and the great distance.

Good. That confirms it. An entrance to the Realm of Recumbency is close. His shade returned, silent and watchful. He naturally lowered his hand to one of his gourds. *Full for now. But I'll need to recharge later, perhaps after.*

He glanced once more toward the stones, then toward the hive. *There is also the boy . . .*

Attica waited until he was certain he wouldn't be spotted and moved to a higher ledge. The Spiralrealm lived in his bones. He'd grown up less than a mile from the first tier's edge, carved his instincts in the dark, hunted monsters like these since he was old enough to bind a shade.

He had a sixth sense for it, Attica was as much a predator as some of the newer flashwraiths he had encountered. He moved like one of them now—half shadow, half ritual. A predator in his own right, no less cunning than the newer breeds of flashwraiths that stalked the tiers.

From this new vantage, the sense he'd carried all along solidified: the Spiralrealm was fractured here. Just beyond the basin, after the hive's far lip, the land fell away entirely. A clean severing.

What had once been tiered ground now gave way to a sheer descent, a vertical drop into the fourth tier. Mist churned in the gap like breath through cracked teeth. He could see down maybe twenty feet, the first few layers of stone smeared in soft glow. Farther out, ten or fifteen feet beyond the ledge, the fog thickened, swallowing depth and shape.

Soon, he thought, gaze lingering on the abyss. *But not yet . . .* He shifted his weight, feeling Luther's presence behind him. A quiet ripple in the mist appeared beside Attica. "Is this what you were looking for? The hive?" Luther asked.

"Yes, unless there are others."

"Not in this region. The broodmother was chased out by the Brethren. I'm surprised they haven't cleared this hive yet."

"Broodmother. I've yet to encounter one."

"They make these hives. They are the worst I have seen. Them, and the mistwhale, but that's just a legend, and if it does exist, it never goes near the Brethren's settlement."

"Mistwhale?" Attica remembered seeing something move through the fog when he had first reached the third tier. "Another I haven't heard of. But for now, that can wait. I need something else."

"What?"

"A necklace," Attica said. "The Mother of Whispers requested I find it. She claims it is somewhere inside."

"I cannot carry it," Luther replied, his tone soft with regret. "But I can find it for you. It would be an honor. And I don't mind helping." The fog curled tighter around him, coiling like breath drawn sharp. "I hate the Lightborn."

"You aren't the only one." Attica rose, his cloak whispering against the stone as he moved. He flexed his fingers, feeling a storm of power gather in his shade. He looked down at the seething mass of flashwraiths, their light guttering and shifting like dying stars.

"You're going to kill them all, aren't you?" Luther asked, mist swelling around him in excitement.

"That's the plan." Attica stepped forward, eyes fixed on the hive below. He moved to the edge, gathered shadow, and leapt into the fray.

CHAPTER THIRTY-EIGHT

Attica dropped into the hive.

The swarm didn't see him coming as mist peeled from his cloak and shadows converged around him, unnatural and sharp, forming shapes of teeth and fury. The tendrils struck with him as he landed, the first emitters just crumpling under the weight of a dozen knives from every direction.

The next fired blindly, light blooming across the hive in a short, searing flash. Attica cut this one in half and was gone before the next could react.

He phased through a portion of the hive wall, aimed at the nest of avian emitters. He exploded into the flock of terrorbirds just as they were starting to take flight, his shade swelling with violence.

Attica ripped through several avians, grabbing one just as its wings lifted it off the ground, slammed it down, and crushed its head with his boot. He cut the wing off another, batted a third to the side with his sword and phased through a fourth, his body reforming solid as he crossed through to the other side, exploding the flashwraith's upper torso.

Power rushed into Attica with each flashwraith he killed. Carnage became his fuel, Attica on a mission unlike any he could remember ever embarking upon.

Kill them all. For what they have done to my fellow Vanguard, for Dayanne and Eli—kill them all.

Two more emitters went down, bodies cut in half. Another sprang toward him, talons at the ready, only for Attica to push his blade through its neck and out of the back of its skull. He wasn't here to test his strength, he was here to unleash, to bring forth the kind of pure, unadulterated hell that the flashwraiths had brought upon his life when they raided the settlement.

He shrieked with anger as he cut an emitter's head off, just as its beam of light went wide and hit a portion of the hive, causing it to light on fire. His shade used the head as a projectile as it launched it directly into the face of another emitter, skull meeting skull with a dull thud.

Attica's rage moved through him with the rhythm of something uncontainable—no longer blood, but ignition. He moved to intercept, shifting his position to wedge himself between the swarm and the hive, not out of strategy but spite. This wasn't his mission. The necklace still waited. Their deaths were a mercy he didn't owe.

But mercy had nothing to do with it.

He dropped into the thick of them like a curse made flesh. Shadows snapped out in vicious arcs, slicing through the nearest emitter before it could turn. Another lunged—Attica caught it mid-charge, drove a boot into its chest, and rode it down hard into the stone. It shattered with a shriek of dying light.

He didn't stop.

He *couldn't.*

His shade unraveled and lashed forward, cleaving a path into the horde. Attica moved with it, flanking a cluster of writhing light-forms.

He vaulted up, landed on an emitter's back, and drove his blade down, next to its spine. Another tried to pulse—he stomped its core until it stopped twitching. The ground hissed with vaporized light and mana.

Attica flashed behind a shrieking emitter and severed its legs at the knee, dragging it down with a twist of sharpened shadow. Its body buckled, flickering. His shade surged beside him, slashing through an avian mid-dive. Wings crumpled and corpses tumbled.

Another avian hit Attica in a rush, wrapping tight around his frame just as two beams of light hammered into him. He staggered, teeth gritted, shadows burning against the flare. But he did not fall. He smiled through the pain. "Come on, then," he hissed as more of them turned. "We're just getting started."

Attica barely flinched as the flashwraiths closed in, their heat pressing against him in waves. He raised one hand. Not in desperation—but invocation.

His new power answered, shadows peeling from the stone like skin from bone, rising from the hive's cracked foundation, drawn from crevices and ancient hollows. A hundred slivered echoes of darkness surged toward Attica then passed, coalescing midair into a single writhing command as he used Shade Swarm.

They struck like a murder of ravenous crows, descending upon a battlefield, silent at first, graceful in their sweep before the unmaking began. Emitters were ripped apart mid-glow. Avians screamed as wings turned brittle and failed. A halo of flaring light burst outward, only to gutter and die in the same breath.

The screams faded, drawn out like threads that snapped all at once.

Silence fell, but it wasn't still. The mist coiled through the carnage, weaving between ruined husks and scorched stone. Nothing moved. Nothing dared.

Attica crouched in the center of it, shoulders rising and falling with each ragged breath. He uncorked his other gourd with a flick of the wrist. The mana hit hard, liquid fire in the lungs, flooding his limbs, pulling tight the edges of his focus. For a moment, it felt like the ground rejected him, like gravity itself recoiled.

Pushing through the sensation, Attica vaulted forward, trailing shadow, his blade one of pure wrath.

Flashes lit the fog like lightning strikes as limbs snapped. Light burst, shrieked, and guttered.

He tore into the next cluster, a force of violence and purpose. One emitter tried to retreat; he drove it into the dirt with a downward slash and crushed its skull beneath his heel. Another shrieked and scattered radiant flares in all directions; his shade formed armor over him, devouring the blasts.

Attica moved through the flashwraiths. Each strike landed with the precision of rage honed over years. His grunts came low and brutal, not words, not threats, just sound carved from fury.

A rhythm of impact and motion, of shadow tearing through light.

Of revenge.

And still, the hive waited. The last of the outer guard collapsed behind him. He didn't look back. Only forward, deeper, closer to its heart.

The interior of the hive unfolded around him—a labyrinth of pulsing light and bone-thin passageways, its walls alive with shifting veins of radiance that slithered like nerves beneath skin. But Attica didn't need a path. He *was* the path.

His shade stretched ahead, a liquid silhouette threading through corridors and chambers, alert to every movement, every flicker, every wrong breath in the dark.

Two brighthowlers dropped from the upper spines with sharp cries, their forms crackling with searing intent.

Attica didn't hesitate.

He turned, launched himself backward, and cast a tendril of shadow to a distant spire on the hive's upper shell. It latched with a hiss, coiled tight, and pulled. His shade wrenched him skyward with violent speed.

An avian emitter dove toward him; Attica met it midair, blade first.

The impact shattered its neck. Light burst from its throat, the flare searing right past him. Essence poured into his chest, feeding his shade as Attica landed on an upper ledge.

He ran, blasts of light at his heels as another avian swept toward him. Attica twisted in the air and sent his shadowblade out, which caught a wing joint and ripped it sideways.

The avian spiraled down, shrieking until the ground silenced it. The last one in the air tried to blind him, but was ultimately too slow.

Attica hurled himself skyward again, the shadows coiling tight around his body, light flaring past him as he sailed higher than any living thing had a right to be. He slammed into the flying flashwraith with a bone-crushing knee, his blade punching straight through its chest.

But there were still emitters. And the two brighthowlers were still alive, still tracking him.

They clicked to one another in soft, insectile bursts, pulses of sound woven into a language older than light. His shade tightened, its edges flickering like torn silk before sealing to his skin—an instinctive recoil.

It remembered.

So did he.

This was the very flashwraith that had taken his eye. The same twin-headed thing that had burned half his world to ash.

Attica stepped forward anyway.

The power within him didn't surge, it *coalesced*, dense and electric, as if every choice he'd made had led to this single, narrow moment.

The first brighthowler lunged, both heads snapping like blades.

Attica vanished through the hive wall to his right, shadow splitting, reforming, then reappeared behind the brighthowler in a burst of silent motion.

He drove his blade into the spinal seam beneath its left skull, a perfect insertion. He ripped the blade free, twisting as he did, and cast half the creature's head and a sliver of neck to the ground with a wet thud.

The rest of its body buckled.

Attica didn't wait.

He seized what remained and slammed it against a jagged outcrop of stone. His shade wrapped around him in sync, hardening just before impact—crushing bone, splintering light. The brighthowler broke apart in his hands.

The second one was already moving. It charged, light flaring wild in both mouths as Attica dropped low, shadow trailing. He slid beneath it and dragged his blade through both knees as he passed.

The brighthowler collapsed mid-sprint and hit the hive wall with a sickening, echoing crack.

Emitters appeared, scrambling to catch up to him alongside another brighthowler. One flanked from the side. The other two rushed from the front.

Attica let them come as raw energy seared through him.

The front brighthowler lunged. He stepped into it, cutting deep into the rib cage with a roar of grief—not a war cry, not anger—*grief.* The sound that came from him was wordless, broken, primal, as it spit light and soon choked on its own blood.

Its body still on his blade, Attica turned toward one of the emitters and bashed it with the brighthowler.

His shade lashed out toward the other on instinct, piercing through its light-filled mouth. It rushed toward another emitter and cut it down in a cross pattern that left the monster twitching in silence.

Attica absorbed their light as a few emitters tried to flee.

"Pathetic." Attica sprinted after them, cutting the pair down with a single swing. His shade brought down another, then two more, as the hive burned, the flames lifting higher. "Find the rest," he told his shade, giving it permission to leave him.

Attica felt its presence go. This would have been something he would never have attempted, but now, now he was confident that it was the right thing to do. Around him, flashes of light told Attica that his shade was doing exactly as he had requested. He stood there, watching it all, breathing heavily until the shadow returned.

"Good," Attica told it as his shade settled around him. "You did good. We did good."

He moved to a higher ridge and watched the hive burn. Attica crouched there, enjoying his show of strength. What he had just done was something no Vanguard would have ever attempted, yet he had killed a literal hive of Lightborn with relative ease.

Attica took a big inhale from his gourd and finished what was left of it, his shade buzzing with power by the time he was finished.

The flames burned higher, Attica taking it all in with a delight that he knew he wouldn't be able to share with anyone else. No one had seen him do this, no one knew what he was truly capable of aside from Eve, Tiago, and now Luther.

And he was fine with that.

CHAPTER THIRTY-NINE

Luther found him a few minutes later, just as the last of the flames began to gutter and die.

Attica stood alone at the hive's edge, the mist curling around his cloak, the ember glow of annihilation painting the sharp angles of his face. Smoke drifted from the shattered core, its twisted architecture still trying to hold shape after death.

He said nothing. Just watched.

The silence around him was total.

No more shrieks, no more pulses of light. Only the wind, the crackle of cooling flesh, and the faint hiss of mana bleeding into the stones. His hands still trembled slightly from the fury that had driven him.

Not from weakness, but from memory. With the help of his shade, Attica had moved through the hive like a beast carved from shadow, every strike an instinct.

Now, it was over.

But not done.

He kept seeing it—his own blood, that bright moment of pain, the wail that echoed in his skull when the brighthowler took his eye. The slow drift of Dayanne's voice, the soft weight of Eli's fingers. All of it crashing against the moment his blade tore through the hive.

It wasn't enough. Attica wanted more.

The boy arrived quietly, his shape forming through the mist, more defined than before, less apparition, more presence. "How . . . ?" Luther asked, his voice barely rising above the smoke. He looked around the ruined hive, wide-eyed and blinking. "How did you do this?"

Attica turned toward him, his gaze unreadable. The mist curled tighter around his boots, drawn to him. "I told you I would kill them all."

Luther took another long look around, awe settling into the lines of his misty face. "You did," he finally said. "You really did." He blinked, almost as if remembering something. "I found the necklace. I thought it would be deeper . . . buried somewhere at the core. But it was just in the wall. I can show it to you."

"Good." Attica stepped off the ledge, dropping down to the hive's blackened floor. His shade caught the fall, softening the landing like smoke catching firelight. He rose without breaking stride and walked past a scorched avian carcass, its body still steaming, its face half dissolved in ash.

Luther waited near the hive wall, one hand lifted toward a narrow vein of crystalline growth, half melted but intact. "This way," he said.

Attica pressed his hand into the cracked hive wall and pulled aside a cluster of fused organic plates. The necklace was there, intact, dark silver, wrapped around a piece of polished stone.

"Thank you, Luther."

Attica turned back toward the basin—the burned-out center of his fury—where the hive lay in ruin, still leaking smoke into the mist.

Something moved.

A flicker, high above. Subtle, weightless. The shape drifted downward through the fog, small and alone, its form outlined in a faint, unnatural glow.

His blood went cold before thought could catch up. The figure slowed as it descended, turning midair, a leaf caught in a dream. And then it drifted past the cliff's lip, vanishing over the edge and into the fourth tier.

Luther stepped closer, gaze trailing the same line through the mist. "What was that?"

"You haven't seen it before?" Attica asked, not taking his eyes off the ledge.

Luther shook his head. "No."

Attica's voice came low, threat evident. "That was the child of light." He stared into the void where it had disappeared. "My next target."

"What is it?"

"That, I do not know. But it is what killed my people and destroyed my settlement."

"A baby?" Luther asked.

"A baby." Attica reached the precipice, the wind dragging at his cloak. Below, the fog churned. The faintest shimmer still lingered at the edge of sight, then was gone.

Attica stood there, unmoving, his fury cooling into something darker. He turned back toward the glowing portalstones he'd seen earlier. The Realm of Recumbency would offer clarity. And, more importantly, a refill.

The pile of portalstones lifted, one by one, as if drawn by an invisible rhythm. Cracked slabs of obsidian and veined quartz rose into the air, turning slowly, aligning with purpose older than speech.

In moments, they formed a floating arch, suspended by nothing, humming with a faint harmonic tension.

"Come," Attica said, motioning for Luther to follow.

The boy hesitated. "You are certain?"

"You have more than earned it," Attica said. "Come and be made real again."

He stepped through, the Realm of Recumbency pulling at him—cool, weightless, reverent.

There was no sky here.

Only spiraling stairwells and shattered bridges, suspended in endless half light bathed in a twinkle of distant stars.

Above it all, Duchess Corvenna remained seated on her throne, unmoving, a sovereign of stillness. Her court stretched out in shadows, silent and half formed, like statues too weary to hold shape.

Attica's shade rippled against his skin, uneasy. Even here, in this haven of rest, there was weight, a fear of the power in this unique space. He stepped toward the fountain at the heart of the realm and lowered his gourds into the slow-spilling stream of essence.

Behind him, Luther stared in wonder.

"Where are we?" the boy whispered. Attica didn't answer at first. He just watched the glow ripple through the first gourd as it filled. "The Realm of Recumbency," Attica finally said as Sebastian came down the steps, the boy in his fox mask.

Sebastian came to stop and examined the two of them. "Ah, you have brought your first resident."

"Yes," Attica said as Luther's form took full shape beside him. The boy was dark-skinned like the others, with a faint orange sheen to his hair and a wiry frame stretched thin over wide shoulders. Too young and lean, but solid now.

"You came back faster than I expected," Sebastian said, his voice amused but not unkind.

"I'm not staying," Attica replied, unslinging his second gourd. "I need to refill and descend."

Sebastian clasped his hands behind his back, watching him with mild curiosity. "Descend? You came from . . . ?"

"The third tier."

"You can't be serious."

"I located the child of light. It's heading to the fourth tier," Attica said as he finished with the gourds.

Sebastian stepped in, lowering his voice slightly. "You want to drop into the fourth tier now? So soon after . . . all that?" He glanced past Attica toward the boy. "You haven't even introduced your new permanent guest."

"This is Luther," Attica said simply. "Luther, Sebastian. Sebastian, Luther."

"Sebastian the Limp," the boy clarified, tone light.

"I will not call you that," Attica replied. "We are more than what hinders us."

"Hi," Luther offered, awkward but earnest.

Only then did Attica really look at them side by side. The two boys were close in age, or at least appeared so—Sebastian standing with the quiet confidence of someone who had survived long enough to wear his place in the world. Luther, thinner, still bore the uncertain weight of someone not yet given time to grow. He might have been slightly taller than Sebastian, but the difference ended there.

He looked scrawnier, softer.

And it struck Attica then: If Luther had truly been sent to complete his trial in that state, already half starved, what chance would he have had against the wraiths of the third tier?

Too early, he thought. *Too soon.*

Sebastian wasted no time circling back, his gaze settling on Attica once more. "The fourth tier."

"Yes?" Attica replied, already feeling the low hum of his shade beneath his skin but not yet loosed.

"You're not ready."

"Not ready?" The words hit something coiled inside him.

"I've seen others go too soon," Sebastian said, his tone even, almost gentle. "They fall faster than they climb. And when they return, *if* they return, they're changed." He paused. "There is also your mask."

Attica's grip tightened slightly around the gourd. "If you think your little warnings will wedge themselves between me and the goal I've set, then you haven't met enough Vanguard. My mind is made up," Attica said, voice flat. Final.

He turned away, finishing with the first gourd and moving to the second, the sound of flowing essence soft against the tension settling between them.

Then Luther stepped forward, breaking the tension. "I've been thinking," he said to Attica. "I owe you more than thanks."

"You don't owe me anything," Attica said.

"I had a skill when I was alive. My shade taught it to me. All Brethren learn their weapon from their shade."

"Same with Vanguard," Attica said as he produced his shadowblade.

"Yes, yours is powerful," Luther told him, "but what I have to offer may help. A weapon—"

"Not here," Sebastian said, interrupting them. "Since Luther is your first guest, he must choose a location." He gestured toward one of the platforms. "Surely there is a worthy space."

"Choose a location?" Attica asked.

"When a new resident arrives, they are given a place. I believe that is common across most of the Spiralrealm. Or it used to be. When you bring someone here, a whisper or a spirit, if you will, they are able to move freely throughout the Realm of Recumbency, or I should say, *your* Realm of Recumbency. But this place will be where you find them. They will be anchored there."

"Anchored?" Attica looked over to Luther. "Is that fine with you?"

"I would much rather be here than roaming the mists of the third tier." The boy approached the base of one of the stairs and took it to the top. As soon he stepped on the platform, the space began to change, providing a bed, a desk, and a bookshelf.

"Ah, good," Sebastian said, "a bookshelf. You've brought more than a weapon, then. Perhaps this will help." A heavy ledger bound in rough leather appeared, already lying open as though waiting for entries. "The information from the flash-wraiths you encounter will be kept in the ledger, which is a way for you to access the Codex. You can tell Luther what to write—"

"You can write?" Attica asked Luther.

"All Brethren can write," Luther said. "Our education consists of writing, reading, and combat."

"I should clarify," Sebastian told the two of them, "the ledger will write itself, but it will be in Luther's handwriting."

Attica looked from the fox-masked man to the bookshelf. "I don't understand."

"Approach it and see."

"What about the weapon I wanted to give him?" Luther asked.

"Yes, blades before prose. It has been that way forever, I suppose. But do it up there," Sebastian said.

Luther took the steps to his platform and Attica followed, noticing as soon as he stepped onto it that it seemed to stretch, the space much larger than it had appeared at the base before the fountain.

"This could help you." Luther raised one hand and mimed a stabbing motion— the shadows around his fingers extended outward in a tight spring, then snapped straight like a striking spear, the tip of which reached a distance of nearly twenty feet. It recoiled instantly. "It is called Ravelstrike." He stepped closer and touched Attica's arm. "And now, it is yours."

"Ravelstrike," Attica said as he mirrored Luther's motion.

His shade responded with a flourish as the power took root. He instinctively understood how to cast it as he shot his palm out. A swirl of shadow traced around it and exploded outward, forming a spear that instantly retracted. "This is remarkable," Attica said as his updated status appeared before him.

Name: Attica, the Lone-Eyed Wolf
Designation: Shadowborn – Tier I
Rank: Vanguard (Exile)
Shard Fragments: 0 / 11
Current Traits:
Shadowblade – Your weapon is born of will and shadow. Its shape reflects you.
Resonant Shade – You can extend your awareness through your shade.
Shade Swarm – Summon nearby shades to overwhelm a target. May fail.
Shadow Phasing – Press through surfaces.
Shade Devour – Absorb the essence of slain foes to empower your shade.
Ravelstrike – Unleash a tethered spear of shadow that extends in a blink and recoils just as fast.
Echoes Granted:
Glimpse of the Unmade – This mask will grant you ghostlike impressions of past figures to uncover lore, paths, or patterns.

"Do you like it?" Luther asked.

"I do."

"You should see the ledger as well now that you have a bookshelf," Sebastian called over to him. "I know it's less interesting than your new toy, but it might be of use . . ."

Attica approached to find text magically appearing on the page. It was joined by a sketch of a lightreaver and its information. This was followed by an emitter.

Lightreaver – Tier IV | Rank B | Cog 2 | Predator
Stealth-oriented flashwraith capable of bending light to render itself near invisible. Exhibits coordinated hunting behavior, often striking in silence and retreating with precision. Limbs re-form into bladed constructs using core essence.
Vulnerable to matching light frequencies and prolonged exposure to darkness. Structurally weakest at the knees.

Emitter – Tier I | Rank D | Cog 0 | Swarm
Small, erratic flashwraiths that release focused light-bursts from their mouths. Highly agile in tight spaces. Crystalline mana nodes in the heels are the primary vulnerability. Most dangerous in packs. Common across upper tiers.

An avian emitter formed on the following page, complete with the Codex information.

Avian Emitter – Tier IV | Rank C | Cog 1 | Predator
Flight-capable flashwraith variant with a skeletal frame and burst mobility.
Attacks from above using precision light-shrieks emitted mid-flight. Throat-
centered gland distinguishes it from standard ground-based emitters.

Sebastian continued speaking: "Anything you encounter will appear in the ledger. And it will categorize them once you have more."

Attica turned the page to find a sketch and the Codex information for the brighthowler. "I've been wondering about their categorizations," he said as he looked at the sketch of the brighthowler. "Their classifications." He focused on the information that came coupled with the brighthowler as Sebastian approached. "This part here," Attica said, his finger on the classification text.

Brighthowler – Tier III | Rank B | Cog 2 | Predator
Aggressive mid-tier flashwraith with dual cranial nodes for simultaneous
threat tracking and projection. Known for its resonance howl, which desta-
bilizes shadows and disrupts shade cohesion. While physically weaker than
ancestral strains, it compensates with relentless pressure and bifurcated
awareness.

Ah," Sebastian said, as if pleased he'd asked. "That part's simple enough. The T corresponds to which tier had the first confirmed sighting. Flashwraiths often keep to a set of tiers. The rank is the overall threat to a trained warrior such as yourself. This is a bit subjective, but D would be a minor threat, followed by C, B, A, and finally S, which would be extinction grade."

"Extinction grade?" Attica asked him.

"To be avoided. The cog listing would be their cognizance, or tactical intellect. Zero would be feral; one would be bestial; two, tactical; and three, sapient. And then there is the type."

Attica examined the brighthowler's information again with this in mind.

Classification: T-III | Rank B | Cog 2 | Predator

So the two-headed brighthowlers were first spotted on the third tier, they are ranked relatively high, they are tactical, and their type is a predator . . .

Before Attica could ask anything else, the air shifted. A portal opened at the edge of the realm, mist coiling inward like breath held too long. Vespasia emerged from the fog, her robes trailing in dusky ripples, red eyes glowing as silence followed her.

Attica descended the stairs to meet her, his movements measured but urgent. "How are they? Eve and Tiago?" he asked. "Did they—?"

"Your companions are safe," she said, her voice quiet but certain. "They are more capable than you think. As promised, I led them to the abandoned settlement above. They've begun searching the ruins. They've encountered a few lesser Lightborn, but nothing they cannot handle."

Attica nodded once, relief tempered by the weight still on his shoulders. He reached into his cloak and withdrew the necklace. "I believe this is yours."

Vespasia extended a light, elegant hand to him and took it with no ceremony, only a faint narrowing of her eyes. "You had no trouble finding it, it seems."

"Luther helped me," Attica said, glancing upward. The boy still stood on the high platform, watching silently.

"Yes," she murmured, following his gaze. "Your first guest." Then her eyes returned to him, sharp now. "And now? You plan to rejoin your companions?"

"No," Attica told her firmly. "I saw the child of light near the hive. It descended into the fourth tier. I intend to follow."

"Ahem."

Attica turned. Sebastian stood halfway down the stairs, arms folded, his voice low. "I highly advise you do not rush into the fourth tier. It will be something you regret. You have no armor, and only an additional weapon."

"I agree," Vespasia added. "You'd be wiser to either meet your companions or linger on the third tier, which is not yet finished with you. There are others worth meeting—alliances worth forging. Before you fling yourself into the fourth like so many others, a death wish burning in your chest, ask yourself if you are truly ready."

Attica didn't answer. He walked to the platform's edge, where the portalstones had already begun to shift, realigning into a new gate. "I will be fine," he said.

Whether it was true or not didn't matter. Attica stepped through, intent on finding and killing the child of light.

PART FIVE

Nocturnes And Preludes

CHAPTER FORTY

Attica stood at the edge of the third tier, the fourth veiled in mist below. The Spiralrealm wound downward in a slow, patient spiral, each level deeper, narrower, older. But here, at this precipice, it did not narrow. It opened. Split.

The drop was vast and unknowable. A wound in the center of his world that led down to a ninth tier that Attica could hardly imagine. He glared down into it, mind quiet and set, focused on the task he had set for himself. The child of light was gone from view, but not gone. He could feel it, like a whisper pressed to the inside of his skull.

It waited below, somewhere in the lightless deep, and he would find the child and slay it soon enough.

"Are you ready?" he asked his shade, his voice more breath than sound.

In answer, the shadow coiled at his back tensed, eager. Attica flexed his fingers one last time. Darkness pooled in his palm, obedient and sharp. He spun, fast and fluid, and unleashed Ravelstrike.

The shadow spear tore into the air, slicing forward in perfect silence. No resistance. No drag. Only clean violence and the whisper of speed.

This is going to be very helpful, he thought, his shade pulsing in agreement, thrumming with anticipation, their bond alive with shared hunger.

"I knew you'd like that," Attica said. "Next time we see avians—they won't have a chance to flap their wings. We strike first. Always."

He took one last breath and went for it. Attica flung himself from the third tier with the grace that only comes from years of traversing the upper spiral, his body cutting downward through the fog. As he fell, the fox mask began to unravel. Once fused to his face, it broke apart, dissolving into pale ash, colorless and soft as it filtered away into nothing.

The remnants of the mask scattered behind him, lost to the Spiralrealm.

Glimpse of the Unmade – Echo dispelled!

Shadowy tendrils lashed out from the walls as Attica neared the bottom, his shade anchoring, guiding and catching. Dark essence unfurled like a net between the shifting stones, coiling and snapping with bursts of tension to slow his descent. He half ran, half slid down the remaining face of the tier, bounding from one jagged outcrop to the next in a blur of black motion.

This was not flight; it was surrender to gravity, directed, but not entirely controlled. A fall into the unknown.

And he welcomed it.

Attica landed low, knees bent in the vapor-thick dark, his cloak whispering around him as he rose. The air here had teeth—colder, sharper, raw. There was less mist than the third tier, but it was heavier somehow. Denser.

Drifting vapors lingered up from the cracked earth, rising from luminous potholes that pulsed with faint, sickly light, adding a hint of illumination to the terrain.

Above, the red-ringed sun of the Spiralrealm felt impossibly distant. Its warmth did not reach here. Only the hush remained.

"We're here," he said, words to ground himself as he pulled his cloak tighter. Attica stepped forward, boots sliding slightly on the condensation-slick ground.

The path sloped down into a shallow basin, each step drawing him deeper, sharpening his senses. The silence here was not peaceful; it was held. Watching.

He halted. His shade snapped still.

Something was near. A feminine figure drifted forward from the fog, moving without sound, without hurry. She trailed a long, radiant cloth that shimmered in slow, silken waves, light-woven veils that floated as if underwater, catching and scattering the dim glow of the potholes.

Her presence bent the atmosphere, deepened the cold. Vapor curled back from her passage.

Attica's eye locked onto her as he tried to find shape beneath the veils, but they danced in concert—always shifting, always concealing. Only the faintest outline of her body was visible beneath the drifting layers, just enough to suggest something human. Or close.

His heart kicked. His fists tightened. This was no lost spirit.

Codex Entry Unlocked!
Name: Lumenbride
Origin: Obscured; first confirmed sighting near a collapsed sanctum in Tier IV
Known Strengths:

– Emits harmonic tones that destabilize shade cohesion over time
– Veiled form can leave radiant sigils that detonate in pulses
– Commands lesser Lightborn with gesture and song
Known Weaknesses:
– Prolonged silence disrupts cohesion; cutting vocal cords reduces threat
– Lacks physical resilience when veils are stripped away
– Avoids direct combat unless cornered
Classification: T-IV | Rank A | Cog 3 | Predator
Notes: Rare and highly dangerous. Presence may signal ritual convergence or nesting behavior.

It's a predator, Attica thought, confirming what his instincts already screamed as the lumenbride paused, tilted her head, and peeled back the veil from her face. A beam of cold white light shone from her skull, illuminating a spread of jagged stone. Then the veil fell back into place, and the light vanished.

His shade bristled, tension spiking.

If I can kill her from here . . .

But before he could act, before he could cut her down with Ravelstrike, the lumenbride turned. Her veils flared outward as she released a soft, harmonic chime.

His shade buckled, fracturing along its edges in seconds.

He gritted his teeth through the static pressure in his skull and went for his opening attack. The spear tore forward, dark and silent, aimed dead center.

The lumenbride floated aside, veils streaming, her body tilting in a motion too fluid, too perfect. The spear passed harmlessly behind her.

Attica surged after her, drawing his shadowblade in the same motion. But before he closed the gap, she sang again, two notes this time, crystalline and high.

His shade convulsed and the world pitched.

The pressure in his skull spiked. It felt like the ground had dropped out beneath him as he staggered, his energy waning. The lumenbride came for him again, claws forming from the inner folds of her light. Attica dropped, rolled, sparks of radiant heat singing his shoulder as he spun away.

"Get control of yourself!" he barked at his shade. It tensed and fueled its power into his shadowblade.

Light-forged claws lashed from her sleeves. Attica dropped and came up low, blade at the ready as he grabbed the lumenbride's ephemeral cloth and pulled her toward him.

She rose, swaying, a figure caught in invisible current, her veils trailing behind her in slow, delayed waves. Then her voice surged, a rising glissando, sharp and unnatural.

The sound cleaved the air.

Attica staggered under the weight of it, his ears ringing. His shade curled back, half flayed by the resonance.

But he held firm. He lunged forward and caught the lumenbride mid-rise. With a snarl, he yanked her downward—hard.

He channeled everything into a point-blank Ravelstrike, the spear forming and firing in one breath.

It punched into her shoulder with a sickening crunch of light meeting dark.

The lumenbride released a discordant shriek, dozens of voices twisting together, collapsing into something primal and wrong. Light poured from her wound in brilliant gouts, her veils flaring and unraveling in wild, convulsive arcs. Her body spasmed. Control faltered.

Glowing sigils flared to life at her feet.

Attica dove aside just as the first one detonated.

The explosion wasn't fire or force. It was pressure and glare, a concussive burst of luminous static that cracked the air itself.

His shade threw itself over him, shielding as best it could. Still, Attica felt the edge as she flared backward, robes trailing, her motion no longer elegant. Erratic and wounded.

Spinning.

Bleeding light until she turned to flee.

New sigils bloomed over the stones as she moved, glyphs of light sparking into existence beneath her every step, marking her path like falling stars.

Attica scrambled to his feet, already drawing again.

No.

He wasn't letting her vanish into the dark.

Not after this.

He leapt sideways as the next sigil exploded. Another pulsed, then another, each detonation causing him to jump to the side as he pursued the lumenbride, who continued to flee, trailing torn veils from where Attica had managed to strip her robes away.

He launched Ravelstrike yet again, but it curved wide as the creature banked into a narrow pass.

Don't let her regroup, Attica thought, his hunter instinct taking over.

He followed into the gap, blade ready, breath ragged, his shade still flickering at the edges of his vision.

Got you, Attica thought as the lumenbride slowed just ahead. He accelerated, preparing to lunge, then skidded to a halt.

The narrow pass opened abruptly into a basin ringed with jagged stone. Pools of liquid mana shimmered in the dirt like broken mirrors, reflecting nothing true.

And there, hunched in the gloom, were figures.

Twisted. Twitching. *Wrong.*

They moved in eerie unison. Too small. Too fast. Limbs stretched wrong, joints crooked in angles no body should be able to bear. Their faces were locked in silent screams, and lanterns burned at the back of their heads, white hot and hollow, casting halos of light with no warmth.

Half a dozen. Maybe more.

The lumenbride hovered above them, veils drifting, voice rising as she began to sing.

Attica stepped back as one of the lantern-headed wraiths shrieked and rushed him, fast as a nerve spark.

He braced for claws, for collision.

Instead, the creature's head ignited in a flash of raw, focused light. A detonation of radiance.

The blast would have reduced him to ash if not for his shade.

It cocooned around him at the last instant, absorbing the worst of the impact. The blast lifted Attica off his feet and hurled him backward, his body slamming against the slope of the basin with bone-jarring force.

He hit the ground rolling, momentum tearing through him, ears ringing, vision splintering like cracked glass.

Above it all, the lumenbride sang. Her melody intensified. No longer haunting, but commanding. A resonance that scraped against his thoughts, each note dragging jagged static across his mind.

Codex Entry Unlocked!
Name: Wretch
Origin: Tier II Outgrowth, possibly hive grown
Known Strengths:
– Lantern-bright heads rupture on death, triggering localized light-burst detonation
– Distorted physiology enables erratic, high-speed movement
Known Weaknesses:
– Fragile structure; typically destroyed with a single focused strike
– Head detonation is proximity-based and can be detonated at range
– Coordination defies known behavior models; likely influenced by unseen signal
Classification: T-II | Rank C | Cog 1 | Swarm
Notes: Do not engage in tight quarters. Coordinated group sacrifice suggests hive-mind architecture or external control.

Attica blinked against the flood of new data, the words imprinting across his vision even as his muscles screamed to move.

At the basin's center, the remaining wretches took a synchronized step forward.

One breath. One beat. One signal.

Attica pushed to his feet, but was too late. The lanterns atop their heads swelled, white hot and pulsing, light intensifying with each step.

He tried to shield himself, tried to run as the world flared white and tore itself apart.

CHAPTER FORTY-ONE

A smaller wretch burst apart mid-lunge, its lantern-head detonating in a blinding flash that struck Attica full in the chest.

The blast hurled him backward, skidding him across the pitted stone, his cloak smoldering at the edges. His shade tightened around his torso, absorbing what it could as the burn petered out.

The wretches moved on him quickly, surging forward in a chaotic pack, a swarm of light-sick madness, every one of them twitching and twitching and twitching as they came.

One leapt at Attica, claws outstretched, shrieking as its head began to pulse, readying its explosion. His shade moved first. It lashed upward like a noose, wrapped tight around the creature's throat, and crushed it. Bone cracked. The light died in an instant, and the body dropped to the ground in a twitching heap.

No burst. No flash. Just silence.

Then the others came. Dozens of shambling horrors, sprinting, twitching in broken syncopation.

None of them slowing.

Attica drew in a sharp breath as the fallen wretch's essence poured into him, a stream of thin, acidic light pulled from the husk. It hit him like static—jolting through his limbs, flaring behind his eye as he locked onto another target.

Attica pivoted, slipped beneath a blur of claws and convulsing limbs, and phased—his body vanishing into the curve of a nearby boulder, stone rippling around him like disturbed water. He emerged on the far side in one fluid motion, already turning to strike.

The shadow spear burst from his palm and slammed into the wretch's chest just as it turned, catching it mid-shriek. The impact cracked its core, the creature failing to detonate. Instead, it unraveled in pure shadow, ripped apart before its body could even register the blow.

More essence surged into Attica, more fuel for the slaughter.

The remaining wretches shifted, eyes gleaming, heads twitching in fractured rhythm. They moved closer now, pulling inward, forming a dense, staggering cluster.

They paused just long enough for Attica's stance to settle and for him to issue a command.

"Now," he whispered.

His shade burst outward, summoning the darkness around and splintering into five flitting forms with needling shards that dove straight into the cluster. Screeches echoed as the swarm tore into them, ripping limbs, disrupting triggers, destabilizing their glow before they could detonate.

One managed to get through.

Attica stumbled back as its head exploded, his vision tunneling slightly as he uncorked one of his gourds.

Essence burned down his throat. His body tensed, then realigned. His shade snapped back into place, fully present again, stronger than ever as he turned his gaze to the lumenbride.

She hadn't fled.

The lumenbride hovered above the clearing's rim, arms lifted, her voice rising once more in slow, aching notes, each one dragging like light through a wound.

Only two wretches remained. They stood at her feet, twitching and dim, their lantern heads flickering faintly in the gloom.

Attica didn't wait.

He surged forward, low and fast, a streak of shadow and fury.

He met the first wretch head-on, twisting mid-stride and forcing its detonation to trigger early. The skull erupted in a burst of white fire that went wide, bathing the stone in hollow brilliance.

He was already turning when the final wretch came stumbling in, arms flailing in a broken lunge. Attica stepped into its arc, pivoted cleanly, and drove his shadowblade through its chest in the same breath.

The head flared, then sputtered.

Its light blinked out just as the body began to fall. Attica stepped past it, already moving, already reaching.

Above, the lumenbride turned to flee. But not fast enough. Attica raised his hand, essence boiling in his palm. The spear he produced lanced through the clearing, cutting the air in a single, ruthless line. It pierced what remained of her shoulder, dragging her down and pinning her veils to the stone.

She dropped, not in silence, but with a sudden, brutal stillness that made the quiet thunder in his ears. The lumenbride tried to sing again, one last trembling note, but Attica was already on her. He ripped the veil aside and drove his fist into her face.

Once. Twice. A third time.

The light shattered. Veins of radiance cracked along her masklike skull, and then she went still, veil fluttering in the shallow wind.

Attica stood over her, chest heaving, one hand clenched tight, the other trembling just beneath his control. The last traces of adrenaline flared through his limbs as essence continued to pour into him—hot, thin, and endless.

He let out a short, guttural growl, baring his teeth as he scanned the bodies. Veils torn, husks cooling. The light had gone out of them.

"Good," he muttered, his voice rough.

He uncorked his gourd and drank deep, the essence slick and bitter, folding into him like smoke into lungs.

But even as strength returned, something else moved beneath it.

A wave of feeling, sharp and uninvited, crept up through his chest.

He saw Dayanne's face. Not in blood or ruin, but in the quiet. Seated across from him at the table of their home, elbows resting, gaze fixed on him in that way she always had, the woman often unreadable.

Attica had never been able to tell what she was thinking in those moments. Only that it mattered. That he should have tried harder to ask. Regret stirred in his gut, slow and viscous. He crouched, grounding himself, but the feeling didn't pass.

Instead, it thickened.

With a sharp breath, he threw his head back.

Above, the sun still burned, blood-haloed and distant, its light a dying echo of fire.

He let out a deep exhale and saw his breath, a reminder of how cold it was. *But I can easily get back to the third tier*, he thought as he examined the wall of rock.

"You're making progress," he told himself. "The child of light first, for what it did, then . . . then . . ." Attica forced the words out. "Then, the Crown of Shadows."

If there was a way for him to get Dayanne back, to get Eli back, he would do it. *Not a question.*

How he would go about collecting the eleven shards scattered through the Spiralrealm . . . that was another story.

"It was rough," he had told Dayanne once, unable to say what he truly meant— that after a long expedition, after days of blood and bone, she was the only thing that mattered. The only thing that made it bearable. It went against everything he was taught. He was raised to be a member of the Vanguard, Attica, the Lone-Eyed Wolf, son of Spiran, Knife of the Glintfang.

But the truth was simpler.

The thought of home. Of Dayanne's body as they grew intimate, the way she always held his gaze. The thought of sanctuary. Of lying on the floor, Eli crawling over him, giggling. Of the good times, the struggles, the triumphs, and ultimately, the tragedy.

And now . . .

Now, Attica knew what their settlement really was: just an outpost clinging to the edge of a dying world.

The Spiralrealm hadn't always been this way; his world fractured the moment the Baffled King lost control, when his council of dukes and duchesses shattered the Crown of Shadows into eleven cursed pieces, the color gone.

That everything since—the tiers, the flashwraiths, the Lightborn, the slow unraveling of hope—were symptoms of that act.

Attica exhaled, slow and unsteady.

The thoughts came too fast, flickering like sparks on dry stone. His shade tightened around him, then eased. "I'm fine," he said aloud, voice low but confident. He rose to his feet and glanced back toward the mist-thick dark beyond the basin. "Let's keep looking for the child of light."

The wind was colder on the fourth tier, dry and scraping.

It dragged ribbons of dust across the ground like slow-falling snow, spiraling through the air in patient eddies. The red glow of the distant sun struggled to reach this depth, its light dulled to a sullen haze that barely kissed the surface of the stones.

Attica pressed forward.

One hand drew his cloak tighter across his shoulders, the other rested lightly on one of the gourds at his belt, the movement more habit than thought. Each step crunched faintly beneath his boots. The ground was firm but slick in places— layers of mineral ash and cracked sediment, thin crusts breaking apart like scabs beneath his weight.

He moved on, guided by instinct alone.

His shade drifted close, silent, offering no direction.

There were no bodies here. No more wretched wretches. No whispering lumen- brides. No echoes of battle or violence—just silence, heavy and thick. The only movement came from faint vapors curling up from fractured potholes, each plume flickering weakly as if it, too, was trying to leave this place.

He passed a ridge where the wind whistled through the teeth of split stones, thin and sharp.

Crouching, Attica examined a shallow print pressed into the ash, too light for a flashwraith, too precise for any known scavenger. The shape shimmered faintly in the gray, as if dusted with powdered light.

A footprint. Fresh, human.

Maybe another Shadowborn? An exile? What was the name of the Shadowborn who lived on the fourth tier?

He couldn't recall.

Attica moved onward. The basin narrowed into a corridor of stone, its walls warped and broken, curved like ribs protruding from a half-buried carcass. The path curved slightly, swallowing light as it wound deeper into the tier.

It wasn't sound. Not exactly. More like something folding into place behind him.

Attica turned and froze.

A man stood at the edge of the clearing.

He was wrapped in a red overcoat, long and heavy, embroidered with black thread. His hair was thick and lacquered, curls sculpted into unnatural precision. Pale powder clung to his cheeks, makeup rimming his eyes in ghostly rings. He looked gluttonous, powdered, exhausted. One gloved hand rested lazily on the hilt of a thin rapier. The other dangled a torn veil fragment, lumenbride cloth, still smoldering at the edges.

Beneath it all, beneath the affectation and wear, there was something dark. A wrongness. Like a demon pretending to be human.

"Well," the man said, voice hoarse and musical, echoing slightly as if spoken through layers of walls. "You made quite the mess back there. Were you planning to clean it up?"

Attica didn't move. His shade hovered low behind him, half formed, bristling.

"I didn't know this place was claimed," he said.

The man smiled, slow and thin. "They always say that. And yet they come."

Attica studied his face for cracks, for flickers of something beneath the mask.

"I'm not here for conquest," he said. "I'm tracking a creature. A child of light."

"Are you?" The man let the word roll over his tongue. "They come with pretty stories, too. Tales of lost things. Holy things. Dead things. I've heard them all."

"I don't tell stories," Attica replied. "Only the truth."

"Ah," the man said, eyes gleaming. "And which version is that?" He stepped forward. No sound. No motion. Just space displaced, his presence arriving before his feet did. "Tell me," he said softly, "which version of the truth do you drape around your neck?"

Attica held his stance. "I'm not looking for a fight."

The man's grin widened, teeth faintly stained. "Do you know my name?" he asked, tilting his head. "The Centurions certainly do. They show respect. They still pay their tithe."

"I have nothing to give you."

"I am Duke Tiberion Astor."

Attica had heard the name before. The duke had once ruled over the Brethren's settlement on the third tier until he was exiled.

"Should that mean something to me?" Attica asked, his tone flat. The pageantry was wearing thin.

"If you knew anything about the Council of the Torn," Tiberion said, "it would."

Attica's jaw tightened, aware that the man standing before him had a shard. "I want passage. That's all," he finally said. "I'm looking for something."

The duke sniffed, his tone turning theatrical. "Passage. Passage! Through my tier? Through *my home*? All the little scavengers want passage! And when I say no, they lie. They *always* lie."

"I'm not—"

"They always lie! I know what you are," Tiberion said, face hardening. "I *know* what you want. And I've encountered enough false shadows in my day." He stepped closer. His red coat ruffling behind him.

"The child of light—"

"There is no such thing."

"I'll be the judge of that. *Passage*." Attica summoned his shadowblade with a hiss of black light, the weapon forming down his arm. "Either you step aside," he said, voice low, "or I go through you."

Tiberion's eyes lit with amusement, something ancient flickering behind them. "Oh, good," he said. "The cub wants to bare teeth." The expression on his powered face sharpened into something colder. "I have a little surprise for you." He smiled once, not kindly. "Wait here, won't you?"

And then he vanished.

No shimmer. No distortion. No sound.

Just absence—as if he had never existed at all.

Attica's breath caught. His shade pulsed wide, expanding in a tight ring around him, feeling for movement, for air pressure, for tremors in the stones.

And then, a sound. Not breath. Not speech.

A step. Heavy and measured. Then another. Two hulking figures emerged from the mist beyond. Flashwraiths, but unlike any Attica had seen before.

They stood eight feet tall, broad shouldered and eyeless, their smooth, featureless heads gleaming faintly in the dim light.

They moved without sound, but not without intent. Each step landed with the weight of ritual, their presence heavy with design.

These were not wild things. They were appointed.

CHAPTER FORTY-TWO

Attica shifted his stance, shadowblade steady, his shade folding close around him, close as muscle to bone.

The creatures paused. Then, in perfect unison, their jaws split open and snapped vertically, cleaving their heads from chin to crown in a single, silent motion.

Attica had never seen a flashwraith do that—but he didn't flinch.

Whatever came next, he would face it.

He was Attica, the Lone-Eyed Wolf.

He had bled for every step that brought him down to the cold hell that was the fourth tier. Attica only had a moment to scan the Codex information before the two enormous flashwraiths descended on him.

Codex Entry Unlocked!
Name: Lightfeaster
Origin: Tier IV Brute Type; possibly essence-rich nest guardian
Known Strengths:
– Consumes ambient essence and regurgitates stored energy as chaotic light-bursts that distort perception
– Thickened hide and powerful frame require sustained physical assault to bring down
Known Weaknesses:
– Lacks eyes; navigates via sound and thermal input
– Light-bursts are delayed post-ingestion; window of vulnerability during digestion phase
– Vulnerable to low-frequency vibration shocks
Classification: T-IV | Rank B | Cog 1 | Brute

Notes: Favored in dense nests or essence-rich zones. Combat should emphasize misdirection and attrition—do not rely on shade cohesion or stealth-based attacks.

The lightfeasters advanced with hunched, ponderous force, each step carrying the weight of something bred for ruin. Their arms swung like falling pillars, wide and swaying, jaws still split open along the vertical seam. Their eyeless heads pulsed with flickers of internal light, casting ghost-shadowed patterns across the stone.

The first one struck low. Its knuckles carved a deep furrow through the earth, stone cracking in its wake.

Attica twisted as the blow caught his side and slammed him into the ridge wall. His shade surged to shield him, softening the impact. But it wasn't enough.

Pain exploded through his ribs, the air ripped from his lungs.

Come on, he thought. *Get it together!*

He forced his body to move, muscles still stuttering from shock. He rolled, boots grinding over loose stone, and came up with his shadowblade already forming.

He slashed toward the nearest lightfeaster.

The blade met flesh, but it felt like striking stone—dense, layered, unyielding. The weapon skipped across the creature's hide, leaving only a shallow line.

The monster turned.

A blast of chaotic light erupted from its mouth, striking him full in the chest.

Attica staggered, disoriented, his vision suddenly fractured. Colors bled into one another, deep reds smearing into gray. Depth vanished. Space inverted.

The world looked like it was folding inward, like everything around him was being sucked into a single collapsing point.

The ground buckled and spun, warping into a spiral, a drain swallowing light.

He dropped to a knee, breath shallow, balance gone.

Move. Move!

Attica lunged sideways on instinct alone, just as the first beast came down with both fists, slamming the earth where he'd stood a heartbeat before.

He vaulted backward, boots skidding, as he clawed for what little focus he could. One hand snapped forward as he summoned a spear of darkness.

It launched from his palm, fast and precise—but then it buckled.

Midair, the spear thinned, distorted, drawn off course as the lightfeaster inhaled essence with its vertical mouth.

The creature sucked in the dark mana like bellows feeding a forge. Ravelstrike hovered, veered, grazed its shoulder, and fizzled out in a thread of mist.

Attica's mind leapt to what he had just learned from the Codex. *It consumes essence. It can pull attacks apart!*

He dove toward its flanks. His shade surged around his fists, shadows hardening with violent intent. He struck the lightfeaster in the side of the head, once, then again, bone flexing beneath the blow.

The beast growled low, then turned and swung. The strike landed clean.

Attica was thrown back, bouncing once across the stone before he hit the basalt ridge with a spine-jarring crack. Pain flashed up his back like lightning. His blade flickered.

Still, he pushed forward again.

He drove another punch into the creature's ribs and felt the solidity of it, like pummeling a slab of moving stone.

The lightfeaster swatted him aside without effort. He slammed into the dirt, shoulders scraping against fractured rock.

Blue blood sprayed from his mouth as he coughed and spat, staining the dust at his feet. Attica looked up as the second beast charged, its jaw glowing, readying another blast of disorienting light.

He planted his feet and sent his shadow outward, snaring the ground, then *phased*, slipping just beneath the brute's arm.

He came up and drove a kick into the back of its knee, hoping to bring it down like it was a lightreaver. The creature buckled slightly.

He followed with a shade-enhanced strike, fast and direct, aimed for the spine.

It landed and did nothing. The lightfeaster's hide was too dense. It was like stabbing into a petrified tree trunk woven from mana-rich brick.

Attica coiled back and ducked a swipe from the first lightfeaster, only to take a glancing hit from the second. His shoulder screamed, his shade struggling to protect him.

A burst of essence detonated nearby.

The pressure in his skull spiked, sudden and sharp, like claws prying at the seams of his mind. His limbs went soft, drained of tension, and his knees nearly gave out beneath him.

Attica stumbled, breath catching, vision swimming. A low ringing started behind his eye, not sound, exactly, more like the memory of sound—something deep and wrong.

His thoughts unraveled at the edges, bleeding outward.

His shadowblade flickered, no longer stable. Mana droplets ran backward, sliding against gravity, peeling away from the blade's edge and unraveling into the air.

It was as if the lightfeasters were pulling his strength out strand by strand.

"What's happening?" he gasped, shaking his hands out like he could dispel the tremor. "What . . . ?"

Another step back.

Another heartbeat lost.

The lightfeasters advanced in perfect sync, their movements slow, deliberate, and unyieldingly brutish.

And in that moment, Attica understood.

They were aware now—fully attuned to the fight's momentum, to the faltering edge in his stance. They could feel the balance tipping, could sense the unraveling.

They knew they were winning.

His strength was bleeding out faster than he could replenish it. Each breath came shallower than the last.

Attica tried to summon the swarm—called for the shades, *any* of them—but none came.

One of the lightfeasters stepped forward, chest glowing brighter now, light pulsing just beneath its hide. The other circled wide, its jaw widening with slow, monstrous patience. Their movements had grown lazy. Confident.

They're herding me, he realized, tasting iron. *Not dumb. Just quiet.*

His muscles locked. Instinct roared through his body. He tried to brace for a final strike, to channel one last burst of shadow, to throw anything.

Something seized him.

His shade exploded from the stone behind him and yanked him backward with violent speed, dragging him across the ridge.

"Hey—!" He barely got the word out.

The last thing he saw was one of the lightfeasters opening its jaws wide, a bloom of light swelling from within.

Then, the world vanished in darkness and dust.

Attica slammed into the far wall of a ravine, the stone cracking behind him as he was pulled backward.

His shade didn't stop.

It dragged him deeper, fast and unrelenting, until it heaved him into a half-collapsed tunnel.

The air was stale here, heavy and quiet.

Attica crumpled, breath ragged, chest on fire. "I've told you before," he rasped, his voice breaking. "I've told you not to do that . . ."

His shade held him close. Not protectively.

Desperately.

Attica couldn't move. Couldn't think. He just lay there, body twitching, waiting for the world to settle around the pain.

Every breath that followed burned. His ribs throbbed with each heartbeat, and the ghost of that last hit still rang in his bones. He spat more blood. His shade loosened slightly around him, then tensed again—protective, but not at ease.

Then he heard it.

Something slower, heavier. Not footsteps. Each impact cracked faint echoes through the stone, like weight settling where it didn't belong. The sound rolled through the earth—distant, deliberate, relentless.

A low scraping breath followed, dragged across the silence like something exhaling through a throat not made for air.

The lightfeasters were still out there; they hadn't given up.

Attica remained still, pressed to the cold floor, every nerve tuned to that sound. The moment stretched, thick with waiting.

Then came a flicker.

Light rippled across the cave entrance, brief and distorted, a reflection seen in broken glass. It wasn't firelight. It wasn't natural.

It bent in spirals, warped and pulsing, threading through the stone like veins illuminated from within.

The cave walls throbbed faintly in response, as if remembering the shape of something that had once passed through them.

Attica closed his eye, but the afterimages stayed.

The light remained wrong, disorienting, like it was trying to rearrange the space around it.

He clenched his jaw hard enough to make his teeth ache, pressing his shoulder into the cold stone wall, as if grounding himself could hold the distortion at bay.

His breath came in shallow bursts, and he fought to slow it, to find control, but the pressure in his skull only grew.

The world around him kept tilting, edges blurring, reality warping at the corners.

Another flicker. A low, almost wet sound, as if one of them was sniffing the air.

The lightfeasters were stalking him, and the only thing keeping them out was the shape of the tunnel—and the fact that his shade had dragged him deep enough into a break they couldn't follow. Not yet.

But they were close.

Then, from deeper in the dark, a whisper: "You're lucky," the voice told Attica. "The duke doesn't usually let anyone leave."

A pause followed. Outside, the lightfeasters kept clawing at the stone, methodical and patient.

"If you want to survive," the voice said, softer now, "you should follow me."

CHAPTER FORTY-THREE

Attica followed the voice, limping through the fractured tunnel with one hand braced on the stone, the other pressed against his ribs. Each breath came tight and shallow. His body was wrecked—bruised through, burned along the shoulder, muscles trembling, and a sudden headache that wouldn't subside. His shade moved close and taut, more a brace than a companion now.

Blood lingered on his tongue as he uncorked the gourd and drank. Only now did he realize how much he'd consumed in the last hour. On the first tier, he would have never drunk this much, if any. Vanguard usually inhaled it in the field, saving direct consumption for injury or recovery back at the settlement.

Now, it was a constant fuel source. Commonplace. Normal for him to top off his levels, which was augmented by the essence he absorbed naturally during combat now.

Another sip and the mana hit him hard, his veins flaring cold. The pain dulled, not gone but distant, enough for him to keep moving.

Then, another sip.

Attica knew he couldn't afford to slow. The lightfeasters were still behind him.

He could still hear the brutes, their heavy, deliberate pounding echoing through the stone. Distant pulses of distorted light leaking through cracks in the rock, bending shadows in unnatural directions. No growls. No shouts. Just the sound of pressure and stone grinding under the weight.

The lightfeasters were still hunting him.

Still tracking.

His shade tightened protectively at his back. Not out of fear, but instinct.

If the beasts rammed the tunnel hard enough, the whole thing might come down.

"Thank you," Attica said, knowing full well that his shade would do everything it could to protect him.

Attica pressed deeper into the cave, moving faster than his body wanted, each step a jolt of pain that lit up his ribs like splintered glass. His breathing was shallow now, every inhale a blade. He was alive only because his shade had dragged him into the tunnel, and even now, he wasn't sure how far he'd have to crawl to escape the beasts behind him.

"They'll stop soon," the voice ahead said, calm and sure, as if he knew the rules of this place better than he ever could.

Attica kept on, limping through the fractured tunnel with one hand pressed against the wall for balance. His shade stayed coiled close, moving like a second spine, senses sharpened, every shift in the air met with tension.

The figure ahead wasn't quite solid.

He could see something that wore the shape of a man outlined faintly in the dark. The edges of him shimmered, warped slightly, like candlelight flickering through water. The whisper moved strangely, not quite walking, not quite gliding, but drifting forward with a wavering, uncertain rhythm.

"Keep your steps soft," the man whispered. "If they hear you, they'll try to come through, even if they can't." He gestured vaguely toward the passage behind them. "It will be bad. Those ones are especially nasty without the right armor."

Attica minded his footsteps. He could still feel the pressure of those things behind the stone, the lightfeasters pressing weight into the shape of the tunnel.

Every few steps, a phantom flash lit behind his eye, sharp, residual. The world tilted slightly at the edges, as if it hadn't fully remembered how to hold itself together. The headache was beginning to ebb, but a faint pressure still sat behind his brow, pulsing in sync with his steps.

He blinked, steadied himself on the tunnel wall, and kept going. "Who are you?" he asked the whisper. "What is your name?"

"I am Kairos. You?"

"Attica, the Lone-Eyed Wolf."

"Ah, a Centurion."

"A Vanguard."

"A Centurion from somewhere else, then," the man said. "Which tier?"

"The first."

"That would explain the fact you didn't run as soon as you encountered the two lightfeasters. You didn't know better."

"Centurions . . . same as the Brethren?" Attica asked.

"Yes and no. You've met the Brethren?"

"Just once was enough."

"Centurions are better, more civil, but equally as violent when provoked. We're almost there. Come." Kairos drifted deeper. Attica followed, limping. The tunnel curved downward, narrowing in places. The stone was layered with old moisture. "Here. Look."

Attica saw two distinct paths. "Which way is the exit?"

"This path splits. One leads to safety. The other . . ." He stopped.

"Where does the other lead?"

"I don't go that way," Kairos said. "Why are you here, Lone-Eyed Wolf? You are not equipped for the fourth tier."

"The child of light," Attica said. "I saw it from the third and came down after it. Have you seen it?"

Kairos was silent for several breaths, the dark pulsing faintly around his outline. "Something passed through," he said at last. "I didn't know it was a child. I didn't pay it much attention. It wasn't from this tier, that much I could tell. And I've been a whisper long enough to know when not to watch things that don't belong." He paused, as if weighing his words. "The Spiralrealm shifts the deeper you go. That thing . . . it brought the shift with it."

"So it came from below," Attica said, repeating the words slowly. It was the first time he'd heard anyone say it aloud.

"It did. At least to my knowledge."

Attica pressed his palm to the stone wall, remembering the shimmer in the mist, the corpses torn open and cast across the settlement like refuse. "I thought it might have come from the third tier. Somehow drawn up."

Kairos's voice dropped. "No. It climbed from much deeper than that. It doesn't belong here. And not wherever you're from, either."

Attica didn't respond. The idea of something climbing *through* the Spiralrealm, ignoring the rules of descent, left a hollow in his chest. The tiers weren't barriers, then. Not anymore.

He turned to face Kairos again.

"And Duke Tiberion Astor?" he asked. "Why would he summon lightfeasters to attack me?"

"Because he thinks you're after his shard."

Attica narrowed his eye. "So he has one, then."

Kairos's form dimmed in the dark. "He certainly does. He keeps it mounted in the skull of one of his former mistresses. It sits on his mantle like a damn trophy. He is a collector, you know."

"Mounted in her . . . head?"

"In her skull," Kairos clarified. "He's a deeply troubled man. It is a weapon. *She* is a weapon."

Attica stared at him. "You've been in his home?"

"I spent most of my life there," Kairos said, his voice quieter now, almost lost in the damp echo of the tunnel. "I was his slave. Until he had me killed."

Attica blinked. "What happened?"

"He killed me for sport," Kairos replied. No anger in his tone. Just something brittle. "Said he wanted to test something."

The silence that followed was thick and heavy. It pressed against Attica's chest, not with fear, but with weight.

He didn't know what to say. Nothing felt sufficient.

So he said nothing.

They walked in silence, the only sound the soft, uneven scrape of Attica's steps and the faint movement of dripping water.

Eventually, they reached a space where the walls narrowed. Just ahead, leaning carefully against the stone, was a small pile of smoothed rocks—stacked deliberately, not naturally placed.

Attica recognized the portalstones immediately.

"Are you familiar with the Realm of Recumbency?" he asked, turning to Kairos.

"I am," Kairos said. "You're not the first exile I've met." His form pulsed faintly in the dark, a whisper of light behind veils of shadow. "Most come through here damaged," he added after a moment. "Wounded. Lost. Few ever leave again."

"What about an older man dragging a shield? I spoke with a whisper on the third tier. She said he came here."

"I vaguely remember something like that, but I can't be certain."

Attica crouched beside the portalstones, brushing his fingers along their surface. The runes were faint, nearly worn away, but they responded to touch. A pulse shimmered through them. He looked back at Kairos. "Do you want to go with me there?"

Kairos hesitated. "To the realm?" His voice caught slightly, as if the question itself had cracked something open inside him. "I would be honored," he said. "If . . . if you'd have me."

"It has to be better than a damp cave in the fourth tier," Attica said. "And I want the duke's shard. I didn't come here looking for it, but after what he's done to you, after unleashing those things on me—I want it."

Kairos tilted his head. "And you want my help to get it?"

Attica met his gaze. "You could just tell me how to reach it. That would be enough."

Kairos gave a faint nod, or something like it. "I can help you in more ways than that. Do you remember those two paths we passed? The other one leads to a guarded grotto that is part of his manor. That's where my spirit first drifted after he killed me. I've been caught here ever since. No one knows that the caves exist except the duke—and me."

Attica turned back to the portalstones. Their faint glow throbbed softly in the still air. "We'll go to the realm first. Right now, I'm hunting the child of light. But after?" His voice hardened. "I can see myself paying the duke a visit."

"No." Kairos's reply was immediate. Firm, but not cruel. "Respectfully, no. You're not strong enough. Not yet. If you couldn't handle the two lightfeasters, you won't survive the manor. You don't know what waits there." He stepped closer, his voice dropping to a near-whisper. "If you try now, you will die."

CHAPTER FORTY-FOUR

Attica stood before the pile of portalstones, watching as the glyphs carved into their faces shimmered to life. The stones began to shift, lifting into the air one by one, their edges folding into place with ritual grace. A doorway formed, light spilling from the space between, warm and inviting.

A strange quiet fell over the passage.

From beyond the threshold, warm air rolled out in gentle waves, brushing against Attica's skin and stirring the edges of his cloak. He turned back to Kairos. "Ready to go?"

The spirit's form flickered slightly, as if the portal's light disturbed the cohesion of his shape. "I've . . . always wondered what lies on the other side," Kairos admitted. "I've seen exiles use these doorways before, but I've never followed."

"And you're sure you haven't seen an older man, my mentor, dragging an enormous shieldwraith? He's an exile too, Hadrian the Unshaken." Attica paused, something catching in his voice. "Last I saw, he was heading in this direction and speaking to his shade."

Kairos considered his question, the glow from the portal refracting through his translucent frame. "No, I haven't. But that doesn't mean he isn't here or beyond. Once I left the duke's manor, I never looked back. But he has been known . . ."

"Known to what?" Attica asked after Kairos trailed off.

"He's a collector, like I told you. I don't want to speculate. But regarding something you said about this mentor of yours, I can tell you that I've seen many exiles speak to their shades," he finally said. "It's common, you know. Does yours not speak to you?"

"If it does," Attica said, "I can't hear it." He felt his shade squeeze him ever so slightly.

"That's a shame. They can be quite helpful."

"Trust me," Attica assured Kairos. "Mine finds other ways to get the message across. It's the reason I found you. The reason I ended up in this cave system at all."

"I see." Kairos drifted a little closer to the portal, his outline softening in the light. "I wish I could say I'd met your mentor. But I don't recall a Hadrian the Unshaken. Perhaps, once you're strong enough to travel deeper, you'll find him."

"Perhaps." Attica turned toward the portalstones, where the opening pulsed gently, a heartbeat of light and stillness. He raised a hand toward it, then motioned for Kairos to follow. "Let's head through."

Kairos lingered a moment longer at the edge, his form shimmering like mist above a pond. Then, silently, he stepped into the glow.

The threshold of their world rippled as they reached the Realm of Recumbency. Attica now stood out on the main platform. Black stone unfurled beneath his boots—slick, ancient, half lit by a source that didn't exist. The platform curved outward into endless dark, surrounded by drifting embers of suspended light and staircases spiraling to nowhere.

Luther was crouched near the base of the inner stairwell, carefully arranging a set of flat white stones into a circle. Each placement was deliberate, his fingers moving with practiced care. Nearby, Sebastian sat cross-legged, his fox mask tilted slightly, watching with that vacant, ever-curious gaze.

Above them, Duchess Corvenna loomed from her perch, still as ever, carved from silence and intent. Yet something about her was different.

Her head had shifted slightly toward the boys—just enough to suggest amusement, or perhaps mild surprise, the kind that slipped past a monarch's usual restraint. It was subtle, but in the stillness of the realm, even a gesture that small carried weight.

She was watching her son play. Or more precisely, watching her son *share* something with another.

Attica let out a breath, the weight bleeding from his shoulders in slow degrees. His wounds still throbbed beneath the surface, but the sharp edges of pain had dulled. He glanced toward the fountain of essence ahead, its pale glow casting soft ripples against the carved basin. He'd refill the gourd later, once Kairos was settled.

"Welcome," Sebastian said, rising with practiced grace as he hobbled down the steps. "I am Sebastian the Limp. Above us is my mother, Duchess Corvenna. That is Luther, a permanent guest." He gave Kairos a shallow tilt of his head and gestured toward the raised platforms encircling the courtyard. "Choose one."

"Just . . . like that?" Kairos asked.

"You are now a permanent guest, and all permanent guests should be treated with dignity," Sebastian told him.

"In that case . . ." Kairos stepped forward, moving past Attica with a quiet steadiness. He was no longer flickering at the edge of sight. Not a whisper, not a ghost, but a broad-shouldered man of middle age, thick through the chest and arms, Kairos's bald scalp caught the realm's muted glow. A heavy hammer hung across his back, and he wore a thick black apron, stiff with soot and age.

He looked like someone who had belonged to the world once. And maybe, for the first time in years, he did again.

Attica eyed the hammer warily. "You have a weapon?"

Kairos turned to him and smiled nervously. "No, no, I'm afraid I'm not that kind of blacksmith."

"You worked for the duke?" Attica asked.

"Not by choice. Duke Tiberion Astor was a cruel master."

Sebastian cleared his throat. "Won't you select a platform? That is why you were brought here, you know."

"Indeed, a platform worthy of a smith." Kairos lumbered toward one of the larger ones. As soon as he reached the platform, sparks of colorless light formed tongs, blades, and mallets as an anvil of dark manastone sank into place beside a fireless forge. A cot took shape nearby, complete with a thick pillow.

Kairos set his hammer down gently on the main table. "Ah, it's good to be somewhere."

"Any luck with the child of light?" Luther asked, still crouched and stacking small white stones on one of the steps.

"The fourth tier has proven difficult," Attica admitted. "But the child is there. Kairos saw him."

Luther nodded, not looking up, his hands stacking white stones with practiced calm. Attica watched him for a moment. The boy's movements were precise, like ritual—more focus than game.

It felt fragile, this quiet. Attica barely remembered being a boy, but seeing Luther play sparked something within him, some desire for an innocence he couldn't remember ever experiencing. Attica exhaled softly at the sight, and for once since he stepped through the portal, he understood why this place had been named the Realm of Recumbency.

Sebastian motioned him toward Kairos's new platform. "I would suggest that you see what your guest has to offer," he told him, his eyes smiling behind his fox mask.

"I will do just that." Attica climbed the steps to the forge and found Kairos waiting. The smith stood behind a wide stone table, one hand resting beside a carved bracelet made of pale mottled bone.

Kairos smoothed his hands over the front of his apron, then gestured to the bracelet. "This is for you."

Attica raised a brow. "Thank you, but—"

"It's a tether," Kairos said before he could finish, his tone calm but firm. "Not women's jewelry. Wear it on your wrist. When you touch a corpse, the bracelet will call the body to me." He nodded toward the open space of the main platform, where the realm's soft light throbbed in low rhythm. "The boys might not like it when it comes, and the duchess certainly won't, but I clean up fast."

"So if I kill something like a flareback," Attica said, "and touch the body . . . this will bring it here?"

"It will."

Attica narrowed his eyes. "How do you know?"

Kairos blinked slowly. "I . . . don't. Not exactly." He paused, brow furrowing. "The bracelet belonged to the duke. I lost access to it after he cut off my hands and left me wandering the fourth until I came here. I believe it will function the same." He trailed off, the memory catching in his throat. Then he shrugged, like shaking off dust. "Aye. Not a moment worth remembering. But now, the bracelet is yours. It appeared on my table. That usually means something. And it makes sense to give it to you."

"It's an echo," Sebastian said, stepping lightly onto the platform beside them. "And a rather good one. Bringing others here often carries its own reward. Some echoes are better than others." He gave Attica a sideways glance. "I believe Vespasia has told you this already."

Attica reached for the bracelet, intent on examining the bonework. The moment his fingers brushed the surface, the piece vanished. It reappeared a breath later, fastened snug around his wrist.

A ripple of cold passed up his arm.

He checked his status to find the item listed as an echo, just as Sebastian had said.

Echoes Granted:
Bone Tether Bracelet – Allows the bearer to mark slain foes by touch, instantly transporting their corpses to the Realm of Recumbency for harvesting.

"Thank you," Attica told Kairos. "You didn't have to."

"I've been waiting a long time for an invitation to the realm," Kairos replied. "You barely knew me, and you offered it without asking for anything in return. That means something to me."

Attica glanced down at the bracelet, the pale bone faintly warm against his wrist. "If I send a body here . . . what happens to the rest?"

"I take what I need." Kairos reached beneath his workbench and produced two butcher's knives. They were old, the blades notched and dark with age, rust crusting the bases of the handles. "Everything else goes off the edge. The boys can help with disposal, if they want. As for the bones—I'll use them. I'll make armor. Good armor. But I'll need more. Stronger materials. From Lightborn you can't kill yet. You might consider returning to the third tier for a time. There is someone there that could be useful to our cause here."

"Our cause?"

"The duke."

"Right," Attica said, "his shard."

"I think that's a wonderful plan," Sebastian said, cutting in. "You are much more suited for the third. And you can easily return through the portal there—"

"No," Attica said. His voice held finality. "I've already told you my plan."

Sebastian blinked. "Ah, yes, *that* plan."

"I still have something to deal with on the fourth," Attica told him. "Then I'll meet my companions on the first. But if I find anything worth sending, it's yours."

Kairos nodded slowly, satisfied. "Good. Once I see what you're bringing, I may ask for certain parts. Specific Lightborn. But we'll cross that mana stream when we get there."

"If I'm going after the duke's shard," Attica said, "I'll need better gear."

"You'll need better *everything*," Kairos replied with a dry chuckle. "But I can help with the armor."

Attica gave a slight bow. "To be continued, then."

"To be continued," Kairos echoed, already turning back to his tools. "I look forward to your offerings."

CHAPTER FORTY-FIVE

Attica approached the fountain and looked up at the duchess. A faint glimmer traced its surface as he unslung one of the gourds, filled it, and went for the other. Once they were both topped off, he turned to Luther's platform, which featured a simple bed and a bookshelf with the ledger on it.

Best to update every time I come here, he thought as he took the steps and stopped before the blank page of parchment.

The ink took shape—a child's handwriting. The new entries appeared, complete with sketches of the flashwraiths Attica had encountered on the fourth, along with summarized information:

Lumenbride – Tier IV | Rank A | Cog 3 | Predator
Rare, veil-shrouded flashwraith known for emitting harmonic tones that disrupt shade cohesion. Radiant sigils left in its wake detonate in measured pulses. Often observed directing lesser flashwraiths through song and gesture. Highly intelligent.

Wretch – Tier II | Rank C | Cog 1 | Swarm
Small, malformed flashwraiths with inverted limbs and lantern-bright heads that rupture on death. Detonation creates a focused light-burst capable of vaporizing nearby targets. Movement is erratic and deceptively fast. Structurally fragile—can be neutralized with a single precise strike. Explosions can be triggered at range with accuracy.

Lightfeaster – Tier IV | Rank B | Cog 1 | Brute
Massive, eyeless flashwraith that consumes ambient essence and expels it as disorienting light-bursts. Emits no vocalization—moves with unsettling silence. Thick hide and brute strength make direct engagement costly.

Perception is based on heat and sound, not sight. Vulnerable during post-ingestion phase, when light-bursts are digesting internally.

Attica stared at the ink for a moment, then closed the ledger.

All good things to know, he thought as he turned back toward the main platform. He waved to Kairos, who offered up a crooked smile. "I look forward to seeing what you send me."

"I'll see what I can find. Luther, Sebastian," Attica said with a wave as he approached the stone gateway, gaze fixed. He paused once the rocks formed. "Sebastian?"

"Coming," the boy said. It took him a moment, but he soon joined Attica, eager to help.

"Two things. I'm wondering about the ledger. I've been updating it, but it doesn't provide as much information as the Codex when I first encounter the flash-wraith. It seems summarized."

"Yes, that," Sebastian said as he brought a hand to his scarred chin. "I believe that is the nature of Luther's gift. His shade, which gave you your Ravelstrike ability, was a record keeper. Or should I say, part of his shade was a record keeper because these shadows are, as you know by now, a combination of many different spirits. If you want someone who can enhance the information, you would need an archivist, or someone whose shade held these stronger capabilities."

"An archivist. A record-keeper type, yes?"

"Correct. They could provide more information as well, more than is available on your Codex. So I suggest continuing to update the ledger when you visit, and be on the lookout for a whisper that can provide the information you seek."

"Should I be looking for particular whispers, people with former jobs?"

"That is a possibility, yes."

Attica grunted in response. "Good to know," he said at last. "My second question." He motioned to the portalstones. "How do I tell it where I want to go?"

Sebastian pointed toward the glyphs flaring along the threshold. "There," he said, tapping a rune marked with a glowing numeral. "Each symbol corresponds to a tier and sub-location. If you simply approach, you'll go to the last portal you opened. But you can cycle between them. Lift your hand, and the stone will show you what's on the other side before you step through. If you wanted to return to the third tier—"

"I do not."

"Yes, yes, I'm aware. You would just lift your hand to one of these stones," Sebastian said as he moved his hand toward the stones marked with the number three. "You'll see the location on the other side before you step through and can choose which one you'd like."

"Thank you."

"Do try not to die," Sebastian said quietly, tone half joking, half serious. "Exiles who take sound advice tend to last longer. The others usually head straight for the deepest tier . . . and then wonder why they don't make it back."

"I will return . . . when I can." He stepped forward, and cold swallowed him at once.

The fourth tier reasserted itself with a bleak, breathless hush. Vapor drifted in loose strands across cracked stone, curling low along the uneven ground. The red-ringed sun above was little more than a distant smear behind a gray veil, faint and failing.

Attica's cloak snapped tight in the wind. Grit crunched beneath his boots, each step a small declaration in the silence.

The mist was thin here. The quiet felt thick.

"Let's see if we can't find it," he said to his shade, then started forward in the most logical direction—though logic rarely held for long in the Spiralrealm.

Attica walked until he heard a clash. A thud, heavy and wet, something massive striking the earth.

The sound led him to a natural hollow in the terrain, ringed with broken ridges and frost-choked cracks. Vapor clung to the rocks like old breath.

There, in the clearing below, three figures circled a wounded lightfeaster.

The beast was immense, towering and hunched, its eyeless head flaring with internal pulses of unstable light. Deep gouges marred its flanks. Its mouth hung open in that terrible vertical split, light leaking in thin threads from between its jaws. It twitched, struggling to rise, massive limbs dragging through the ash-crusted stone.

The trio moved in tight formation. Precise. Coordinated.

One was fast, striking quick and low with a shadowglaive. Another moved with more weight, wielding a brutal hook-ended pike that dragged a dark trail through the dust. The third, an older woman with white hair braided back from a battle-lined face, stood just behind them. She was wrapped in a heavy cloak, armor stitched with shadow-threaded leather braces across her chest and shoulders. Her shade mirrored her posture, long-limbed and blade-edged, a silent twin waiting for the signal.

Attica crouched low behind a jagged ridge and watched.

Centurions, he thought. The name stirred from memory, Shadowborn who had remained on the fourth tier.

The lightfeaster lunged, its split jaw flaring wide, but its footing failed.

It slipped on blood-slick stone, light spilling from its chest in jagged pulses. The younger Centurion with the pike drove it deep into the creature's shoulder. The glaive followed, slashing across the vertical jaw, cutting off the buildup of disorienting light.

A single whistle cut the air. The older woman's shade launched forward like a loosed bolt and drove a coiled spike of shadow through the beast's neck.

The lightfeaster spasmed, its limbs twitching in frantic pulses. Then its chest bloomed with collapsing light. The glow flickered once.

Then it was still.

No celebration. No words. Only motion.

The three moved quickly, stripping the corpse with clinical efficiency. Essence first, drawn clean and bottled in dark glass gourds. Then the shoulder bones. The jawbone. Clean cuts. Experienced hands.

The two younger Centurions said little. When they finished, both looked to the older woman, waiting for her signal. "Flickercrabs will get the rest," she told them. "Let's wrap this up and move out."

Flickercrabs? Attica wondered. *Sounds like some sort of scavenger. Another threat.* He stayed low, waiting for them to move on.

When they finished, the three vanished into the northern pass, leaving the corpse behind.

Attica crept forward.

The lightfeaster was still warm, though dimming. Attica reached down and touched it. He felt the bracelet on his wrist flare cold. A second later, the hulking body was gone—ripped from the world and delivered to Kairos back in the Realm of Recumbency.

I can't believe that actually worked, Attica thought as his shade curled with satisfaction.

"Yes, a good thing," Attica told it. "But let's see if we sent him something useful first."

He rose and his shade moved forward, checking on the Centurions.

Once it was clear the three couldn't be able to sense him, Attica followed, keeping his distance. Attica kept his distance, stalking behind them as they cut deeper into the broken terrain. His shade restrained itself. *These aren't mindless flashwraiths,* he thought. *These are highly trained Shadowborn. Any reckless move and their shades will find me.*

He tracked the warrior through fractured stone paths and narrow cliffs. The three moved in silence, occasionally breaking formation to check vantage points, flanking blind corners. They headed deeper into the tier, away from Kairos's old cavern.

Attica didn't care what they were after. Not really. Nor did he care to see their settlement or how Shadowborn could live in such a cold environment. He only wanted to know if the child of light would cross their path.

The Centurions rounded a ridge and disappeared from view.

Attica followed, careful to stay just outside the range of sound. The terrain opened into a wide outcrop, ringed by fractured stone and steep ledges.

An ideal place to rest or . . . to stage an ambush, he thought as he stopped short, Attica crouching low behind a jagged lip of rock.

A fire flickered below.

Not wood-fed but fueled by essence. He could feel it, mana rising in soft, pulsing heat. The glow wasn't harsh, but it was wrong in this tier, too clean.

Attica watched, puzzled. He'd only seen essence used to light settlement lanterns—never for warmth. In the field, it was a waste. A risk. Especially here. But they'd done it anyway, which meant they weren't afraid of what could lurk in the dark.

Or maybe they're too tired to care . . .

He scanned the clearing. Two Centurions had dropped their cloaks and were stretching beside the flame, speaking in low tones. Their leader stood a little farther back, arms folded, the fire at her back, posture sharp.

". . . You remember the broodmother's hive?" one of the men asked, his shadows flickering idly around his knuckles. "The one near the hollowed cliffs?"

"How could I forget? Took us two days to clear it. Crabs still picked the corpses clean."

He groaned. "I think this one was worse. Has to be."

"You always think the current fight is the worst one."

"That's because it always is."

The two laughed. The older woman made a small sound—half amusement, half warning. "Less talking. More watching."

She hadn't sat. Her stance stayed ready, shade active.

She knows, Attica thought. The realization settled in cold. Of course she does. She's waiting. "Let her shade know I come in peace," Attica whispered.

His shade moved forward—and met a force that caused it to tremble. Attica felt its response: a buzz, followed by another tremor that petered out as the shadow returned to him.

He adjusted his cloak and stepped carefully over the ridge into view.

"Stop right there," the woman said, still at ease. Her men tensed. She whistled, and they relaxed.

"I'm not here to take anything from you," Attica told her, voice even. He lifted his hands. "I'm looking for something."

Her gaze didn't waver. "You're exiled," she said flatly. Not a question.

"I am."

"From where?"

"Just passing through."

"Is that what you call shadowing us for over an hour?" she asked.

"I'm tracking something."

"That still doesn't answer my first question. Where are you from?" she pressed again.

"Up top."

"There are three tiers above us," she said. "Be more specific—unless you want to sound like you dropped in by accident."

"The first," he said.

That earned a pause. One of the younger Centurions looked up, suspicion edging his voice. "All the way from up there?"

The woman studied him now, hard and deliberate. A pale scar ran from her cheekbone to the edge of her jaw—healed poorly, like it had been stitched with fire. Her face was lined by battle, not time.

When she spoke again, her voice had shifted. Quieter. "Welcome, for now."

"Like I said, I'm just—"

"Passing through, I know." She motioned to the fire. "Sit, Shadowborn. You've followed long enough. You've earned a rest. Let's see if you're worth trusting."

CHAPTER FORTY-SIX

The mana flames burned low and steady in a wide ring of carved stone. Their warmth was faint, more illusion than comfort, but it pushed back the worst of the chill and hinted—however briefly—that this clearing was a place the dark dared not reach.

The two younger Centurions sat in a loose arc, backs to the stone, their uneasy gazes locked on Attica. Their leader remained standing, cloak pulled tight around her broad shoulders, posture still watchful.

Eventually, one of her men used his shadow to move a large rock over, giving her a proper place to sit. "Thank you," she told him as she returned her focus to Attica. "You've got that look, you know."

"What look would that be?"

"The kind that doesn't sit until it's sure no one's going to stab it."

"I've earned that look," Attica said.

"You're exiled," she replied. "Of course, you have. What's your name?"

He hesitated—just long enough for the silence to stretch and settle around the fire. Then he stepped forward, slow and deliberate, lowering himself near the edge of the light with one leg tucked beneath him. His shade moved with him, coiling into place but never truly relaxing. It remained alert, eyes fixed on the flame, its surface occasionally shivering with tension.

"Attica," he finally said. "The Lone-Eyed Wolf."

The younger Centurions exchanged a glance and the faintest of smirks, but neither spoke.

The woman didn't flinch.

"You may call me Gwendalyne."

"No last name?" Attica asked, watching her closely. "A name given once your trial is complete?"

She raised an eyebrow but didn't blink. "Is that where you earned yours?" Her gaze shifted, catching the line of the scar beneath his left eye. "Ah. Your eye. Lost during your trial."

"A brighthowler," Attica told her, voice steady. "It was the first one our people had seen in a long time. But I killed it and returned with both heads and the lanterns lit."

The pride in his voice slipped through before he could mask it, and his shade flared subtly, its edges rising, as if echoing the memory of the kill.

Gwendalyne watched—measured, not unkind, but unimpressed. Her fingers drummed a few times against the tops of her knees.

"You are a Centurion?" he asked, shifting the weight of the conversation.

"I am," she said. "And you?"

"Vanguard. But I suppose we have similar responsibilities, or at least, we did when I wasn't exiled."

"How did you become exiled?" Gwendalyne asked carefully. "There is always a story."

"You've met many?"

"The third and fourth tiers are transient in nature."

"The Brethren on the third were less than inviting," Attica said, which drew the attention of one of the men seated with his back to a rock. He scraped ash off his boot with a flint blade and spat at the ground.

"That doesn't surprise me. We are the same people," Gwendalyne said, motioning between the two of them, "We should get along, but we often do not. There are Shadowborn and Lightborn."

"Our people called them flashwraiths."

"I've heard the term from our Seer," she said. "But you never told us your story. Why were you exiled?"

"It wasn't by choice." Attica paused. The memory pressed hard against the edge of his voice. "One of ours went missing during her trial. We went out to find her and were ambushed by lightreavers—"

"That far up?" she asked, brow furrowed.

"Yes. The first time anyone from my settlement had seen such a thing."

Gwendalyne tilted her head slightly. "This is the second time you've told me you or your Vanguard encountered something *for the first time.*"

"Would you be surprised," Attica said, "if I told you there was a third?"

A smirk pulled at her lips. "I would not."

"A shieldwraith. A few years ago. We brought it back to the settlement. It released a beam of energy down into the Spiralrealm."

He offered her a moment to absorb the weight of that. "Remember that detail; it will become relevant in a moment."

"It is remembered," she said. "And no, I've never seen one." Her two men shifted slightly at that. From their low grunts, neither had either.

"As I was saying," Attica continued, "we went out to find the girl—Livia. A future Vanguard. What we found instead were emitter corpses. Dozens. Her body among them."

"She died fighting them?"

"No . . . or yes. I'll never know," he said. "But that's when the ambush came. Two from our party were killed. I was nearly taken apart myself."

He paused, then added, softer, "It wasn't random."

Gwendalyne's gaze narrowed. "What do you mean?"

"It was planned. I felt it. You know how it is—we're hunters. We know when we're being stalked." He looked past the fire for a moment. "Everything about it felt like a trap." He drew a breath, held it. "And while it was happening, our settlement was attacked. My people were killed."

"I'm sorry to hear that." Her voice was even, but not unkind. "But how did you come to be exiled? You said you were wounded."

"I made it back to the Sanctum," he said, skipping over what came before—Dayanne, Eli. That was too much to relive, too much to offer to someone he barely knew. "The Seer told me to drink from the flask, and I did."

"I see."

He hesitated again. There was more—names, faces, memories—but they caught somewhere in his throat. "New powers came," he said instead. "I killed as many flashwraiths as I could." A silence settled between them. The fire popped once, sending mana sparks into the mist. "And that," he said finally, "brings us to the fourth time I encountered something new."

"Another?"

"Another. A giant." He paused. "Perhaps I should count this one as two."

"Two?" Gwendalyne asked. "Speak clearly."

"The flashwraith was the largest I've ever seen. But inside its skull . . . I saw it. A child of light. Floating. Watching. It was *inside* the thing's head."

One of the younger Centurions shifted. His eyes flicked to his companion, then back to Gwendalyne. She didn't look at them. She was nodding—slowly, carefully. "So now, you're hunting the anomaly?"

"Is it that obvious?"

"You're not wearing armor. You've come from the first tier in what I'm guessing is a matter of days or less. Yes. It is that obvious." She met his gaze, steady. "Revenge wears its own mark, Lone-Eyed Wolf. Like a brand no cloak can hide."

Attica nodded once. "I will kill it," he said. "We already brought down the giant."

"We?" Gwendalyne asked, glancing around the perimeter.

"Two of the remaining Vanguard," he said. "They're on the second tier now, trying to obtain a sample of the Painter's blood."

"The what?" one of the younger men asked, voice edged with disbelief.

Gwendalyne silenced him with a wave of her hand. "Continue," she said. "We may share a common enemy."

"You're hunting it too?" Attica asked.

"Something came up from below. Maybe a week ago. No traceable light signature, but the footprints it left behind were massive. And just recently, one of our scouts saw something flashing in and out of existence, or maybe drifting down from the third. We're not sure which."

She stood slowly, cloak shifting around her frame.

"It was the child of light," Attica said.

"Yes, I believe so. And that's why we're here. To kill it, if we can. Or drag it to the settlement and end it there."

Attica stared into the flames instead of meeting her eyes. The heat softened the chill in his bones, but it also slowed him. Not tired, exactly—just . . . still.

But the fire inside him remained.

"I will kill it," he said. "Not you. Not your men."

"For your people?" Gwendalyne asked.

"For my people. For the Painter, the settlement, and the Spiralrealm."

And for Dayanne and Eli. Though he didn't say their names aloud.

Gwendalyne studied him for a moment longer. "And then what, Lone-Eyed Wolf? What will you do?"

"Then I will wander the Spiralrealm." He didn't mention the crown, or the shard held by Duke Tiberion, not yet. "I will wander the Spiralrealm and kill others like it."

"In that case," she said, "we join forces."

"We do?"

"You want it dead. So do we. Our reasons differ, but the Painter has brought us together. We'd be fools not to accept the grace of that." She regarded him for a moment, and for the first time, something softened in her voice. "And if I'm being honest, you look like a man who's been walking too long. One who could use a friend."

"Friendship isn't something I've thought about in a while."

"Then it's long overdue." Gwendalyne turned back toward the flame. "You're welcome to stay the night, Lone-Eyed Wolf. We move at first light, track this thing down, and handle it. You can take the kill. We'll assist."

Attica considered refusing. On instinct. But the fire felt good. And the quiet? Even better.

"In that case, I'll stay," he said.

"I think that's a wise choice."

He leaned back, just enough to stretch his legs and settle against the stone. His shade wrapped around him—alert, but no longer tense.

No one spoke again.

The wind fluttered along the cliff's edge, soft and steady, signaling the coming night.

The next day came with no true dawn, no morning hope—only a deepening of the cold and a thickening of the wind. Light didn't rise so much as drain in, gray and brittle, filtered through clouds that never broke. The fire had burned to a dull ring of ash, and the warmth they'd shared felt like something imagined rather than remembered.

They broke camp in silence. Gwendalyne took the lead, her cloak snapping behind her in the gusts, while the two younger Centurions moved with quiet discipline, falling into rhythm behind her without a word, their steps measured and efficient.

Attica walked a little apart from them, not quite trailing, not quite leading—just separate. His cloak was pulled tight around his frame, shoulders hunched against the cold. His shade drifted low to the ground, formless and quiet, moving like an extension of the wind.

No one offered conversation, and he didn't ask for it. His thoughts were still for once, a rare and welcome silence inside his skull. *One task*, he told himself. *The child of light dies. Then I figure out what's next.*

The terrain of the fourth bristled, shearing from the edges of exposed rock. The longer they walked the more fractured their paths became, the way ahead often treacherous with its narrow switchbacks carved into jagged ledges, long-dead crevasses yawning beside them interspersed with furnace-like hoodoos and skeletal stone arches.

As the trail narrowed to a single choke point, the first burst of light flared.

A sharp *pop*—followed by a crackling ripple across the ground.

Then another.

"Flickercrabs!" Gwendalyne said, her shout accompanied by a prompt:

Name: Flickercrab
Origin: Tier IV Subterranean Cluster Species
Known Strengths:
– Emits blinding light pulse upon impact—contact triggers chain reactions in nests
– Stonelike shell grants excellent camouflage in natural terrain
– Flash bursts can disorient, alert nearby flashwraiths, or trigger ambushes

Known Weaknesses:
– Harmless when isolated; minimal threat outside of clustered environments
– Shell is brittle under focused strikes; light pulse only activates when startled
– Predictable movement patterns; rarely deviates from territorial bounds
Classification: T-II | Rank D | Cog 0 | Swarm
Notes: Nests often placed in natural choke points—commonly followed by ambush predators.

Small, stone-colored bodies erupted from narrow crevices, their segmented backs hissing open to reveal clusters of pulsing glands. With each twitching movement, they unleashed bursts of blinding light—chaotic flares that scattered sharp brilliance across the cliffside.

One of the Centurions staggered backward as his shade flickered in confusion. The other surged forward, shadowglaive coalescing in his grip as he brought it down with a sharp crack. The blow split one crab in half—but the impact triggered another burst of light, brighter and closer.

The entire ledge lit up in a cascade of fiery explosions.

Cracks in the stone came alive with motion—dozens of flickercrabs skittering out in all directions. Their shells scraped against the rock with a dry, insectile chattering as they poured across the path in unpredictable patterns.

Attica narrowed his eyes against the brilliance. His shade tensed, shifting close around him in layered defense. "They're triggering a cascade!" Gwendalyne called out, her voice level even under pressure.

Attica surged forward and booted one flickercrab hard into the wall, shattering its shell with a crisp and satisfying crunch. A second one scurried past, too fast to catch. His shade lashed out, striking with a focused burst of pressure that cut a flickercrab in half.

Attica spun, slipped past a disoriented Centurion, and drove his palm into the center of another crab mid-leap, grounding it hard and silent. He tapped it with his hand and sent it away to Kairos, Attica assuming the smith would have some use for it.

More flickercrabs surged in waves, three dozen or more, scuttling through cracks and over the ledge, their pulsing bodies flaring in chaotic bursts. The chain reactions were growing wild now, bright enough to draw the eye of anything else roaming nearby.

To the east, two crabs collided in a flare of sparks, triggering a massive chain detonation.

Attica threw up his arm just in time. Light overwhelmed his vision, and static tore through his ears like distant screaming.

The world snapped back a breath later. He was already moving.

He dropped low, slid down a loose slope of shale, and grabbed a jagged rock from the scree. He hurled it into a cluster of flickercrabs—shattering their formation and scattering them like splintered glass.

He pressed forward without pause. His shadowblade formed clean down his arm, and he ended two more with swift, precise strikes.

No flourish. No wasted effort. Only motion and intent as the Centurions finished off the rest.

By the time the final flash faded, the ledge was strewn with twitching husks and steaming corpses.

The low hum of the fourth tier returned.

Attica stood over a shattered crab shell, exhaling through his nose. He crouched and sent it away with a touch. "Kairos is going to hate us," he told his shade, which shimmered behind him and reformed into a thin veil across his shoulders. The gesture felt like ritual now, one corpse at a time, one offering after another.

"You seem as if you've fought these before," Gwendalyne said, her voice unreadable, more observation than compliment.

"I've fought worse," Attica replied.

She didn't argue.

The other Centurions stayed silent. One of them cast him a sideways glance—not suspicion, but reassessment. The kind of look you give a man you thought was shaped from wax, only to realize he was carved from stone.

"You moved like you knew where they'd burst," Gwendalyne added.

"Just instincts," he told her, voice steady. He didn't mention the Codex. Not yet. He wasn't sure how much she knew, or how much he wanted her to know.

One of the younger Centurions murmured something under his breath but fell quiet when Gwendalyne glanced his way. She crouched beside a cracked shell, turned it over in her hand, and studied the inner lining. "We're close to something," she said, rising slowly.

Attica felt it too. The mist was thinning, but the air was heavier. Not colder, just wrong.

His shade drifted out a little farther, testing the trail ahead without being told. "Definitely," he said. "We're close. I don't know if it's the child of light or not, but it's something."

Gwendalyne scanned the path, eyes narrowing as she measured more than just distance. The terrain fractured into uneven shelves beyond them, mist gathering in pockets like held breath.

"Stay sharp," she told her men, her voice low but clear. "Where there are flickercrabs . . ."

She didn't finish the thought. She didn't need to.

The silence ahead was too deep. Something was waiting.

CHAPTER FORTY-SEVEN

The group pressed on through the jagged terrain of the fourth tier, each step met with the grind of loose stone beneath their boots. Harsh, spiraling gusts of dust tore through narrow passes and caught in the folds of their cloaks, blinding them in bursts and making every turn feel uncertain. The wind wasn't constant, it came in surges, like the breath of something sleeping just out of sight.

They moved up and down crumbling hills, senses sharpened, always scanning the haze for flickers of light, subtle signals of flashwraith movement half hidden in the gloom.

"Stop," Gwendalyne said suddenly. Her shade flared beside her, low and bristling like a guard dog on a short leash.

Through the mist, it emerged: a silhouette rising from the fractured stone, a monument half buried by time.

Her men fell silent at once, the weight of it pressing down on the trail. The figure ahead was massive—too still, too deliberate, too symmetrical to be mistaken for anything natural.

Nearly twice the height of a person, hunched under the weight of its own plated mass, the floating sentinel hovered in a clearing of broken stone and snowy dust. Its armor was thick, jointless, seamless, like it had been poured into form and left to harden. A carved ring circled the front of its faceless mask marking a singular, darkened eye at its center.

Codex Entry Unlocked!
Name: Shieldwraith
Origin: Tier VII Obelisk Type, possibly construct-class hybrid
Known Strengths:
– Emits focused light beam through central eye, capable of incinerating targets in seconds

– Near impervious to all conventional attacks; armored on all sides
– Some can deploy long, retractable tendrils to crush or impale targets at mid-range
Known Weaknesses:
– Vulnerable only when the eye is open; puncturing it disrupts internal core stability
– Movement is slow and deliberate; possible to outmaneuver in open terrain
Classification: T-IV | Rank S | Cog 1 | Engineered
Notes: Shieldwraiths are rarely mobile unless provoked or triggered by ancient protocols. Do not engage.

The shieldwraith didn't move.

But the air around it shimmered. Heat distortion bent the mist in wavering lines, warping the cold in quiet pulses. Snow at its feet had melted into a dark ring of exposed stone, steam rising in slow curls that caught the light and vanished.

It floated inches above the ground, silent, anchored by nothing.

"What in the name of the Painter . . . ?" one of the Centurions whispered.

"That's a shieldwraith," Attica said, mostly to Gwendalyne.

Her eyes widened. "You mean the one you brought back to your settlement? The one that shot a signal down into the Spiralrealm?"

"Exactly . . ." His voice stayed low, measured, but his stance was alert. "We kill this here, and we haul it off the edge. That's the only way. You do *not* want this thing anywhere near your people."

"Haul something that big?" one of her men asked. "That . . . that's not possible."

Attica didn't look at him. "I watched a man twice your age drag one. It's not light, but it's not immovable. Aim for the eye. And get out of its way."

As if stirred by the words alone, the shieldwraith's core began to glow. Soft at first, dim and pulsing, then brighter, with a steady, rising intensity. Like a slow, furious heartbeat swelling behind its armor.

Something rippled outward. Pressure. Weight. A hum just beneath hearing, felt more than heard.

Attica's shade flickered sharply, drawing closer. Gwendalyne's hand dropped instinctively to her side, calling her weapon into form.

Then it moved.

Without warning, a tendril whipped from the shieldwraith's flank—long, razor-edged, more blade than limb. It struck the stone beside one of the younger Centurions with enough force to fracture the ledge. Another tendril lashed out a heartbeat later, forcing him back with a shouted curse as he scrambled for footing.

"Get clear of the front!" Attica shouted.

A beam of pure light erupted from the eye, carving a molten line through the earth as it swept toward them. The Centurions dove—one dragged the other down just in time.

The tendrils lashed again, fast despite the shieldwraith's bulk. Its size was deceptive, the creature able to cover ground quickly when attacking. Its limbs kept the Centurions on the defensive, circling wide, unable to close.

Only Attica advanced. His shade surged beneath his feet in frantic bursts, accelerating him in quick lunges as he slipped between the tendrils. He waited, timed it, and when the eye widened again, he struck.

His shadowspear arced from the palm of his hand and punched through the open eye just as the next beam began to charge.

The shieldwraith reeled, light flickering, but it didn't fall.

Attica surged forward before the others could react, his shadowblade already coalescing along his arm, Shade rippling like smoke around the weapon. He launched himself straight into the shieldwraith's center mass and drove the blade deep into its eye.

The creature shuddered; light flared behind the cracked lens.

But it didn't fall.

Still hovering, the shieldwraith began to rise, lifting vertically into the air with a low, grinding hum.

Attica didn't let go. He clung to it, legs braced against its armored plating, dragging his blade free and stabbing again as his feet scraped against its surface. The eye blinked in bursts of blinding light, but Attica kept striking, the force of each blow amplified by his shade.

"Die already!" he snarled, hammering a fist into the eye with his off hand.

The impact rang out, shade force rippling through his knuckles. The cracked eye splintered wider, jagged lines widening with every hit.

He was still rising with it, but now, the shield was starting to falter.

The light swelled and shattered.

A fizzling shock wave burst around him as the brilliance flared and broke apart, sending the shieldwraith plummeting toward the ground, the monster bleeding out in threads of smoke and burning essence.

Attica's shade surged beneath him, snapping upward just in time to launch him clear of the collapsing form.

He landed hard, boots skidding across fractured stone as the shieldwraith crashed into the earth behind him. The impact split the ground open with a thunderous crack, debris and dust billowing into the air like smoke from a broken forge.

Its tendrils twitched weakly, no longer weapons, just remnants, moving as if trying to remember how they were once alive.

Attica didn't hesitate.

He stepped through the dust, climbed onto the fallen giant's chest, and drove his blade into the eye one final time.

He pressed his hand onto the surface of the shieldwraith, intending to send it back to Kairos.

Nothing happened.

The realization that followed was staggering. *It's not dead. Just like the one we brought to the settlement. But . . . I've already stabbed its eye enough times that I should have killed it . . .*

"I need your help!" he called to the Centurions, who seemed dumbfounded by what he had just done. They joined him cautiously as Attica pointed to the sides of the shieldwraith. "We need to flip it."

They hesitated, the three still stunned by the sheer size of the flashwraith. Gwendalyne recovered first. "In case it tries to signal?"

"Exactly."

She whistled, and her two men moved into position without hesitation. Between them, they rolled the shieldwraith onto its back with a slow, groaning effort, the weight of it grinding against stone until its ruined eye pressed flat to the ground.

"I thought you said it wasn't heavy," one of them grunted, sweat already beading along his brow.

"We moved it, didn't we?" Attica replied. He crouched beside a tendril and hefted it. It coiled, dense and flexible, but heavy. "Now its tendrils. We tie it, and we drag it to the edge."

"Yes." Gwendalyne stepped up to survey the terrain ahead, scanning the horizon with practiced precision. "I know this place. There's a break about a mile north, a clear drop into the fifth tier. If we do it from here, we'll have to haul it uphill. We take it there instead."

"Then we go north," Attica confirmed.

A strange grin tugged at the corner of her mouth. "The fifth tier's settlement will *hate* us for this. But we've already cut diplomatic ties."

They set to work, cutting and coiling the shieldwraith's tendrils, wrapping them around its armored bulk. Even dead, the thing resisted—its weight shifting awkwardly, its form fighting every inch as if some last instinct clung to the body. But once bound, it moved.

They took shifts—two dragging, two watching the perimeter.

Attica didn't complain. His mind kept circling back to Hadrian. The old man had done this alone. *Alone.* Attica glanced up at the skyless gloom above the fourth tier, wondering if Hadrian was out there wandering the Spiralrealm.

Would he be hunting shards? Which tier could he be on? Is he even alive?

Only time would tell.

* * *

Attica and the three Centurions reached the ledge just past midday—if *midday* still meant anything this deep in the Spiralrealm.

The light overhead wasn't light, not really. Just a smudged gray luminance filtering through mist and hanging dust. The air was colder here, sharper, edged with a swirling grit that coated everything it touched.

Attica had grown used to the cold. It lived in his blood now.

Still, something about this place unsettled him. The wind moved too cleanly, too quietly.

Ahead, the path narrowed between two warped pillars of stone, curving slightly inward like half-melted guardians. Beyond them, the ridge opened onto a wind-scoured shelf that jutted out above the void.

Attica stepped forward and looked down.

The fifth tier churned below, its surface obscured by thick fog that clung to everything like breath on glass. Here and there, spires jutted through the mist— stone formations twisted by time and pressure, jagged silhouettes reaching upward as if remembering something older than the spiral itself. Attica could see no movement, no lights, no life. Only the broken geometry of a world that had sunk too far to be named.

He raised his gaze toward the vast spiral that wound through the air above and below them, tiers upon tiers lifting and descending into obscurity. The column was massive, impossibly so—an axis of world-wrecked gravity around which the Spiralrealm had formed or fractured.

If not for the mist and dust, he could have seen the other side of it. Could have seen other paths, other lights moving, other exiles climbing or falling or disappearing into their own battles. Each tier vast enough to hold cities, empires, whole forgotten histories.

"What's even down there?" he asked Gwendalyne as he released the tendrils they'd used to drag the shieldwraith. "Have you been?"

She stepped to his side, her cloak catching in the wind.

"The fifth? No. It's a complex tier. The anchor between the upper four and the lower spiral. Factions fight for footholds there. Lines shift constantly."

"So you avoid it?"

"At all costs," she said. "Centurions stick to the fourth. Sometimes the third."

"But that causes other problems," one of her men added.

"I'm not saying we sneak around the third tier," Gwendalyne told Attica, "but . . . that's often how it turns out. We've had agreements with the Brethren in the past. Something always breaks them."

"That's the part I don't understand," he said. "My people heard stories— rumors, really—that there were other Shadowborn. But we never saw any. No signs. No evidence. I don't think we'd have fought them," he added, voice softer. "I think we'd be relieved. To know we're not alone in all this."

"I've never thought of it that way," Gwendalyne said, her smile fading. "But neighbors have a way of becoming invaders."

"I suppose if the Brethren were just one tier below us and always beating their chests . . . it would get old," Attica said. "And you've got the duke on this tier. He mentioned you pay tithe."

"Duke Tiberion Astor is a necessary evil," Gwendalyne replied, her tone carefully measured. "There's little we can do. As long as we pay tribute, he keeps to his manor and leaves our people alone. But make no mistake—he has immense power. And he can command certain Lightborn."

"I'm aware," Attica said.

"But not creatures like *this one*," she added, gesturing toward the collapsed shieldwraith. "He doesn't control the wild ones. He keeps a curated army at his manor."

"Ah, his manor," Attica echoed, recalling the cave where he had met Kairos and the secret entrance to the duke's estate. "And if you could, you'd end him?"

Gwendalyne met his gaze, steady and unblinking. "We've learned the hard way that even whispers can reach his ears."

"I understand."

She stepped toward the edge and nodded to the shieldwraith. "Speaking of unwanted guests—let's be done with this."

Attica joined her, pausing at the edge. Something shifted in his stomach, low and deep, like the body bracing for a fall.

The cliff dropped sheer and black for hundreds of feet. Far below, mana shimmered in slow, rising currents—twisting around stone spires like phosphorescent veins pulsing through the bones of the earth.

The sight made the world feel thinner. Smaller.

Together, without a word, they gave the shieldwraith its final push. It slid slowly at first, catching on a rough lip of stone. Then, as if accepting its fate, the living shield tilted and dropped, vanishing into the void.

A dull flicker of reflected light spiraled after it.

No impact. No sound. Only wind.

"That's one hell of a message," Gwendalyne said, rubbing her shoulder. "I'm sure we'll hear from the fifth soon. Or not. We can always say we didn't tip it over the edge."

"Solid plan," Attica said.

They stood there a moment longer, staring into the churning fog below. The space didn't feel empty—it felt *vacant*, like a room recently abandoned, where the heat still lingers but the presence is gone.

After a pause, they turned and began the walk back. The trail felt lighter without the shieldwraith's weight dragging behind them—but somehow, it felt slower too.

Gwendalyne fell in beside Attica, her steps measured against his. "You said you watched a man drag one of those things alone, yes?"

"I did," he replied. "My mentor, Hadrian the Unshaken. After his exile. He dragged it down to the third tier. I helped him get it that far, but I don't know what happened after. You never saw an older man—bearded, worn, dragging a shieldwraith in a harness?"

"I would've told you if I had."

"Yeah," he said quietly. "I figured."

She nodded, and for a while, nothing more passed between them. The wind whispered across the trail, threading through their cloaks as they pressed forward, boots crunching softly over loose stone.

The path narrowed, the mist thickening ahead.

Gwendalyne raised her hand, signaling them to stop. The four froze, eyes shifting forward. Ahead, something floated just beyond a cursed rise of jagged stone.

A figure.

Small. Still. Not glowing in the way flashwraiths did, but *radiant*, the air around it pulsing with soft, rhythmic waves of light. Attica stepped forward without thinking.

His shade tensed but did not stop him.

The child of light hovered there, silent and strange. Numinous in a way that didn't belong in the Spiralrealm—untouched by grime or shadow, clean in a world that had long forgotten how to be clean.

The child didn't run, didn't speak.

It simply turned to face them.

CHAPTER FORTY-EIGHT

The child of light twisted slowly within a shell of flickering essence. The orb surrounding it twitched and frayed at the edges—neither solid nor smoke, but something in between. Like glass blown from starlight, too new to hold its shape. It bled light in irregular waves, golden at the core, paler as it reached the edges, like a flame caught in wind it couldn't quite resist.

Inside, the child's form was faint. Small. Still undefined. Not fragile, but unfinished.

For a second, none of them moved. The Spiralrealm itself felt quieter, like it was watching how they would react.

Then Gwendalyne inhaled, sharp and steady, and motioned them forward. Her shadowspear held low at her side, not yet thrown. Her men fanned out wide, splitting formation, each step measured. Careful, but ready to strike.

Attica held still a second longer.

"Don't rush it," he warned, his voice tight, his eye squinting against the radiance. "If it wants to vanish, it will."

Gwendalyne gave a low whistle. Her Centurions shifted farther outward, spreading into a flanking arc.

The child turned slightly, the orb of essence around it pulsing once. Then it moved—slow, deliberate, just fast enough to beckon them forward, a lure wrapped in light.

They gave chase.

"I said don't rush it!" Rather than watch them ruin his chance, Attica surged ahead, shade flickering around his limbs, his stride whip fast across the broken terrain. The child wasn't fleeing. Not really. It moved like it was playing with them.

Enhanced by the power drawn from the Painter's blood, Attica pushed on, shadow swarming his limbs as he caught the child's trail. His body moved faster than thought, faster than instinct, each motion fluid with deadly precision.

The Centurions fell behind, and in seconds, he was within striking distance.

"Got you," he growled, raising his hand to summon the spear.

This wouldn't be like last time. No hesitation. No failure.

Kill the child. Let the pieces fall where they may.

Ripples of shadow coursed over him, lashing down his arm as the weapon formed—dense, honed, humming with quiet rage. He drew his palm back, poised to hurl it through the child's heart, when the child turned to face him.

It didn't run. It didn't scream. The child of light simply *looked* at him as the sphere of essence protecting it burst.

Small. Still. Lit from within by a quiet pulsing flame. Its light curled softly in the air around it, like breath against frost.

The child held no weapon. Made no sound. But its eyes, blazing and wide, fixed on him with a familiarity that hit deeper than shadow.

Attica had seen those eyes before.

Not here. Not now.

The spear in his hand unraveled into smoke, vanishing before it ever left his grip.

Behind him, Gwendalyne shouted a command, but it was too late.

His gut screamed, louder than any logic. Not a warning—but a command.

Protect the child.

Attica's shade moved first.

It surged outward, a blur of motion and dark force, intercepting her as she lunged, the woman intent on striking the child. A tendril of shadow snapped around her mid-leap and flung her sideways into a jagged rock.

Her shade caught her mid-impact, shielding her from a broken spine, but not the pain. She hit hard, groaning as she rolled to one knee, stunned by Attica's betrayal.

The others froze. So did the child. So did the world.

Realizing this could be his last chance—and finally gaining control—Attica took a half step toward and produced his shadowblade, which hummed with summoned essence as it slid down his arm.

Yet he couldn't move it; he couldn't bring his arm up to strike.

One of the Centurions roared from behind and charged. Attica pivoted, blocking the man's shadowglaive just as it swung in, the air crackling with essence. His shade lashed low, swiping the man's legs out from beneath him. He hit the ground with a hard grunt.

The second Centurion came in tighter, stabbing forward with his pike.

Attica met the strike with a sharp sidestep, deflecting the thrust with the back of his blade. He spun and drove a shoulder into the man's ribs, sending him sprawling.

Ahead, the child reached for Attica, tiny fingers glowing faintly, its eyes filled with curiosity.

Attica's arms dropped, his blade faltering. His grip had gone numb. His breath, held too long, finally escaped.

In the light, he saw it again—not the child of light, but the real *Eli*, and behind his son, *Dayanne,* her arms beckoning Attica toward her.

And suddenly it was clear, her voice so strong that it made his knees buckle. Her eyes were calm, knowing. "When the time comes, you must protect the child of light," Dayanne had told him that fateful night of Eli's birth, the night she had consumed some of the Painter's blood. "You must—"

Attica took the child's hand, and his shade didn't resist. It relented, as if it too recognized her.

"Eli," he whispered as he cradled the child in one arm, the blinding glow around her dimming. The veil of essence peeled back to reveal her shape—small, fragile, naked, her features soft but unmistakable.

A girl.

She weighed almost nothing, the child bearing a faint smile on her face as she looked up at Attica. His heart thundered. His shade coiled around them both, a second cloak as the Centurions approached, weapons lowered but tension rising in the air like static.

Gwendalyne led them, her hardened gaze fixed on Attica, weapon at the ready. "What are you doing?" she asked. Her voice was calm but brittle, ready to snap.

Attica held the child closer to him, essence buzzing against his chest. "I . . . I don't know."

"Hear me, Lone-Eyed Wolf: She's a threat."

"She's a *child.*"

"She killed your people. You told me yourself. She was inside the giant's head. That was her."

"I know what I saw." Attica said, voice rough. He didn't mention Dayanne or Eli, he didn't even know if what he had just seen was true, but he had to go with his gut for now, and his gut was telling him not to let them kill it, to protect the child. "She's innocent," he said, quieter now. "She *feels* innocent. Eli," he started to say again, remembering his son.

Gwendalyne didn't respond to that. Her eyes flicked to her men and back to Attica. "Last chance. Hand her over now, Lone-Eyed Wolf. We'll make it quick. We'll make it clean. And we'll forget what you just did to us."

"No."

"Have you lost your—"

"*No,*" he said again, with the kind of firmness that could move a mountain.

"Then you will die." One of the male Centurions surged forward, fury in his stride.

Attica turned, stepped aside, and struck with his free hand. The blow cracked across the Centurion's jaw, sending him sprawling across the stone.

The man rose again, bright blue blood at the corner of his mouth, and charged.

Attica moved with more force this time, sidestepping and driving him back with a clean, decisive strike. His shade rippled around his arm, restrained but pulsing, a clear warning.

"Stay back," Attica said, voice low but firm. "You know where this leads. You've seen what I can do."

The second Centurion hesitated, glancing at Gwendalyne. She raised her hand, stopping him. "Enough." She stepped forward alone now, her eyes locked on Attica. Her voice dropped. Cold. "You will pay for what you've done here today."

Attica swallowed hard. "I know I will. That is my burden to bear, not yours." He held the child closer. "Eli," he whispered, remembering his son.

"I believed in you," Gwendalyne said.

Attica's voice broke, barely more than breath. "I'm sorry. You have to understand that this isn't what I wanted, isn't what I planned."

Gwendalyne stared at him for a long moment and finally turned. She walked a few paces and paused, as if waiting for him to call her back. To change his mind.

Attica said nothing. She nodded once—maybe to him, maybe to herself—and vanished into the mist. Her men followed without a word.

Silence returned as Attica stood alone with the baby girl in his arms, the wind shifting around them, the weight of his choice slowly settling in.

What have I done? he thought as he looked down at her. At first, all he felt was a flicker of disgust—revulsion at what this thing had cost him.

But then the child of light giggled.

She looked up at him, her face haloed in warmth, and spoke a single word: "Eli."

PART SIX

SOME KIND OF MONSTER

CHAPTER FORTY-NINE

Attica set the child on a flat stone and began to pace, his breath shallow, thoughts racing. "What have I done?" he whispered. "How could I—" He stopped, glancing into the mist where Gwendalyne and her men had vanished.

"Eli," the child of light said softly. "Eli?"

"No," Attica whispered, crouching in front of her. "You're not Eli. You're . . . something else."

She tilted her head at him, birdlike, curious.

Her eyes—too wide, too knowing—gleamed with the hush of light. She looked more human now: small limbs, round cheeks, skin faintly luminous like she'd been dipped in moonlight. Not dark like Attica's, but pale in a way that felt borrowed, as if color hadn't fully decided her fate. Wisps of hair curled at her crown, soft and fine. Her fingers opened and closed with a slow, untrained rhythm.

She smiled. That unsettled him more than anything else.

What if I just walked away? he thought as he looked her over, casting away the thought that she had actually spared him for some reason. *I could walk away, and tell Eve and Tiago I couldn't find her. As for Gwendalyne, I could just stay clear of the fourth tier. No, the duke is here, but I can use the portalstones to reach him through the cavern. The Centurions would only know he was gone once he stopped collecting tithe.*

Attica looked toward the opposite side of the tier, where he knew he'd eventually encounter the wall that led up the third. *Maybe I go there and ask Vespasia.*

"Eli." The girl touched her chest and said the name again. "Eli."

"You are not Eli, you are some kind of monster. But it seems . . ." Attica couldn't believe the words that came out of his mouth next. "It seems that I am temporarily responsible for you." His vision of Dayanne returned, her words that night. *Did she really tell me to take care of this thing?* Attica stared at the child for a moment.

"Eli."

Attica closed his eye and let out a deep, troubling exhale. "Stop." He kneeled and lifted her again. She pressed her head against his chest and made a soft, vibrating sound in her throat.

"Good," he whispered to the child now in his arms. "Rest."

"Eli."

"No. Stop," he said, already walking. "Vespasia?" he called out into the gloom, hoping she'd actually come to the fourth tier. She didn't answer. He tried again, a bit louder this time, but not loud enough to draw too much attention to himself.

His steps carried him across uneven ground, where wind-carved ridges had split the stone. Dust eddied with every footfall, fine as ash, clinging to the edges of his boots. Loose shale slid underfoot as the trail twisted through dead gullies and half-fallen arches, the sky above pale with high mist.

The child barely weighed more than a whisper. And still, with every step, his thoughts dragged, heavier and heavier.

Attica still couldn't process what he'd just done. Only that he had done it. He had stood against his own kind to protect a Lightborn child. And for what? *You now cradle the very thing that annihilated everything you loved.*

A child. A weapon. Maybe both.

I know what I saw back at the settlement, but it didn't seem like the child herself was orchestrating the attack. She was merely in the giant's head . . .

He kept walking, thoughts slamming against the inside of his head as he resisted the urge to turn, or leave the child, or kill it. He didn't know, but at least a destination gave him some sense of purpose.

The trail narrowed at the base of a shale ridge, mist pooling near the edges.

His shade tensed. Then he heard them scuttling.

Flickercrabs burst from the cracks around the path, a dozen, maybe more. All of them pulsing with light, shells flexing, claws clicking in rhythm as they prepared to detonate.

Attica shifted his grip on the girl.

"Stay close," he told her, his shadow coiling into a defensive arc.

The first crab lunged and the child simply raised her hand.

A flick of light flared from her palm.

Not a beam.

Not a weapon.

Just an unseen pressure.

The flickercrabs reeled back, stumbled as the light dimmed around them. One tipped and tumbled into a crevice. Another twitched once and lay still. The others scattered, back to their holes.

Attica stared at her once they were gone. "You . . . helped me?"

She reached for his face. "Eli."

"Don't . . . don't touch my face. And you need to learn a new word." Attica glanced toward the jagged rise leading back to the third tier. "Let's get up there. See what Vespasia has to say."

He shifted the child in his arms, tucking her close, one hand pressed firmly against her back. His shade climbed ahead in darting bursts, anchoring to ridges and broken ledges, guiding them upward. Each foothold came with a crunch of stone and a ribbon of dust trailing into the dark.

The girl didn't make a sound. She clung to him, her small fingers curled in his collar, breath warm against his neck.

By the time Attica crested the top, his arm ached from holding her steady, but the climb had steadied something in him. He stepped forward and exhaled slowly, not from strain, but from everything that had just happened.

What have I done? he thought again as the child shifted in his arms, head resting against his shoulder like she belonged there.

She was quiet now, so calm that he didn't want to call out for Vespasia. He whispered her name instead, which of course, woke the child.

"Eli?" the small girl whispered.

"No, no Eli. You are *not* Eli. I don't want to tell you that you're a monster again—"

The mist thickened, swirled, and parted. Two pale hands emerged from the swell of darkness. One hand lifted, pulling back a dark hood. "The Lone-Eyed Wolf returns," Vespasia said. Her red eyes flared on the girl in his arms. "Not what I expected."

"I'm not sure what I've brought," Attica said. "Or what I just did."

"I'm not fully certain what you've done either. As I've told you before, my purpose is simple: to guide the exiled to the Gate of Whispers."

"And the gate only exists on the third tier?"

"Correct."

"But you've been to the ninth before. The bottom."

She didn't answer right away. "That's not what matters now. What matters is this—what you've done. I didn't expect you to spare the child. But you did." She studied him a moment, voice softening. "You need to speak with Duchess Corvenna."

"Corvenna doesn't speak," he reminded her.

"She will when necessary." Vespasia's eyes lingered on the child. Then, without another word, she floated back, the mist peeling away around her. "Have your shade lead you to the nearest portalstone. One isn't far from here."

"My shade?"

"It can sense them, you know." She paused, her gaze distant. "Did you truly think I was going to hold your hand through all of this?"

The child giggled again. "Eli!"

"Is that the name you've given her?" Vespasia asked.

"No. Absolutely not. She keeps saying the name."

"She is Lightborn," Vespasia said, and this time her voice held something colder. Not fear but something older. Caution worn thin by memory. "Whatever innocence she wears now, it is borrowed. You'll soon learn what that means."

Attica stiffened. "Maybe you could tell me."

She turned, just slightly. Her voice softened this time, though her expression did not. "Your Codex. It didn't tell you anything?"

"It did not."

"Then you'll need to speak to the duchess, as I've already told you. Unless you want to head past the fourth tier and find someone else who might know." Her eyes traced around his form. "Trust your shade. It will guide you. And take care of her in the meantime. She may be Lightborn, but she is still a child."

"Why else would I have brought her here?" Attica asked.

But Vespasia was already gone.

CHAPTER FIFTY

Attica stared into the mist, agitated for a number of reasons. He hadn't expected Vespasia to hold his hand, but he knew she was capable of parting the mist with her whispers, which would make the journey easier.

But that part didn't bother him as much as what he had done back in the fourth tier. Not only had Attica made an enemy in Gwendalyne and the Centurions, he had also done exactly what he told Eve he *wouldn't* do. He had spared the child of light, and now . . .

"Eli," she said with a cute hiccup. She covered her mouth, surprised.

Attica clenched his eye shut and groaned. "You don't understand me anyway. You are Lightborn. You have no knowledge of the common tongue. But you do," he said to his shade, which curled around him. "And the Mother of Whispers claims you are able to lead me to a portalstone. So by all means." He motioned to the path ahead. "Lead."

His shade uncoiled from his legs and drifted forward, its form almost human now—floating, legless, shivering with intent. It turned northwest and moved without hesitation. Attica followed—it was impossible to see more than a few feet ahead. Even on the first tier, where every ridge and tower had once been familiar, this kind of fog would've turned the world into guesswork.

The child murmured in his arms as he came to a flat stretch of uneven stone, parts of which were smooth, as if they'd been polished. Occasionally, his shade peeled back and surged forward again, as if testing the path for danger.

"Good," Attica told his shade. "And . . . thank you."

He glanced down yet again. The child clung gently to his side, her breath warm against his collarbone. This thought caused him to pause for a moment as he realized something he hadn't thought of yet.

She's breathing . . . like me . . .

Attica examined the child. "Eli?" she asked.

"Stop." He refocused on his shade, which curled toward a narrower pass, marked by the ruins of an ancient settlement. Old columns rose into the air here, some collapsed into others. They were made from cracked stone, worn and slick in places with lichen-like decay.

His shade hesitated at the fork then took the rightward bend.

Attica kept on its tail, shifting the child in his arms. "I'm trusting you," he reminded his shade as they pressed on, through the long-abandoned settlement.

His shade thrummed as it came to a sudden stop. Its body bristled, flattening outward, tendrils raising like hackles. A soft, silent resistance.

Attica's gaze drew taut. "What now?"

The shadow didn't move. It just held position, firm, blocking him from advancing. Attica frowned. "There is nothing to fear. Why have you stopped?"

No response. He stepped forward anyway, right through his shade's resistance. It relented, but not without tension. He could feel it in the drag against his boots, the way it clung to his calves like cold water.

The mist ahead parted as Attica pushed through to a narrow clearing, wider than most of the paths they'd crossed. At its center: strips of flesh laid out like ritual bones piled, and a makeshift cutting board carved from what looked like a pelvis bone.

A Brethren camp.

Attica froze.

Four figures rose from the far side in layered armor with helmets made of jaw fragments, every plate darkened with soot. No women among them.

The tattooed hunters stared not at Attica, but at the glowing child in his arms.

She blinked back at them, face calm. Unafraid. "Eli," she said playfully.

"What are you?" their leader asked, his voice sanded down to something harsh.

"I am exiled. I have the permission of your Seer to pass," Attica said, figuring it would be worth an attempt.

"What is it that you carry?" the man asked him.

"What does it look like?"

"Eli," the child said with a giggle.

The Brethren drew their weapons. Shadows poured from their arms, spiraling into organic blades, hornlike and serrated.

Their leader spoke. "You carry a Lightborn child. Even if you have been granted passage by our Seer, which I would have to confirm, you harbor the enemy. There is only one kind of punishment for this sort of blasphemy."

Attica didn't move, not yet. The child leaned her head against his chest again. *Four against one*, he thought as his shade strengthened around him. *Four against one who has drunk the Painter's blood.* Attica cleared his throat. "It would be unwise—"

The Brethren surged forward, spinning with their blade-grafted limbs. Attica shifted the child to his off arm and moved in tight, his shade exploding outward.

The first lunged, weapon high. Attica ducked, drove his knee into the man's gut and spun him to the ground with a crack of bone and shadow.

"Eli!" the child of light shouted with glee.

Another Brethren came from behind. Attica blocked the swing. His shade whipped around and slammed the man flat.

The third Brethren bore down on him, taller, heavier, his weapon more like a fused hammer of bone. Attica stepped into the strike, rolled the child slightly in his arms, and summoned a spear that pierced the man's throat.

The fight stopped for a brief moment as Attica held the man there. He cast his arm aside and let him fall to the side in a heap.

Their leader's eyes filled with rage. "You killed—"

"I didn't want this," Attica said, chest rising and falling with fury.

The three remaining Brethren didn't exchange glances. One of theirs had died by the hands of another. There was only one response that was appropriate and Attica knew it was coming.

The first Brethren charged; Attica speared him clean through, the man rising and falling. The child of light giggled again, soft and bright.

"Quiet," Attica told her as the mist thickened—no longer fog, but a tide, rising around them like breath from a vast, unseen mouth. It swallowed the world in slow gulps, until Attica could see only shadows, only shapes. The air hummed with pressure, like something ancient was shifting just beneath the veil.

Another Brethren lunged, head low to guard his throat. The shades clashed with a hiss like tearing cloth. Attica stepped into the chaos, shadowblade drawn. He phased through the strike—a clean swing that should have ended him—and emerged behind the man, cutting him down with finality.

"I warned you," Attica said as he turned to their leader, the man nearly completely obscured by the mist. Attica shifted the child's weight over his arm, prepared for the fight to get worse, when the ground beneath them changed.

Not a rumble. Not a quake. A *pull.*

The mist poured down the slope behind them like a slow wave, cold and vast. The air turned sharp with pressure. His shade flared, not in aggression, but in reaction.

Attica turned just as something titanic shifted through the fog—light coiling within it like breath trapped in glass. It didn't walk. It drifted, vast and deliberate, swimming through the mist as if the Spiralrealm were water and it had always belonged.

There were no legs. Only the slow undulation of veiled fins, trailing like torn banners through the haze. Its body stretched on forever, all ridged curves and overlapping mass, like the knotted spine of a drowned cathedral.

The Brethren leader turned—just in time to see its mouth open up.

The fog folded inward, and he was gone, swallowed whole.

Codex Entry Unlocked!
Name: Mistwhale
Origin: Tier III Legend-Class Entity
Known Strengths:
– Massive size allows it to swallow targets whole; movement near silent within deep mist
– Emits strobing bioluminescent pulses across its body that can disorient, entrance, or trigger memory lapse
– Able to phase in and out of dense fog, vanishing entirely from sight and shade detection
Known Weaknesses:
– No confirmed weaknesses
Classification: T-III | Rank S | Cog 3 | Leviathan
Notes: Widely regarded as a myth. Records suggest these beings are tied to deeper phenomena in the Spiralrealm. Approach with awe—and caution.

Attica's shade stopped moving entirely, like prey beneath a hunting sun as the mistwhale turned its focus on him.

The child reached out, small hand extended, palm up. "Eli," she whispered.

The mistwhale didn't respond. It simply hovered there, watching. Then, slow as a dying breath, it turned.

Its long, translucent tail shimmered like starlight as the mistwhale vanished into the gray, leaving the world changed forever.

CHAPTER FIFTY-ONE

Even with the mistwhale gone, Attica remained tense, blade drawn, child in one arm. He stood there, his shade tense around him as he relived how the massive flashwraith had just swallowed a man whole. Before him lay three dead Brethren, their deaths something no one would ever have to know about yet something he would have to process.

I killed my own kind for . . . He looked at the child of light.

"Eli," she said.

This time, he ignored her mimicry. "You stopped that thing," he said, awe-struck by what she had just done. "You waved your hand and it . . . it stopped. What are you?"

"Eli," she said again. She noticed a glint of something around his neck and reached for Dayanne's necklace.

"No, that's not for you." He wanted to hate the child, yet there was some-thing about her that he was starting to begrudgingly like. And she seemed to need him in the same way Eli had, the way a child needs a parent.

He looked up at the hazy sun as he realized he hadn't asked Vespasia about Eve and Tiago. He had been so wrapped up with the child of light, and the fact that he had brought her to the third tier, that he hadn't asked about his companions.

"Eli?"

"Eve is going to hate you," he told the child. He turned his focus to his shade. "How much farther to the portalstone?"

His shade buzzed in a positive way, a sensation Attica had long since come to recognize.

The trek took no more than thirty minutes. Thankfully, the direction veered away from where the mistwhale had vanished; Attica didn't think he could handle another surprise like that.

He reached a small pile of stones—nondescript, just like a hundred others he'd passed. The portalstones didn't glow. They didn't hum. Not yet. But when he waved his hand over them, the glyphs on them glowed and they lifted and locked into place, forming a gateway of shadowed stone.

Attica stopped just shy of stepping through. He was told he couldn't bring Eve or Tiago through, but he had never tried. Would the same hold true for the child?

"I'm going to set you down," he told the child, lowering her to the ground.

Her gaze rose to meet his as sadness bloomed across her face, swift and silent.

"I don't think I can bring you through."

"Eli?" the child asked, on the verge of what Attica knew would be tears.

"She can go through," Vespasia said, the hooded woman stepping out of the mist and once again startling Attica. "I thought I was clear about that earlier."

"Have you been with me the whole time?" Attica asked.

"You seem to think that I constantly surveil you."

"No, it's not that, I'm just wondering if all the mist and whispers are somehow connected to you."

Her red eyes shifted into something that resembled pleasure. "You're learning."

"My companions? Where are they, and more importantly, how are they?"

"They are at your settlement and have taken it upon themselves to bury more of the dead and mark their graves."

"So you're telling me they're safe. Were they able to drink any of the Painter's blood?" Attica asked as he lifted the child again. He bit his lip as he awaited Vespasia's answer.

"No, I'm afraid not. All they found was the flask. But that doesn't mean there isn't more out there. And there are certainly more whispers. Have you been listening to them?"

"I've been busy."

"The more you aid, the better chances you have of collecting the shards. You aren't the first exile to get lost in the spiral, you know."

"I'm not lost. I had a mission," he said, lifting the child in his arm, "and . . ."

"And?"

"And now, I don't know. I'm following your advice by taking her to the realm."

She gestured a pale hand to the portal. "Then follow away."

Attica pushed through the arch created by the portalstones, mist giving way to light. He emerged onto the main stage of the Realm of Recumbency, which floated in an endless abyss, platformed steps suspended in the void, lightless and vast.

The forge crackled faintly on one of the platforms. Kairos stood beside it, sweat glistening along his bald head as he worked a curved fragment of carapace into something harder, darker. He glanced up as Attica approached and wiped his hands on his apron.

"Stop sending flickercrabs," he said, still focused on his work. "The lightfeaster you sent? Nasty bugger, and missing some parts, but—" He looked up and saw what was in Attica's arms. The hammer nearly slipped from his fingers. "You . . . found it?"

Near the steps, Sebastian placed flat white stones into a ring. Luther sat beside him, watching how he placed them, a smile on his face. It was only after he placed the last form that Sebastian glanced at Attica, something shifting behind his fox mask. "What is that?" he asked, pointing.

Luther seemed equally shocked. "How did you—?"

Vespasia appeared beside Attica, the Mother of Whispers born from the quiet seam between breath and mist. Her form coalesced from the air itself, sharper now, more solid than usual. She pressed her hood back and bowed slightly to Sebastian. "The child of light's name is Eli," she said.

Attica shot her a glance. "That's *not* her name. She just keeps saying—"

"Eli," the girl said, tapping her chest with one finger. "Me . . . Eli." She laughed at this.

"She speaks?" Kairos asked as he took a step closer, the smith clearly visibly uneasy with what Attica had brought through.

"Just one word," Attica said. "Two, now."

"Me, Eli," the child said.

"Fine," Attica told her. "You . . ." He looked down at her, at the innocent bright smile on her face. "You can be Eli. I can't believe I'm saying that."

"Welcome to the Realm of Recumbency, um, Eli," Sebastian told her. "I would say choose a platform, but perhaps, well, perhaps you could choose one at a later time."

"Eli!" she chirped.

Vespasia moved past Attica. "Sebastian, we need to speak to your mother."

He blinked. "The duchess does not—" His mouth fell open. His masked face tilted down as his feet lifted an inch from the stone, arms slack, back arched in a way that made his hump even more visible. A low, breathless sound escaped his throat—half gasp, half inhalation. Then, a voice spoke through him. *"Vespasia."*

"My sovereign." Vespasia dropped to a knee and stayed there for a moment before she floated back to her feet and gestured toward Eli. "The exile has come across something."

Above the fountain, the duchess remained perched on her strange throne, unmoving and expressionless, yet her voice echoed through her son's lips as she spoke: *"It has always been considered a false prophecy. If the crown were ever shattered, the Painter's grace cast aside, the color would leave the Spiralrealm, and the only way for it to return would be through a Lightborn child."*

Sebastian's head tilted, eyes blank as he looked down at Eli, who looked like she was mere seconds away from falling asleep in his arms.

"*But we know now that this is not the case,*" the duchess said through her son. "*The only way to restore order and color would be through the Crown of Shadows, uniting the shards. The child in your arms isn't the only one. There have been others born of light. None have lasted. None have restored color to the Spiralrealm. They grow. They change. And when the light matures, they become what they truly are.*"

"What they truly are? What do you mean?" Attica asked the duchess.

"*Eli will not stay a child for long, Lone-Eyed Wolf. The girl will age. And when she reaches adulthood, she will become a monstrous flashwraith. The most monstrous.*"

A quiet ripple passed through the realm, causing the stones Luther and Sebastian had stacked to fall.

Attica's grip on the girl tightened just slightly. "How long does she have?"

"*It has happened to every child of light since the shattering of the crown, since its shards were distributed, stolen, and stolen again. This is why it is widely considered a false prophecy. She has a year, maybe less. That is the time before she changes. And while you can bring her here, she cannot stay here. What you do with her now is your choice, Lone-Eyed Wolf.*"

"She's powerful. She has already done things like stop flickercrabs and . . . and . . ." He hesitated, the image vivid in his mind. "She stopped a mistwhale."

Sebastian staggered and dropped to his knees, one hand pressed to his chest, eyes wide with alarm. "What just happened?" he asked.

"Your mother," Luther said gently, still seated at the base of the steps. "She spoke through you."

Attica slowly turned to Vespasia. "You really didn't know this? You, who scours the tiers?"

"About the children of light? I knew," she said. "But I've been instructed by the duchess to bring any and all anomalies to her. That is all." Mist rose around her feet, slow and pulling, a tide slipping over stone. "I am not your guide, Lone-Eyed Wolf. I never was. And I've already helped you more than I've helped others. My task is eternal. I lead the exiled to the Gate of Whispers. That is all I will do going forward. For you, or for the next exile. Friend or not."

Attica said nothing as she faded away.

The child looked up at him, her expression dim with confusion. "Eli?" she asked, blinking. "Me . . . Eli?"

CHAPTER FIFTY-TWO

Attica held Eli, the weight of Duchess Corvenna's words still heavy in his chest. There had been other children of light, enough to falsify the prophecy.

The only way is to get the shards . . . Eli is destined to die, he thought, still in shock he had actually agreed to call her that. He took in the Realm of Recumbency, the endless void of the space as he glanced from the expressionless duchess to her son, Sebastian the Limp, the masked boy already rejoining Luther at the stairs.

She only has a year. Maybe less . . . Attica didn't know what to do with that part of what he'd just learned. He had already made enemies by protecting Eli. And if she truly was destined to change into something monstrous, then every bridge he burned along the way would be for nothing.

Yet when he looked down at the child, he still felt the urge to protect her.

Eli.

Not *his* Eli, but an Eli all the same, an innocent child who had named herself. The duchess's revelation had been heavy—but she had said the prophecy once promised a child of light would restore color and order to the Spiralrealm.

Maybe the prophecy wasn't false after all, maybe it could still come to pass . . .

And if I could be part of that . . .

Eli placed her head on his collar bone. The soft essence that clung to her seemed to settle against the dark pulse of his shade, as if they'd always belonged together. What could have become a quiet moment, one in which Attica wondered even more about what he had done, was interrupted by Kairos.

The smith approached, the big man wiping his hands on a blackened cloth sticking out of the pocket of his apron. "You look like you're trying to stitch up a wound with nothing but thought. Don't. Place her there," he said, motioning toward Luther and Sebastian. "Place her there with the boys. Come with me."

Attica hesitated, but eventually stepped toward the base of the platform and gently lowered the girl beside Luther and Sebastian.

The child of light blinked at them, curious about the game they played. "Eli," she said. "Me . . . Eli."

Luther smiled at her. "Hello, Eli, I'm Luther, and this is Sebastian."

"Eli," she said, pointing directly at the fox mask.

Sebastian hesitated. "You . . . want me to take it off?"

"Eli!"

Luther glanced up at him. "I've always wondered why you wear it."

"I'll show you some other time," Sebastian said, voice quieter now.

"Eli!" She swiped her hand forward, knocking over a small stack of white stones with deliberate defiance. The tiny collapse scattered across the floor.

Luther groaned. "That took me forever to make."

Eli pointed at the mask again. Sebastian looked at her for a long moment, then glanced toward the throne where the duchess sat unmoving.

"Come on," Kairos said, gesturing for Attica to follow him again. "Let's talk over here." Once they reached his platform, the big man returned to his place behind the worktable. "The lightfeaster bone is good, but if you want armor that'll last longer than a single tier, something to take on the duke, I'll need better material. Flareback. Lightfeaster. Maybe even a wretch."

"Got it," Attica told him.

Kairos leaned closer. "But if you do plan to go after that bastard's shard, you really want something that will last, bring down a mistwhale."

Attica raised an eyebrow at him. "Have you ever actually seen one?"

"Alive? No. But I've seen its bones. The duke has quite the collection, you know. And with it, I could forge something for you that would help. Your shade can shield you, sure. And you've taken hits most couldn't, Painter's blood and all that. But you'll need more. Bring me the bones of a mistwhale and you'll be surprised what I can do."

"Just like that, huh?"

Kairos shrugged. "Just like that."

"I watched that thing swallow a man whole. It appears to be able to vanish and reappear on a whim. Not to mention it moves in the deep mist of the third tier, nearly impossible to track. If we're being honest, I don't even know how to kill something like that."

"Then find someone who does. There are whispers, and some of them used to forge weapons. In fact, I happen to know a weaponsmith out there, somewhere on the third tier, an old colleague of mine named Joan."

"Did you say Joan?" Attica asked.

"That's her, best I knew when I was alive. I don't know where you'll find her, but that's where she used to work, at the Brethren's settlement when the duke was in charge."

"I . . . I actually know her."

Kairos placed both of his big calloused hands on the table and leaned forward. "Do you, now?"

"She helped me get into the Brethren's settlement when I needed a few drops of Painter's blood."

"Did she?" Kairos said, interest sharpening in his voice.

"It was her, Joan, I swear it," Attica said, recalling the voice that had guided him to the settlement, and later, scouted ahead once he took the hidden passageway.

"Good, that'll make things easier. I suspect if you listen closely enough, you'll hear Joan's voice among the sea of whispers. Just ask for her name when you're ready. Now, the mistwhale. Maybe I'm just being greedy. I'm definitely being greedy. Or maybe I want a real challenge. I also want that. But bring it down, and I'll make you something worth wearing. Like any artist, I want materials that carry potential."

"Noted."

Kairos paused, his expression tightening slightly. "Speaking of which . . ." He scratched the side of his nose, squinting thoughtfully. "Yeah. I think I can swing it. Made something like it before."

"Made what, exactly?"

"A sheath," Kairos said, grinning. "Though you don't need one for the kind of shadow weapon you carry. You need one for a child."

"So I don't have to constantly carry her," Attica said. "That would be helpful . . ."

"You're catching on. Between the bones you sent and a bit of fabric, it won't take long. Just give me a few minutes."

"That fast?"

"What can I say?" Kairos asked with a shrug. "I'm good with my hands." Using a blend of stitched hide, reinforced thread, and a lightweight bone frame, Kairos began working on a child harness—part sling, part shell.

While he worked, Attica descended to the main platform, then emptied and refilled his gourds in the fountain. He lingered a moment, watching Eli as she played with the stones, tapping them together in odd, rhythmic patterns that seemed to amuse her more than anyone else.

Sebastian folded his arms, clearly annoyed. "She's doing that on purpose."

"She's just playing," Luther said without looking up.

"Eli . . . me!" she said joyfully. Attica offered no comment. Instead, he wandered to the other side of the platform.

The Realm of Recumbency and its numerous platforms stretched far in all directions, stone islands adrift in the void, connected by paths that shimmered only when you stepped near them. Some were simple, flat, and bare. Others bore strange shapes: partial arches and half-built thrones.

Attica ascended a narrow set of stairs and ended up on a small circular platform. Empty, quiet. A fine layer of dust coated the stone, undisturbed.

He stood there for a moment, his cloak stirring faintly in the windless space as he looked across the vastness of the realm. Other platforms drifted in the distance—some near, others so far they melted into the void. All were unoccupied.

Attica moved to Luther's platform. He approached the bookshelf, where the ledger sat open, its surface shimmering faintly. He turned to a blank page and the ink began to move, starting with a crude sketch of the flickercrab.

Flickercrab – Tier IV | Rank D | Cog 0 | Swarm
Burrow-dwelling crustacean native to Tier IV's lower stonework. Shell resembles lichen-covered shale, near invisible when still. Startled flickercrabs emit a pulse of searing light—harmless alone, but devastating in clusters. Chain-triggered bursts can disorient and expose travelers to greater threats.

A shieldwraith took shape on the next page:

Shieldwraith – Tier VII | Rank S | Cog 1 | Engineered
Obelisk-born construct cloaked in seamless armor, impervious from all angles but one. Emits a piercing light beam through a single central eye—lethal within moments. Some variants wield tendrils, retractable and precise, used to impale or crush. Core destabilizes if the eye is breached.

The final entry was for the mistwhale, which had Attica wondering the same question he had wondered once Kairos told him he could use its bones: *How do I kill this thing?*

Mistwhale – Tier III | Rank S | Cog 3 | Leviathan
Colossal entity said to drift through the densest fogs of Tier III. Body pulses with strobe-light bioluminescence, disrupting memory, perception, and will. Can vanish from all senses without warning. Can swallow prey whole. No confirmed weaknesses.

When he returned to the forge, Kairos was fastening the final knots of the harness. "Ah, perfect timing!" he said as he showed Attica the harness.

It was shaped to cradle Eli snugly along Attica's back, secured by two cross-latched bands across the chest and one adjustable strap at the hip. A curved neck brace kept her from slumping while she slept. Even better, the design allowed Attica to swing the harness forward when needed—letting him check on her quickly without unfastening the rig entirely.

Attica nodded, impressed by his craftsmanship. "You're a genius."

"When inspiration strikes, it hits like a comet. Let's try it on, shall we?" he asked.

Attica tested the movement, sliding the frame around to cradle the girl in front of him, then back into place. The weight was centered, his arms free. "This will really help."

"That was the plan."

"Thank you."

"Thanks for the challenge. A mistwhale, if you really want to challenge me, bring it. And don't forget to find Joan."

"I'll see what I can find," Attica said, remembering he could use the portal-stones to return to the third tier's earlier location. *But before I go looking for Joan, I need to check on Eve and Tiago . . .*

Attica heard Eli giggle. He looked over and saw her knocking over the boys' white stones again. Sebastian scowled. Luther just laughed.

He watched them a moment longer. Eli looked so small. So innocent. But the light within her was growing.

Someday, she would be a threat.

The duchess had warned him—he could not simply leave her behind. *Whatever I do next . . . and whatever happens when I face Eve and Tiago*, Attica thought, *I won't be able to undo it.*

And still, he approached the child and took her into his arms.

CHAPTER FIFTY-THREE

Attica stepped through the portal with Eli secured tightly to his back, her small weight steady in the bone-framed harness. Bone-gray mist licked at his boots as he emerged onto the fractured edge of the third tier near the Gate of Whispers.

The fog path split ahead; his natural instincts told him that it would eventually lead him to the cliff wall that would allow him to scale up to the second tier.

"I thought you said you wouldn't help me," he told Vespasia under his breath as he started on the path. "Thank you, anyway."

The whispers came once he focused, faint and distant. Attica paused for a moment, wondering how he would pick Joan the weaponsmith out of the crowd. It seemed impossible, but he got the sense that if he sat there for a moment, he would be able to distinguish her voice from the others.

Maybe it's simply a matter of asking and receiving . . .

Or so he hoped. Attica had his shadowblade, and Ravelstrike was certainly a power that would come in handy once, and if he decided to deal with the duke. But he had a feeling he would need more.

He'd seen what the fourth tier offered.

Lumenbrides. Wretches. Lightfeasters.

There are bound to be other things, he thought.

The path cracked beneath his boots, the stone dry and uneven, as he followed the break in the mist. Attica curved around an enormous black rock that hunched over a narrow ravine. The way it split the land reminded him of the giant from the settlement. The one Eli had once inhabited.

Attica still wasn't certain what that was, or what it had to do with her, and he certainly had no clue as to why it attacked the settlement. But he was convinced now that Eli, the girl curled silently on his back, breath warm, had nothing to do with that part. How could she? She was barely a toddler, even if she could say two words.

His shade spread out around him, scanning ahead as they neared the base of the second tier's climb. "This won't be long," he told Eli, who stirred behind him, small fingers pressing lightly against the fabric of his cloak.

She responded with a sniffle. Attica paused, instantly recognizing the sound. He turned the harness around to find her pouting, her lips parted like she was hungry.

"What do you eat anyway?" he asked as the answer came to him naturally. Attica took one of his gourds from his belt and uncorked it. He brought it close to her face so she could smell the essence, Eli's eyes glowing with delight.

"Careful now," he said, tipping it to her lips.

She drank, light pulsing faintly along her skin. Not a flare, not dangerous— just a shimmer of contentment, soft and dim. Her fingers curled around the rim as she fed.

"Good, good." Attica fought the urge to touch her. He'd held her often enough by now, but there was still a hesitation in him, like gentleness was something he'd forfeited.

"Good," she said, burping. Eli burped again. "Good. Me . . . Eli. Good." She continued laughing, and Attica couldn't help but smile at her.

Once, before his son was born, he had discussed what it would be like to have a daughter with Dayanne.

"She would be just like you," Dayanne told him at the time. "A Vanguard."

"Or a Spectralist like her mother."

"No, we have plenty of those, but Vanguard keep us safe, and that's exactly what she would do."

The memory twisted in his chest, sadness filling his heart as he remembered the conversation.

Eli burped again and laughed. "Good, me . . . Eli. Good!"

"You are . . ." Attica couldn't call her a monster this time, not with the way she was looking up at him, content, her eyes starting to blink as sleep came over her.

"Rest," he whispered, and his shade helped him reposition the harness. She tucked back into place, drowsy and warm.

The climb to the top came easy. His shade guided his footing, anchoring him across the steeper ridges. Attica moved with care, whispering once or twice for it to take extra caution with the child on his back.

He reached the second tier, the mist thinner here.

Attica recognized Turtle Rock the moment he saw it—its wide, flat face jutting from the fog like the snout of some buried creature. He and the other Vanguard used to carve into it after long climbs.

"Let's take a look," he told Eli, even though she had started sleeping. He approached the rock and effortlessly moved to the top, where he found the carving he'd made six years ago. It was a crude portrait of Dayanne, etched with the blunt edge of a black stone he had picked up below. "Remember this?" he asked his shade, which patted him lightly as if to confirm it had.

He let out a deep breath and noticed that the child was lightly snoring.

"Things were good," Attica said to himself as he walked to the other side of the rock and stopped. A massive form shifted in the clearing ahead, heavy and unmistakable.

Codex entry unlocked!
Name: Flareback
Origin: Tier III Apex Type
Known Strengths:
– Explosive nodules across back and shoulders can detonate at will, releasing blinding bursts and searing heat
– Capable of consecutive detonation, producing a spontaneous combustion
– Some have exhibited shock-wave stomps that release radial blasts of light
Known Weaknesses:
– Nodules are volatile; precise strikes can trigger fatal chain detonations
– Reacts poorly to deep shadow interference—shadow veils reduce effectiveness of flare bursts
– Limited agility; can be misled by decoys or struck from elevated positions
Classification: T-III | Rank B | Cog 1 | Brute
Notes: Avoid engaging in open ground without coordinated support.

It was surrounded by flaylights, but less than Attica had seen before.

Codex Entry Unlocked!
Name: Flaylight
Origin: Tier I Symbiote Type
Known Strengths:
– Swarm behavior triggered by disruption or aggression near host creature
– Emits flickering light pulses that can alert nearby flashwraiths
– Mild contact burns; can singe exposed flesh and temporarily blind if swarmed
Known Weaknesses:
– Extremely fragile; easily destroyed with minimal force
– Lacks independent intelligence; reliant on host for direction and protection
– Drawn to high-mana signatures, making them predictable once identified

Classification: T-I | Rank F | Cog 0 | Swarm
Notes: Commonly cluster around high-threat flashwraiths.

He tried to take cover, but the beast had already sensed something. It grabbed a stone and hurled it in Attica's direction, his shade pulling it out of the way in time.

Rather than head for cover, Attica dropped into the open, summoning his shadowblade as the creature's nodules pulsed red hot across its back. Its skin there cracked like molten glass, waves of heat pouring off it in bursts.

If it explodes . . . he thought.

"Eli," he said as he prepared to engage the monster. "Now would be a good time to work your magic!"

No answer.

The flareback stomped, and a ripple of light scattered across the ground, throwing sparks into the haze.

"Eli!" he said again, voice sharp. But she didn't answer.

There was a time when Attica would have never risked taking on a flareback alone, a time when he would have, his shade slingshotting him forward, as far away from the gargantuan flashwraith as it could.

But things had changed.

I guess it's on me, then, he thought as the flareback surged forward, claws carving trenches in the rock as it continued to swell with light.

Attica vaulted to the side as a flareback's attack scorched the ground. His shade whipped around him, forming a veil of darkness that blunted the worst of the heat, but he still felt it tear across his face like a furnace wind.

He landed in a crouch, jaw tight.

"Eli?" the child asked, stirring.

"Good! How were you sleeping through this?" Attica asked as he dodged left, barely escaping another shock-wave stomp that sent a radial burst of light crackling through the tier. The stone fractured. Pale grit scattered.

An opening presented itself—Attica lunged forward and struck upward. His shadowblade dug into the flareback's underside but didn't pierce deep enough.

The big brute spun fast, faster than it should have for its size.

Attica's shade came to his rescue.

It slammed into the monster, briefly separating from him. His shade snapped back to Attica as he produced a spear from the palm of his hand, just at the moment the nodules on the flareback's body began to boil, their lights intensifying.

He unleashed the spear, which slammed into the largest nodule, dead center.

The detonation was immediate.

Attica stepped back as the flareback ruptured—light surging along its spine, flashing white in a rising sequence of muffled thunderclaps. The flashwraith buckled, its form twisting as it fell in a blaze of scorched bone.

"Eli? Eli, good?" the child asked.

"No. Eli not good," he said, coughing. "Eli was very much *not* a team player back here."

Behind his back, Eli shifted. "Eli . . . good. Me . . . good."

"I don't know how your powers work," Attica told her as he approached the flareback, its nodules still smoking. He touched the creature and sent its corpse to Kairos back in the Realm of Recumbency. "That should give you something to play around with," he said for the smith.

"Eli?"

"No, Kairos. And don't worry, you're good." He spun the child around to take a look at her. "You are . . . a good girl."

She giggled and reached out to his face. "Good."

"You are going to be the death of me. Aren't you?"

She laughed again, her hand still reaching for his face. Attica bent his head slightly toward her. Eli ran her hand over his nose and stopped at the place where his eye used to be.

"Eli," she said, her head tilting slightly. "Eli."

"This is an eye," Attica told her. "Or it used to be." He pointed at his other eye. "Eye."

"Eli."

"Eye."

"Eli."

"You'll figure it out one day," he told her. "And if what the duchess said is true, that day will be closer than we think."

She said her name again and smiled. "Good!"

Attica could make the final climb to the first tier in his sleep. He knew this stretch of the Spiralrealm too well, the ridged slopes that curled like folded strata. This particular section of the first tier had practically been shaped by the harsh weather and years of Vanguard patrol. It was like walking across a memory, dulled by dust and quiet.

"Home," Attica told Eli once he stepped onto the cliff. "Can you say home?"

"Eli?"

"My home," he told her, a hint of sad pride in his voice.

"Home," she said, sounding the word out. "Home."

"Good."

"Good."

He shifted her so she could take it in. Attica touched his chest and swept it toward his surroundings. "This is my home, the first tier, the highest up from the bottom, if that means anything to you. I'm guessing it does." He frowned as he looked out over the gray stones—barren and pitted like the surface of a dead moon. Craters pocked the slope, their rims broken, their centers long cooled. Nothing moved. For a moment, it seemed like even the wind had forgotten this place.

"Me home."

"No, you are not home. I don't know where your home is. I am home," he told her, "*Me* home. My home." He touched his chest again. "Me."

"Eli . . . home?"

"Eli's home is somewhere much deeper," Attica said.

"Home," she said as he transitioned her onto his back.

"Yes, but not yours, mine. And you . . ." He was about to tell her she should be familiar with this place, but he did not. Attica had seen her there during the destruction of the settlement, but the more he came to know the child, the less he thought she would be capable of something terrible like that.

Instead, he started walking, boots scuffing stone. His breath steady, his mind not. He glanced toward the dim horizon. The path ahead was short, but the conversation that waited wasn't.

His shade moved beside him in low, cautious loops, like it could feel his hesitation.

It knew he was stalling.

"What am I even going to say to her?" he asked under his breath. He walked in silence for a few more minutes and then answered himself. "I could just tell Eve that I found a prophecy. That I fought for it. That I brought it here."

The child of light. Eli, he thought, envisioning the look on Eve's face once she heard what he had decided to call it.

He would try his best to explain everything that he knew, how Duchess Corvenna had called the child of light prophecy *false*, that Eli's predecessors hadn't lasted long enough to change anything. But that he didn't fully buy it.

Couldn't there be two ways to restore color to the Spiralrealm? The child or the shards?

More importantly, this was what Dayanne would have wanted. She had told him that night; he was convinced now what she had said. *When the time comes, you must protect the child of light.*

And if Attica was destined to take on stronger and stronger flashwraiths, it would be good to have Eli at his side. The girl had stopped the mistwhale with nothing more than a glance. Yet she had done nothing when the flareback charged . . .

She doesn't have the proper training, Attica thought, pushing ahead. *And when she gets older, I can train her myself.*

He envisioned what this may look like as the terrain leveled, stone giving way to a black-gray soil that was almost like clay.

"Here we are," he said aloud, more for himself than her.

The smell hit him—smoke and iron and death, long settled but never forgotten.

The settlement beyond would never heal. Collapsed towers, gutted buildings, ash-scattered paths—his childhood home was ruined beyond repair. The corpses were gone, the bones buried. But the scars remained.

"Home . . ." Attica stepped over a broken support beam, boots crunching against old debris. The air smelled of soot and memory. Nothing here had healed, not really.

Then: footsteps echoing fast.

He looked up just in time to see a streak of white hair dart from the far side of the ruin. "Attica!" Tiago called out. "He's back!"

Attica froze, heart clenched.

He wasn't ready for this.

Not for them. Not yet.

But Tiago reached him in seconds, breathless, smiling in that crooked way he always had when relief hit before the logic of a moment could catch up.

"How did it go?"

"It . . . went," Attica said, voice quieter than intended. His words hung strangely in the air, too brittle, too unfinished.

Then he saw Eve.

She followed behind Tiago, shoulders tight, face unreadable as ever, fierce as ever. Her eyes sharpened. They swept over him in full, top to bottom, scanning for blood, for damage, for anything out of place.

She didn't see the child yet.

Not fully.

But her head tilted. A flicker of caution passed across her expression. The shimmer around Attica's shoulders, faint, pulsing, was hard to miss.

"Attica," she said, slow and wary.

"Hello," he replied. The word felt wrong in his mouth. Too ordinary for what was coming. "Look, before we get into it, there's something I need to show you."

And then, like a stone dropped into still water:

"Home!" the child called from behind his shoulder, voice bright, delighted. "Me home!"

Eve's mouth dropped open in horror.

CHAPTER FIFTY-FOUR

Just hold on," Attica told Eve, slower this time—measured, controlled. "I need to show you something." His voice was steady, but every part of him was braced. This wasn't going to be easy. Not with Vanguard, especially with the fact their shades certainly knew by now what he was hiding behind his back.

"What are you trying to tell us?" Eve asked, her tone clipped.

Tiago opened his mouth, a question forming, but Attica cut him off with a raised hand. "First," he said, "you have to trust me. Trust that what I'm about to show you isn't as . . ." He searched for the right phrase. Found nothing that fit.

Eve's eyes narrowed. "What have you done?"

"Nothing yet," he answered. His shade tightened around him, a brace of silent resolve. Coiled, waiting. "And I'd prefer to keep it that way. Something has changed. I've already spoken with Vespasia. I know that—"

"Home!" The child's voice pierced the tension.

"Attica," Eve said, her voice sharpening, darkness flaring around her. "What is behind you?"

"Eli?" the girl whispered. "Eli . . . good. Eli home."

That was all it took.

Eve's expression changed, but not toward softness, not the same way Attica was certain Dayanne would have reacted if he had shown up with a stray. She would have knelt, asked the child's name, checked for injuries, even while the world burned behind her.

Dayanne had carried warmth like other people carried knives, other people like Eve, who had been raised for war from an early age.

Eve's instincts were armor, not shelter.

Strength was what she offered. Mercy was something she'd never been taught to hold, and it was also one of the reasons she was spawning her weapon now.

Attica had been forged the same way, trained to deny mercy, yet here he was with a Lightborn child strapped to his back, his eye locked on the whipsword uncoiling at her side, the weapon gleaming like oil in fractured light.

"Don't," Attica said. His voice held steady. "Eve, you don't understand. Neither of you do. Not yet. Just let me explain."

"You brought the child of light . . . here?" Tiago asked, his tone veering into disbelief. "Why would you? Why?" His eyes bounced between them. "Am I missing something? Is this a hallucination caused by the Painter's blood?"

"Let me show her to you first," Attica told them both. "You know me. You both do. She's safe." He stepped forward slightly, hands open. "I wouldn't bring something dangerous. Not to you and not here. Not to the settlement." He gestured to the broken ground around them. "I was born Vanguard. I spent most of my life here on the first tier. You know I'd never betray that. Just give me a moment. Let me explain."

He reached behind his shoulder. His shade moved with him, loosening the bindings of the bone-forged harness. Attica swung it forward, slow and deliberate, until the child faced them fully.

Eli blinked and her golden eyes sparkled. Light shimmered faintly across her skin. She smiled and reached a hand toward Tiago. "Me? Eli."

Tiago staggered a half step back, his shadowdaggers forming with a sudden flash.

"Speak clearly, Lone-Eyed Wolf," Eve said, raising her blade at him. She had only ever called him this once, in a sparring match in which she lost her temper.

Attica held his ground. "Weapons down, *now*. I'm going to tell you both everything. And then you can decide how you want to handle it."

"You really brought it here." Tiago's voice cracked—disbelief, but more than that. *Betrayal.* He looked at Attica not as a comrade, but as a man watching his hero fall.

"Eli . . . Good . . ." the child said, confused by the tension.

"I'm only going to tell you once more," Attica said, his voice low, just above a growl. "Put your weapons away. You're not going to kill her." His eye locked on Eve's. "You'd have to kill me first. And you're not going to be able to do that."

That stopped them.

The wind moved through the broken beams of the ruined settlement, catching loose dust, tugging at cloaks. No one spoke for a breath. Then, slowly, Eve and Tiago's shades began their retreat. Weapons dissolved into smoke and silence.

The standoff unraveled—not with peace, but with a grief threaded through the stillness.

Eli tilted her head. She giggled, as if none of it had touched her. "Eli good," she said brightly. "Me good! Home? Home!"

The sound scraped against the silence.

Eve stared at Attica, her mouth agape. Her face changed, not with rage but something closer to despair. "What have you done?" she finally asked, her voice frayed, trembling.

A single tear ran down her cheek, clung to the edge of her chin, and fell. Yet she maintained her glare. "Why have you let this thing bewitch you?"

"She—"

"You named the little monster Eli? Shame on you!"

"She named herself—"

"How would she even know how to say it if she hadn't heard it from you? Have you lost your mind? That thing is a *flashwraith*. A monster."

"Monster?" Eli asked. "Monster. Eli, monster? Eli, home?"

Tiago blinked, unsure now, looking to Eve for direction. But she had none to give. Her shade flared in agitation as she turned in place, pacing sharp lines into the dirt. "You . . ." She finally stopped and turned to Attica. "You need to go."

"I came here—"

"To what? Show us the baby flashwraith you took it upon yourself to adopt?"

"Hear me, Eve."

"I've heard enough. That thing destroyed our home." She gestured madly at the settlement. "You and I both saw it. You swore to kill it. You had not one, but two chances now. And you show up with it strapped to your back? Where did you even . . . ? That doesn't matter. You need to go. You need to go now."

"Eve, at least let me explain why I spared her. At least let me explain what I learned from the duchess who created the Realm of Recumbency."

"Explain—" Eve started.

"Actually," Tiago said, interrupting her, "we should hear him out. I don't trust the thing either, but we owe him that."

"Me? Monster? Eli monster?" the child asked.

"Shhh," Attica said as his shade helped him return Eli to his back. "Here's what I know, or what I was told: There is a prophecy that a child like this will help restore color and order to the Spiralrealm. Thus far, this hasn't been the case. There have been others, but they weren't able to do so."

"And you think this baby will somehow be the one?" Eve asked. "What about the shards?"

"The crown is the other way. And she won't be a baby for long," Attica said. "She will age to adulthood in a year, and that's . . . that's about all the time she has."

"What aren't you telling me?" Eve asked, her voice splintering.

Attica couldn't hide the grimace that formed on his face. She knew him too well. They'd grown up side by side, shaped by the same shadows. He couldn't lie to her. Not well.

"What I'm not telling you," he said slowly, "is that at some point . . . she might turn into a monster. But—"

"What?" Eve hissed. "Say that again."

"Eli? Monster?" the child asked softly from his back. "Me . . . monster?"

"No, you're good. Eli good. Eli is not a monster. Let me finish," Attica told both of them. "I'm going to try, Eve. Dayanne—"

"What does she have to do with this?"

"The night she gave birth. She drank from the Seer's flask and had a vision. I didn't remember it until I came into direct contact with the child. But now I do. Dayanne said I had to protect her."

Eve stepped closer, her expression twisting. "You'd believe a ghost over what you're seeing with your own eyes? Over what we *know* now? The Lightborn is a false prophecy. The child is a curse. You said it yourself—she'll become something else before the year is out."

"I know," Attica said, his voice hoarse. "But I have to try."

"Dayanne was hallucinating, Attica. Just like Tiago was when we gave him two drops from the Painter's flask."

"I still have to believe her."

Eve folded her arms, the woman trembling with disgust. "Really? You believe a ghost over me? After everything we've seen? Everything we've been warned about?"

Attica didn't answer right away. Then, with a steady breath and lifted chin: "I've been changed by all this. You know that. And I think Eli can change things too. If there's even a chance that she's the key to restoring color and order to the Spiralrealm, I have to take it. If that means chasing shards across the Spiralrealm, prying them from the dead grips of mad dukes and fallen duchesses, then so be it. If it means descending to the ninth tier, then I'll go alone." He looked down. Then back up. "And if it becomes clear that she can't help . . . that she *won't* help . . . then I'll do what has to be done."

"You'll kill her?" Tiago asked quietly. "Attica, I don't want to doubt you, but—"

"You've already had two chances," Eve cut in. "And you didn't do it."

She stepped in, voice taut. "You really think after raising this . . . this thing for a year, you'll have the strength to end it? You think you'll even want to?"

"You don't need to worry about that," Attica said, steady but low. "If it comes to it, I won't let her suffer. If she turns into a flashwraith, that's exactly what will happen. She'll suffer." He looked away. "I won't let it happen."

Eve shook her head. "I don't know what to tell you. But I'm not going to babysit that thing with you for the next year."

"I figured," Attica said. "And maybe that's for the best. At least until one of you drinks the Painter's blood. Vespasia told me there are more options out there, if you keep searching."

"We can do that," Tiago said, once Eve didn't answer. "Catch up to you. Powerwise."

Eve said nothing. She turned, ran a hand through her hair, and faced away—shoulders tight, fists clenched.

"How would we even find you?" she asked. "There are nine tiers."

"Go to the third," Attica said. "Call for Vespasia. She'll hear you. I'll ask her to. She claims she isn't helping me . . . but she always shows up when I need her most." He paused. "If either of you drink from the Painter's flask, you'll be able to speak to her directly." And with that, he turned to leave.

Tiago stepped forward, cautious now. "Wait."

"Yes?" Attica asked.

"Let me see her again."

Attica turned the harness, lifting Eli gently so Tiago could see. The child's light caught in his eyes, reflecting in their dark centers like twin stars. "She looks just like a Shadowborn child," Tiago said quietly. "But made of light."

"She does," Attica replied.

Tiago nodded once. "Good luck. I guess. I . . . I don't know."

He shifted back to Eve, who still hadn't moved. She stood with her back to them, fists clenched, eyes fixed on some point beyond the ruins. She didn't speak. Didn't turn.

Attica waited a beat longer than he needed to.

Then, slowly, with more regret than he could ever remember bearing, he walked away.

And this time, no one called out to him.

CHAPTER FIFTY-FIVE

The wall between the first and second tiers was no stranger to Attica's boots, especially with the help of his shade. It moved ahead of him, easing the climb, gripping ledges where his balance faltered. He descended with practiced ease, his eye shut against the wind and grit, letting his thoughts drift behind him.

The child didn't stir, her silence a rare gift.

But the shame Attica carried was not. It clung to him like smoke that wouldn't lift—bitter, cloying, impossible to shake. He had vowed to kill the child. Twice. And both times, he'd failed to follow through. If he'd truly known Eve and Tiago, truly understood the limits of their faith in him, he should've seen their reactions coming.

Eve was never going to go along with it, he thought as he started his trek across the second tier. *And Tiago? Who knows? He might have been just foolish enough to join me, but now . . .*

He hadn't expected forgiveness from Eve. He hadn't even asked for it. But he had still hoped. And Tiago—he'd said nothing cruel, not outright, but the weight in his stare said enough.

They'll move on, Attica thought. *Maybe someday they'll understand, and when that time comes, they know how to contact me.*

Behind him, Eli stirred with a soft yawn.

"Shhh," he murmured. "Let's not give ourselves away. In fact . . ."

". . . Eli?" she asked, still half asleep. "Monster?"

"Yes, good. Eli sleep. Eli not monster. Eli sleep."

"Eli . . . sleep."

"Good. Another word. An important one. Sleep, child," he told the girl. Attica focused on his shade. "It's time. Go ahead and check our passage to the edge. I'd prefer not to have any encounters if we can help it. Not right now, anyway."

Attica felt the presence of his shade leave him as it rushed ahead. He closed his eye. And was presented with a limited perspective of what lay ahead. It was still familiar enough territory, and there didn't seem to be any flashwraiths in their path.

His shade returned and curled itself protectively around him.

"Good," he said. "Let's keep going."

They crested a low ridge, a blackened rise where the terrain opened in a swath of land with deep pits. Attica paused. Below them, the second tier unfurled— bone-pale stone broken by deep fractures, ash-thick paths twisting through clefts in the land like veins beneath burned skin. Fog huddled in the hollows, slow-moving and strange, curling around the remnants of structures long lost to collapse.

Attica scanned the horizon.

There.

A flicker, then another.

Small bursts of white against the gray signaled a herd of flashwraiths. Judging by the size and rhythm, probably a pack of emitters, but there could be a glint-fang as well. Maybe one larger among them, a flareback, something shielding the others. And there were definitely some flaylights.

He watched the pattern. No sharp detonations. No erratic pulses. They weren't agitated, and he didn't plan to draw their attention.

"We keep moving," he told his shade.

It buzzed in a way that told him it agreed.

Attica pressed on until the edge of the second tier came into view, sheer and jagged, broken in parts from a landslide long ago. He began his descent. His shade gripped a narrow outcrop and helped vault him downward, catching his weight when his boots skidded on loose gravel.

Eli shifted once in the harness, then stilled. No sounds, no mimicry. Just breath against his back, warm and rhythmic.

The fog of the third tier reached Attica before his boots truly found solid ground. The world felt heavier here, damp and hungry. Moisture clung to every surface, which glistened like something that refused to dry.

Attica paused for a moment, his hand naturally coming to the polished pearl with red rings around it that Dayanne had once worn. He glanced up through the veil of murk toward the sun, barely visible through the gloom.

I hope you've set me on the right path, my love, he thought. His fingers closed around the pearl.

Tight.

Then slowly, he let go.

Attica dipped his head and listened. The whispers came almost immediately— threading through the stones in soft currents, brushing his ears like wind that knew its way through bone.

Not speech, not truly. More like memory trying to form a sentence.

Some were faint. Others much louder. Another wept. And one warned him about visiting the third tier.

"Joan?" he called back, his voice cutting through. He tilted his head back and closed his eye. He tried calling for the weaponsmith again. "Joan?"

Then, a reply. Faint, westward. Barely audible.

"That's her," Attica told his shade as he set off. "This way, and be ready. There are bound to be other flashwraiths on the third that we've yet to encounter."

"Eli?" the child asked. "Eli . . . sleep . . ."

Attica fought the urge to turn the harness around and check on the girl. "Yes, sleep," he whispered. "Just like that."

He moved through the dense fog, every step soft, deliberate. Light scattered like abandoned kites, slicing through the haze without direction or warmth. *The mistwhale could very well be out there*, he thought, recalling the enormous beast. "Shhh . . ." he told Eli before she could make another sound.

"Joan," he called again, the whispers swimming in and out of his head.

"I'm here," came a reply, not as far away as he would have thought. He followed her whisper through the rockfall and the dead flora, around bones that no longer remembered what shape they once belonged to, and the markings of a crumbled outpost, ramparts etched with crude carvings.

The mist coalesced slowly, drawing itself into the shape of a long-limbed woman wrapped in threadbare robes, a leather apron buckled over them, her sleeves rolled to the elbow, hair pinned off to one side. Unlike Kairos, her presence felt more anchored here. Attica could almost see her clearly, her features brushing the edge of recognition.

Joan drifted forward, the tips of her sandaled toes skimming just above the stone, untouched by the Spiralrealm. "You're back," she said. "And curiously . . . you have a companion."

"Yes, Eli," Attica said.

Her voice cut through the fog again. "Odd to see Shadowborn with something that is clearly Lightborn. The other whispers are all curious. You are the talk of the tier, for what it's worth. Yet you call my name."

"You told me your name when we first met, but you never told me what you once were," Attica said.

"What do you mean?"

"The duke's weaponsmith. Back when he ruled the settlement. Kairos said that was you."

"I suppose I didn't mention that, but to be fair, you never asked."

"I had access to the realm then. If I'd known . . . I would have invited you."

"And now?" Joan asked. "What brings you back to me, Lone-Eyed Wolf? What piece of my forgotten life have you uncovered?"

"Kairos mentioned that you once served Duke Tiberion Astor."

Joan paused. The mist around her pulsed faintly, contracting inward.

"He was a cruel master," she said at last, her voice quieter than before.

"So I've heard," Attica said. "That's why I'm here."

"Is it?"

Attica's shade curled tighter around his legs. "I need a weapon," he said. "Kairos said you were the right person to ask."

The fog pushed closer to him, the outline of her face intensifying. "You need a weapon to kill the duke?"

"Not immediately. First, I need armor. Kairos wants me to bring him the bones of a mistwhale so he can forge it. What I do with it after remains to be seen."

"And when the armor's done?"

Attica didn't hesitate. "Then the duke."

Her presence darkened subtly, the edges of her form thinning into vapor. "Did he do something to you?"

"He sent his trained pets after me. Nearly had me killed on the fourth tier. I don't plan on giving him a second chance."

"And what do you want from him?"

"A shard. One of the crown's. Kairos said he keeps it embedded in the head of a mistress, mounted like a trophy."

Joan made no sound at this, but she did recoil slightly.

"I already owe you for first leading me into the Brethren's settlement," Attica told her. "I haven't forgotten. So tell me—what would it take to bring you to the Realm of Recumbency? To forge me a weapon worthy of killing a mistwhale . . . and a duke?"

CHAPTER FIFTY-SIX

I believe I told you before that I don't need anything from you," Joan said, the space around her folding and refolding in restless swirls.

"Then you will come to the Realm of Recumbency with me?"

"Gladly. If Kairos is there, it shows me that you are a trustworthy individual. But that doesn't solve the problem of your weapon."

"What do you mean?"

"Kairos needs the bones of a mistwhale to make a unique armor set, yes?"

"That's right."

"And I need something if I am to create a dark essence weapon worthy of battling someone with a shard. Specifically, I need a particular type of black ember." She swept her misty hand in the direction of the Brethren's settlement. "It is enshrined in the Painter's church."

"The Painter's church?" Attica remembered passing it once, the building angular and with a stained-glass display on the second level.

"Yes," she said. "Bring me that, and I will be able to help you."

"Gladly. Can you lead the way to the hidden entrance? I don't think walking up to their gates with Eli will be the best way to approach."

"Just a few words," Attica replied, his gaze steady on the whisper. "But she's a fast learner. Let's keep it at that."

"I see." Joan drifted forward, her form curling into a ribbon of mist that slipped between broken rocks and slick earth. "In that case, follow me."

He did so at a distance.

Eli was quiet now, her warmth pressed against his back like a fading ember.

They moved west, away from the broken spires and ash-streaked monuments that marked the edge of the tier. The path wound wide, deliberately, across terrain littered with shattered pylons and stone relics sunk half deep into the earth. Rotted beams jutted from old ruins, and every so often, the fog peeled back just enough for Attica to glimpse old etchings on boundary posts, long since worn down by time and absence.

He kept his eye moving, watching the ridgelines above for movement.

They were too close to the settlement now. He couldn't risk being seen. Not after what he'd done. Not with Eli glowing faintly against his spine.

Would they know? Probably.

Especially with the Brethren's Seer whisper-bound to this tier. Especially with the way Attica and the child's presence seemed to linger now in the air between voices.

The idea of approaching the main gate with a Lightborn child on his back was almost laughable.

I might be able to use Shade Swarm and Shadow Phase, he thought, *but that doesn't mean I can take on an entire legion of shade-armed men . . .*

The land pinched narrowly ahead, and the stone rose with it—a bluff of jagged obsidian veined with old crystal scars. The path bent hard toward the cliffside, where petrified trees leaned like sentinels and runoff from old floods left gouged ruts in the rock.

Joan came to a stop.

The entrance was just as Attica remembered.

Hidden in the stone's shadow, half swallowed by crumbled rock and moss. A narrow tunnel yawned beyond it, choked with dust and silence. It led downward—into a forgotten basement in the Brethren's settlement, a place no longer in use.

Joan said nothing. She didn't need to. Attica adjusted Eli's harness, glanced back once at the fog behind them, and stepped forward.

"Their Seer will know you're coming," Joan told Attica. "He speaks with whispers, and while I certainly won't say something, others may."

"I assumed so. We will cross that bridge when we get there. First . . ." Attica squinted up at the sky. "We wait until it is a bit darker."

"I will be here," Joan said as she vanished.

"Eli?" the child asked once she was gone.

"Yes, Eli. We break for a moment, and prepare."

He knelt and unstrapped the harness. Eli stirred, blinking in the dim. He set her down gently and watched her wobble upright near the tunnel entrance.

She took two steps forward then floated, her legs dangling above the ground.

"Yes, I know you can float," he told her. "But you should also be able to walk too. Stay here." He brought her down to the ground, where she stood on two feet again. "Hold her steady," he told his shade. It wrapped around her gently, anchoring her in place.

Attica took ten paces back, then turned and gestured for Eli to follow. "Come here."

His shade let go, and Eli drifted forward, a few feet above the ground.

"No, that's cheating," Attica said as he approached the girl again. "Walk. I'll help you." He took her hands and positioned Eli with her feet on top of his. "Like this," he said as he showed her how to walk. "And I keep forgetting you need clothes. I don't actually know how that would work. Your skin is made of the same material as a flashwraith, which would burn normal clothing. Kairos will know what to do."

"Me Eli?"

"Yes, you're Eli."

She looked up at him with big eyes. "Eli . . . good?"

"Eli is getting better. Walk." Attica helped her walk and repeated the word again.

"Eli . . . walk?"

"Yes, good!" He stopped and handed her back off to his shade. "Let's try again," Attica told her as he took a few steps away.

"Eli, good?"

"Yes," Attica said as he motioned for her to catch up. "Help her," he instructed his shade once she started to wobble. Eli caught herself.

"Walk," she repeated as she neared Attica. "Walk!"

"Yes, walk, good!"

"Eli good walk." She kept at it, wobbling in a wide arc, circling back to face him again.

"Good, good," he told her as he sat cross-legged and gestured for her to sit with him.

Rather than sit in front of him, she floated forward and lowered into his lap.

"At least let me get some essence for us," he said as he produced his gourd. Attica took a whiff of it, satisfied with how recharged it made him feel. He brought it to her lips and she drank some.

"Good."

"Yes," he told Eli, "it is good. And later . . ." Attica looked up at the sky. *Technically tomorrow*, he thought. "Tomorrow," he said aloud. "Tomorrow, early in the morning, Eli, quiet."

"Too-mar-row?" she echoed as she stared at him with big bright eyes.

"Today." Attica to the sun, which was starting to vanish into a lightly glowing orb as it always did at night. "To-day. Sun. Bright. Tomorrow. Next sun. I'm probably trying to teach you too much," he told her quickly. "Tonight? Later tonight? Forget that part. *Quiet.* That's the word I want you to understand." He raised a finger to his lips. "Shhh, quiet. Say it with me, *quiet.*"

Eli covered her mouth with both hands. Wide-eyed.

"Actually, yes," he said softly. "That's it."

"Quiet?" she asked, muffling her mouth.

"Yes. Quiet. Tomorrow, quiet." He spread his hands to show the shape of the red-ringed sun and how it dimmed through the Spiralrealm's cycle. "Tomorrow, quiet."

"Tomorrow," she said, more certain this time. "Eli. Quiet."

"Exactly."

He tapped his chest. "Now—me. I sleep."

She mimicked him, touching her chest. "Eli."

"Yes, you are Eli."

"Eli . . . monster?"

"Eli is not a monster, yet," he said under his breath.

She pointed at Attica's face. "Eli?"

"No," he told her as he realized what she was asking. "I'm . . ." He didn't know what name to give himself. Not Attica. Too sharp. Not Lone-Eyed Wolf. Too long. And certainly nothing like Father.

"Eli?" she asked again. She pointed from herself to Attica.

"Wolf. You can call me Wolf." He touched his chest. "Wolf."

She smiled. "Wolf. Eli. Wolf. Home."

The words hit him harder than he expected. He looked away, tried to breathe through it.

"Sleep," he said, quietly. "Eli, sleep. Wolf, sleep."

Rather than remain on the ground in front of him, she hovered forward and relaxed into his lap, warm and certain. The night pressed in around them, but for the first time in days, Attica didn't feel like it was closing.

Sleep wasn't going to happen, not with what lay ahead.

Attica watched the sky darken further, the red-ringed sun pulling tighter into itself above the Spiralrealm as he came up with a plan when he inevitably encountered a Spectralist.

Joan said the Seer will know I'm coming, and he'll probably send Mara . . . Attica had never been great at lying; he didn't have that kind of cunning, not like some of the other Vanguard, people like Cassian, who once romanced two Spectralists for years, neither aware of his actions until it all boiled over in the end.

I think it makes sense, though. A child from the settlement . . . Attica glanced at Eli, who was back in her harness now, her breathing steady, her small frame radiating a powerful warmth that never faded.

Or I could just leave her here, resting. Just for an hour. Sneak in, deal with whatever comes, and return. Long enough to get in, get the ember, and leave.

No.

He knew he couldn't abandon her like that. But he couldn't smother her beneath his cloak either—not without risking her light bleeding through the fabric and catching a passing glance.

There was his shade, which could shroud her, but only for a little while, and never completely.

The basement might be the solution. I could leave my shade there to guard her, or Joan could, and head to the Painter's church, retrieve the ember, and be done with this question. But I'll still have to lie to Mara and whomever she brings.

With the help of his shade, Attica positioned the harness on his back.

"Eli?" she whispered. "Wolf, Eli?"

"Yes, Wolf and Eli are going," he told her. "Eli quiet. Remember?"

"Too-mar-row," she mumbled, half asleep. "Quiet."

"Quiet. Now, quiet. Shhh . . ."

"Quiet." Eli's head settled near his shoulder blade, warm and soft.

"Good, let's go."

Attica took the narrow path through the hidden break in the wall, the tunnel just as he'd left it—tight, damp, and quiet, the stone walls slick with condensation and ancient carvings. The air smelled faintly of earth and rusted metal, as if the Spiralrealm itself was sweating.

He moved carefully, ducking lower with each step until the ceiling forced him to crawl. Attica grimaced, but kept going, grateful for his shade as it extended protectively around Eli, shielding her from the scrape of stone and the weight of the dark.

"Thank you," he told it as he finally came to the stone ladder that led up to the basement.

Attica slid the stone aside and pulled himself up. "Eli, quiet," he said.

She didn't reply.

"Good."

He had just begun to adjust the harness when his shade flared—an instinctive warning.

Then the entrance to the cellar door creaked open. Mara stepped into the room, half shadowed at the top of the stairs. She tilted her head as she looked him over. "Your mask is gone."

"It is," he said.

". . . I didn't expect for you to be missing an eye."

"You are blunt."

"Sorry," Mara said as she placed her hand on the back of her neck. "But I have to ask."

"Yes?"

The Spectralist studied him from the landing. "You were given passage. Why sneak? The Seer doesn't understand. And what is that glow behind you?"

"I brought someone," Attica said carefully. "And I need you to—"

Her eyes narrowed on his harness. "What's behind you?"

"What I'm going to show you may cause alarm but, um, believe me, she's just like us," Attica said, going with the lie he had devised. "You have to trust me." He unfastened the strap and carefully swiveled the harness around. "And your Seer would know of her presence already anyway."

Eli blinked at the light, her head lolling slightly. "Eli good."

Mara gasped.

"She's not mine," he said quickly, "but she is a survivor from my settlement. I am responsible for her—"

"Wolf, Eli? Home?" the child asked, sleepy-eyed.

Mara started to back away. "This feels. . . ."

Attica cut in, his voice low, worn. "The Mother of Whispers told me where to take her."

Her mouth tightened. "I don't speak to whispers. The Seer does."

"Then ask him," Attica said. "Or don't. But I need to go through, *now*. You have to trust me, Mara. I don't want this to get out of hand."

The moment hung between them. Cold. Weighted.

Attica tensed. "Please, Mara, you have to—"

Her foot clipped the edge of the stair. She stumbled, caught herself, and turned.

"Don't—" he called as she started to flee. Attica gritted his teeth. "Do something," he told his shade, who lunged ahead, slick and fast across the stones.

Mara screamed, sharp and loud, piercing the hush.

It was too late now.

The warning had gone out. The Brethren would come. And Attica still had to reach the church.

CHAPTER FIFTY-SEVEN

Attica didn't slow once he heard Mara's scream. His shadow darted ahead of him, pulling her into the basement shadows.

"Please," he said, realizing too late how this must have looked as his shade pinned her down.

"Do it, then. I'm not afraid," she spat, glaring over at him. "I will die for the settlement."

"I'm not going to kill you, Mara. I need something from the church. I—"

There was movement outside. Attica could hear it.

He stood there for a breath, listening. *Another bridge burned*, he thought as Mara spoke again. "They will not let you take anything. Your best bet, if you value your life or the life that . . . that Lightborn monster . . . would be to leave the way you came."

"Eli . . . monster?" the child asked.

"I promise Mara, as strange as this seems now, this will make sense someday." Attica's shade dragged her aside and held her down as he took the stairs to the exit. He reached the top and cleared the doorway and went directly into the Brethren's settlement.

"Wolf?" Eli asked, the child jostling against his back, sleepy, confused.

"Wolf is good. Eli, stay quiet."

Attica turned toward the path he'd once taken with Mara and the other Spectralist, boots striking the stone with force as he ran. The church wasn't far, but neither were the Brethren. Their voices chased him, sharp and rising, echoing through the narrow streets.

He wove through alleys of the settlement, the route half memory, half instinct.

His shade pressed close, scanning ahead, urging speed. By the time he reached the front of the church, the Brethren were already there, waiting.

Three of them. Then five. Shadow weapons forming down their arms as they swarmed toward him.

Attica's own shadowblade took shape. There were no warnings. No words. Just the sudden appearance of more enemies as the Brethren emerged from the alleys, circling fast.

"Eli?" the child whispered.

"Do not worry," Attica told her as the first Brethren lunged. He ducked under the swing, countered, drove his blade in shallow and slipped free before the Brethren's blue blood could slick his grip.

Another came from behind.

Attica twisted, his shade forming a second spike that pierced the man clean through. He placed his other hand on the man's face as he fell, Attica slamming the back of his head into the ground with the help of his shade.

More closed in.

Tendrils of darkness flared around him as his shade beat away enemy shadows. One of the larger of the Brethren surged forward, his shadow weapon a tree-trunk-sized club.

His shade tried to intercept, but it was stretched too thin, defending on too many fronts. The blow caught his shoulder, snapping pain through bone.

"Wolf!" Eli whimpered.

The big man swung again, and this time Attica was able to phase through it.

He stepped through him and twisted toward him with his shadowblade, where he was able to cut across the man's back. Ravelstrike finished it, the tip of Attica's spear bursting from the front of the big man's chest.

More Brethren rushed in. Another blow. Another breath. A cut across his arm.

Attica kicked the next Brethren attacker into the church steps, just as two more appeared from the far side of the chapel hall. "Lightborn!" one of them yelled. "Kill the Lightborn!"

Their voices were thunder now, echoing through the broken city. Their eyes were fixed not on him—but on the child of light glowing faintly across Attica's back.

He gritted his teeth and charged into the fray.

Attica fought like a storm collapsing inward, fast and absolute. The streets of their settlement filled with the sounds of shouts and the cries of pain as Attica moved into a protective, killing frenzy.

But it wasn't enough. There were too many. He couldn't shield her forever.

A shadow arrow slammed into his shoulder, striking the same place the club had bruised. Hands and shades closed in, tearing at him. Attica fought them all off as he fell to one knee, shielding Eli with his body.

"Get away from her!" he growled.

"Wolf!" Eli cried out.

The sound was small—but what followed was anything but. Light tore from her body blinding and absolute, a rupture in the world itself. It surged outward in silence, a shock wave of pure radiance that had no heat and no mercy.

Everything it touched ceased to exist.

When the light finally receded, it left behind a crater nearly thirty feet wide, the earth hollowed and scorched, edges fused to glass.

A few Brethren caught at the edge of the blast writhed in place, their bodies partially consumed, skin fused to armor, lips moving in slurred, broken prayers.

The rest were gone. Reduced to blackened silhouettes—burnt echoes stamped into stone, some frozen mid-scream, others with arms raised as if trying to shield themselves from the impossible.

The silence that followed didn't feel empty. It felt *accusatory.*

"What have you done?" Attica asked as he looked from Eli to his smoldering surroundings. He focused on her again, Eli staring up at him with all the love in the world.

Somehow she had spared him while leveling everything else.

He glanced around again, horror taking shape on his face as a new realization struck: *A baby did this* . . . It was worse than any flareback explosion, any targeted blast of essence. Nothing compared to the destructive power of what Eli had just unleashed.

"Let's get inside," he finally said, voice raw.

"Eli . . . Wolf?"

"Eli, good. Wolf . . ." Attica let out a deep breath. "Wolf, good enough." He took one last look at the vapor around him, the ash and light-burned bones. "There will be more soon," he told his shade. "Let's go."

Attica took the scorched steps of the Painter's church and shouldered through the opening. Once inside, he turned to check the crater, expecting to see more Brethren charging in, but finding nothing aside from burned bodies and plumes of smoke.

"Where is it?" he called, voice low and hoarse. "Joan, where is it?"

A curl of mist slipped from the shadows. He couldn't see her face clearly, but something in the way Joan watched him had changed. "Your child killed . . . I don't know how many."

"She's not my—"

"Eli?" the girl asked.

"She was protecting me." Attica moved past a pew and under an archway. "Where is it, Joan? I'm here for your ember, not to . . ." Another rough breath out. He looked down at his injured arm to see blue blood. *Refuel,* he thought as he went for his gourd.

He pulled his gourd free, took a long sip, and pressed on, listening as voices started gathering outside. *The Brethren are angry and afraid. I don't blame them,* he thought as he glanced back at the open doorway. No one crossed the threshold.

"Wolf . . ." Eli said quietly. "Eli good?"

"Good, Eli good. Quiet."

She had saved him. That much was true. But the way she had done it, Attica had no name for it. No scale to measure it by. It wasn't just power. It was finality.

"This way," Joan told him finally.

He pressed onward, following her voice. The church groaned around him, old beams shivering in the silence.

Don't rest. Don't assume you're alone.

He passed through the reliquary, vaulted and narrow, the walls carved with the third tier's mountains in sharp relief. At the end stood an altar, tarnished low to the ground with a silver box sitting on it. Joan's mist twined around it protectively, like a hand shielding flame, yet she couldn't lift it. "Here."

Attica approached slowly. He knelt, fingers trembling slightly, and opened the lid to find a black ember inside, a coal without fire, but not inert. He sensed an inner warmth that would soon be reignited. "Good," Attica said. "This is what we came for."

"Good?" Eli asked, her voice quivering.

"Do not worry. We will be out of here soon." He closed the box, tucked it under one arm, and tightened Eli's harness with the other. Her glow had faded, but not completely.

He looked toward the entrance of the church.

They will be waiting outside . . . Attica didn't need to use his shade to confirm this—he could hear them. And they knew it. They could likely see him as well, some able to send their shades forward.

Then . . . how?

He stepped back into the chapel's main hall and looked up at the stained glass above. "I think I found our exit. Make sure Eli is secure," he told his shadow.

Attica jumped, his shade boosting his ascent as he sailed up and through the stained glass and out onto the church's sloped rooftop.

The Brethren below shouted at the sudden movement on the church's roof as Attica took off running toward the nearest exit.

He jumped to a rooftop, nearly lost his balance, and continued as shadow arrows and barbed lines of dark essence streaked through the air.

Attica ducked one and parried another; his shade batted a few down as two men slingshotted themselves to the rooftop. He tore through one of the men and shoved him off the roof and to his death. His body moved faster than thought— muscle, instinct, training. But his mind was somewhere else, still catching up.

They wouldn't stop. Not after what they'd seen. *There's always Shade Swarm. But these are enemy shades. What would happen if . . . ?*

Attica took a running leap and landed on another roof, the tiles giving way. A shadow arrow struck right where his foot had just been as he continued his mad dash toward the outer walls of the settlement.

"Come on," he said as another Brethren landed. *Come on . . .*

His shade flared to match the man's shadow, allowing Attica to hit him with Ravelstrike. The man blocked it using a conjured shield made of dark essence, something Attica hadn't seen before. In doing so, the man left himself open for Attica to simply rush past him and vault to the next roof, a tower near the front of their settlement.

So close . . .

Attica jumped once more, landing on the far rooftop, his shade flinging him toward the top of the final wall. Fingers digging into mortar, boots scrabbling, Attica's shadow helped pull him up and over.

He dropped down in front of the Brethren's settlement. "Portalstone," he gasped to his shade. "Find one. Now. And thank you. Thank you for everything."

His shade didn't hesitate. It dove into the terrain, pulsing outward as it took control, half dragging Attica forward.

The mist thickened as they moved.

Behind him, shouting.

Behind him, Eli . . . laughing?

She doesn't understand what's happening, he had to remind himself. *What she just did . . . how many people she just killed . . .* Attica didn't look back. His focus remained on the terrain, the thick fog ahead, until he reached the outline of an old campsite, where he found a pile of rocks.

He staggered toward it.

"Here we are," he said as he held his hand over the portalstone. The rune-covered stone lifted of their own accord, forming an arched doorway, the Realm of the Recumbency beyond. "Joan?" Attica asked.

"I'm here," she said, her misty form appearing.

"Good, let's—"

A second whisper cut through her presence. Attica stepped back as an old man's face rose from the mist, cracked with age, his voice heavy as he spoke: "The Brethren know what you have done," the man said, "and what you have taken."

Attica froze, realizing this was a message from the Brethren's Seer.

"You are now our enemy, Lone-Eyed Wolf. We will hunt you until the ember is returned and the Lightborn monster is dead."

And with that, the whisper faded.

PART SEVEN

Wolf and Eli Hunt the Mistwhale

CHAPTER FIFTY-EIGHT

Attica stepped through the portalstone, the third tier collapsing behind him in a rush of mist and fractured light. He emerged into the stillness of the Realm of Recumbency, his shoulders still heaving from the sprint through the Brethren's chaos, his skin damp with sweat, grit, and lingering fear.

The air here felt too calm. Too measured.

The strange quiet of the place—its floating platforms, spiral staircases, and half-lit arches—felt dreamlike after the carnage he'd just survived. A place untouched by what hunted and often, what *he* hunted, in the Spiralrealm.

He stood still, breath tight in his chest, heart not yet caught up to the calm.

Then Eli stirred in his arms. "Home?" she asked softly. "Eli home?"

"Yes," Attica said, voice hoarse. "Home."

Beside him, Joan's form solidified—not as vapor this time, but rooted, real. The mist that once veiled her had cleared. She stood tall and long-limbed in her threadbare robes, the leather apron buckled neatly across her front. Her sleeves were rolled to the elbows, hands calloused, hair pinned to one side in quiet defiance of the realm's weightless quiet.

Attica handed her the silver box. "The ember," he said, his voice dry, scraped thin.

Joan took it gently, cradling it like something that still burned.

"Thank you," she said. "And believe me, as mad as all that was back there, it will be worth your time."

Footsteps echoed from above, soft but deliberate. Sebastian descended first, the fox mask catching the light. "I see you've brought another," he said, voice quiet, measured.

Luther followed close behind, arms already reaching. Attica unfastened the harness and passed Eli into his grasp, careful, steady—like handing over something sacred.

"Home?" she asked, more delighted now, her voice light.

"Yes," Luther told her, a smile creeping into his voice. "Home. Let's go play for a while." He carried her to the steps, where he had carefully stacked white stones into miniature terraces, creating a small imagined settlement.

Above them, the duchess sat unmoving, still as stone beneath her veil, draped in silence. Watching.

Attica exhaled, but the breath wasn't deep enough. It felt caught in his chest, like his lungs were still in another tier. "I need to sit," he said, mostly to himself.

Across the platform, Joan crossed to Kairos, who had already stepped down from his forge. He gave her a brief nod, his eyes drawn to the ember in her hands, but he said nothing.

Sebastian remained beside Attica. "If you need to rest, you should choose a platform. You can have one too, you know."

"You never told me that."

"You never asked."

"That's going to be your answer to everything, isn't it?"

"Only when it's true."

Attica smirked, weary but faintly amused. "I suppose the best answers come when they're needed."

"They do," Sebastian said with a shrug, the fox mask tilting slightly, unreadable.

"Anyway, before I find a place to rest, I'll update the ledger."

Attica climbed to Luther's platform and approached the bookshelf of the large leatherbound ledger. Two new entries took shape as he looked down at the blank page, the entries etched in shifting ink alongside rough sketches:

Flareback – Tier III | Rank B | Cog 1 | Brute
Apex-class brute lined with volatile nodules that detonate on command, flooding the field with light and heat. Known to chain-combust in rapid bursts or unleash radial shock waves through seismic stomps. Fragile nodules can be targeted for fatal chain reactions.

Flaylight – Tier I | Rank F | Cog 0 | Swarm
Symbiotic insectoids that swarm around larger flashwraiths. Triggered by sudden movement or aggression near their host, emitting pulses that signal nearby threats. Contact causes light burns; enough of them can blind.

Attica took another look around the Realm of Recumbency.

Rest hadn't been something he'd considered when coming here. But now, with the fighting behind him and the air around him still, the idea didn't seem so distant.

If there was peace to be had, even briefly, he would take it.

He made his way to the fountain and topped off his gourds. It had become part of his rhythm now, this quiet act of maintenance. A ritual.

And he was aware, acutely so, of how rare it was, how blessed he was to have access to what seemed like an endless flow of essence when most would die for even a taste.

As Attica sealed the second gourd, his eyes drifted across the open space, looking for a platform to call home. He chose the platform directly opposite the duchess, who hadn't moved, the woman still as carved obsidian, draped in her silence.

She holds court from the center, he thought. *Across from her feels right. Close enough to watch, far enough to think. I'll see everything from there.*

He climbed the spiraling steps and stepped onto the chosen platform.

A bed rose from its center—simple, wide, carved from the stone itself with a soft pad on top. Beside it, a throne-like chair emerged, turned toward the fountain and the endless fall of the Spiralrealm beyond. There were cushions, too.

Attica blinked. *Comfort? That's a surprise.*

He let out a breath and sat down. For a long moment, Attica didn't move. He just breathed.

The memories came in flashes—the Brethren surrounding him, the light Eli had unleashed, the crater it left behind. It had been beyond anything he'd ever seen. Not magic. Not combat. Something else entirely, something that would only make enemies.

The third tier wouldn't forget what she had done. Attica hadn't yet decided what to do with the feeling of having protected something that powerful— something he'd been raised to fear, even hate.

But he sensed there could be a breaking point soon.

Luther and Sebastian played with Eli down near the fountain. She laughed, her glow dimmer now as she waddled between them, her steps steady. She was walking instead of floating.

On the other side, Kairos had joined Joan at her forge, listening as she recounted what had happened, her quiet voice rising just enough for Attica to hear bits of it.

"Vespasia?" Attica asked aloud, slouching deeper into his new chair.

Mist gathered like kneeling servants, drawing close until her shape emerged at their center—hooded, still, and unmistakably sovereign. "You look comfortable," she said, her voice a quiet echo, like it slipped past his ears and settled straight into his mind.

"How come no one told me I get my own platform?"

"You didn't ask," she replied, echoing Sebastian.

"How are they doing?"

"Define *they.*"

"Eve and Tiago. I told them if they ever needed me, they could call out to you. That you'd let me know."

"And you assumed I would simply honor that?"

"I don't have another way to reach them. The third tier's dangerous, and they don't know what it's become."

Vespasia tilted her head slightly. "Where you've made quite the stir."

"And on the fourth."

"I can't recall another exile who's caused this much noise."

"It was never my intention to complicate anything."

A small grin tugged at her mouth. "Is that how you justify it? That it wasn't your intention? You arrive seeking revenge, and instead, you take in a child—one made of light—and turn two factions against you. Surely, you must have thought some of this through. Surely, you could have guessed how this might play out."

Attica's fists tightened, then loosened again. The throne was soft. And she wasn't wrong. "Life got in the way."

"That's what makes it interesting." She turned slightly, her gaze drifting toward the spiral horizon. "As for your companions," she continued, "they're fine. Still on the second tier. Resting near an ancient monument your people never explored."

Attica frowned. He knew the place.

A hollow stretch of stone tucked between ridges, long avoided by instinct and tradition alike. Few dared speak of it.

Attica had only seen it once—from a distance. Massive pillars jutted from the earth like broken teeth, blackened by time, carved with spiraling marks that shimmered faintly in moonlight. Cracked tombs littered the ground around them, many half swallowed by dirt and root, their openings shaped like mouths too wide to be natural.

Some said it was a sacrificial site from before the spiral fractured. Others claimed it was a tomb for something that never quite died.

It had always repelled him.

Even now, thinking of Eve and Tiago camped near its shadow sent a ripple of unease through his chest.

"Thank you," he said quietly.

"I take it they didn't like Eli."

"They didn't know what to make of her," Attica told Vespasia. "I barely do."

"You're not making many friends out there," she said.

Her words lingered longer than her presence. She vanished before he could answer—the Mother of Whispers dissolving back into mist, as if she'd never been there at all.

Attica sat in the quiet she left behind.

He let the silence stretch until footsteps echoed lightly across the stone. Kairos and Joan approached together, their conversation trailing off as they neared.

Kairos gave a faint nod toward the chair. "Looks like you've settled in."

"It seems."

He gave Attica a once-over and grunted. "Don't blame yourself. The Brethren had a choice. They could've listened. Isn't that right, Joan?"

Joan nodded. "You did warn them."

"Eli responded to protect you," Kairos said. "She cares for you."

Attica looked toward the fountain, where the child laughed as she fell into Luther's arms.

Joan's voice followed a beat behind Kairos's. "After some discussion, I've decided what to make for you. Something strong enough to kill a whale . . . and a duke. That *was* the request, wasn't it?"

"It would be ideal," Attica said. "Yes."

"Good." She didn't wait for approval. Turning away, Joan crossed the courtyard and stepped up to what would become her new forge. The stone shifted beneath her feet, rising and reshaping into the tools of her craft—racks for shadow-tempered molds, a low-bellows forge, and broad, heavy tables sculpted from glassy black stone. The air shimmered faintly around her, thick with potential.

Kairos stayed behind. "If you ever want to talk," he said, gesturing toward his platform, "I'm around."

Attica met his gaze. "I just need a moment. Thanks."

"Suit yourself."

Kairos turned and followed Joan, disappearing into the heat and hammer-song of her forge.

Attica leaned back into the chair and closed his eye. For the first time in what felt like weeks, he let himself rest.

CHAPTER FIFTY-NINE

Joan stood at the center of her platform, sleeves rolled up, apron ready to be streaked with soot. Something shimmered in her hand, sharp-edged and black, not a weapon, exactly, but the echo of one.

Attica, who had just woken up, examined her for a moment from his throne-like chair. He leaned his head back and stared at the endless expanse overhead, then pushed to his feet.

"Let's see what she's made," he told his shade as it curled tighter around him.

He crossed to her platform and found Joan grinning when he arrived.

"You finished it already?" he said as he smoothed his hand through his long dark hair.

She placed her hands on her hips, pride in her eyes, soot on her brow. "With an ember like this, I can shape quickly. I've been done for over an hour."

"I was asleep that long?" He blinked a few times and looked around.

"You were. And before you ask—yes. Bring me more embers if you find any, and I'll forge more."

"I wasn't going to ask."

"Well, now you know how this works."

"I was going to ask what this one is."

"A beauty, isn't it?" She lifted the artifact, admiring her handiwork. It looked like a gauntlet that was sleek and segmented, the piece crowned with an enormous crow's head at the end. The beak gleamed faintly, shaped of hardened shadow, ridged and serrated like the spine of a saw. "Slip your arm inside. Let it bind."

Attica obeyed.

The gauntlet unraveled into smoke and sank through his sleeve and into his skin, wrapping his arm in black filaments of essence that feathered out and disappeared. A pulse followed—a sharp hum of connection—as the crow's head reformed over his forearm.

A whisper of system text followed:

Name: Attica, the Lone-Eyed Wolf
Designation: Shadowborn – Tier I
Rank: Vanguard (Exile)
Shard Fragments: 0 / 11
Current Traits:
Shadowblade – Your weapon is born of will and shadow. Its shape reflects you.
Resonant Shade – You can extend your awareness through your shade.
Shade Swarm – Summon nearby shades to overwhelm a target. May fail.
Shadow Phasing – Press through surfaces.
Shade Devour – Absorb the essence of slain foes to empower your shade.
Ravelstrike – Unleash a tethered spear of shadow that extends in a blink and recoils just as fast.
Carrion Crow – Summon a shadow-formed crow that snaps, clings, or hurls you forward with predatory precision.
Echoes Granted:
Bone Tether Bracelet – Allows the bearer to mark slain foes by touch, instantly transporting their corpses to the Realm of Recumbency for harvesting.

"Carrion Crow?" Attica asked, flexing his fingers. Like his shadowblade, essence flowed down his arm—this time forming the outline of a massive crow's face. A feathered beak shimmered into shape, curved and jagged, already twitching like it could smell prey.

"Ever seen anything like it?" Joan asked.

"Can't say that I have."

"It's built for the kill—and the chase."

He said nothing, watching the crow's face re-form along his forearm, twitching again. It looked dangerous, almost sentient.

"Summon the beak with a flick of your wrist," Joan explained. "It lashes out and can snap through limbs, weapons, even tendrils of light."

Attica raised his arm. The beak extended with a crackle of condensed shadow. Light from the fountain below danced along its serrated edge.

"But that's just the first function," she continued. "It can also cling and grapple. Let's test that."

She gestured, and her platform responded. The stone rippled outward in perfect silence, widening, a feat Attica had witnessed once before—when Luther granted him the Ravelstrike.

But this time, it felt heavier. More deliberate.

From the far edge of the expanded floor, two figures began to form.

They rose slowly from the surface—shadow-forged emitters, hollow-eyed and thin, their limbs too long, torsos wrapped in layers of seared essence, like brittle armor. Their movements were twitchy, almost unfinished, as if they hadn't yet remembered how to exist.

Each pulse of their cores cast a low, sickly glow, a heartbeat of dark light that made their silhouettes shimmer against the stone.

They didn't breathe. They didn't speak. They simply stood there, waiting to be unmade.

"First: sever," Joan instructed.

Attica flicked his hand forward. The crow's beak launched like a striking viper and clamped down on the nearest emitter's neck. With a wet snap, the head was severed cleanly, and its body dissolved in a hiss of steam and scattered light.

Joan let out a short laugh, pleased. "Good. Just how I wanted it to work. Now for something larger."

The second emitter flickered once, then faded. In its place, the air churned.

A flareback took form—towering and broad shouldered, its frame layered in plated shadow muscle and lacquered bone. Volatile nodules bulged along its spine and shoulders, glowing faintly with unstable light. Every movement caused them to shimmer, pulsing with barely-contained detonation.

The ground beneath it cracked with weight, smoke leaking from its mouth in slow streams as it stared at Attica with a low, hungry hum.

Joan stepped back, folding her arms. "Try to cling to it."

Attica raised the gauntlet, the crow's silhouette forming again in shadow and shape. He felt the beak thrum with tension.

And then he let it fly.

This time, the beak didn't snap—it latched on.

He felt it lock, deep and brutal, embedding itself. The flareback flailed, but Attica held fast, dragged across the platform until he twisted loose and dropped to his feet. He stepped back, shaking out his arm as the flareback faded away. "I could see using this on a creature ten times that size. Whale-sized."

Joan smiled. "Exactly the point."

"And the third function clings?"

"Sometimes your shade is busy or strained. This lets you *move*, regardless."

She pointed across the courtyard to another platform.

"Grapple."

Attica didn't hesitate. He summoned the crow. It shot forward like a bolt and struck the far edge with a sharp crack. The moment the beak latched on, it pulled hard. Attica lifted from the ground, shadow trailing, and sailed across the gap. He landed with a thud on the opposite platform.

He heard a laugh below.

He looked down to see Eli clapping, Luther beside her. She bounced in place, pointing at him mid-waddle. Attica let himself smile—just a little. He used the crow to vault back to Joan's forge.

"So," she said. "You see how versatile it is."

"I do." He looked from the crow fading on his hand to the smith.

"You see how it could help you kill a mistwhale and stop the duke."

"I do. This is an incredible weapon ability, thank you."

She leaned against her table, smiling wide. "Then my work here is done. And Kairos will begin once you bring him the mistwhale. Good luck out there. I'm not the type to say you're going to need it, so I won't." She straightened. "But just know—I'm thinking it."

Eli giggled as Attica strapped her into the harness. "Eli? Wolf?"

"Yes, Eli and Wolf are going back out there," he said, resisting the urge to place a hand on her head. A father's gesture. Not yet. Not quite. He'd grown fond of the girl—far more than he wanted to admit. And that fondness wasn't going anywhere. But trust was another matter.

He didn't trust himself. Not with how he felt. Not with what she might become.

Even with Dayanne's voice in his memory, her instructions that night . . .

I just don't know, he thought as Eli looked up at him, those big bright eyes searching his face with quiet certainty.

"Home?" she asked.

"Yes," he said softly. "We're home."

Then, after a breath, "And in a way . . . we're going home. Another home."

She shuddered. "Monster."

"There will be those," he said gently. "There always are." *And none of them will touch you*, he thought.

"Eli good? Eli . . . bad?"

He blinked. "Who taught you that last word?" Attica looked over at Luther and Sebastian.

Luther only shrugged. "She learns quickly."

"Eli good? Eli bad?" she repeated.

Attica exhaled and gave in. He lifted her gently. "Eli good," he said. "Eli is a very good girl." He held her a moment longer. Then let go, allowing her to float in front of him.

He turned and looked back—first to Joan and Kairos, heads bent over their work. Then upward, toward the duchess, still seated. Still watching.

"Eli sleep?" the child asked as she hovered just a bit closer. His shade retrieved her and placed the girl in her harness.

"Sure," Attica said, just as the Spiralrealm's pull began to stir through the stones before them. "Eli can sleep."

Before he could step through the arch, he heard Sebastian call out to him.

"Wait," the boy said as he limped over.

Attica turned. "Yes?"

"You're going after the mistwhale now?"

"I am."

"It's not like other Lightborn," Sebastian said. "It's hard to track."

"I'll figure it out," Attica replied. "I've been tracking flashwraiths my entire life."

Something moved behind Sebastian's eyes. For a moment, his body shifted—feet rising just slightly off the ground, shoulders drawn low, hunch moving higher as his mask tilted downward.

When Sebastian spoke again, his voice was not his own: *"The mistwhale mourns."*

Attica's brow furrowed upon hearing the new voice. "Duchess?"

"The whispers of the third conceal its mourning song," she said through him. *"Hear that song . . . and you will find it."*

The moment passed. Sebastian straightened, his body his own again as he was lowered. He blinked fast, confused.

"So you'll just track it?" he asked, as if nothing had happened.

"I will," Attica said. "Don't worry about that. And if I find more guests for the realm, I'll bring them through. Until then . . . keep Luther company."

He turned toward the arch. The duchess's words echoed in his mind.

Listen for its mourning song . . . Attica looked back once more and offered her a final nod as he stepped through.

The moment his boots touched the stone of the third tier, something shifted beneath it. A cold current rippled through the terrain—sharp and immediate.

The Spiralrealm felt . . . aware. The air constricted around him like breath held too long as Eli settled against his back, already half asleep.

A whisper surfaced, an older man again: *"Your presence has been noted, Lone-Eyed Wolf. The Brethren will find you."*

CHAPTER SIXTY

The Spiralrealm's red-ringed sun hovered above, a wound above the fog, casting long blood-tinged bands through air that refused to hold still.

Attica stepped carefully, boots muffled on ash-coated stone. The child dozed lightly against his back, her limbs tucked close, heat radiating faintly through the harness like a heartbeat trapped between them. His shade curled low and wide, sweeping ahead in slow, searching patterns.

Somewhere behind him, the whispers trailed—thin, distant, but never gone. One voice in particular echoed louder than the rest: *"They know you are here, Lone-Eyed Wolf,"* the man said. *"They will find you."*

"Then let them come," he said, which he had decided would be his go-to response when threatened by a spirit from that point forward. By now he'd accepted that it didn't matter—what he said, what he felt, how far he ran.

Let them come, he thought, internalizing the words as he pressed onward across terrain that felt more like scar tissue than stone.

Fractured ridges rose on either side, sutured by gullies where radiant light had once burned through the Spiralrealm's surface. Mangled boulders leaned at strange, off-kilter angles, as if they'd been frozen mid-collapse. The ground was soft in places like it could be up on the second, but most of it remained hard and unyielding.

Attica paused beneath a broken arch, the top half blackened and split. Crude carvings marked the stone—vulgar etchings cut deep by Brethren blades.

"Eli, Wolf?" the child asked quietly.

"Yes," Attica said. "Eli and Wolf."

"Eli, Wolf, good."

"We are good enough. We're hunting a mistwhale." He kept walking as he spoke, voice steady and low. "Remember the big flashwraith you scared off with just a flick of your hand? We need that one."

"Bad?"

"Is it bad?" he repeated. "If that's what you're asking, I don't know. I don't know what's good or bad anymore. Everything is gray." He swept his hand toward their surroundings. "Like the Spiralrealm itself." Attica paused, sighing. "And look at me. What I'm doing is bad, but it's also good. You're too young to understand me, but everyone wants me to kill you."

"Eli?"

"Yes, Eli is good. What most people think is good is . . . actually bad. And what you did back there to the Brethren, that was . . . gray." He glanced back at her over his shoulder. "Sorry for trying to have a philosophical conversation with a child."

"Eli good. Wolf good. Home good. Monster bad. Sleep good."

"And eating is good," Attica muttered, making a slow gesture with his hand. "Eat."

"Eat good."

"Yes," he said with a dry smile. "Now you know another word."

Attica descended a steep incline, boots grinding over loose stone slick with soot. The ground below was carved with long, deliberate grooves—not the work of wind or water. These weren't natural.

Something had passed through here.

Something massive . . .

It hadn't walked. It had dragged itself across the Spiralrealm like a dying god—its weight carving furrows through ash and rock alike, the kind of movement that suggested pain, purpose, or both.

The fog broke as he reached the basin below, parting just enough to reveal the shape of the land.

A wide bowl of scorched terrain stretched out before him, flanked by ridges shaped like thorns—jagged and uneven, as if the tier itself had tried to defend against whatever came this way.

At the far edge of the basin, a shallow pool shimmered beneath a film of slick, radiant scum, almost gelatinous in the dim light, pulsing faintly. There was essence above it, but not a lot.

Attica slowed. His boots pressed carefully into the ash as he spotted the first impression.

Tracks.

He crouched low, one hand brushing the soot aside, eyes scanning the fractured terrain.

"Wolf?" Eli whispered behind his shoulder, voice small.

"Shhh," Attica breathed. He touched the edge of one track.

Three-pronged. Deep.

The claw marks bit through the ash, gouging straight into the stone beneath.

"Glintfang," he said quietly.

His shade tensed in response, rippling across his back in a subtle wave, its edges hardening without being told.

The shape was unmistakable—broad forepaw, the inner digits flared slightly, spacing too deliberate to be wild. More canine than feline. But leaner. Hungrier. A predator evolved for pursuit, not ambush.

And where there is one . . . He stood slowly, gaze lifting to the ridgelines.

The silence he'd noticed earlier wasn't silence anymore.

It had shape now. A weight. As if the Spiralrealm had inhaled—and was waiting to see if he noticed.

Something was listening. Something close.

Be ready, he mouthed, a message to his shade.

A sharp howl split the fog—high and sudden. It knifed through the air, designed not just to call, but to disorient.

The noise echoed across the basin, bouncing off the stone in strange spirals. It seemed distant, maybe a quarter mile off, but Attica knew better. Sound in the Spiralrealm lied.

It's closer than that, he thought, his arms naturally tensing.

The cry that followed caused the hairs on the back of his neck to stand to attention.

It was lower, drawn out, a sound that dragged like something wounded—or ancient.

This one carried depth, resonance. Like it came from beneath the tier itself, brushing up against the edge of thought.

It was a response, the exact sound Attica had been hoping to find.

"The mistwhale is answering the glintfang . . ." he whispered, barely audible.

Attica took a step back as the light bent strangely through the fog, colors dimming and slurring like oil dragged over water. Time seemed to hesitate and resume.

They were close.

The beak of Carrion Crow bloomed down his arm; Attica was ready to use his new weapon. "Shade, expect an ambush."

"Bad," Eli said softly. "Bad."

"I know," he told her.

He felt it before he saw it. A ripple of motion in the mist, then the click of claws.

Codex Entry Unlocked!
Name: Glintfang
Origin: Tier II Predator Class, native to upper-spiral slopes
Known Strengths:

– Emits pulses of hunting light from eyes and chest to dazzle and corner prey
– Exceptionally sharp senses—can track by heat, mana trails, and sound
– Hunts in coordinated packs, using light-burst howls and flanking
maneuvers
Known Weaknesses:
– Light-bursts have brief cooldowns; vulnerable between pulses
– Pack cohesion can break if alpha is eliminated
Classification: T-II | Rank C | Cog 1 | Predator
Notes: Fast, coordinated, and highly territorial. Often mistaken for lesser threats—until the first light-burst howl pulse signals the pack.

Attica turned just as a shape detached from the cliff above—jaws wide, shard fangs gleaming, aimed straight for his throat.

He met the creature midair, driving Carrion Crow forward with brutal precision.

The beak skewered through hide and bone in a clean, fluid strike.

A second glintfang launched in from the side, faster than the first. Attica tore the corpse free and hurled it into the oncoming shape. The two collided mid-leap, snarling bodies crashing together in a flurry of fur and fangs.

Bones cracked.

Essence burst outward in ragged pulses of light.

Before either could hit the ground, his shade surged wide—tendrils unfurling like black fire as the third came from behind. Fast and silent.

It never made contact as Attica's shadow caught it mid-pounce, limbs still tucked for the potential strike. Tendrils snapped shut around its body, crushing its midsection with a sound like dry wood snapping under pressure. It slammed the creature into the stone, hard enough to crack the ledge.

He barely turned.

The fourth glintfang came in low, slicing for his legs.

Attica shifted his stance and let it pass. In the same breath, he summoned his shadowblade, the curved weapon forming down his forearm. One clean arc and the blade sliced down through spine and sinew.

The glintfang's body folded instantly.

The alpha emerged from the mist with weight behind every step—larger than the others, its shoulders thick with muscle, one flank marked by a long, pale scar. Its fangs glinted in the dim light, but its mouth stayed closed.

No growl.

No sound.

Its pace was slow, deliberate, almost regal in its restraint as it continued studying him.

Attica crouched low, drawing in a steady breath, every muscle coiled beneath his cloak. His shade tightened around him, anticipating the moment.

"Wolf?" Eli asked.

He didn't have a chance to hush her as the alpha lunged, faster than it had any right to be.

But Attica didn't dodge. He turned into the motion, slipping just past the snapping jaws, his body moving with the kind of instinct born from hunting beasts like this his entire life. His hand snapped out, catching the beast's tail just as it whipped past.

With a sharp breath and a twist of his hips, he heaved.

The strength of his shade poured through him, amplifying the movement.

The alpha jumped toward him, legs flailing for purchase. Attica pivoted with the motion, dragging it through the air in a wide circle before slamming the beast full force into the last glintfang still struggling to rise.

The impact cracked across the basin like a war drum. Both beasts hit the stone hard, limbs tangled.

Attica didn't hesitate.

Carrion Crow took shape once more in his grasp, the weapon forming as if summoned by the act of breath itself. He stepped forward, drove the sharp end into the alpha's chest with all the force he had left, and pinned it to the ground.

The creature spasmed once beneath him, back arched in a final reflex. Attica placed his foot on its neck and used Carrion Crow to rearrange its guts. He grunted and released his hold. Fog drifted back into the space, curling softly around the bodies.

"Good," he finally said, breath slow and measured, the weight of the fight settling across his shoulders.

"Good," Eli chirped with a soft giggle, breaking the stillness.

His shade tightened and finally relaxed.

Attica took a sip from his gourd and then cycled it over the first corpse, essence flowing clean and sharp into the vessel. He moved from one body to the next until the gourd pulsed with fullness. After, he sent the bodies to Kairos. "At least they're not flickercrabs," he said as he got to his feet.

"Wolf?" Eli asked.

"You could say that."

Attica raised his hand to his mouth, formed a ring with his fingers, and released a single sharp howl—high and precise, the same call the Shadowborn had long used to lure glintfangs and signal one another across distances.

The sound unfurled into the mist, lingered in the air, then vanished.

For a moment, there was nothing.

Then the Spiralrealm responded. Not with a howl. Not even a voice. A rumble stirred in the bones of the third tier—low and vast, too deep to be air alone. It rolled through the mist, threaded with something more than sound.

There was tone to it, shape. A long, mournful resonance that didn't touch the ears so much as settle in the spine.

Attica narrowed his eye, gaze fixed on the horizon. "The mistwhale," he said quietly, a smile forming. "This is how we find it."

CHAPTER SIXTY-ONE

Attica moved low through the fog, shadow silent, keeping close to the broken ridgelines that carved into the third tier. He brought his hands to his mouth and produced the call of the glintfang.

Then he waited. A tremor rolled through the mist in response. Not a sound, but a pressure. A breath that shifted the world without stirring the air.

There you are again, he thought, angling toward the source of the mistwhale's reply.

The Brethren would come soon. Their Seer could hear the whispers—same as he could now. As they had before, some voices called for help, soft and scattered. But one stood apart. Cold. Certain. It only warned: *You are being watched. Your time is short.*

Attica smoothed his hand through his hair. *The faster I finish this, the better chance I have of avoiding another fight with the Brethren.*

Eli kicked lightly against his spine. "Quiet," he whispered.

Another kick. "Eli . . . Wolf?"

"Do something about her," he told his shade.

It responded, tightening the harness, holding the child steady.

"Bad!" Eli protested, flaring with light.

Attica sighed and turned the harness, pulling her around to face him. "What's wrong?"

"Eli, good," she said, serious now. "Good."

"I know you are."

She reached toward the ground and kicked.

"Wait. Do you . . . want to walk? You do, don't you?" he asked as he studied her. "You want to move, stretch your legs, I get it. You were walking around back in the realm."

"Eli?" she asked, tilting her head.

"I hear you." Attica pointed toward a steep cleft ahead. "But if you're going to walk, let's go there, up to the second."

He shifted course, weaving through the fog until he reached the jagged stone shelf. It rose from the ridge like a torn page, a scar in the terrain that gave his shade plenty of anchor points as it helped him scale up to the second.

The Brethren don't climb this high up, and the whispers don't carry cleanly between layers of the Spiralrealm, he thought. *They may know I'm up there, but I doubt they'll chase me. If they do, I'll have the advantage.*

He continued his climb, his shade weaving beneath his boots in anchored curls, helping him scale the narrow face. Eli squirmed against his back.

"Almost there," he told the child of light.

With his shade's aid, Attica crested the shelf and stepped onto the rim of the second tier—a narrow stretch of cracked stone and dead scrub, where the slant of sun above currently painted everything in shades of bruised red.

Eli kicked again. Then again.

"All right, all right," Attica said, crouching to unfasten the harness buckles. "I get it."

She dropped into his arms with a soft sigh, her small weight folding easily against his chest. One hand rose at once—her finger tapped his cheek, then pressed to the bridge of his nose.

"You're relentless," he told her. "You know that, right? Stubborn like Eve."

"Eli . . . walk."

"Yes, Eli walk. But first . . ." He scanned the ridge. It was still. The terrain ahead looked clean—flat, stable, soft enough underfoot. The kind of place you could pause, if only for a little while. "Let's check for unwanted guests."

At this, his shade unraveled at his side, slipping forward in a fan of writhing tendrils. It spread low across the ridge, rippling like oil across wet stone. A moment later, it returned—quiet, coiled, indicating nothing nearby. No flashwraiths.

"Good," Attica said. "Thank you. Take care of her while I check the fog below."

His shade eased beside Eli, one darkened tendril curling gently around her waist. She didn't resist. Her steps were still awkward, but better now. Stronger.

"We'll rest here," he said aloud, more to himself than anyone else. "Just for a bit."

Attica retrieved his collapsible monocular from a pouch.

He walked to the ledge of the second tier.

Below, the fog churned in slow, heavy waves—each one layered with sediment and light, thick as smoke and just as evasive. The sun above had dropped behind a wisp of cloud, casting long, fractured bands across the upper mist, less like sunlight, more like veins of red glass suspended in shadow.

This had once been a Vanguard watchpoint. Scouts used to gather here, peering down into the third tier for flashes of movement. Back then, no one ever saw more than flickers. They would speculate about what they could be, but no one would venture down. It was forbidden.

Attica remembered some of these scouting missions as he raised the monocular to his eye and swept slowly across the basin.

There.

A glimmer. Faint, but not random—a pulse that didn't match the rhythm of the fog. It moved with intention.

Is that you? he wondered, narrowing his eye, following the faint beat of unnatural light.

The mistwhale was closer than expected. Too close.

To be certain, he lowered the monocular and cupped his hands to his mouth once more. The glintfang call echoed from him, sharp and clear.

A moment passed.

Then came the reply in the form of a flash.

Bright. Brief. Then nothing. No wind, no echo, just stillness, just stillness, like time had missed a step.

He turned from the ledge, eyes lingering a final second on the silent basin, then walked back toward Eli and his shade.

"Come here," he said, kneeling. "Feet."

"Wolf?" Eli waddled over and stepped carefully onto his boots. He steadied her by the arms, his shadow-dark hands wrapping gently around her glowing wrists.

Together, they began to move, his steps low and measured, hers nested inside his, light on his boots.

They circled the ridge in silence, father and not-quite-daughter, dancing slow over ash and stone, her laughter soft and free in the windless air.

No one watched. Yet somewhere below, the mistwhale stirred again.

"You're learning fast," he said.

"Wolf slow," she whispered.

"Slow?" He raised an eyebrow. "Where did you learn that word?"

"Loo-thur. Fast. Slow. Loo-thur."

"Right, when I was resting," he said, chuckling under his breath.

Attica didn't know how long they walked, but for once, he didn't feel like a weapon waiting to be drawn.

And this time, he knew to cherish it.

For Attica, the quiet never lasted.

Not long after, the fog thickened as Attica descended from the ridge, drawn once more to the third tier and the weight of his hunt.

The ground beneath his boots began to change—gradually at first, then unmistakably. Stones jutted up at strange, unnatural angles, as if pushed from below by something that didn't belong. They leaned and twisted, the ground buckling in slow ripples, like pressure had folded the earth from within.

Ahead, the mist condensed into something denser than fog, thick as a wall and pale as chalk, swallowing the path in featureless silence. It didn't drift. It pressed, heavy and colorless, with no visible end.

Eli clung quietly to his back. Not asleep, but calm, content from the rhythm of their walk.

Attica raised a hand to his mouth and gave the glintfang call again: low, sharp, clipped. Eli giggled softly at the sound but said nothing. He repeated the call, slower this time.

The answer came faster than he expected.

A ripple passed through the fog—not light, not shadow, but something between. It shimmered through the air like heat over water, but colder, wrong.

Then came the sound.

A low, guttural tone rose and cracked at the edges, as if trying to imitate the call of the glintfang. It echoed with something deeper, older, too large for the throat that tried to make it. The noise wasn't sound alone. It had texture, like wet stone dragged across a dry one.

The fog shifted and the light dimmed around him after a series of bright flashes.

A tremor passed through the ground beneath Attica's feet as he stepped into the place where the mistwhale had just been, its presence lingering like heat after fire.

A pale shimmer drifted around him. The path ahead looked drained, as if the light had been siphoned out, pulled toward something still hidden.

Following it, Attica stepped into a place beyond imagining.

Dead trees ringed the clearing—tall, petrified, their trunks split and hollowed by fire or worse. Broken branches lay scattered. Gray dust coated everything in uneven swaths, and the air carried the faint, acrid scent of scorched bone.

He slowed at the grove's edge, where the trail narrowed into a trench. It wasn't deep, but wide enough to swallow a full Vanguard patrol. Still, Attica moved forward.

It's near . . .

He summoned Carrion Crow. The gauntleted weapon unfurled across his arm, shadow and feathers falling together. Its edges formed, the crow's head forming sleek and sharp over his fist.

The air around him constricted.

This is it.

Attica's shade drew in tight, coiling along his spine like tension made flesh.

"Ready?" he whispered. It buzzed in response. Not words, but intent.

Behind him, Eli stirred against his back, silent but no longer calm.

The fog parted, revealing the mistwhale.

Massive and unhurried, the beast drifted through the basin, its body shimmered with fractured geometry, light bleeding off it in slow spirals, pulsing at odd intervals like distant stars flickering beneath skin.

The sheer scale of it struck first.

Larger than any fortress. Larger than anything *should* be.

Its tail dragged deep furrows through the ash, wide enough to reroute rivers, carving new scars into the Spiralrealm with every ponderous stroke.

The sound it made was not a roar. Not quite.

It was breath: immense, low, and unbothered. A sound that passed *through* things instead of around them.

Attica crouched, centered his weight, then moved. His shade surged, launching him forward with explosive force as Carrion Crow extended mid-strike, its crow-beaked spearhead erupting from his arm in a sharp lance of shadow.

The blow landed.

The weapon sank deep into the mistwhale's flank, embedding with a jarring shudder.

"Wolf!" Eli cried, clutching tighter.

"Hang on!" he shouted—to Eli, to his shade, to himself—as the mistwhale pulled them deeper into the fog.

Stone blurred beneath him, fog peeling back in wild spirals. Attica fell, knees scraping the ground, boots skipping across uneven terrain, the force nearly tearing him loose as he maintained his hold on the mistwhale, his weapon lodged deep into its side.

Ahead, the mistwhale twisted, its groaning light pulsing in a chaotic strobe. It tried to rise, tried to flee, but he was hooked now, tethered.

The Spiralrealm collapsed into motion and light and weight.

And still, Attica held on.

His arms burned. His shade screamed through every tendon, wrapping him and Eli in layers of shadow, shielding them from the jagged remains of petrified trees as they tore past.

"I will bring you down!" he shouted, his rallying cry half lost to the wind and the roar. "Let's do this!"

CHAPTER SIXTY-TWO

The mistwhale surged forward through the fog, dragging Attica in its wake. Carrion Crow held fast—its shadow-forged beak buried deep in the creature's translucent hide. The tether vibrated like a strained nerve, each tremor driving deeper into his arm as he held on, determined to bring the titan down. The beast twisted every few seconds, bucked, and tried to shake him loose.

Attica didn't let go.

He'd caught the beast in a moment of stillness, when the monstrosity floated through the fog like it was remembering something.

Now came the violence.

Stone formations cracked apart as the mistwhale barreled through them—monoliths reduced to hail. One shattered just ahead. Attica hit the ground running, vaulted over a spike, landed on a slick outcrop, and snapped the tether again, flinging himself forward with brutal speed.

The Spiralrealm blurred around him as he held tight, trails of fog tearing past in tattered ribbons. Eli clung to his back in silence.

The whale moved like it didn't care about the world it was destroying, but it wasn't mindless.

It turned and began tracking Attica, each exhale shimmering with blinding light. The mistwhale cut right and loosed a warbling cry; Attica's shadow unraveled beneath him, causing him to lose his grip on the creature.

A radiant flare seared through the fog.

He barely managed to dodge the blast as he leapt from a ledge and latched back on. Carrion Crow struck true—again embedding deep. He slammed into its flank, shade-wrapped, anchored by will.

Carrion Crow throbbed, straining deeper.

The mistwhale shuddered. A long, low tremor moved through it, more breath than cry. The sound lingered, deep and mournful, as Attica slipped from its back once more. He landed at the edge of a ridge. The creature hovered in the fog ahead, still and immense. Then it released the sound again.

Is it . . . sad?

Attica recalled what Duchess Corvenna had told him about the mistwhale's mourning song. Earlier, it had mimicked the glintfangs' howl, but this was different. This was something new.

The cry held him in place. Just for a breath, he couldn't move—staggered by the raw grief in its voice.

"Bad," Eli whispered. "Monster . . . good."

"No," he hissed, fingers tightening as he regained his focus. "Monster . . . bad."

Carrion Crow formed down his arm. He fired it at the mistwhale and vaulted up the creature's spine, sprinting along translucent flesh as it took off again. It smashed through a stone arch and circled backward.

The mistwhale rolled, deliberately trying to buck him off.

Attica read the motion just in time. He jumped clear, landed hard on a stone hoodoo shaped like a chimney, and fired Carrion Crow again as the rock gave way beneath him, the tower of stone collapsing into dust.

The tether caught, and he yanked himself forward, the shadowblade forming along his other arm in one smooth pull. He dragged it across the mistwhale's side.

A burst of light exploded from the wound.

Attica flew, tumbled through fog, and landed hard on his side, once again protected by his shade, which also covered Eli.

"Thanks," he said as his vision swam red. Attica pushed to his feet just as the mistwhale turned. Its jaw opened unnaturally wide, revealing rows of light-fangs. Not for tearing or devouring, but siphoning.

Attica sprinted toward it, shadowblade in hand, and slashed across the underside of its mouth as it passed.

Behind him, Eli started crying. Not loud. Not afraid. Just whispering the same words, over and over. "Monster good . . . monster good . . . monster good . . ."

The light around her was flaring, growing brighter by the second.

"Eli—" Attica shot forward with Carrion Crow and once again scaled to the mistwhale's back. He pulled the weapon out and drove it in again. The whale lurched, dragging them both into a trench where the fog grew thicker, heavier— near black.

Attica struck again, finding another point in its spine. He plunged in with his shadowblade next, hoping to make a deeper wound. His third blow found something vital.

A burst of light erupted from the wound, flinging him back.

The mistwhale bellowed as Attica hit the ground hard. Once again, he was aided by his shade as he rolled and rose in one motion depositing him on his feet.

"Thanks again!" Attica said, winded, yet still determined. Dark essence plumed across the trench beyond as the mistwhale drifted fifty yards farther. It rose a few feet higher into the air then folded in on itself and collapsed.

The fog curled around the fallen body.

"Did it," Attica said, voice haggard. He dropped his shoulders as he waited for his heartbeat to steady, ignoring Eli's quiet sobs. "Now I just need to finish this."

The mistwhale's body trembled once, then again, and began to rise.

Attica was just taking a step toward it when four figures broke through the fog—cloaked in bone-gray armor, shadows laced around their limbs like leashed smoke. The Brethren.

The lead one raised a whip of shimmering dark essence. Another held a curved shadowblade that pulsed in time with the red-ringed sun above. All wore helms of bleached flashwraith bone, faces hidden, eyes lit with cold, unwavering light.

Attica turned, readying Carrion Crow.

Behind him, the mistwhale cried out, a sound like a bell collapsing inward as it twisted once and vanished into the fog.

Gone.

Attica looked back to where it had just been. The only trace was a trail of glimmering light dancing along the fog.

Eli didn't say a word. Yet Attica could sense her small hands clenching behind him, not from fear—something else.

She's upset at me, Attica thought as he turned back toward the Brethren.

"You are making a mistake," he told them, before their leader could threaten him. It was the only warning he would provide.

The first of the Brethren lashed out with his shadow whip. Attica blinked past it, reappearing beside him, blade reaching over his knuckles. One clean slash across the back of the knee and the man stumbled.

He pivoted as the second came from behind. Attica pierced the man's chestplate with Carrion Crow, anchoring deep. With a great tug, Attica yanked the man forward and drove his shadowblade into his gut.

A third approached from the right, weapons forming over both arms.

Attica's shade didn't hesitate. It pushed past the Brethren's own shadow and took his legs out. The man fell; Attica met him at the ground, ramming his shadowblade through a gap in the armor beneath the sternum. The blade tore through him and burst out the back.

His shade surged forward to meet another incoming shadow and quickly overwhelmed it. Attica struck the man with Ravelstrike, and let him fall to the side.

He circled back to the first—the one he'd hobbled.

The man was trying to rise, his shade flaring to protect him.

Attica used Carrion Crow to finish the man off in the fastest way possible. His helmeted head rolled to the side as his body dropped.

He hated to fight his own kind, but he knew they'd never stop. He knew this because he was Vanguard. He would have never stopped, and the Brethren were twice as fanatical about combat.

It gave him no pleasure to kill them all, but it did buy him some time . . .

The whispers of what he had done would reach their Seer, and he would likely send more. *But there will be a breaking point*, he thought, *one in which they learn hunting me is futile. Unless they truly plan to exterminate themselves for revenge . . .*

The mist drifted low, veiling the bodies. Blood steamed faintly where it met the cold air, turning the ground into a canvas of scattered limbs and dark, broken armor stained blue.

Attica stood at the edge of it now, breath slowing, ears ringing with the silence that follows violence. He uncorked one of his gourds and drank—just enough to push the fatigue back, to steady the ache behind his ribs. The essence burned down his throat like memory.

He exhaled once, then looked to the horizon, where the fog seemed to circumambulate a series of cone-shaped stones.

The mistwhale is still out there, badly injured too . . .

"Eli?" he asked, voice quieter. "Hungry?" He turned his head. "You okay back there?"

The girl didn't answer. He squinted as he looked ahead, at the way the fog had closed around them, the trench quiet.

"Eli?" he asked again. When she didn't reply this time, he turned the harness with help from his shade.

Her eyes wouldn't meet his. She stared just past him, defiant.

"Seriously?" he asked the girl. "I know you don't fully understand what's happening here, but it has to be done. We need the mistwhale's bones. I do. Wolf does." He held out the gourd. "Please. Drink."

She took it. Slowly. Her glow dimmed, her breath evened. Her silence eased—but didn't vanish.

Attica nodded. "I'll make it quick. I promise."

CHAPTER SIXTY-THREE

Attica stepped away from the dead Brethren. The fog parted for him, thin and reverent, curling around the dead but never touching him.

"Let's look for a better place to talk," he told Eli.

He kept her in front of him as he moved through the mist. Attica found a place where the ground dipped—a hollow between two stone outcrops, far enough from the bloodless wreckage behind him.

He crouched, careful not to jostle her, and began unfastening the harness. "I'm going to let you down," he said softly.

Eli didn't answer, but she didn't resist as he eased her down, placing the child of light on unsteady feet.

She tilted her head back, blinking up at him, lips still pressed in a line. Attica dropped to one knee so they were eye to eye and placed a hand on her shoulder. "You're upset," he said. "Mad at me. Mad at Wolf."

"Bad . . ." She pouted. "Bad." Eli shut her eyes for a moment, like it pained her to string the next set of words together. "Wolf bad."

He sighed. "You think what I did was wrong. I get it. I know it looked cruel. And maybe it was."

"Wolf bad," she started to sob again.

"Don't, please don't cry," he said as he noticed the light flickering around her, forming a bright halo. "Eli." He hesitated. "The mistwhale might seem good to you. Maybe you forgot it swallowed one of the Brethren men whole. Do you remember that? Hold her," he told his shade.

He pushed away from her and clamped his hand around his other fist to mimic a mouth.

". . . Bad?" she asked.

"Yes, bad. All flashwraiths are bad. You . . . you are not bad, but people think you are because—" He stopped, catching himself.

He was seconds from arguing with a child about the morality of Lightborn monsters, an argument that would have exposed him considering all he had done, and if she was logical enough to figure it out, what he *should have done* when they first met. He shifted course. "My point is: Kairos needs bones to make armor. Remember Kairos?" He puffed out his chest, ran a hand over his head in imitation of the smith's baldness.

To his surprise, Eli nodded.

"You do?"

"Loo-thur?" she asked.

"Luther is one of the boys you played with. Luther and Sebastian. Kairos was—" He bulked up again and mimed hammering. "Kairos."

"Kay-rose," Eli said, nodding.

"Yes." Attica pointed into the fog. "He needs the bones. For me." He touched his chest. "For Wolf." He gestured wide to suggest the whale's size. "That thing is a monster."

She bit her lip. "Monster," she echoed.

"Good. You're getting it." He kept a hand on her shoulder, ignoring the way her glow made his eye ache, the way it scorched the edges of his sight. "I need armor. Kairos will forge it from the mistwhale's bones. I know that's a lot to understand, but—"

"Why?"

Attica tilted his head, studying her. "Why?"

"Why need?"

"Armor," he repeated. "You're asking me why I need armor." When she didn't say anything else, he asked his shade to steady her. Attica grabbed a flat stone and placed it over his chest, knocking against it with his fist. "Armor."

"Are-moor," she said.

"Yes. I need the bones for armor." He tossed the stone away. "Protection."

She frowned. "Why?"

He exhaled. "For Dayanne and Eli," Attica said, the first answer that came to his mind. While he needed the armor to get the shard from the duke, the real reason he was going through with any of this was for Dayanne and Eli.

She pointed to herself. "Eli. Me Eli."

"Two Elis," he told her, holding up two fingers. "You and another. My son."

She blinked.

"I know. It's confusing," he said, instantly regretting he even mentioned it.

The girl tilted her head the other way. "Two Eli?"

"There was another Eli," he said. "Someone I lost. You are not him. But you . . . matter too. And this"—he gestured vaguely between them—"has grown too complicated for simple answers." He placed a hand back on her shoulder again. "When you're a little older, I'll explain better. And at the rate you're grow-ing . . . that might be soon."

She stared at him for a long moment. Then stepped forward. He bent lower as she wrapped her arms around his neck. "Wolf," she said. "Wolf . . . good. Eli . . . good."

Attica closed his eye, surprised that she was hugging him.

For a moment, the Spiralrealm felt different. Not safe. Not forgiving. But quiet enough to believe, if only for a breath, that something in this cursed gray world might still be worth saving.

And just at the moment Attica felt at peace with his world, he heard the mist-whale in the fog, moaning, the beast down, ready for the slaughter.

"We have to go," he told Eli as she continued to hug him.

"Wolf good," she said softly.

Attica moved through the fog toward the sound, Eli back in her harness, quiet against his back.

"The whale is close," he told his shade. "I can feel it."

It buzzed in response.

Each low call from the creature sent tremors through the ground. The world at his periphery warped—light dimming, thickening, taking on weight as he con-tinued his hunt.

Attica pressed forward, head down, instinct locked to purpose. He spotted the mistwhale drifting between two shattered stone pillars, vast and low to the ground. Its flanks leaked pale radiance from wounds that hadn't yet sealed.

It wasn't fleeing, but it hadn't surrendered either.

Here's my chance—Attica's train of thought was broken by the child on his back. "Eli?" he asked, making sure she was fine.

"Eli good," she said.

"Then you understand. Let's finish this," he told his shade, which tensed around him, feeding off Attica's energy as he moved forward, feathered shadows trailing down his arm.

He launched Carrion Crow; the weapon struck the mistwhale's side, tether pulling tight.

In moments, Attica was flying, the child of light strapped to his back.

Stone blurred past. Wind screamed. His shadow curled tight around Eli and him as they slammed through a broken ridge, rock shattering. Attica ran when he could, hurled himself forward when he couldn't, caught in the wake of some-thing vast and merciless.

The mistwhale twisted again, spraying beams of concentrated light that sheared through the mist.

Still, Attica held fast.

When his feet found ground, Attica bolted forward with all the speed he could muster, closing the gap beneath it. He struck—once, twice—driving the shadowblade into the whale's underbelly. The creature screamed, the sound rising through the fog like metal torn in half.

It lifted, then twisted.

The tail came sweeping through the air.

Attica ducked the first pass, rebounded on the tether, and vaulted up onto the whale's back. His boots slid across translucent flesh, veins glowing beneath his feet. He slashed again.

More light spilled. Blinding. Fever hot.

The mistwhale rose hard and slammed sideways into a rock wall—dragging Attica with it through the fog.

Carrion Crow went taut. A jolt snapped through the weapon, and Attica was flung hard to the right.

"Argh!" He clipped a jagged outcropping, pain lancing through his ribs just before he slammed into the ground in a bone-jarring roll. His head snapped sideways against a bulbous rock, and the world went white, then black.

Attica settled on his side, the breath driven from his lungs, his shade surging instinctively to shield Eli from the worst of the impact.

"Get her . . . away from here," he managed to tell his shade, barely hearing his own voice over the roar building in his skull as everything faded away.

He awoke moments later with a ragged gasp, eye popping open as he jerked upright.

The mist had thickened, not just in depth but in weight. Attica lay on his side, limbs trembling as he tried to drag the world back into shape. "Eli . . ." he whispered.

His hands moved first, checking for injury, confirming that his body still obeyed him. Then his thoughts turned fully toward the child. "Eli?" He reached for the harness. "Eli?" he asked again, growing alarmed until the light hit his face.

Eli floated just ahead—suspended above the cracked stone.

The mistwhale loomed before her, motionless but not dead, bleeding light from half a dozen open wounds, its head hung in obedience.

Attica pushed himself upright, stumbled, and finally found his footing. "Eli—" he said, overcome with joy that she was okay.

The girl merely turned to him, calm, her glow soft and steady.

"Wolf," she said, and drifted aside, giving him the opening he needed. "Wolf good. Monster . . . bad."

Attica didn't need any more permission than that.

He charged ahead, summoning both Carrion Crow and Ravelstrike. The weapons bloomed from his arms—one a tethered spear of shadow, the other an oversized crow's head, both heavy with built-up momentum.

He drove them both forward.

Carrion Crow pierced the core. Ravelstrike followed, a crushing double attack.

The mistwhale came crashing down. Light detonated outward in a current of radiance that flattened the surrounding ridge and carved a crater where none had been.

The creature moaned once—a long, shuddering exhale—and went still. The last threads of the mistwhale's light unraveled into the air.

Attica staggered toward it, breathing hard, weapons fading as he reached a hand out to the beast. "We . . ." He sank to his knees as Eli hovered over to him. "No, you. *You* did it. Thank you."

CHAPTER SIXTY-FOUR

Attica returned to the Realm of Recumbency, half carried by his shade, the stone beneath his boots uneven, his breath shallow. Eli clung to his back in silence.

He took in the giant carcass laid out across the main platform, the one he had just sent there by simply touching the mistwhale's dead body.

"By the Painter," he whispered as pale light seeped from the creature's wounds, diffusing slowly into the twilight, the scene gruesome, dark, but necessary.

Kairos was already at work with his knives, cutting into the mistwhale and removing hunks of flesh. Joan stood beside him, sleeves rolled, hands dark to the elbow as she helped him cut pieces away, the two intent on reaching its bones. Luther helped as well while Sebastian stood off to the side, watching it all take place.

"Where does it all go?" Attica said as he approached.

"Eh, over the side," Kairos told him. "That's what Sebastian said to do."

She can't like this, Attica thought as he looked up to Duchess Corvenna, who sat on her throne overlooking it all, her face blank. *Then again, she's the one who told me how to track the damn thing . . .*

Luther approached. "I'll take her," he said as Attica already started to turn the harness around.

"Loo-thur!" Eli said as Attica passed her into the boy's arms. She went quietly, looking up at him with her usual intensity. Her glow softened against his chest.

"She's learning quickly," Attica reminded him.

"Just like Sebastian said she would."

"I don't think you understand what I'm trying to tell you here. Be careful what you say around her." He grinned at the boy. "She's already arguing with me."

"Noted," Luther told him.

Attica's gaze lingered on them for a moment—then moved past, toward the platform with the ledger on it. A sketch of the glintfang appeared, followed by a brief text:

Glintfang – Tier II | Rank C | Cog 1 | Predator
Pack-hunting predator with light-burst glands in the eyes and chest—used to dazzle, isolate, and corral prey. Tracks by heat, mana trace, and sound. Strikes in flanking patterns, often preceded by a piercing howl pulse. Packs unravel quickly if the alpha is felled. Fast, territorial, and never alone.

Once he took care of this ritual, Attica headed back down, where he refilled his gourds at the fountain. He went ahead and drank one, still not used to having such ready access to pure essence.

"Good, right?" he asked his shade, who squeezed his shoulders.

After one more look around, and deciding he would prefer to rest than help butcher the mistwhale, Attica climbed the stairs to his platform. He reached the top and dropped into his chair without ceremony.

Below, Luther and Eli sat on the steps playing with white stones while Kairos and Joan finally reached the mistwhale's bones and Sebastian continued to watch them work. "Take a load off," Kairos called up to him. "It won't be much longer now. Take a little rest. You bloody earned it!"

Attica soon found that he couldn't relax.

Even as Kairos and Joan butchered the mistwhale and began work on the bone-forged armor, his thoughts kept drifting—to Eve and Tiago, and the space between them now that he had Eli with him. His thoughts spun and spun until he finally gave in to the pull.

"Vespasia," he said. "Are you there?"

The mist gathered, threading into the shape of the woman, her eyes burning red beneath her hood.

"I see you've found some place comfortable," she said. Her gaze shifted to the mistwhale carcass, which Kairos had begun to drag toward the edge of the main platform. The work was slow, deliberate. "Before you ask, your companions are still on the second. I'm assuming that's why you called me."

"It was, thank you. And thanks for checking on them. I don't know how I'm going to reconcile any of this. But I'll try."

"You are exiled, and they are not. I do not know if there's much more I can tell you, but I can say this: If I were you, I would abandon your desire to reconcile with them. If they ever find enough of the Painter's blood to meet you in exile, they will become your competitors, not your companions."

"I don't believe that has to happen."

"You, who has only recently been exiled, who has never been past the fourth tier, and who knows little of the Crown of Shadows. How many Seers were there in your settlement?"

"One."

"And if there had been two?"

"There weren't two," he replied flatly.

"But if there had been?"

"I see the point you're trying to make. But I still don't think it applies. If being a Seer requires some mythical object, what does it matter who holds it? Couldn't it be shared? A council?"

"There *was* a council," Vespasia said. "You should be familiar with the Spiralrealm's history by now. Or were you in too much of a hurry last time to understand the full picture?" She didn't wait for an answer. "There was once the Baffled King. He wore the Crown of Shadows, a gift forged by the Painter—the same being who created this world. Do you know why he was baffled?"

"I don't," Attica admitted.

"Because the crown itself corrupted him. He shattered it—regrettably. And he created the Council of Torn to manage its shards. If you ask me, he should have cast it into the abyss. It is too powerful an object for any one person to possess aside from the Painter."

"The abyss?"

She tilted her head. "What do you think lies at the bottom of the Spiralrealm?"

"I don't know."

"Now you do," she said. "The abyss. Instead of tossing the crown in, he shattered it, and in doing so, stripped the color from the world. The council was meant to protect us from what the crown might become if it was ever put together again, but even that has failed."

Attica gestured up toward the fountain, where the duchess still sat. "You said she wore the crown."

"Briefly. The duchess was close with the Baffled King, and he tried to give it to her at the height of his lunacy. She created this realm, and others like it, but at a cost. Once it was shattered, she got trapped in a place neither here nor there, neither of the Spiralrealm or this multitude of realms she has created. She sits in quiet watch across numerous Realms of Recumbency, damned and kept alive by duty—and by her son, Sebastian the Limp."

Attica frowned. "Sebastian said the shards could give me the power to bring Dayanne and Eli back."

"You mean your partner and child?"

"Yes."

"Then yes. The crown's shards could grant you that power."

"But it sounds like there's a price."

Vespasia stepped closer. Her eyes dimmed slightly, voice softening. "There could be. But you seem to have found another option now."

Attica followed her gaze. Eli was seated near Luther, sleeping while Luther and Sebastian spoke in quiet tones. "The duchess said it was a false prophecy."

"All prophecies are false—until they're realized," Vespasia said quickly. "So if your goal is reunion, you have two options. One forged in grief. The other in trust." She paused, letting that sink in. "And there's something else you should know," she added. "Since your next step is the shard, yes?"

"Yes."

"If you manage to get the shard from Duke Astor, it could give you immense power—more than you know. Like the Painter's blood, it reacts differently in each bearer. You have a good heart, but there's rage inside you, Lone-Eyed Wolf. If you're not careful, it will become your compass."

He didn't argue.

"And then there's the girl. She's destined to become a monster," Vespasia reminded him. "Not because she wants to. But because of what she is. And soon, she'll realize the distance between what she is and what you are." Her form began to unravel. "Be wary of when that day comes. It will be sooner than you like."

CHAPTER SIXTY-FIVE

Kairos stood on his platform, a big smile on his face as Attica approached. The armor was finished, the pieces laid out on the table, bone forged, blood cleansed, and glimmering with faint residual light. Joan was beside him, wiping something clean with a rag, sleeves already darkened from her work.

"You're late," Kairos said.

Attica shrugged him off. "What can I say? I wanted to give it time to cool." He swept his hand toward the main platform, the mistwhale carcass gone. "You clean up quick."

"Over the edge, just like I said. Is there no better way to hide the evidence?" Kairos rubbed his hands together. "But enough chatter. You killed a mistwhale, and I promised you I would create something worthy out of its bones." The smith gave a sharp nod. "Strip. Let's get it on you."

Attica peeled off his cloak first, then the layers beneath—his clothes stiff with dried blood and the dust of the third tier. His skin, like all those born Shadowborn, was deep and lightless, a shade darker than shadow itself, a kind of black that seemed to swallow torchlight.

"And new clothes too," Joan said as she approached, the woman barely flinching at the sight of Attica's scars, which gleamed faintly where the light managed to catch angles. "You'll need them, too."

"I'm not the best tailor," Kairos admitted, "but the duke had me making all kinds of things, clothes being one of them. I also made something for Eli." He gestured to a cloth on his table.

"I've been meaning to ask about that . . ." Attica said.

"Well, now you don't need to." Kairos motioned him closer. "Joan and I will help you get it on."

Once he undressed, Attica turned his back to the two of them, allowing the pair to snap pieces into place. He felt his shade tense and whispered for it to relax as he looked down, examining his new layer of protection.

The armor had been carved from the inner bones of the mistwhale—curved white plates overlapping like the ribs of a serpent, fitted to allow full movement without sacrificing defense. The chest was reinforced, a smooth plane over the sternum etched with a faint spiral. The shoulders were lower-slung, the arms layered in three segments each. The legs were lighter still, with pliable ridging near the knees.

It wasn't beautiful, but it was strong, and it fit perfectly.

Kairos fastened the final piece and stepped back. Joan handed over a set of fresh robes and a cloak, both dark and cut to drape cleanly over the armor.

Once he was dressed, Attica pulled the harness across his back, adjusted the straps, and stood still for a breath.

"How does it feel?" Kairos asked. "Move around, see if it feels natural."

He moved his arms forward and back. "I like it. It's light. Much lighter than I would have expected."

Kairos grinned. "Good, right?"

"Better than that."

"Amazing?"

"Amazing," Attica said.

"And that's not the best part. There is a method to my madness, a reason I requested mistwhale bone—"

"It refracts light," Joan said for Kairos.

"Hey, I was going to tell him that part—"

"Sorry!"

Kairos rolled his eyes in a playful way and continued: "Flashwraiths use light-based attacks. I shouldn't have to tell you this," he said, growing serious. "You've witnessed the horrors of what they are capable of. We all have. But here it is: This armor can fully absorb light attacks from . . ." He ran his hand over his bald head. "Well, I can't say what kind of monsters are south of the fourth tier, but anything above it—this will entirely absorb their attacks."

"Which leaves my shade free to handle other things," Attica said.

"Yes, exactly that. The armor holds, the shade doesn't have to spend all of its power fueling your shadow weapons and protecting you. It will still spend some of it, but this armor specifically gives you more protection than you've ever had before, at least against certain light attacks, like direct beams." Kairos cracked his knuckles. "Good, right?"

Attica gave a small nod. "How many more compliments would you like?"

Joan laughed. "He'll never let you forget it, if that's what you're asking."

"I do wonder one thing," Attica said as he examined the armor yet again. "What about my phasing ability? Will I still be able to do that?"

"Try it," Kairos said.

Attica stepped forward—and vanished. He reappeared an instant later near the forge, his boots scuffing stone.

Kairos didn't blink. "That answers that."

Joan summed it up. "Anything we make you will work with what you already have. We're pros, remember?" She winked at him. "Of all the whispers you could have brought here, you chose two of the best. Congratulations are in order."

"Don't get ahead of yourself there," Kairos told her.

"Do you know a better weapon or armorsmith on the third or fourth?" she asked.

"I can't say that I do . . ."

Attica adjusted the harness again, tested the balance. "Thank you, both. I have one final question for you," he told Kairos. "I'm going to portal to the fourth and will choose the same cavern where I met you. I wanted to ask about the other exit, the one that leads straight into the duke's grotto." Attica looked at him. "What should I expect?"

Kairos exhaled. "What to expect, what to expect. Well, for one, Duke Tiberion Astor is a collector. He collects things. Trophies. Creatures. Things of interest. With the shard, the duke controls flashwraiths. You've already met some of his toys."

"The two lightfeasters," Attica said, recalling the brutes that he wasn't able to beat. *There are also lumenbrides, wretches, and flickercrabs on the fourth tier*, he thought.

Kairos grimaced. "The duke likes his feasters best. He doesn't have an army of them, but there are quite a few."

"Lumenbrides?"

"I don't think he has one of those, or at least I never saw one. But . . ."

"But?"

"The cave. They did float their way into the cave. As a whisper, I was able to usher them out—I hate the things—so you might run into one there."

"Potential lumenbride in the cave, good to know. Anything else? What about the shard?"

Kairos shook his head. "Not much. I only know where he kept the shard, but never got past the outer halls. My job was to craft. Slaughter. Build things the duke liked." He hesitated. "Sculptures," he said finally. "He'll have more than a few of them in the courtyard. Don't let them bother you or the child. They're harmless."

"Until they aren't," Joan told him.

"What do you mean?" Kairos asked her.

"He has the shard. He might have had you build them for a reason."

Kairos bit his lip, eyes narrowing as he absorbed this new potential horror. "I didn't consider that. Either way, you've got the tools now to handle anything he can throw at you."

"Thank you again." Attica turned toward the stairs.

Down below, Luther sat with Eli, who had just woken and begun stacking white stones into a careful tower. The tower wobbled. Eli tapped it once, and it fell.

She started laughing, her bright eyes shifting up at Attica as he approached with clothing. "Wolf. Wolf . . . ready?"

Attica stepped through the portalstone, Eli now tucked securely into the harness on his back.

"Bye-bye," the child of light said, waving to Luther and Sebastian as they vanished behind the threshold.

"Another new phrase," Attica told her. "The boys will have you speaking fluently in no time."

The calm hush of the Realm of Recumbency gave way to the cold austerity of the fourth tier. The world here stretched out in gray-white silence, the landscape smothered in a soft coat of ashfall and bone dust. Cracked stone ran like veins across the ground. Above, the red-ringed sun hung half obscured in the haze—faded, bruised, and seemingly forgotten.

For a long moment, Attica didn't move.

He stood and breathed it in. The cold. The quiet. The ache.

He imagined the world awash in color again—the way it had flared when he lit the lanterns during the trial, the way it had pulsed inside him when he drank from the Painter's blood. A memory, sharp and impossible. A world that had never truly belonged to him.

He adjusted the harness gently and turned, Attica already used to the armor.

The silhouette of the cave stood ahead—low-slung, jagged, a wound in the cliffside he remembered far too well.

He reached up and swiveled Eli around, settling her so they were face-to-face.

"We're going to do something that will be very difficult," he said softly. He pointed toward the cave. "Monster."

"Monster?" Eli echoed, unsure.

"Bad monster," Attica said. "Eli and Wolf, good. Monster, bad." He paused, watching her expression shift. "And . . . I don't know how much you'll be able to help me this time." He faltered, not sure of how to explain risk to the little girl.

"Eli . . . help?" she asked.

"Yes, Eli can help," he said. "But Eli shouldn't worry. Eli . . ."

He looked into her eyes, and something cracked. "Eli is a good girl. And this is dangerous. That's a big word, I know. It means . . . it means I really should be leaving you somewhere safe." He exhaled, voice tightening. "But I can't do that. I won't do that. So Eli—"

"Eli help?" she repeated.

"Yes and no. Did Luther teach you the word *yes*?"

"Yes."

"Did he teach you the word *no*?"

"Yes."

Attica squinted. "Am I . . . Fox?"

She blinked, then grinned. "No, Wolf."

"Are you Eli?"

"Yes," she said. Then held up two fingers. "Me Eli two."

The words hit harder than he expected. Attica looked away, not ready to relive the loss of his actual child and the fact that she was now cognizant enough to understand there had been another.

"Let's just keep moving." His shade drifted closer to help, stabilizing Eli as he turned her around and secured the harness again.

Once she was settled, Attica pushed forward. Boots crunched softly against the ash, dust curling through the broken edges of stone.

He slowed as they neared the cave. The shadows here didn't fall in natural directions. They curved inward, toward something deeper. The temperature dropped, and the cold scraped against his exposed fingertips.

He stopped at the threshold. "A lumenbride could be in there," he warned his shade. "They affect you more than they affect me. If you sense one, we pull back." He hesitated. "I don't know what Eli would do to something like that. But . . ." He remembered the ghostly flashwraith, the veiled horror. "I'd rather she didn't see one. It could give her nightmares."

As usual, Attica's shade didn't respond, a fact that didn't make him feel any better as he stepped inside the cave. He pushed forward, his mind fixed on reaching the duke's courtyard when something twitched.

What's this? he thought as stone-colored bodies shifted along the high walls, small, segmented creatures half blended into the cave's jagged architecture. Their backs hissed open, exposing clusters of pulsing glands that flashed with unstable light.

Flickercrabs.

There were dozens, possibly hundreds.

Their shells twitched in sequence, glands opening, closing, opening again— each one a tiny strobe in a sea of barely suppressed brilliance. A misstep, a startled shade, the wrong breath, and they would all go off.

The whole cave would go with them.

Attica froze. He hadn't sent his shade forward. He had planned to keep it close, ready for a lumenbride.

But the flickercrabs were worse in numbers. If they started a chain reaction here, the cave itself could collapse on top of them.

He stepped back slowly. Very slowly. Eli stirred gently on his back.

Attica didn't look at her yet. Not yet as the cave began to shift. Instead, he kept his voice low and calm, as if they were still back in the realm, speaking in the quiet of the upper platform. "Eli," he said. "We have company. Flickercrabs. I don't know how—"

"Eli help," came her reply, voice cheerful. "Eli help."

CHAPTER SIXTY-SIX

The flickercrabs surged ahead, a living tide of clicking limbs and twitching glands that lit the cave in bursts of disjointed brilliance. Their hardened bodies skittered over the rock, scattering in waves as they fought for space, competing to be first into the open light.

Eli floated just behind them, her hand raised, small and steady, the infant in total command of the cast of flickercrabs. Light shimmered around the girl as she moved ahead, soft but growing brighter by the moment, her path absolute, her purpose unspoken but clear.

Attica followed, boots crunching quietly in the wake of the chaos.

He didn't rush. He could feel what was coming, the pressure of it, the tension.

His shade unraveled behind him, twitching and coiling in near silence, boiling with anticipation. They were close now. The moment before battle, that unbreathable stretch of time between knowing, hoping, and doing.

"Wolf?" Eli called over her shoulder, not turning, her way of checking.

"Wolf good!" he said back, his way of answering.

Ahead, the flickercrabs accelerated.

They raced over one another, their shells clicking, pincers scraping stone, their light growing increasingly erratic. The air buzzed with static, their hissing bodies twitching in barely controlled sequences.

The pressure rose as the cavern narrowed, funneling into the final turn.

Then, the exit came into view.

The duke's grotto was massive, hollowed out by years of obsessive detailing. Strange bone sculptures rose from the floor like half-finished bodies, some humanoid, some beastlike, all twisted. Their limbs were carved with deliberate wrongness. Their mouths hung open in frozen, silent screams.

And standing among them—

The lightfeasters.

More than Attica expected. At least six of them, thick-bodied, glowing from within, their jagged heads pivoting at once toward the incoming flood of crabs.

"Now!" Attica shouted.

Eli didn't hesitate.

She pulled back and lowered her hand.

The moment her palm dropped, the flickercrabs *poured* out—not tumbling but erupting, cascading down the incline into a space unlike any Attica had seen before. The entire swarm ignited. Their glands flared with molten veins, their segmented backs pulsing gold and orange as the internal heat reached a threshold.

Then they exploded, chain reactions rippling through the grotto, hurling shrapnel across the sculptures, through the air, and directly into the lightfeasters.

The blasts came in staggered waves—flashes of white and red, followed by thunderous concussions that cracked the stone seating and sent carved limbs flying.

Shells and claws. Essence and heat.

The whole grotto bloomed with destruction.

And through it all, Attica kept back, shielding Eli, his new armor and his shade protecting him. He waited until the explosions stopped and turned to the grotto. "It's my turn," he told Eli as he put her into her harness and had his shade transition her to his back. "Let's do this!"

Attica stepped over a cracked jawbone, boots grinding through shell fragments and ash. As the smoke thinned, he saw the space for what it truly was.

This isn't a grotto, it's . . . an amphitheater!

Circular. Tiered. Built for display, not defense, the grotto being just another place for the duke to showcase his trophies, to force grotesque performances. Now that Attica was standing inside it, the symmetry clicked into place.

Of course the duke would build something like this, he thought. *He was never a warrior. He was a collector. A performer. A god in a kingdom of dust. And now, a dead man . . .*

Attica squinted through the haze toward the manor beyond, which loomed above the amphitheater like a cathedral, a towering sprawl of darkened stone and bone-forged archways. Windows flickered with strange light, and the walls were reinforced with something pale and organic, not quite bone and not quite steel.

Shadowborn and Lightborn hands had shaped that place. Attica saw it in the awkward pitch of the stairs, the rough-hewn buttresses, the way the structure leaned under its own contradictions.

What he'd once thought was a grove, some sort of sanctuary for the macabre, was in fact a stage—and he had just taken center stage.

Attica stepped forward through the fallout, his dark cloak trailing behind him, the heat still rippling off the new armor that hugged his frame. His shade hovered close, twitching and low, its form unreadable but alert.

Three lightfeasters remained, and he planned to kill them all.

The lightfeasters stood at the far end of the grotto, their thick hides steaming, chests rising in uneven pulls. The explosion had torn into them, but not enough. Not nearly enough. Only one limped—its left foot shattered from the flickercrab blast. The other two were injured as well, their heads twitching, glowing mouths split vertically, each movement tracking for sound, for heat.

Attica didn't wait.

"Go for the injured one first." His shade peeled away at once, slipping off in a serpentine blur—low and fast, its form streaking like smeared ink across the far wall. The lightfeasters reacted instantly, all three of their twisted heads tracking the wrong direction.

Attica broke left, body low, cutting across the amphitheater's wreckage. He didn't charge—he closed the distance with careful momentum, conserving energy, calculating every footfall. The injured lightfeaster was already moving—unsteady but fast. Its left leg dragged behind it, flaring with white-hot light where the foot had been half shorn away.

It turned toward him once it sensed his presence and lunged. Not graceful, not precise, just raw mass tumbling forward.

Attica dropped into a slide, letting its swing carve the air over his head. He rolled beneath it, tucking hard against the ground before coming up behind the thing's flank.

The lightfeaster staggered forward, unable to stop its own momentum as his shade returned. It reconnected with him in a cold rush of instinct just as he conjured his shadowblade down his right arm.

Attica struck low, driving the blade into the creature's damaged flank. It didn't cleave cleanly, not through hide this thick, but it bit *deep.*

The lightfeaster shrieked—high and gurgling, a wet, unnatural howl. The sound hit, forcing Attica to brace as the other two responded to the cry.

They began their charge.

Attica kept his shadowblade in and twisted hard. The wounded creature tried to turn, sluggish, its movement lurching as one leg buckled beneath its weight.

Attica followed through, his next attack sinking into the beast's side, wedging beneath the plated hide. The lightfeaster convulsed once, limbs flailing wide, then collapsed in a trembling heap.

One down . . .

He barely had time to pivot, as the second one closed in fast, undeterred by the death of its kin.

The vertical seam of its skull split wide, raw light unfurled from within. Pulses of brilliance poured outward in jagged, convulsing bands, too fast to track, too intense to resist.

Attica staggered, immediately disoriented.

The pressure wasn't sound. It wasn't radiance. It was something deeper, something psychic, like hands pressing in from every direction, trying to fold his senses inward, to turn thought to static.

His vision flared, white first, then a hot red bloom that pulsed behind his eyes. Eli screamed.

The sound pierced the fog in his mind, snapping something loose. Just enough. Just barely.

I have to end this! Attica thought, going for Ravelstrike.

The spear surged into being, formed with a lurch of will and bone-deep instinct. He raised his arm to launch it forward but never got the chance as a burst of light tore out of him.

No heat. No harm.

Just a perfect ring of searing brilliance, soundless and fast, passing through his chest.

It slammed into the charging lightfeaster.

The brute didn't react.

Didn't even flinch.

The lightfeaster stood frozen—then its body began to split.

Its torso sheared apart, the upper half sliding backward as if on invisible rails. Its arms twitched. Its mouth hung open, frozen mid-breath. The lower half lingered for a single heartbeat, then collapsed in a hiss of steam and ruptured light.

Attica turned his head, slowly, to the child on his back. "Eli . . . ?"

"Eli help," she said. "Eli help Wolf!"

A strange stillness passed over him—not disbelief, but something close as the third lightfeaster charged.

No hesitation. No strategy. Just instinct and fury.

The beast scrambled toward him, clawed feet pounding through ash and bone.

Attica moved just as fast. He raised his arm toward the lightfeaster and launched Carrion Crow.

The weapon struck low, latching onto the creature's sternum with a wet crunch. It howled, momentum sending it stumbling as the tether yanked it off balance.

Carrion Crow detached with a flick of force as Attica closed the gap, sprinting hard, forming his shadowblade down his other arm.

He reached the monster and stabbed deep into its shoulder just as its skull mouth began to split open. His shade joined in, tendrils wrapping the creature's face. It didn't just restrain, it ripped, the vertical maw torn apart in a spray of broken light and sinew.

The lightfeaster dropped and the world stilled.

The duke's amphitheater hung in silence, a slow, dangerous kind.

Attica braced himself for more lightfeasters as his shade curled around him. It buzzed, not in fear or anticipation like he would have expected, but in excitement.

"What is it?" he asked, softly, still not ready to let his guard down.

Behind him, the child stirred as well. "Eli . . . Eli know," she told him. "Eli know!"

Attica turned his head. "Eli knows what?"

His shade's energy shifted again—urgent now. Focused. Buzzing not just with tension, but recognition, as it started to pull Attica forward.

"Stop!" he told his shade as Eli squirmed in her harness behind him.

"Eli know," she said again, more insistent. "Eli know!"

Attica gave in to the child once she started kicking him. He turned the harness around and looked directly into her bright eyes. "What is it—?"

"Hay . . . Hay-dree-an." Eli pointed toward the manor ahead. "Hay-dree-an."

CHAPTER SIXTY-SEVEN

W here did you hear that name?" Attica asked Eli. He looked deep into her bright face and asked again. "Where did you hear the name Hadrian?"

"Hay-dree-an." Eli's gaze fixed on the manor, her fingers curling toward it again. Attica followed the direction of her hand, expecting the stairwells—the obvious path. But her fingers pointed slightly lower, off to the side.

Not the grand entrance.

A smaller door, half hidden in shadow, tucked against the foundation. It looked like it led somewhere below.

Attica's shade took it from there as it pulled toward the lower entrance. "Fine, I'll go that way, but I am in charge," he reminded it as he resisted his shadow's urge to push him forward. "And Eli, you're going on my back again."

"Eli walk."

"No, Eli cannot walk. We are literally walking into the lair of a monster. You need to stay—"

"No. Eli walk."

Attica shook his head. Eli shook her head in response.

He felt a sensation from his shade, one that he took as an affirmation. "You will look after her?" he asked, intuiting what his shade was suggesting. "Fine," Attica said as he took her out of her carrier. "But she's not walking. She needs to float."

Eli interpreted exactly what he meant, as she hovered into the air. "Eli walk."

"No, you are floating. Eli float. Walking is on the ground," he told her as he pointed down. "But we can deal with that later."

"Hay-dree-an," she said as she turned toward the lower exit.

Attica followed after her. "You are going to be the death of me," he said under his breath as he remembered the attack she had pulled off earlier, from his back, facing the wrong direction. *A disc of light passed through me and killed the light-feaster,* he thought as she reached the door to the basement, his shadow right beside her. *She can phase light the same way I can phase with shadow, but her ability is much more concentrated . . .*

Eli pointed at the door. "Walk."

"You mean *open*."

"Oh-pen," she said, growing brighter.

"Don't do anything crazy. I'll open the door," he told her. The lower entrance groaned as Attica pushed the door open, stone grinding against stone.

The light radiating off Eli was swallowed by the narrow corridor that lay ahead. Attica's nostrils flared. It didn't smell like a basement. It smelled like a slaughterhouse.

He paused at the threshold, letting his eyes adjust. Eli floated beside him, fearless as ever, her glow illuminating the way.

"Not a basement," Attica finally said. "Something worse."

Eli, who was already halfway down the stone stairs, looked up at him. "Bad."

"Yes, bad," he told her as he caught up, not sure if he should teach her the word dungeon.

They descended a set of stairs that seemed to grow from the ground, the walls that surrounded it either carved of bone or meant to look like it. The ceiling above was arched in a repeating rib pattern, as if they had entered the carcass of a dead god. At the bottom, the white ground was stained with blood and discarded bone.

"Eli," Attica said. "Stay close."

"Bad. Monster," she told him.

Attica stepped beside her and led the way. They came to the first door, one marked by iron bars sculpted to look like large femurs. The door was locked, and behind it—flesh. A lot of it.

A flashwraith, maybe, Attica thought, *or what is left of it. It's not prompting a Codex entry, meaning it is either something I've encountered before or something entirely unrecognizable . . .*

Whatever it was, it was no longer moving, the creature's shape having collapsed in on itself like its bones had been siphoned out of its body. They passed another cell, one defined by a slick heap of skin and an unbearable stink as Eli continued muttering the same phrase, "Bad monster. Bad monster."

The third cell had a series of mangled skeletons in it, arranged in a way that looked as if they had fought and then clawed over one another for something.

Human by the looks of the armor around them, Attica thought. *Centurions? Brethren?* There was no telling. The next cell spelled out a different scene as Attica came to a single skeleton. Whoever it had been, they were seated against the wall, skull cocked back as if mid-laugh.

"Bad," Eli said as she continued deeper into the dungeon, past chambers filled with bodies that had no pattern—some rotted and wet, others dried and crumbling. A few were even clean, their doors unlocked, waiting for a future guest.

Attica couldn't tell how long the hall stretched—only that it curved downward like the Spiralrealm itself, deeper with each turn, its angles more organic than architectural. His shade moved slower now, as if disturbed. Attica felt the tension creep back into his spine.

The final chamber waited at the end, its arched door locked. Eli paused before it, her light shimmering, reacting to something within.

Attica stepped closer, squinting into the dark. *Is that . . . ?*

The lock snapped, wrenched open by his shade. He spun toward it. "Why did you—"

It didn't answer. Instead, his shade stretched long and thick beneath him, slithering around his legs like smoke. A sudden pressure rose behind his back and shoved him forward.

"Hey!" Attica stumbled across the threshold of the final cell and into a circular chamber. It was empty, save for one thing: chains hanging from the far wall, fastened to the wrists of a man with a long white beard.

A cough echoed from the emaciated man's chest as he raised his head.

Attica stopped breathing. "No . . ."

"Hay-dree-an," Eli said. "Good."

"How did you—" Once again, Attica felt his shade. *Can it communicate with her?* he barely had time to process the thought before he snapped back to the present moment. He rushed forward. "Hadrian!"

The man looked up, blinking, his eyes completely white. "Lad? Is . . . is that you?"

"Free him," Attica told his shade. It lashed out at Hadrian's cuffs. The older man fell forward and Attica caught him, his scent ripe, Hadrian's shade all but nonexistent by this point. Attica could sense it, but just barely.

"Lad?" Hadrian asked as Attica sat him up carefully.

Eli floated closer to the old man. "Hay-dree-an."

"Please, Eli," Attica started to say.

Hadrian grinned—and in doing so revealed that most of his teeth were now missing. "Your child."

Attica's spirit sank. Moments ago, he'd felt confused, angry, even hopeful. But now? Now he saw it clearly. Hadrian, though weaker, hadn't changed. The decay had continued.

"Can you see me?" Attica asked as Hadrian reached for his face.

He placed his hand on Attica's chin. "You've changed."

"How did you get here?" Attica asked slowly.

"I killed the shieldwraith. I know how to do it now," he said as he glanced in Eli's general direction. "So . . . bright. Even I can see it and . . . and I'm blind! What is wrong with the child?"

"Eli good," she said, confused.

"Eli is her name?" Hadrian asked after she spoke. "Eli . . . yes, a good name. Why are you traveling with a child? You yourself are barely old enough to go outside of the walls alone, lad!"

Attica fought the rising flood of emotion. The last time he'd seen Hadrian was two years ago, before the settlement fell, before his world had unraveled at the seams.

"Eli good," she said again.

"You *are* good," Hadrian told her. He coughed again and pressed his back against the wall. "I figured it out."

"What have you figured out?" Attica asked.

"All of it. The shieldwraith does not die easily. Even if you pierce its eye, even if you tie it down, beat it, and drag it. Your shade can kill it. From the inside. The shieldwraith is hollow, just barely, but hollow enough that Arminius was able to destroy it. Arminius . . ." He laughed bitterly. "Arminius is nearly as dead as me! Poor fellow. He no longer speaks to me . . ."

"Arminius, your shade," Attica said.

"Yes." Hadrian lifted his bony arm. "He's still here, I think. But we are weak. I haven't had essence in . . . a year. I do not know how long. I can't even remember what it tastes like."

Attica went for his gourd. Before Hadrian could say anything else, he placed it into the older man's hand. "Here."

Hadrian looked down at it, sensing the essence. "You . . . you would share, lad? What about the settlement? You must conserve it for the others."

Attica started to tell Hadrian what had happened but stopped himself. *It would break his heart*, he thought as he tried a different explanation. "Do not worry about the settlement. These are . . . reserves."

"Reserves? Is this a new practice?"

"Yes, a new Vanguard practice," Attica said. "Please, drink up." He helped Hadrian uncork the bottle.

The older Vanguard blinked a few times as he inhaled the essence. A newfound sharpness came over him. "The duke put me down here. You came . . . to rescue me."

"So you remember? You remember what happened? Drink," Attica said excitedly.

Next to him, Eli leaned in closer toward Hadrian. "Drink, Hay-dree-an, drink."

"Eli is . . . your daughter? Ha! In that case, your daughter is pushy."

"She's not—" Attica never finished what he was saying, as Hadrian brought the gourd to his lips.

He stopped just shy of drinking it. "I remember . . . I remember they killed the shieldwraith. You helped me bring it. Yes, it was you! I don't remember much before aside from drinking from the Seer's flask. Lad, why are you here? You know I am dying, right?" He looked down at his skinny arms. "I should be dead already. My shade has kept me alive, but I do not know why. Arminius never said. Or did he?" Hadrian peered up at the ceiling.

"Drink, please, it will help."

"I really thought I'd be a whisper by now," he told Attica. "Right! I remember now. I had a guest in my Realm of Recumbency who can find particular whispers. I wanted to use it to find my brother, but I never got around to it."

"So you visited the Gate of Whispers?" Attica asked.

Hadrian peered at him for a moment. "You know of Vespasia and the Gate of Whispers?"

"I do."

"Then to answer your question, yes, I visited." He inhaled more essence. "I solved some puzzle, a difficult one, but Arminius helped. Then . . . then I met them, the fox boy and his mother. I don't recall their names."

"Sebastian and Duchess Corvenna."

"That's them! And there was one whisper whom I encountered on the fourth tier. Where are we?"

"The fourth tier," Attica said.

"I see. Then . . . this is where I discovered her. I suppose." He offered Attica a toothless grin. "You really want me to drink this, don't you? I can feel your shade nudging it toward me. So pushy!"

"I do, Hadrian. Please drink."

"It won't save me, you know. But I think . . ." Hadrian took another inhale from the gourd. "I think it will give Arminius and me the power we need for one more fight, one more hunt."

"Yeah?" Attica asked, recognizing the tone in Hadrian's voice, one he hadn't heard in years.

"I do, lad. Together, we handle the duke, the monster who locked me away here," he said, growing serious. "Then, and only then, do I die." Hadrian drank. His eyes flared with power—alive, for the first time in years. "On my terms."

CHAPTER SIXTY-EIGHT

Hadrian drained the gourd and rose. There was a sharp clarity behind his white eyes now, a glow that held against the dungeon's gloom. His shade steadied him—first step unsteady, second more sure.

"What happened to your eyes?" Attica asked, taking the empty gourd back.

Hadrian touched his face. "The duke didn't like their color." His shade shrouded him for a moment and snapped back. "Ah, thank you, Arminius." Hadrian focused on Attica again. "He knows we're here."

"He should. I killed his pets, the lightfeasters."

The older Vanguard ran a hand down the length of his arm. "By the Painter . . . I didn't realize how close to dead I am. Look at me, skin and bones." A grin broke across his face. Not mad this time, just aware. "You realize what is about to happen here, right, lad?"

"What do you mean?"

Hadrian stepped closer and placed a hand on Attica's shoulder. His fingers were bone thin, but the weight of them felt heavier than any command. Eli hovered nearby, her soft light catching the sharp lines of his withered face. "This is it for me."

Even though Attica was now taller than his old mentor, he felt small beneath the gesture. "It?" he said.

"We do this," Hadrian said, "and I die happy, I die proud."

"You just needed essence—"

"Essence cannot fix what has happened to my mind." Hadrian squeezed Attica's shoulder. "It would take an endless supply. I remember now. The Painter's blood exacerbated my mental decline, as the Seer said it would. It reacts differently to everyone, you know."

"I always wondered about that," Attica said.

"It prolonged my life, and it gave me something else. Knowledge. Knowledge of our world, the Spiralrealm, more than I could have ever imagined. The essence you gave me, it has briefly brought me back, I can feel it. I can't see it due to my eyes, but I can feel it."

"Then we get you to your Realm of Recumbency. There's a fountain there. You can choose your own platform—"

"No, no. That won't do. I can also feel something else: I will die here today, in the next hour, in the way I always wanted. With honor and power."

"That's what you always wanted?"

"I suppose not *always*, but it is what I want now, Attica," he said, becoming increasingly clearer by the second. "The Painter's blood drove me to the verge of insanity, but there was a time in the third tier, and on the fourth, where I was able to be myself again. Yet even then, even with the constant flow of essence, my mind kept faltering. You don't know what it is like to lose your mind."

Attica looked at him and saw what remained of the man he once was. "It's here, you have it now," Attica said softly as Hadrian lowered his hand.

"Hay-dree-an, good," Eli said, her light shining brighter.

"Do not be tricked by my sudden clarity. It will not last long," Hadrian said. "And may you never experience the loss of memory. Speaking of which . . . I'm just realizing now I have so many questions. How is Dayanne? Eli?"

"Me . . . Eli," the girl said. "Two. Eli two."

Hadrian turned to her voice. "I don't understand."

"I didn't want to tell you," Attica said. "I didn't want to explain everything."

"I see." Hadrian took another step, rolling his shoulders as control returned. "Well, if I'm going to die here today, a day like any other day in the Spiralrealm, I . . . I would like to know. At least let me know what it is I'm dying for."

"The settlement is gone," Attica said, just coming out with it. "I think it was the signal from the shieldwraith, the one you killed. It was overrun by flashwraiths. I was severely injured. The Seer made me drink her entire flask. Only three Vanguard remain—Eve, Tiago, and me. They are on the second tier, hoping to find some of the Painter's blood so they can be awakened as well."

Hadrian let out a long, ragged breath. "All dead?" he whispered. "Dayanne? Your child?"

"Eli two," the child of light said as she showed Hadrian her fingers.

He turned to her, even though he couldn't see them. "And this girl? She is Lightborn?"

"She is. But she could . . . I don't know how just yet," Attica said, "but there is a prophecy that a child like her could restore color to the Spiralrealm. So that's where I'm at. I am hoping to get the duke's shard but . . . also . . ."

"I see, you have two paths, then."

"I don't know if Eli is a path. She only has a year before everything changes."

"Eli?" the girl asked, looking from Hadrian to Attica. ". . . Good?"

"Yes, you are a very good girl."

"I . . ." Hadrian stood erect and smiled at Eli. "I believe you are a very good girl as well. And you," he told Attica, "you very well could do it. I've spent countless hours imagining a world of color, a world in which Light- and Shadowborn aren't enemies. And to see . . ."

Both their shades shook, which caused the ground around them to tremble.

"Well, I guess that cuts this short. It seems like the duke wants us to come out and play," Hadrian said. "He is a theatrical fool, a weak man. You cannot hide Eli, so perhaps you head out first and distract him. I will use what power I have left to end it from there, and you take the shard."

"An ambush," Attica said.

"Yes. And after, I will release my hold on this body before my memory lapses. I think I have . . . I don't know how much longer, but we should go. We should do this. I am so very proud of all you have done," he said, his white eyes softening, "and I'm incredibly sad to hear of the loss of Dayanne and your child. But there is always darkness before the light. You know that phrase."

"I do. I always thought it meant something else."

"Anything means what anyone wants it to mean, and now it means something else to you. Eli," he told the girl, "you are good. No matter what, be good and be well."

"Eli . . . yes," she said.

"And you, Attica—remember: He's just another monster." Pride traced across his grizzled face. "We were born for this, raised for it, Attica, the Lone-Eyed Wolf, son of Spiran, Knife of the Glintfang; and me, Hadrian the Unshaken, son of Cato, the Shaded Fists, both Vanguard, defenders of the settlement. We do this together. We do it now. Before . . ." The strength in his voice thinned. "Before I lose what little wherewithal I have left. Understand?"

"I do," Attica said.

"Do you really?"

"I do."

"Good. Then let's make this count."

CHAPTER SIXTY-NINE

Attica paused at the top of the dungeon stairs, just shy of the sunken amphitheater where he knew the duke waited.

"Eli," he said, glancing back at the child of light on his back. "If you can help, do it. If not, that's fine. But don't be afraid. You are strong. Strong." He flexed his muscles to show her what he meant.

She reached a hand out toward his bicep. "Wolf strong. Hay-dree-an strong. Eli strong."

Behind him, Hadrian stood tall for the first time in years, his shade steadying his frail frame. "Stick to the plan," he said with a grunt. "Go out there with one thought only—make it count."

"For the settlement."

"And for the Painter," Hadrian said. "Kill or be killed. We've reached that point."

"Kill or be killed," Attica said, internalizing the words.

He gathered the shadows. The lost shades came to him like moths drawn to flame, a storm of whispering black swelling with hunger and purpose. They circled him, faster, tighter. The pressure built. He could feel their power now—alive in his veins, screaming for release.

Attica stepped through the door.

The amphitheater opened up before him, the ruined sculptures still scorched from the earlier carnage. The duke stood at its center, dressed in a tailored red coat, his face powdered, rapier at his side.

Attica didn't give him time to speak.

He closed the distance in a blink, the swarm of shades converging ahead of him, a sea of blackness unmoored, hungry for something to drown.

The duke didn't flinch.

He swept his hand forward and sent an arc of light scything through the shadows, scattering them like ash in wind. Attica gritted his teeth as he spotted the shard.

There it is . . .

The duke raised a bleached skull, its bone lined with intricate etchings. Embedded in its forehead was the black shard.

"You really thought it would be that easy?" the duke asked. With a flick of his fingers, two of the grotesque sculptures lining the amphitheater stirred. They groaned, bone grinding against bone.

Towering twenty feet high, the giants moved like puppets—dragged forward by something that loathed them. Their bodies were sculpted from flashwraith remains, twisted into joyless war things by Kairos. Wings hung in tatters. Limbs were hacked from spines, bent at unnatural angles. Rib cages had been torn apart and reassembled into crude armor. Their faces were a patchwork of creatures, stitched into something barely human.

Attica didn't hesitate.

Carrion Crow formed in a ripple of black feathers down his arm. He hurled it at the nearest giant, striking it in the clavicle. The tether yanked tight. Attica flew, landing hard on its shoulder.

"Deal with the bones," he told his shade, "like Hadrian did the shieldwraith!"

The skeletal colossus twisted to throw him—but froze as shadow rolled over it, into the crevices of its body. Its core shuddered. Cracks spiderwebbed across its surface. Then it caved inward as his shade tore it apart from within, hollowing it to collapse.

Attica rode the disintegrating statue down into a plume of dust and grit.

He landed and turned to the other monster only for the duke to step forward, his red coat flaring behind him.

"I always knew you'd come for it. They always do." He lifted the skull, fingers stroking the shard embedded in its brow. The duke kissed it. "And when they do, I handle them. I collect them, you see? This is my world, and you Shadowborn are insects to me."

"Bad," Eli said from Attica's back. "Bad!"

The duke tilted his head, his powdered face twisting with theatrical disdain. "Don't worry, I have space for you and that little monstrosity on your back. A place beneath the estate. You'll see it soon. And how odd, really. Shadowborn taking care of Lightborn, as if either of you have a chance."

Near Attica, the bones of the shattered colossus he'd just brought down rattled and rose, not into a humanoid shape this time—but something worse. The fragments reassembled into a creature with bladed limbs and a long hooked tail, glowing with unstable essence. Its body swirled with fractures, as if barely holding form, but the power it radiated was undeniable.

Attica's eye snapped back to the duke's shard. The black jewel in the skull's forehead glowed even brighter now, alive with heatless light.

He braced himself as the second intact colossus thundered forward, shadowblade moving down his arm.

A halo of light tore past him, silent and sharp. It hit the second giant square in the torso. The thing lurched, split, and folded apart—bisected before it could take another step.

"Eli . . ." Attica breathed.

"Eli help," she said from her harness. "Eli . . . kill."

Attica turned back to the fractured beast. It lunged for him; he met it with a hard strike of his shadowblade, carving into the monster's forelimb. Bone cracked. Essence sprayed. He twisted and leapt back just as the beast reared for another charge.

A beam of concentrated light slammed into him, fired from the duke's outstretched palm. His new armor held. The blast scattered across its surface as Attica rolled clear, just in time to evade the creature's next lunge.

Across the amphitheater, Hadrian emerged from the shadow's edge—creeping behind the duke, just like they'd planned.

But something was wrong.

Attica could see it now in the brief glimpse he got of his mentor. Hadrian wasn't sure where he was. He took a few unsteady steps, hesitated, blinked toward the mottled sky as if searching for a forgotten name, the man mumbling to himself.

"No . . . no . . ." Attica said under his breath as the fractured beast came for him again. He ducked the blow and rolled forward, sprinting toward the duke.

The air split with a sudden burst of force—silent, sharp, and brutal. It hit Attica like a hammer to the chest, launching him off his feet. He flew backward toward the manor steps, spine first. His shade flared around him at the last moment, cushioning the impact in a swirl of shadow.

"Eli—"

"Wolf?" Eli asked as his shadow helped him stabilize.

"Wolf good, Eli—" He turned back to the duke just as the man plucked the shard from the skull in his hand. He kissed the skull once more—soft, almost reverent—then slammed it to the ground. It broke apart in a burst of brittle bone.

The duke held the strange stone for a moment, his eyes filling with madness and delight as he brought it to his forehead, where the black jewel sank into his skin.

Essence flared, light and shadow together, writhing around the duke in convulsing arcs. Power snapped outward, carving lines into the ground as the air warped. Pressure collapsed inward. Reality frayed at the edges as the muted tones of the Spiralrealm inverted.

And behind him, Hadrian stumbled in circles, lost.

Kill or be killed, Attica thought as he broke into motion.

The shard hadn't yet disappeared beneath the duke's forehead. His hand still pressed over it, holding the jewel in place.

If I can reach him. If I can—

The duke's free hand snapped outward toward Attica.

An unseen force seized Attica by the throat, lifting him off the ground in a single violent motion. He tried to cut himself free, but his shadowblade passed through empty air—useless against the invisible grip. His shade shrieked, lashing out with wild tendrils that struck nothing.

"Wolf! Wolf!" Eli fired burst after burst of haloed light, but each flickered out before it touched the force that held him suspended above the amphitheater.

Attica's vision dimmed at the edges.

The duke rose to meet him, one hand pressing to the shard in his brow, the other clenching the air, as if throttling something unseen.

Essence was ripped from Attica in violent strands, yanked loose from muscle and bone. He saw it spilling out—tendrils of shadow unraveling from his body, tangled with threads of light, the sound deafening.

"Eli," he gasped through clenched teeth, realizing the truth.

The duke was pulling essence from both of them.

Two streams—one black as pitch, the other radiant white—spiraled together around the man, forming a cyclone of raw, impossible force. The air crackled with it.

Attica tried to move but his limbs betrayed him. His lungs seized. Vision collapsed to a pinprick, a spinning star swallowed by dark punctuated by the duke's increasingly maniacal laughing.

"Eli . . ." he whispered. "Dayanne . . ."

This was it. Attica knew it.

He would die here—or worse, be locked away in the dark, forever cut off from the ones he still hoped to save.

And at that moment, at the moment that Attica started to lose both consciousness and the battle, a shadow burst upward, sudden and sharp.

Hadrian screamed as he vaulted into the air, his shade flaring, shadowblade drawn. He drove his weapon through the duke's back, the jagged tip bursting from his gut in a gout of dark fire.

The duke's expression finally cracked.

His grip on Attica fell apart, causing Attica to plummet toward the ground. His shade caught him and Eli at the last second, softening the fall as Hadrian and the duke battled above.

Air tore into Attica's lungs as he regained full consciousness. Strength surged back—jagged, raw. He pushed to his knees, vision swimming into focus. "Eli?"

". . . Wolf?" the child whimpered from his back.

"Eli good?"

"Good . . ." she said.

Another crash split the clearing, shadows and sparks erupting where they met, the amphitheater filling with static and dust.

Attica pulled himself to his feet, shadowblade forming down his arm as he stumbled toward the smoldering impact site. He reached the duke, who lay sprawled behind the older man, convulsing, trying to reach something glowing and failing as he bled profusely from the chest.

The shard.

It throbbed with both light and dark, a trembling unity of contradiction.

Attica dropped low and severed the duke's arm at the elbow. The man shrieked. Attica drove his blade through the same puncture Hadrian had made. He lifted the duke and slammed him to the stone.

His body didn't rise again.

Silence followed as Attica's shadowblade melted away.

". . . Wolf?" Eli asked in a tiny voice.

Rather than reply, he turned the harness around to check on the girl.

She reached her arms out to him.

Attica lifted Eli from the harness and held her close. "Eli, Wolf, good," he whispered—then, at last, let her go.

The child of light rose into the air, glowing softly as he turned toward the scene before him. He looked from Hadrian to the shard, which lay nearby, glowing, untouched.

Attica made his choice.

He rushed to his mentor's side and knelt beside him, the stone beneath them slick with blood. Hadrian's eyes fluttered open.

"Lad," Hadrian rasped. "You were always a good lad . . ."

Attica took his hand, pressing it tight. "Hadrian—"

Eli floated over them, quiet. "Hay-dree-an . . ."

Confusion spread across Hadrian's face as he looked at Attica, blue blood pooling at the corner of his mouth.

"You . . . shouldn't be outside the settlement. You're just a boy . . ."

His breath hitched once then stopped. Hadrian's body went still, head rolling gently to the side.

Attica stayed kneeling, holding the hand of the man who had raised him, who had taught him more than survival—who showed him what it meant to live with purpose.

At last, he stood.

Attica turned to the shard, head bowed, the soft glow from Eli casting light over the wreckage—the only warmth left in the ruin.

The shard rose into the air, beating with power.

All he had to do now was reach out and take it.

FLASHWRAITH CODEX

Each Lightborn creature encountered in the Spiralrealm is classified according to the following criteria—Tier, Rank, Cognizance, and Type.

- T-# (Tier): Indicates the tier of first confirmed sighting, from T-I to T-IX. If sighted on multiple tiers, this is sometimes classified as Upper Spiral or Deep Spiral.
- Rank (Threat Level): Measures the overall danger to a trained Vanguard cell.
  Scale:
  D – Minor Threat
  C – Moderate Threat
  B – High Threat
  A – Lethal Threat
  S – Extinction Grade
- Cog (Cognizance): Represents tactical intellect and behavioral complexity.
  Scale:
  0 – Feral
  1 – Bestial
  2 – Tactical
  3 – Sapient
- Type (Behavioral Archetype): Defines the creature's combat and environmental role:
  • Predator • Swarm • Behemoth • Guardian • Brute • Engineered

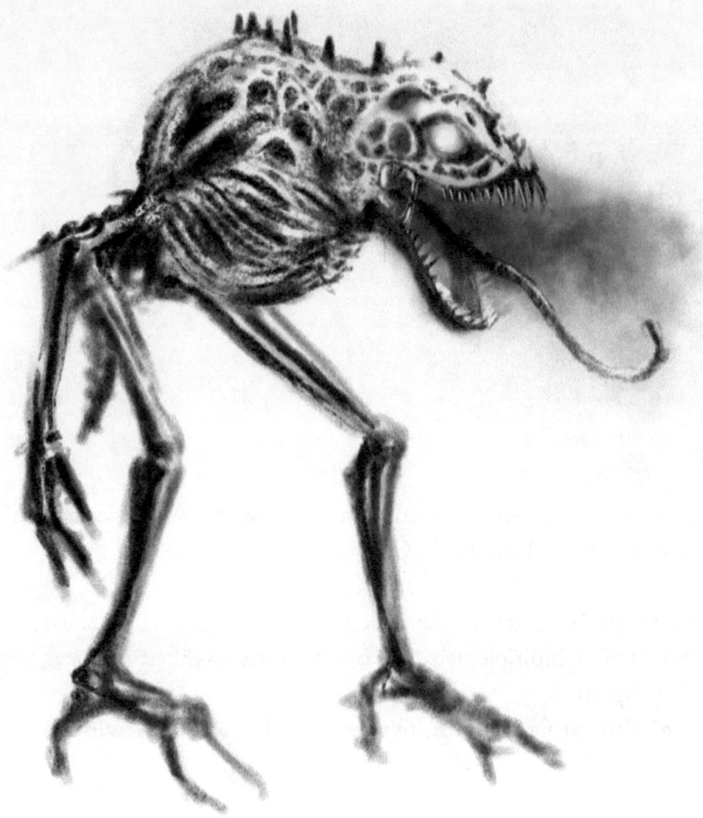

Avian Emitter

Origin: T-IV Variant; initially mistaken for ground-based class
Known Strengths:
– Capable of true flight despite skeletal frame
– Emits shriek-light while airborne, can target from above with precision
– Exceptional burst speed and vertical mobility
Known Weaknesses:
– Bone structure is hollow and brittle under sustained pressure
– Light gland is throat-centered, not heel-bound
– Becomes disoriented in high winds or enclosed spaces
Classification: T-IV | Rank C | Cog 1 | Predator
Notes: Often underestimated due to resemblance to standard emitters. Do not engage near cliff edges or open air unless prepared for aerial pursuit.

Brighthowler

Origin: Mid-Spiral Mutation, possibly naturally occurring
Known Strengths:
– Dual cranial nodes allow simultaneous tracking and threat projection
– Emits a resonance howl that destabilizes nearby shadows
– Highly aggressive, difficult to flank due to bifurcated awareness
Known Weaknesses:
– Head-strike vulnerability—severing one disables coordination
– Reduced physical force compared to ancestral forms
– Often overcommits in melee, exposing flank
Classification: T-III | Rank B | Cog 2 | Predator
Notes: Rare but increasing in number. Intelligence borderline strategic, prefers direct engagements over ambush tactics.

Emitter

Origin: Common Upper Spiral Variant
Known Strengths:
– Emits concentrated light-bursts via oral cavity
– Agile and erratic in close quarters
Known Weaknesses:
– Crystalline mana nodes located in heels—primary kill point
– Light burst has a cooldown; vulnerable afterward
– Panics when isolated or cornered
Classification: T-I | Rank D | Cog 0 | Swarm
Notes: Frequently encountered in packs. Low individual threat—lethal only to the careless or overconfident.

Flareback

Origin: Tier III Apex Type
Known Strengths:
– Explosive nodules across back and shoulders can detonate at will
– Capable of consecutive detonation, producing a spontaneous combustion
– Some have exhibited shock-wave stomps that release radial blasts of light
Known Weaknesses:
– Nodules are volatile; precise strikes can trigger fatal chain detonations
– Reacts poorly to deep shadow interference
– Limited agility, can be misled by decoys or struck from elevated positions
Classification: T-III | Rank B | Cog 1 | Brute
Notes: Avoid engaging in open ground without coordinated support.

Flaylight

Origin: Tier I Symbiote Type
Known Strengths:
– Swarm behavior triggered by disruption or aggression near host creature
– Emits flickering light pulses that can alert nearby flashwraiths
– Mild contact burns, can singe exposed flesh and temporarily blind if swarmed
Known Weaknesses:
– Extremely fragile; easily destroyed with minimal force
– Lacks independent intelligence; reliant on host for direction and protection
– Drawn to high-mana signatures, making them predictable once identified
Classification: T-I | Rank F | Cog 0 | Swarm
Notes: Commonly cluster around high-threat flashwraiths.

Flickercrab

Origin: Tier IV Subterranean Cluster Species
Known Strengths:
– Emits blinding light pulse upon impact; nests trigger chain reactions
– Stonelike shell grants excellent camouflage
– Flash bursts can disorient or trigger ambushes
Known Weaknesses:
– Harmless when isolated
– Shell is brittle under focused strikes
– Predictable movement patterns
Classification: T-II | Rank D | Cog 0 | Swarm
Notes: Nests often placed in natural choke points—commonly followed by ambush predators.

Glintfang

Origin: Tier II Predator Class, native to upper spiral slopes
Known Strengths:
– Emits pulses of hunting light from eyes and chest to dazzle and corner prey
– Exceptionally sharp senses—can track by heat, mana trails, and sound
– Hunts in coordinated packs, using light-burst howls and flanking maneuvers
Known Weaknesses:
– Light-bursts have brief cooldowns, vulnerable between pulses
– Pack cohesion can break if alpha is eliminated
Classification: T-II | Rank C | Cog 1 | Predator
Notes: Fast, coordinated, and highly territorial. Often mistaken for lesser threats—until the first light-burst howl pulse signals the pack.

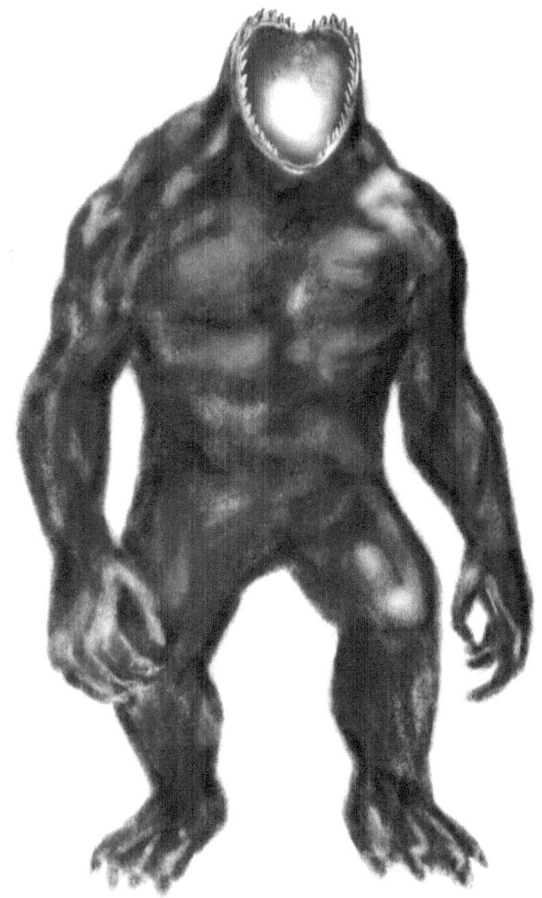

Lightfeaster

Origin: Tier IV Brute Type, possibly essence-rich nest guardian
Known Strengths:
– Consumes ambient essence; regurgitates energy as chaotic light-bursts
– Thickened hide and powerful frame
Known Weaknesses:
– Lacks eyes, navigates via sound and thermal input
– Vulnerable during digestion phase
– Susceptible to low-frequency vibration shocks
Classification: T-IV | Rank B | Cog 1 | Brute
Notes: Favored in dense nests or essence-rich zones. Combat should emphasize misdirection and attrition.

Lightreaver

Origin: Lower Spiral Variant, possibly engineered
Known Strengths:
– Invisibility through refracted light
– Coordinated tactics, hunts in packs
– Adaptive melee weapon formation from limb-core essence
Known Weaknesses:
– Overloads when forced to clash with matching light frequencies
– Susceptible to prolonged darkness saturation
– The knees are its weakest point
Classification: T-IV | Rank B | Cog 2 | Predator
Notes: Entry incomplete. Further observation required.

Lumenbride

Origin: Obscured; first confirmed near a collapsed Sanctum in Tier IV
Known Strengths:
– Emits harmonic tones that destabilize shade cohesion
– Veiled form leaves radiant sigils that detonate in pulses
– Commands lesser Lightborn with gesture and song
Known Weaknesses:
– Prolonged silence disrupts cohesion
– Lacks physical resilience once veils are stripped
– Avoids direct combat unless cornered
Classification: T-IV | Rank A | Cog 3 | Predator
Notes: Rare and highly dangerous. Presence may signal ritual convergence or nesting behavior.

Mistwhale

Origin: Tier III Legend-Class Entity
Known Strengths:
– Massive size, can swallow targets whole
– Emits bioluminescent pulses that disorient or erase memory
– Able to phase in and out of dense fog
Known Weaknesses:
– No confirmed weaknesses
Classification: T-III | Rank S | Cog 3 | Leviathan
Notes: Widely regarded as a myth. Records suggest ties to deeper phenomena in the Spiralrealm.

Shieldwraith

Origin: Tier VII Obelisk Type, possibly construct-class hybrid
Known Strengths:
– Emits focused light beam from central eye
– Near impervious to conventional attacks
– Deploys long tendrils to crush or impale at mid-range
Known Weaknesses:
– Vulnerable only when eye is open
– Movement is slow and deliberate
Classification: T-IV | Rank S | Cog 1 | Engineered
Notes: Rarely mobile unless triggered by ancient protocols. Do not engage.

Wretch

Origin: Tier II Outgrowth, possibly hive grown
Known Strengths:
– Lantern-bright heads rupture on death
– Erratic, high-speed movement
Known Weaknesses:
– Fragile, destroyed with a focused strike
– Head detonation can be triggered at range
– Behaviors suggest external control or hive mind
Classification: T-II | Rank C | Cog 1 | Swarm
Notes: Do not engage in tight quarters. Coordinated sacrifice hints at collective control.

ABOUT THE AUTHOR

Harmon Cooper is the bestselling author of nearly one hundred books across the LitRPG, cultivation, and progression fantasy genres, including the Pilgrim, Cowboy Necromancer, Cozy Abyss, Shadowborn Exile, and War Priest series. He began writing LitRPG in 2015 and hasn't looked back since. Born and raised in Austin, Texas, Harmon then lived in Asia for five years before relocating to New England and ultimately settling in Portugal.

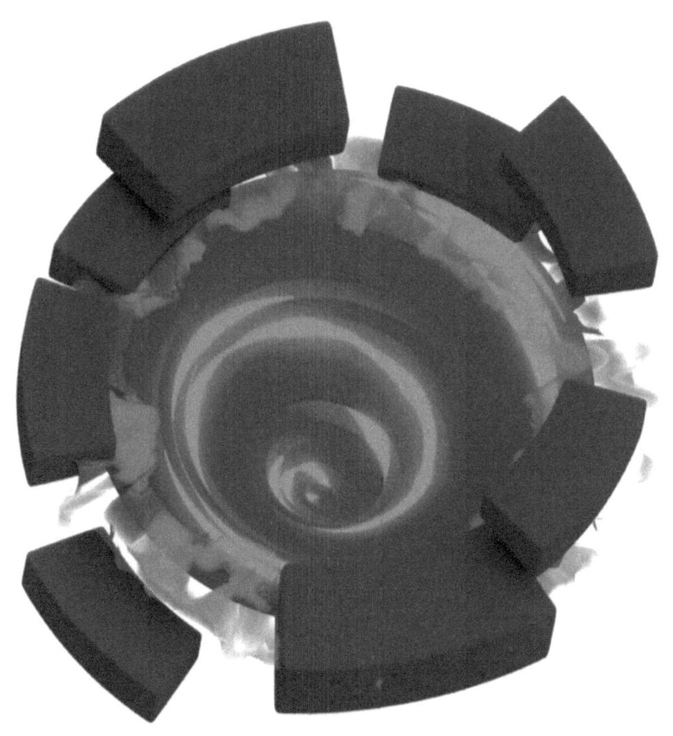

RESPAWN YOUR CURIOSITY

follow us on our socials

podiumentertainment.com

@podiumentertainment

/podiumentertainment

@podium_ent

@podiumentertainment